Homecoming

Kate Morton was born in South Australia and grew up in the mountains of south-east Queensland. She has degrees in dramatic art and English literature, specializing in nineteenth-century tragedy and contemporary gothic novels. She is the author of *The House at Riverton*, *The Forgotten Garden*, *The Distant Hours*, *The Secret Keeper*, *The Lake House* and *The Clockmaker's Daughter*, which have all been global number one bestsellers. She began her latest novel, *Homecoming*, after leaving the UK to be near family in South Australia. Inspired by themes of home, belonging and family, her novel is set in London ('the city of my heart') and the Adelaide Hills, and is filled with secrets and mysteries, mothers and daughters, and a big old house on a hill.

You can find more information about Kate Morton and her books at katemorton.com or Facebook @kate mortonauthor and Instagram @katemortonauthor

KATE MORTON

Homecoming

PAN BOOKS

First published 2023 by Mantle

This paperback edition first published 2024 by Pan Books
an imprint of Pan Macmillan
The Smithson, 6 Briset Street, London EC1M 5NR
EU representative: Macmillan Publishers Ireland Ltd, 1st Floor,
The Liffey Trust Centre, 117–126 Sheriff Street Upper,
Dublin 1, D01 YC43
Associated companies throughout the world
www.panmacmillan.com

ISBN 978-1-5290-9408-4

Pan Macmillan does not have any control over, or any responsibility for,
any author or third-party websites referred to in or on this book.

1 3 5 7 9 8 6 4 2

A CIP catalogue record for this book is available from the British Library.

Typeset in Sabon by Jouve (UK), Milton Keynes
Printed and bound by CPI Group (UK) Ltd, Croydon, CR0 4YY

Visit **www.panmacmillan.com** to read more about all our books
and to buy them. You will also find features, author interviews and
news of any author events, and you can sign up for e-newsletters
so that you're always first to hear about our new releases.

For my family

PROLOGUE

And, of course, there was to be a lunch party to mark the new year. A small affair, just family, but Thomas would require all the trimmings. Unthinkable that they would do otherwise: the Turners were big on tradition, and with Nora and Richard visiting from Sydney, neither frippery nor fanfare was to be skipped.

Isabel had decided to set up in a different part of the garden this year. Usually they sat beneath the walnut tree on the eastern lawn, but today she'd been drawn to the stretch of grass in the shade of Mr Wentworth's cedar. She'd walked across it when she was cutting flowers for the table earlier and been struck by the pretty westward view towards the mountains. *Yes*, she'd said to herself. *This will do very well.* The arrival of the thought, her own decisiveness, had been intoxicating.

She told herself it was all part of her New Year's resolution – to approach 1959 with a fresh pair of eyes and expectations – but there was a small internal voice that wondered whether she wasn't rather tormenting her husband just a little with the sudden breach of protocol. Ever since they'd discovered the sepia photograph of Mr Wentworth and his similarly bearded Victorian friends arranged in elegant wooden recliners on the eastern lawn, Thomas had been immovable in his conviction that it represented the superior entertaining spot.

It was unclear to Isabel exactly when she'd first started taking guilty pleasure in causing that small vertical frown line to appear between her husband's brows.

A gust of wind threatened to rip the string of bunting from her hands, and she held tight to the highest rung of the wooden ladder. She'd carried the ladder down from the gardening shed herself that morning, quite enjoying the struggle of it. When she first climbed to the top, a childhood memory had come to her – a daytrip to Hampstead Heath with her mother and father, where she'd scrambled up one of the giant sequoia trees and looked south towards the city of London. 'I can see St Paul's!' she'd called down to her parents when she spotted the familiar dome through the smog.

'Don't let go,' her father had called back.

It wasn't until the moment he said it that Isabel had felt a perverse urge to do just that. The desire had taken her breath away.

A clutch of galahs shot from the top of the thickest banksia tree, a panic of pink and grey feathers, and Isabel froze. Someone was there. She'd always had a powerfully developed instinct for danger. 'You must have a guilty conscience,' Thomas used to say to her back in London, when they were new to one another and still entranced. 'Nonsense,' she'd said, 'I'm just unusually perceptive.' Isabel stayed motionless at the top of the ladder and listened.

'There now, look!' came the stage whisper. 'Hurry up and kill it with the stick.'

'I can't!'

'You can – you must – you took an oath.'

But it was only the children, Matilda and John! A relief,

Isabel supposed. Nonetheless, she remained quiet so as not to give herself away.

'Just snap its neck and get it over with.' That was Evie, her youngest, at nine.

'I *can't*.'

'Oh, John,' said Matilda, fourteen going on twenty-four. 'Give it here. Stop being such a pill.'

Isabel recognised the game. They'd been playing Snake Hunt on and off for years. It had been inspired by a book initially, an anthology of bush poetry that Nora had sent, Isabel had read aloud, and the children had loved with a passion. Like so many of the stories here, it was a tale of warning. It seemed there was an awful lot to fear in this place: snakes and sunsets and thunderstorms and droughts and pregnancy and fever and bushfires and floods and mad bullocks and crows and eagles and strangers – 'gallows-faced swagmen' who emerged from the bush with murder in mind.

Isabel found the sheer number of deadly threats overwhelming at times, but the children were proper little Australians and delighted in such tales, relishing the game; it was one of the few activities that could be counted on to engage them all despite their different ages and inclinations.

'Got it!'

'Well done.'

A peal of exultant laughter.

'Now let's get moving.'

She loved to hear them gleeful and rambunctious; all the same, she held her breath and waited for the game to take them away. Sometimes – though she never would have dared admit it out loud – Isabel caught herself imagining what it might be like if she could make them all disappear. Only for a little while, of course; she'd miss them dreadfully if it were

any longer than that. Say an hour, maybe a day – a week at
most. Just long enough for her to have some time to think.
There was never enough of it, and certainly not sufficient to
follow a thought through to its logical conclusion.

Thomas looked at her like she was mad if she ever said as
much. He had quite fixed ideas about motherhood. And
wifedom. In Australia wives were frequently left alone to
deal with snakes and fires and wild dogs, apparently. Thomas
would get that faraway glint in his eye when he expounded
on the subject, the romantic sentimentalist's fascination with
the folklore of his country. He liked to picture her a frontier
wife, enduring hardship and keeping the home fires burning
as he gallivanted around the world making merry.

The idea had amused her once. It had been funnier when
she'd thought that he was joking. But he was right when he
reminded her that she'd agreed to his grand plan – had leapt,
in fact, at the opportunity to embrace something different.
The war had been long and grim, and London was despic-
ably mean and milk-washed when it ended. Isabel had been
tired. Thomas was right, too, when he pointed out that life in
their grand house was not anything like a frontier existence.
Why, she had a telephone and electric lights and a lock on
every door.

Which wasn't to say it didn't get lonely sometimes, and so
very dark, when the children had gone to bed. Even reading,
which had long been a source of solace for her, had started
to feel like a rather isolating endeavour.

Without losing her grip on the ladder, Isabel craned to see
whether the curve of the swag was going to fall high enough
to accommodate the table beneath. Getting it just so was a
trickier task than she'd imagined. Henrik always made it
look easy. She could have – should have – asked him to do it

before he'd finished work the previous day. There'd been no rain predicted; the bunting would have been fine to hang out overnight. But she couldn't. Things had changed between them recently, ever since she'd come upon him in the office that afternoon, working late when Thomas was in Sydney. She felt embarrassed now when she asked him to do menial jobs around the place, self-conscious and exposed.

She was simply going to have to do it herself. Really, though, the wind was a menace. She'd made the decision about the western lawn before it started up; she'd forgotten this was the less sheltered side of the garden. But Isabel had a stubborn streak; she'd been like it all her life. A sage friend once told her that people didn't change as they aged, they merely became older and sadder. The first, she'd figured, she couldn't do much about, but Isabel had been determined not to permit the latter. Thankfully, she was, by nature, a very positive person.

It was only that the windy days brought with them agitation. They did lately, anyway. She was sure she hadn't always felt this turbulence within her belly. Once, in a different lifetime, she'd been known for having nerves of steel. Now, she was as likely to be overtaken with a sudden surge of alarm from nowhere. A sense that she was standing alone on the surface of life and it felt as fragile as glass. Breathing helped. She wondered whether she needed a tincture or tea. Something to settle her thoughts so she could at least sleep. She'd even considered a doctor, but not Maud McKendry's husband in the main street. God forbid.

However she did it, Isabel was going to put things right. That was the other New Year's resolution she'd made, although she'd kept it to herself. She was giving herself one more year to regain her equilibrium. People were depending on her, and it was time.

She would turn thirty-eight at her next birthday. Practically forty! A greater age than either her father or mother ever reached. Perhaps that was why she had been overcome lately with memories from her childhood. It was as if sufficient time had passed that she could turn around and see it with clarity across the vast ocean of time. She could barely remember crossing that ocean.

It was ridiculous to feel lonely. She had lived in this house for fourteen years. She was surrounded by more family than she'd ever had – God knew, she couldn't escape the children if she tried. And yet, there were times when she felt terror at her own desolation, the gnawing sensation of having lost something she could not name and therefore could not hope to find.

Down on the curve of the driveway, something moved. She strained to see. Yes, someone was coming, it wasn't her imagination. A stranger? A bushranger sweeping up the driveway on his horse, straight out of a Banjo Paterson poem?

It was the postman, she realised, as the brown-paper-wrapped parcel he was carrying came into focus. On New Year's Day! One of the virtues of living in a small country town where everyone knew each other's business was service outside usual hours, but this was exceptional. A flame of excitement flared inside her and her fingers turned to thumbs as she tried to tie the bunting so she could get down to intercept the delivery. She hoped it was the order she'd written away for some weeks ago. Her liberation! She hadn't expected it to arrive so soon.

But it was maddening. The string was tangled, and the

wind was teasing it around the flags. Isabel struggled and cursed beneath her breath, glancing over her shoulder to observe the postman's progress.

She didn't want her package delivered to the house.

As he reached the nearest bend of the driveway, Isabel knew she would have to let go of the string if she were to scramble down the ladder in time. She vacillated for a moment and then called out, 'Hello!' and waved. 'I'm over here.'

He looked up, surprised, and as another gust of wind made her grip the ladder tight, Isabel saw she'd been mistaken. For although he carried a parcel, the stranger on the driveway was not the postman at all.

Christmas Eve, 1959

Later, when he was asked about it, as he would be many times over the course of his long, long life, Percy Summers would say truthfully that he'd thought they were asleep. The weather had been hot enough for it. Throughout December, the heat had pushed in from the west, crossing the desert centre before driving south; there it had gathered, hanging unseen above them and refusing to budge. Each night they listened to the weather report on the wireless, waiting to hear that it was due to break; but relief never came. In the long afternoons they leaned over one another's fences, squinting in the golden light as the shimmering sun melted into the horizon beyond the edge of town, shaking their heads and lamenting the heat, the blasted heat, asking one another, without expectation of an answer, when it would finally end.

Meanwhile, tall and slender on the upsweep of hills that surrounded their river-run valley, the blue gums stood silent, streaky skins glinting metallic. They were old and had seen it all before. Long before the houses of stone and timber and iron, before the roads and cars and fences, before the rows of grapevines and apple trees and the cattle in the paddocks. The gums had been there first, weathering the blistering heat and, in turn, the cold wet of winter. This was an ancient place, a land of vast extremes.

Even by usual standards, though, the summer of 1959 was hot. Records were falling in the place where scores were kept, and the people of Tambilla were feeling every bit of it. Percy's wife, Meg, had taken to rising with the dawn to get the day's milk delivery inside the shop before it had a chance to spoil; Jimmy Riley said that even his aunties and uncles couldn't remember it so dry; and in everyone's mind, especially with the memories of 1955 so fresh, was the risk of fire.

'Black Sunday' the papers had taken to calling it. The worst fires seen since the colony had been formed. Second of January had dawned four years ago, heavy with a sense of disaster brewing. A dust storm had rolled in overnight, gathered from the dry plains to the north; scorching wind gusts of a hundred kilometres per hour. Trees bowed and leaves hurtled along the ravines; sheets of corrugated iron were wrenched from the tops of farm buildings. Electric power lines broke free, sparking multiple blazes that raged and grew and finally met to form a great hungry wall of fire.

Hour by hour, the locals had fought it hard with wet sacks and shovels and whatever else they could find until at last, miraculously, in the evening, the rain had started to fall and the wind had changed direction – but not before forty or so properties had been lost, along with the lives of two poor souls. They'd been calling for a proper emergency fire service ever since, but the decision-makers down in the city had been too slow to act; this year, in the face of eerily similar conditions, the local branch had taken matters into their own hands.

Jimmy Riley, who worked as a tracker for some of the Hills farmers, had been talking about land clearing for ages. For thousands of years, he said, his ancestors had conducted regular slow burns, reducing the fuel load when the weather was still cool, so there wasn't enough left to start a fire when the earth was baking and the north-westers howling, and the merest spark was all it took. It seemed to Percy that men like Jimmy Riley, who knew this country from the inside out, weren't listened to anywhere near as often as they should be.

The most recent call had come through from Angus McNamara down near Meadows the week before. The mild, wet years since '55 had resulted in rich growth and the forest of Kuitpo was thick with foliage. One stray lightning bolt, one dropped match, and the whole lot would go up. They'd been at it all week and had finished slashing in time for Christmas. Just as well – storms were forecast over the weekend, but there was every chance the rain would pass them by and they'd be left with dry strikes instead. Meg had been less than thrilled when Percy told her he'd be gone during the busiest time of year, but she knew it had to be done and that Percy wasn't one to shirk. Their boys had been drafted in as proxies at the shop and Meg had grudgingly agreed that it was no bad thing for the lads to have some real responsibilities. Percy had left them the Ford utility and taken Blaze on the run down to Meadows.

Truth be told, Percy preferred to go on horseback. He'd hated putting the ute up on blocks during the war, but you couldn't get petrol for love nor money – what little there was had been requisitioned by the army and other essential services – and by the time they were able to pull the motor down again, he'd got out of the habit of driving. They'd kept the ute for bigger deliveries, but whenever he could, Percy saddled up Blaze for the ride. She was an old girl now, not the fearsome young filly who'd come to them back in '41, but she still loved a run.

The McNamara place was a big cattle property this side

of Meadows that most people referred to simply as 'the Station'. The house was large and flat with a wide verandah running all the way around and a deep iron awning keeping the heat at bay. Percy had been offered a spot in the shed to sleep, but he'd been happy to take his swag out under the stars. He didn't get much chance to camp these days, what with the shop keeping them so busy and the boys growing up. Sixteen and fourteen they were now, both taller than him and with boots as big; each preferring to spend time with friends rather than camp with the old man. Percy didn't begrudge his boys their independence, but he missed them. Some of his best memories were of sitting around the campfire telling stories and making each other laugh, counting the stars in the night sky, and teaching them real skills, like how to find fresh water and catch their own food.

He was giving them each a new fishing rod for Christmas. Meg had accused him of extravagance when he brought the presents home from town, but she'd said it with a smile. She knew he'd been looking for something to soften the terrible blow of losing old Buddy-dog in the spring. Percy had justified the cost by reminding her that Marcus, in particular, was becoming a fine angler; he could do worse than to take it up full-time. Kurt, the elder of the two, would be heading to the university when he finished school. He'd be the first in their family to go, and although Percy tried not to make too much of a fuss over his glowing school reports, especially not in front of Marcus, he was proud as punch – Meg was, too. Even with the recent distraction of Matilda Turner, Kurt had managed to keep his grades from slipping. Percy just wished his own mother were still alive to read the things Kurt's teachers wrote.

*

Heat ticked in the underbrush and bone-dry twigs snapped beneath Blaze's hooves. They had left the Station first thing and had been travelling all day. Percy steered the old girl along the track, slow and steady, sticking to the dappled shade where he could. Ahead was the edge of Hahndorf; not much longer and they'd be home.

With the day's warmth on his back and the monotonous drone of hidden insects buzzing in his ears, a somnolence had come over Percy. The dry summer air brought back memories of being a boy. Of lying in his bed in the small back room of the house he'd shared with his mother and father, training his ears on the noises outside, closing his eyes so that he could better imagine himself into life beyond the window.

Percy had spent most of his twelfth year in that bed. It hadn't been easy for a lad who was used to roaming free to be struck down. He could hear his friends out in the street, calling to one another, laughing and jeering as they kicked a ball, and he'd longed to join them, to feel the blood pumping in his legs, his heart punching *one-two* at his rib cage. He'd felt himself shrinking, fading away to nothing.

But his mother came from strong Anglican stock and wasn't the sort to stand by while her son's self-pity threatened to swallow him up. 'Doesn't matter if your body's grounded,' she'd said, in that firm, no-nonsense way of hers. 'There's other ways to travel.'

She'd started with a children's book about a koala with a walking stick, and a sailor and a penguin, and a pudding that miraculously re-formed each time it was eaten. The experience was a revelation: even as a small child, Percy had never been read to. He'd seen books on his teacher's desk at school, but – influenced by his father, perhaps – had assumed them objects of punishment and toil. He hadn't realised that inside their covers were whole wide worlds, filled with people and places and hijinks and humour, just waiting for him to join them.

When Percy had heard the children's stories enough times that he could recite each one under his breath, he dared to ask his mother whether maybe there were others. She'd paused, and at first he thought he'd crossed an unseen line; that the stories were going to evaporate, and he'd be left alone again with only his broken body for company. But then his mother had murmured, 'I wonder?', and disappeared deep into the coach house in the back corner of the garden, the place where his father didn't go.

Strange to think that if he hadn't been stricken with polio, he might never have met Jane Austen. 'My favourite,' his mother said quietly, as if confessing a secret. 'From before I met your father.' She hadn't the time to read it *to* him, she said – 'The whole town will starve if I'm not there to sell them their milk and eggs!' – but she'd placed the book in his hands and given him a silent, serious nod. Percy understood. They were co-conspirators now.

It had taken Percy a while to get used to the language, and some of the words were new, but he hadn't anywhere else to be, and once he was inside there was no turning back. *Pride and Prejudice, Sense and Sensibility, Emma*; they'd seemed at first to describe a world quite unlike his own, but the more he read, the more he came to recognise the people of his town in Austen's characters, the self-importance and ambitions, misunderstandings and missed opportunities, secrets and simmering resentments. He'd laughed with them, and wept quietly into his pillowcase when they suffered, and cheered them on when, finally, they saw the light. He had come to love them, he realised; somehow, he had come to care for them – figments of a faraway author's imagination – with the same wholeheartedness he felt for his parents and his very best friends.

When he had exhausted the small stock of books his mother kept in her secret box in the shed, Percy convinced her to borrow new ones for him, three at a time, from the travelling library. He would read with his back to the door, ready to tuck the illicit novel away beneath the sheets at the sound of his father's footsteps in the hall. His dad would come upstairs after work each night to stand by Percy's bedside, a big man rendered helpless, frowning with impotent frustration as he asked whether Percy was feeling any better and silently willed his son's useless legs to recover.

And perhaps all that willing worked, because Percy was one of the lucky ones. He wasn't much good with a football anymore, and he was too slow on the cricket pitch, but with the help of a pair of splints, he slowly regained the use of his legs and, in the years to follow, an observer would've been hard-pressed to guess that the boy offering himself up as umpire was any less physically able than the other lads.

Percy didn't give up his reading, but neither did he shout about it. Fiction, non-fiction and, as he got older and his changing feelings made him a stranger to himself, poetry, too. He devoured Emily Dickinson, marvelled at Wordsworth, and found a friend in Keats. How was it, he wondered, that T.S. Eliot, a man born in America who'd made a life for himself in London – city of history, of Englishness; foreign to Percy, mysterious and grey-stoned – could look inside Percy's own heart and see there so clearly his own considerations about time and memory and what it meant to be a person in the world?

These thoughts he kept to himself. It wasn't that his secret was guilty; rather that he knew already that the other boys in Tambilla didn't share his interest. Even Meg had looked at him uncertainly when, during their courtship, he'd ventured to ask after her favourite book. She'd hesitated before answering, 'Why, the Bible, of course.' At the time, he'd taken the response for piety – which was unexpected, and a bit surprising given some of the other things they'd said to one another. Later, though, when they'd been married for a year or two, he'd brought it up again and she'd looked confused before dissolving into laughter. 'I thought you were checking on my virtue,' she'd said. 'I hadn't wanted to disappoint you.'

Blaze was lathered with sweat, so Percy stopped at the trough in Hahndorf's main street to let her have a drink and a rest. He climbed down from the saddle and looped the horse's reins over a post.

It was after three, and the street was in shade, courtesy of the hundreds of giant chestnuts, elms, and plane trees running down each side, planted more than half a century before. Some of the businesses were still open, and Percy was drawn to the window of a nearby woodturner's workshop, where a couple of shelves displayed an assortment of hand-made items: bowls and utensils, some decorative carvings.

Percy went inside. 'There's a little wren,' he said to the girl behind the counter. The sound of his own voice was a surprise; it was the first time he'd spoken to anyone all day. 'May I have a closer look?'

The girl went to take it down, bringing the miniature figure back to Percy.

Percy marvelled as he turned it this way and that. He held it up to the light, admiring the fragile set of the bird's neck, the jaunty sweep of its tail feathers. The likeness was remarkable, the workmanship fine.

'Is it a gift?' said the girl.

He placed the carving back on the counter with a nod. 'She collects them.'

The shopgirl offered to wrap the wren. She had a little piece of Christmas paper and a length of fine silver ribbon in the back room where she'd been readying her own gifts, she said; it was as well to use the rest today. 'Won't be much call for it tomorrow, will there?'

After he had paid, Percy tucked the tiny wrapped present in his pocket and wished the girl a merry Christmas.

'To you, too, Mr Summers,' she said. 'And give my best to Mrs Summers.' He must have looked surprised because she laughed. 'We're in the CWA together. Mrs Summers is going to love that little wren. She told me once that she has a special fondness for birds, that she's loved them ever since she was a child.'

Percy couldn't recollect the first time he'd laid eyes on Meg. In truth, she'd always been around. For a long while, she was just one of several younger kids making up the gang of them that used to gather in the dusty paddocks or on the edge of the river after rain, looking for what passed as sport. She'd been a dirty little thing, but he hadn't judged her for that; they were all country kids who didn't have much use for spit and polish, unless it was to front up to church on Sunday, and even then only under threat of a thrashing from their mothers.

But he'd come across her one day when he was out by the disused copper mine, not far from where the trains ran through from Balhannah to Mount Pleasant. He went there when he wanted to escape his father's well-meaning attempts to 'toughen him up'. She was sitting on the windowsill of the old stone crusher house, her face a hot mess of tears and snot and dirt. At the time, he'd wondered how on earth she'd got herself up there, a tiny scrap of a girl like that. It was only later, when he got to know her, that he realised the angelic face belied a tough-as-nails survivor's spirit.

Percy had called out to ask her what was wrong, and at first she'd refused to tell him anything. He hadn't pushed it; he'd simply got on with his business, reading for a time in the shade of the big circular chimney before giving his legs a stretch, then poking about in the overgrown spear grass, searching for flat stones to skim across the dam. He could feel her watching him, but he made no further overtures. It must have looked like fun, what he was doing, though, because without a word she appeared at his side and began searching for her own skimmers.

They continued in a companionable silence, broken only on occasion when he whistled his appreciation at a bouncer she'd tossed along the water's surface. At lunchtime he split his sandwich with her. They ate without talking, but for the updates he gave when he spotted a bird of interest.

'Sacred kingfisher,' he said, pointing at the stout puffed-up chest in the lowest branch of a nearby she-oak.

'Is not. It's a kookaburra.'

He shook his head. 'Same family, but see how her darker feathers are turquoise? Just watch – she'll dart out when a lizard or beetle catches her fancy, and you'll see how they glisten in the sunlight.'

'What's that one, then?'

'A red wattle.'

'And that one over there?'

Percy spotted the black-and-white bird with its bright yellow beak. 'Noisy miner. Can't you tell? She doesn't stop calling.'

'What about that one?' The girl pointed up at a small bird with a vibrant blue breast and long, straight tail feathers that jutted skywards.

'That's a blue wren – a superb blue wren, to be precise.'

'I like her best.'

'She's a he.'

'How can you tell?'

'The male birds are prettier. The female is brown, with only the tiniest bit of green on her tail.'

'Like that one over there?'

Percy strained to see where she was pointing. 'Yes, just like that.'

'You know a lot of things,' she observed.

'Some,' he agreed.

When it was time to leave, he asked Meg if she wanted to go with him. He could give her a lift back to town, he said. It was getting dark, and he could smell rain on the way. She hesitated a second before telling him that she wasn't going back at all: she had run away from home, that's what she was doing out here.

Percy realised then how little she was; her face was defiant, her arms wrapped tightly across her body, and yet there was a part of her, he could tell, that hoped he'd force her to return with him. Her vulnerability filled him with a sudden sense of deep sadness. Of anger, too. It was common knowledge that her daddy couldn't keep his fists to himself when he was raging. He'd had a bad war, was all Percy's mother would say about him. 'But show me a man who had a good one.'

Percy understood what she meant: that generation of men had learned that the only way to forget the things they'd seen and done, the mates they'd lost to the mud and the guns, was to drink themselves numb and take their nightmares out on those at home. Percy was luckier than most. His father was strict, but he wasn't violent. Violence would have required him to be present and he was far too distant for that.

The first big splats of rain began to fall. 'All right,' Percy said. 'But it's going to be cold out here tonight.'

'I have a blanket.'

'Clever girl. And I suppose you're right for dinner?'

'I brought some bread.'

He tucked his book back inside his backpack. 'Sounds like you've thought of everything.' He checked Prince's saddle, tugging on the stirrups. 'Only they said on the wireless that it's going to storm tonight. And bread isn't much chop on a cold, wet night.'

A cloud of uncertainty darkened her brow.

'You know,' he continued, 'my mum had a stew on the stove when I left this morning. She cooks it all day, just like my nana used to, and she always makes too much.'

'What sort of stew?'

'Lamb scouse.'

The girl shifted from one foot to the other. Her hair was quite wet now, her braids forming two limp ropes over her shoulders.

'I don't suppose you'd like to come and have a bowl or two? I can bring you back here afterwards.'

She hadn't stopped at two bowls; she'd had three, Percy's mother watching on with quiet pleasure. Susan Summers took the duties of Christian charity seriously and to have a waif arrive on her doorstep on a wild, wet winter's night was a welcome opportunity. She'd insisted on giving the girl a bath and, after the stew had been served and the dishes cleaned, tucked her up on the daybed near the crackling fire where she promptly fell into a deep sleep.

'Poor little pet,' Percy's mother said, observing the child over her half-glasses. 'To think she planned to spend the night out there alone.'

'Are you going to tell her parents where she is?'

'I have to,' she said with a firm but troubled sigh. 'But before we let her go, we'll make sure she knows she's always welcome here.'

Percy had resolved to keep an eye out for her after that, and he hadn't had to look too far to find her. She started spending afternoons in the shop, talking to Percy's mum, and before he knew it, she was working behind the counter on weekends.

'The daughter I never had,' his mum would say, smiling fondly at Meg as she totalled up the accounts and made a list of reorders. 'Kind and capable and not at all unfriendly on the eye.' Later, as Meg grew from a child into a woman: 'She's going to make someone a very good wife one day.' More pointedly, but not unkindly, her glance darting to Percy's stiff leg: 'A fellow with limited options would be fortunate to marry a girl like that.'

Hahndorf was behind them now and they'd entered the familiar territory of undulating hills that rolled towards the rise of Mount Lofty. Rows of leafy grapevines basked in the late afternoon sun and the warm air carried with it the faint scent of lavender from Kretschmer's flower farm.

Blaze picked up her pace as they neared the Onkaparinga

Valley Road. Apple orchards gave way to olive groves, and when they crossed the Balhannah bridge she began to toss her mane, pulling gently towards the water. Percy tightened his grip on the reins, pressing a palm against the horse's neck. 'I hear you, old girl.'

Meg would have a lot for him to do when he got back. There were always last-minute orders to go out on Christmas Eve and attendance at Reverend Lawson's 6.30 p.m. church service was not negotiable. But it had been ten hours since they'd left the Station, with only a couple of short breaks. No matter how keen he was to get home, it didn't seem right not to take Blaze for a swim.

He continued west into the afternoon sun, but on the outskirts of Tambilla encouraged Blaze away from the street and down a steep grassy gully. The creek was narrow here, a tributary of the Onkaparinga River that rose in the foothills of Mount Lofty and wound its way through the valley. Blaze met the water gladly, nosing the reeds as she continued downstream. She reached the gap where the wire-and-wood fence had pulled away from its post and Percy hesitated briefly before giving her a small prod of consent. He was on Turner land now, but the house itself was still some distance away.

It was from this very direction that he'd approached the house the first time he saw it. Funny – he hadn't thought back to that day in years. He'd been thirteen years old, returning to the shop after making a delivery. The polio might have taken away his speed on the cricket pitch, but up on Prince, his father's horse, he was no different from anyone else. His father had approved wholeheartedly – anything was better than finding his son inside with a book in hand – and took it a step further by offering Percy after-school work.

On horseback he could cover all of Hahndorf, out as far as Nairne, and then back towards Balhannah and Verdun. Piccadilly Valley strained things a bit, but his father was never one to turn down an order, so Percy just learned to ride faster. He was supposed to take the most direct route, but Percy always went cross-country. This was his place, these hills his home, and he loved them.

There were hardly any houses on Willner Road, and never any deliveries to make, but he went out of his way to ride along it because he liked the smell of wattle, and the road was lined with large, silvery-green bushes that erupted with yellow pompoms each August. It was late in the season, but on this particular day, in this particular year, there was still an abundance. Percy had taken a deep breath, savouring the sensation of the sun on his shirt and the pleasant earthy fragrance of eucalyptus and soil and sun-warmed flowers, and he'd leaned forward to lie across Prince's broad back, letting the rhythm of the horse's gait lull him like a baby in its mother's arms. In such a way he travelled for some time, until a call overhead drew his attention.

He blinked up towards the sheer, bright sky, where a couple of wedge-tailed eagles were turning lazy wheels together on the warm thermal currents. He followed them with his eyes before encouraging Prince onto the verge, through the gap in the fence, and onwards in the direction of the pair. The top of the hill above which they were circling was covered with dense foliage. Percy began to wonder whether he might discover their nest. He'd heard that there'd been eagles sighted up near Cudlee Creek, but he'd never known them to settle this far south.

As Prince proceeded boldly uphill through the lank lean gums, Percy scanned their highest limbs. He was looking for a platform made from sticks and covered with leaves. Glancing between the lattice of branches and the sky – determined not to lose the eagles themselves – he didn't initially realise that he had crossed an invisible line into a different type of terrain. It was the altered sound that caught his attention first, as if a domed lid had been lowered and the canopy had suddenly drawn closer.

There had been a profound shift in the foliage around him, too, he now noticed. The run of gums and long yellowing grass had been infiltrated by other vegetation, so that silver trunks mingled with thick woody oaks, textured elms and cedars. Tangled brambles covered the ground and leafy creepers scrambled upwards, stretching between the trees so that it was difficult to find a large enough break through which to glimpse the sky.

The temperature had dropped by degrees within the shaded world. Birds were chattering to one another above him, silvereyes and lorikeets, swallows and honeyeaters and wrens. The whole place was teeming with life, but there was little chance, he realised, of spotting his eagles' nest.

He was turning Prince around to head back into town when a light caught his eye. The afternoon sun had hit something beyond the trees, causing it to shine like a torch through a gap. Curious, Percy urged Prince onwards up the dense, wooded slope. He felt like a character in a book. He thought of Mary Lennox as she discovered her secret garden.

The blackberry bushes had become too thick to ride through and Percy dismounted, leaving Prince beneath the shade of a thick-trunked oak tree. He chose a strong whip of wood and started carving his way through the knotted vines. He was no longer a boy whose legs didn't always do as he wished; he was Sir Gawain on the lookout for the Green

Knight, Lord Byron on his way to fight a duel, Beowulf leading an army upon Grendel. So keen was his focus on his
swordplay that he didn't realise at first that he'd emerged
from the forested area and was standing now on what must
once have been the top of a gravel driveway.

Looming above him was not so much a house as a castle.
Two enormous floors, with mammoth rectangular windows
along each face and an elaborate stone balustrade of Cor-
inthian columns running around all four sides of its flat roof.
He thought at once of Pemberley, and half-expected to see
Mr Darcy come striding through the big double doors, riding
crop tucked beneath his arm as he jogged down the stone
steps that widened in an elegant sweep as they reached the
turning circle where he stood.

He knew then what this place was. This was the house that
Mr Wentworth had built. It was a ridiculous folly, most
people said, a grand stone hall like that, out here in the middle
of nowhere. Only love or madness, they said, or perhaps a
good dose of each, could have inspired a man to envisage – let
alone build – such a house. There was no shortage of impressive stone dwellings in the Hills; from the earliest days of the
South Australian settlement, the wealthy gentry had snapped
up land on which to build country residences where they
could wait out the summer in a kinder climate. But this house
was like nothing Percy had seen before.

Mr Wentworth had had the plans drawn up in London
and tradesmen shipped all the way from England. The cost
had been astronomical – forty times the price of the next
best house in South Australia. Imagine spending all of that
money, people whispered incredulously, only to end up rat-
tling around alone in an enormous monstrosity.

Percy agreed that the house was enormous – no one with

eyes could argue against that – but he didn't think it a monster. On the contrary. It reminded him of the illustration on
the frontispiece of his favourite book.

After that first day, he returned whenever he could. He
didn't tell his friends about the house. Not at first. A strange,
possessive feeling came over him whenever he thought about
it. The house had chosen to show itself to *him*. But being the
sole keeper of such a tremendous secret soon became a
burden, and he grew tired of being alone, and the value of
the news was irresistible and got the better of him. He
regretted the disclosure as soon as it was made. His friends
wanted to race up to the house immediately. They wanted to
see it for themselves, to go inside. When they smashed the
window to gain entry, Percy felt the breakage like a wound.

Once or twice, he'd followed his mates inside. Most of the
furniture that Wentworth had ordered and shipped from
England was still there, covered with dust sheets. A large
portrait of the old man hung on the wall above the stairs.
Percy had sensed the eyes of the painting upon him –
accusatory, betrayed – and he'd felt ashamed. Later, when he
learned the story of Edward Wentworth, he realised why.
The house had been built for love, but the young woman
who'd inspired it had died from sunstroke on the sea voyage
out to Australia. Mr Wentworth, who'd been waiting for her
on the dock in Adelaide when the news arrived, never
regained himself, bolting the doors so as to remain alone
with his grief. The house became a shrine to his broken
heart.

Eventually, Percy's friends grew tired of the place and
moved on to new adventures. Percy, too, became busier: he
married Meg, they took over the shop, and then there was
the war. Next thing he heard about the house was that a

fellow from Sydney had bought it. Turner was his name, and once the war ended, word spread around the town that he and his English wife would be moving in that spring.

That had been fourteen years ago now. There'd been a lot of changes to the place since then. The land had been cleared and the bones of Wentworth's garden discovered within the wildness and restored. Tradesmen, local and otherwise, had been engaged, and a great deal of money spent (or so the local rumour mill went) to bring the house itself back to order.

Percy had been up there many times with groceries, and never failed to marvel, as he made his way around the graceful curves of the restored driveway, at the transformation. Sometimes, when he stopped to let Blaze catch her breath at the westernmost point of the climb, he would gaze up through the formal gardens towards the house and admire the verdant sweep of lawn and stone walls, the crab apples and camellias, and for a split second, if he let his eyes glaze, he would glimpse instead – as if through a veil – the overgrown, primordial approach as it had been for so long before the Turners had come . . .

But he wasn't going near the house today. Blaze had no interest in the climb up Wentworth Hill and Percy hadn't the time. He loosened the horse's reins and followed her lead. He knew where she was going. The old girl was making her way north to a place she loved, where the willow-lined banks widened, and the riverbed grew deep enough to form a waterhole, perfect for swimming.

The first thing he saw that was out of the ordinary was the jaunty flag suspended from a branch of the largest willow tree.

Percy pulled Blaze up short and lifted his hand against the

sun. The scene came into focus. Several folks were lying beneath the tree, he realised, on blankets, and with baskets nearby. They were having a picnic. In the tree, along with the flag, someone had threaded a paper Christmas chain from branch to branch.

Percy was mildly surprised. In the middle of summer, at that point in the waxing afternoon, most sensible people were inside, doing their best to escape the heat; he hadn't expected to come across anyone out here. He stroked Blaze's warm neck, deliberating. He was trespassing, and although he knew they wouldn't mind – Mrs Turner herself had invited him to cut across the paddocks whenever he was running deliveries – he didn't want to be seen to be overstepping the mark, taking advantage of her kindness. Like any man in town, he'd been made nervous by Mrs Turner when she first arrived. New people rarely moved to Tambilla, let alone to take up residence at the Wentworth place, and she was refined, dignified, very English.

He ought to turn around and leave. But if she were to wake and see him slinking away – well, wouldn't that be worse? More incriminating somehow?

Later – and he would be asked many times over the days, weeks and years ahead, including in the coming hours by the policemen in their interviews – he would say that a sixth sense had told him things were not quite as they seemed. Privately, he would wonder whether that was right; whether the scene had really seemed eerie or he simply remembered it that way because of what came next.

All he knew for sure was that, faced with the choice, he had given Blaze a gentle nudge and started towards the Turner family beneath the willow tree.

*

The sleeping children, he remembered thinking, looked like the etchings in his mother's precious family Bible, brought with her grandparents when they emigrated from Liverpool. Beautiful children they were, even the boy, John. Blond curls, like their father must have had when he was a child, and striking sea-blue eyes – all except the eldest girl, Matilda, whose dark hair and green eyes made her the spitting image of her mother. He knew Matilda a little. She had been in Kurt's class at school since they were small and lately the two had become sweet on one another. She was lying in the shade nearest the tree trunk, her straw hat on the ground beside her. The warm wind ruffled the hem of her skirt. Her feet were bare.

The other two children were on the blanket with their mother, wearing trunks with towels wrapped around their middles as if to dry off. John was on his back, while the girl, Evie, was curled up on her side, her right arm outstretched. Percy was reminded of the many times he'd taken his boys swimming – in the creeks and lakes of the Hills, but also down at the beach, to Port Willunga and Goolwa and the other places that his own father had taken him when he was a boy, to fish and hunt for pipis. He could almost feel the happy post-swim drowsiness that came from having sun-dried skin.

An old-fashioned wicker crib hung from the straightest bough of the willow. It was Meg who'd told him that Mrs Turner had finally been delivered. They'd just come in from church a month or two before and she'd stopped at the hall mirror to unpin her hat and straighten her hair.

'Did you hear that Mrs Turner's had her baby?' she'd called after Percy, who was by then in the kitchen filling the kettle. 'Tiny little thing with a serious face.'

'Is that right?' Percy had answered.

'That's four now, and better her than me,' Meg had said with a laugh. 'Never let yourself get outnumbered. That's my motto.'

He'd since seen Mrs Turner in town. A couple of weeks ago, she'd been carrying the babe in her arms, and he'd nearly knocked them over on his way out of the shop. He'd coloured with embarrassment, but she'd smiled at him as if it were no inconvenience at all to be trampled.

Percy had been carrying a large sack of flour for delivery, so he couldn't lift his hat in greeting and had settled instead for a nod. 'Mrs Turner, how are you?'

'I'm well, thank you – we're both very well.'

His eyes had followed hers then to the small face in the blanket she held. A pair of ink-blue eyes stared up at him, pale brow knitted in that attitude of false wisdom that all newborn babies share and then shed with their first smile.

'So tiny,' he said.

'It's true what they say. One forgets.'

Meg joined them on the footpath then and started cooing over the baby, making elaborate apologies to Mrs Turner meanwhile. 'Not usually forgetful, my Percy, but when he does make a mistake, he's always sure to make it worthwhile. I trust you were happy with the fish paste I sent over?'

'It was delicious, Mrs Summers, and far too generous. I was coming to see you, to ensure you add the charge to my account. I've been meaning to telephone, but my mind hasn't been my own lately.'

'I don't wonder why,' Meg said, reaching up to rub the tip of her finger against the baby's cheek. Her ease was so contrary to Percy's own discomfort that he felt even more oafish by comparison. 'These little ones have a way of taking over, don't they? And what a lovely babe she is, too: so pretty.'

She. Percy hadn't realised Meg knew. He'd made a quick study of her face, searching for signs of grief or envy or anything else of note. But she was only smiling at the slumbering child.

To see Mrs Turner lying there on the blanket now made Percy's cheeks burn, as if he'd crept up on purpose. There was an intimacy to the set-up beneath the willow, a vulnerability: here was a family asleep together, evidence of their lunch still laid out haphazardly on the blanket between them – plates and cups, sandwich crusts and crumbs of cake.

The stillness of the scene struck him then. It was almost unnatural.

He took his hat from his head. Afterwards, he would wonder what it was, precisely, that made him do so. He was aware of the sound of his own breath: in and out, in and out.

Something was moving on the younger girl's wrist, he noticed. He took a careful step closer. And that's when he saw the line of ants crawling straight across her body, over her arm, and on towards what was left of the picnic food.

Everything else was static, silent. No one's features twitched in sleep. No one yawned and readjusted as the breeze grazed their skin. Not a single chest lifted or lowered.

He went to Mrs Turner and knelt beside her head. Dampening his finger, he held it near her nose, willing it to cool with an exhalation. He realised that his finger was shaking. He looked away into the middle distance, as if that might somehow help him, as if by concentrating his senses he could force her to breathe.

Nothing. There was nothing.

Percy backed away. He stumbled over the lunch basket, flinching at the jarring noise of cutlery and crockery clanking together. Still no one stirred. Not one of them so much as moved a muscle.

With trembling hands, Percy jammed his hat back on his head. He tried to stop his thoughts from racing, tumbling, colliding with one another. Realisation, shock, fear – he tried to clear his head of the lot of them so he could work out what should happen next.

Blaze was nearby, and without another moment's hesitation Percy grabbed her reins and found his way into the saddle, urging her onwards in search of help.

PART ONE

CHAPTER ONE

London, 7 December 2018

Whenever Jess felt angry or sad or even just inexplicably unsettled, she paid a visit to the Charles Dickens Museum on Doughty Street. There was something enormously comforting about sitting down to a pot of English breakfast tea after a wander through the museum's rooms. Sometimes she listened to the audio guide, even though she'd heard it enough times to have memorised the information, because she liked the narrator's voice.

She had discovered the museum during her first months in London. She'd been twenty-one, living in the attic of her schoolfriend's mother's aunt, working part-time in a run-down pub near King's Cross station. One day, having arrived too early for her shift, she'd decided to take a roam around the area. It was her favourite thing to do, to walk and to look, to pinch herself in wonder at being here, in this place of cobblestones, pint glasses and mews houses, of poets and painters and playwrights, of the great skulking, ageless River Thames.

In the spirit of exploration and discovery, she'd granted herself the freedom to turn in either direction at random when she reached the end of a road, which was how she happened to be walking along Doughty Street, past a row of neat brick houses, when she noticed a sandwich board on the pavement outside number forty-eight, announcing it as the Charles Dickens Museum. A thousand childhood hours spent lying in her grandmother's garden in Sydney, book in hand, had come back in an instant, and she'd hurried up the concrete stairs and pushed open the shiny black door. Time had dissolved; the novelty of being in England, of finding that the names and places she'd come across in novels were *real*, was still fresh, and Jess had been utterly awed to think that Dickens himself had once walked through these halls, eaten at this table, stored his wine in the cellar downstairs.

She'd arrived late for work that day and earned herself a warning, followed shortly by a second, which had led in turn to her dismissal. In a stroke of good fortune, unemployment had begot opportunity, and the next job vacancy she answered had been for a small travel company in Victoria that required her to write, among other things, copy for their newsletter. And so, in an instance of rare, perfect synchronicity, she had always felt that she had Dickens to thank for giving her a professional start as a journalist.

Her preferred room at the museum changed frequently, depending on her mood and the circumstances of her life. Lately, she'd had a lot of time for the study. She liked to stand in the corner, where the edge of the desk met the window, and gaze upon Robert William Buss's unfinished painting of Dickens asleep in his old wooden chair, the characters he'd conjured to life filling the air around him. She enjoyed picking them out, each one overlaid with the memories she carried from the first time she'd met them. It was an extraordinary proposition: that the imaginings of an English writer from a previous century had woven themselves into the lived experience of a little girl growing up in far-away Sydney.

Today, though, as she'd considered the painting, it had occurred to Jess that there was something almost menacing in the way the characters seemed to be haunting their author, surrounding him, entrapping him, refusing to grant him peace even in sleep. Jess knew that state of mind. It was precisely how she'd been feeling, ever since she'd had The Idea. In fact, she'd felt that way, to some degree or another, her whole life: once an idea announced itself, she thought about it obsessively, worried it this way and that, did not stop until she'd solved it, found it, finished it. She had it on good authority that the trait drove other people mad and had been told variously that she lacked discipline, that she was distracted company, that curiosity killed the cat. No one could ever deny, though, that the trait had served her well in her work.

This particular idea had come to her a week ago. Jess had caught the Tube home from the library, and when she hopped off at Hampstead she'd noticed that one of the disembarking passengers was a very old lady struggling under the weight of a pair of bulging Sainsbury's bags. Jess had offered to help and ended up walking the woman home to one of the dark brick Georgian houses on Well Walk, between the pub and Gainsborough Gardens. It was during the walk, and afterwards as they shared a pot of tea, that Jess came to hear her new friend's life story, including that her house had once belonged to John Keats. Further, that as a newlywed she'd discovered a letter the poet had written to Fanny Brawne tucked deep inside a crack between the stair treads.

This marvellous fact had got Jess thinking about all of the other houses she walked past each day. The ever-present history, the tangible layers of time wherever one cared to look, was an aspect of London that she still found deeply stimulating, even after almost twenty years. Wouldn't it be something, she'd thought, to pick a street at random and interview the current residents of each home, weaving their present-day situations together with whatever she could learn about the previous occupants and, indeed, the histories of the houses themselves? It would be a celebration of the ubiquity of stories and all those unseen parallels that threaded together to form the framework of our lives. How many points of interest there must be – some small and intimate, others more exceptional – hiding in the dusty stair-wells of the city.

In the time it took Jess to traverse the short distance from Well Walk to her own small house in the shadow of New End School, she had sketched out an entire series in her mind. She unlocked the door, kicked off her shoes, and went straight upstairs to her study. As darkness settled and the blue light from her monitor cast its glow on the floor around her, the number of research tabs open on her screen multi-plied. By the time she stood up again, she'd produced a detailed outline, a snappy pitch, and a list of editors who might be interested in publishing it.

After the exhilaration of the idea, though, had come the excruciating wait. Jess was still getting used to it after so many years in full-time work. The last editor she'd contacted had been in touch the day before to say that the idea showed promise, but that he'd have to take it 'further up the chain' and would 'reach out' again before the weekend. Today was Friday, thus Jess was on tenterhooks. There was no chance she'd be able to focus on anything else, and so she'd walked all the way from Hampstead, through Primrose Hill, across Regent's Park, to arrive at the museum in time for opening. It hadn't taken long for her to find herself in the tearoom, where she was now finishing off a pot of Darjeeling and a slice of banana bread. She understood she'd committed the cardinal sin of the freelancer: becoming emotionally invested in an idea before she had the go-ahead from an editor willing to purchase and print the finished article; she couldn't afford to write for her own edification.

Newsroom budgets were being slashed, small independent papers were closing, news was being syndicated rather than gathered locally. Scores of journalists had been let go and they were all trying to eke out a living now as freelancers. 'It'll be good to have the flexibility,' they'd insisted to one another in the beginning, with nervous optimism; but there'd been too many of them and too few publications to go around. Readers, they were told, were impatient with long-form stories now, so word counts and word rates were being cut in tandem. It had become almost impossible to make a living. A few of Jess's friends had gone back to study, some were 'taking a break', while others were selling property or even mining bitcoin.

'What about a screenplay?' her friend Rachel had asked, trying to be helpful. 'I read that everyone's getting something made. Netflix, Amazon, you can't go online without hearing how content-hungry they are. Who's that journalist who wrote that movie – *Bonfire* something?'

'Tom Wolfe? *Bonfire of the Vanities*?'

'Yes! Him! Write something like that.'

'He didn't write the screenplay; he wrote the book.'

'Then write a book. You're a writer, aren't you?'

Rachel was well-meaning and had almost certainly not deserved the withering glance Jess shot her. Jess did, in fact, know several ex-journos who were writing books, but only one had signed a book deal, and the least said about him and his new life, the better. She did not mention that *Bonfire of the Vanities* (the defining novel of the eighties!) had, in fact, been a serialisation first – twenty-seven parts in *Rolling Stone* magazine. (Twenty-seven!)

At her table in the back corner of the museum tearoom, Jess poured the last of the Darjeeling into her cup. She was setting the pot back when a flyer on the table with a small sketch of Dickens caught her eye. Now *he* wouldn't have let a global downturn get him down. The man's industry had been legendary: fifteen novels, five novellas, ten children, copious short stories, poetry and plays, international tours, and a not insignificant amount of society-changing philanthropic work. Then again, he had also enjoyed the benefit of having a wife to pick up the slack – and, it would seem, his wife's sister, too.

Jess twisted her napkin tightly and pressed it beneath her knife. The fact of the matter was, she missed being immersed in a long-form project, sinking deep into research and losing herself to an idea. She missed pursuing answers and sharing stories. She knew it sounded cringingly earnest, but at her best she had considered herself to be doing vital work: speaking truth to power, holding governments and leaders to account by shining a light on behalf of those who couldn't. Surely, in this age of fake news and social media conspiracies, long-form journalism was more important than ever? It wasn't that she was expecting to change the world, exactly; she just yearned to be doing something with meaning.

'Paying your mortgage has meaning,' said Rachel.

And what a mortgage it was. Rachel was right. It was the height of privilege to expect that her work should bring her purpose as well as the money to pay her bills. To work for spiritual fulfilment was a luxury not afforded most people on the planet. Nonetheless, it was difficult to see that the world needed yet another puff piece on fast fashion or urban coffee trends. Jess sometimes felt that she was polluting the earth with rubbish just as surely as if she were manufacturing plastic straws.

She picked up her phone again and frowned at the screen. Still nothing.

There was a chance that he would email, but he'd said that he would call.

Jess checked her email.

She checked her phone's volume.

She set the phone down and glanced up as a family arrived noisily into the tearoom. The immediate effect was of hum and motion, and it took a moment to assess the situation: a crying baby in a carrier on the man's front, a rain-bedraggled child of five or so dragging on the woman's arm, an uncowed toddler with a clear list of demands and a mind to make them heard. They were casting about for an unoccupied table, brightly coloured backpacks bumping chairs and walls as they manoeuvred through the cosy space.

Jess met the mother's eyes and recognised that here was a human at the end of her tether. 'I was just leaving,' she offered, indicating her empty cup.

Jess decided not to go back upstairs into the museum. She would head to the library instead; perhaps even pull up a bit of research for the Well Walk piece. Not start it, she wouldn't do any of the writing, she'd just make sure that she was ready when the call came through.

She was still digging about in the bottom of her bag as she pushed open the museum's front door and stepped out into the street. With the first raindrops to hit her head came the image of her umbrella sitting on the kitchen bench at home. She glanced upwards and the low grey sky glowered back; she would be drenched by the time she got to the Tube. She was about to go back inside when she spotted the cab turning from Guildford Street. A cab was a luxury she could ill afford these days, with every spare penny going on her mortgage, but as thunder rumbled in the distance she stuck out her arm to wave it down. She would just have to limit herself to a single glass of wine when she met Rachel for their Friday evening drink. Her own fault for having let herself be charmed into buying in a part of London where a large glass of rosé could set you back twenty quid.

Her phone rang at the precise moment that she was clambering into the back of the taxi. She jammed it between her chin and ear. 'Hello – would you hold for a minute?' she said, sliding onto the rain-spattered seat and setting down her bag. 'British Library, please,' she told the driver. She reached to pull the door shut with a thud, and as the driver executed a neat turn and started heading west, gave her attention back to the caller. 'I'm sorry,' she said. 'I'm here.'

'Jess? Is this Jessica Turner-Bridges?'

Jess steeled herself, trying to keep her hopes contained. 'Speaking.'

She would always remember the warm smell of the taxi's heating and the efficient swiping of its windscreen wipers. The shock of the call's content was compounded by the fact that she'd been expecting a very different conversation. Because it wasn't the editor of the magazine supplement at all, but a voice from long ago and far away, a different life, bringing her the worst report possible; news she had dreaded receiving ever since she'd left Sydney for London.

CHAPTER TWO

'But how did she fall?' Rachel was ensconced in their regular spot in the dim, cushion-backed booth at the back of the tapas place, downstairs on the corner of Heath Street and Church Row. 'Doesn't she have a nurse who's engaged to look after her?'

'It was his afternoon off,' explained Jess. 'She was meant to be in the library writing letters – that's where Patrick left her. I don't know what she was thinking. She'd had her main meal. Her bedroom's just across the hall. She shouldn't have had to go anywhere else.'

And certainly nowhere near the stairs on the top landing. This was the part that Jess had trouble comprehending. In all the time she had lived with her grandmother in the house overlooking the harbour, she couldn't recall Nora ever going near the attic. Jess wasn't supposed to go up there either. It was one of the few places her grandmother had forbidden her from playing when she was a child, because the staircase was so steep and dangerous. Naturally the warnings had only acted as an enticement – Jess had spent a lot of time sneaking into the A-framed room – but never once had Nora breached the door or shown any interest whatsoever in climbing the stairs herself. With a home the size of Darling House, she hadn't needed to. Everything of value, and some besides, had a storage place in a cupboard or desk or drawer in the main downstairs rooms.

Jess eyed the glass of wine she'd been nursing since she and Rachel met. It was the wrong day to have chosen to limit herself, but in the end she hadn't had much choice. She'd been so shocked by the phone call in the taxi, and so intent on learning as much from her grandmother's housekeeper as she could – thank God Mrs Robinson had forgotten her shopping bag and returned to Darling House to collect it – that she'd asked the driver to take her all the way home to Hampstead. With the roadworks in New End, he'd ended up circling back around West Heath Road and the whole exercise had cost close to twenty-five quid. 'I just can't figure out why she'd have gone up there. It's not even a proper staircase. It's steep and dimly lit.'

Rachel, delicately: 'How old is she now?'

'Nearly ninety. And I know what you're thinking, but she's as sharp as a tack.'

Rachel nodded kindly, but Jess could tell that she didn't really understand. Nora wasn't a little old lady doddering about, forgetting where she was going and accidentally climbing the stairs to the attic when she meant to walk across the hall to bed. Nora was formidable and fiercely bright; age had not wearied her in the slightest. She had founded the Nora Turner-Bridges Group after her divorce, back when women – particularly the single sort – were allowed to be secretaries or shopgirls and not much else; nearly sixty years later she still telephoned the office each day for a report.

The fact that Rachel didn't know Nora opened a chasm between them and Jess felt a sudden ache in her chest, an isolating sense of panic. She wanted to explain that Nora was wise and bold and ferociously loyal. That she had taken Jess in and loved her like a daughter and never made her feel that it was inconvenient to be saddled with a child again;

that she had made Jess believe she was a longed-for, precious gift. A second chance, Nora used to say, on the only occasions Jess had known her to get that sad, distant look in her eyes. They had been each other's second chance.

A pompous bearded man at a nearby table laughed percussively; Jess glanced his way and the loneliness was gone as quickly as it had arrived. She said simply, 'Nora isn't like other people. She's her very own climate system.'

'Sounds like someone else I know.'

Jess had heard the sentiment a lot when she was growing up, not least from Nora herself, who'd used to be fond of telling Jess she was a 'true Turner', especially when she'd excelled at school or pushed herself to a place in the swim squad or excoriated the opposition debating team. Jess had enjoyed the comparison enormously back then. Now, though, considering her life's recent downward trajectory, it embarrassed her. 'No,' she said firmly. 'Nora's one of a kind.'

Rachel put her hand on Jess's. 'Tell me what the hospital said.'

'I know almost none of the details. By the time I finished the call with Mrs Robinson and dialled the hospital, the doctor was gone and the nurses had just changed shift. I'd hoped they'd be able to tell me more, but the nurse I spoke with didn't have any information beyond what was written on Nora's chart: she fell, she hit her head and broke her wrist, she was stable but sleeping. They said to call back in the morning.'

'Morning in Sydney must be soon?'

'Eight o'clock tonight.' Jess checked her watch. There was still an hour to kill. 'Her doctor will be on the ward again then. Once I've spoken with him, I'll know whether I need to go back.'

Rachel was surprised. 'To Australia? When?'

'Tomorrow night. I've already held a seat; I've got until the morning to confirm.' She did not mention that she'd only had the points to book a one-way flight.

'You'll miss the awards.'

'I know.'

'But we already bought the revenge dress!'

'Alas, it might have to wait for another chance. If Nora needs me . . . who else is there?'

'Your mother?'

'Please.' Jess rolled her eyes.

'Are you sure you're not considering going back *because* you'll miss the awards?'

'Definitely not.'

Rachel took a sip of wine, her gaze wandering pointedly beyond Jess's left shoulder.

'I'm *not*. I can assure you, I'm absolutely fine in that regard.'

'Then if the doctor says your grandmother's okay, why don't you leave it a few more days? Do both. Go to the awards, wear that fabulous dress, show the Lad how absolutely fine you are, and impress the hell out of every editor you meet. Then you can board your flight, victorious, first thing Tuesday morning. Go home for Christmas.'

'Maybe,' said Jess, more to placate her friend than because she was genuinely considering it. The truth was, once she'd allowed herself to imagine missing the awards, a sense of deep relief had come over her. She wasn't pining for Matt, and she truly would be fine if she ran into him. She'd seen him a few times since they broke up, Maxine too, on one occasion; they were all being very grown-up about it. But there were limits. 'I'll think about it.'

'Good,' said Rachel, sliding out of the booth. 'Now, finish your drink, for God's sake, so we can order you another when I get back.'

Jess's gaze followed Rachel as she disappeared towards the loo, before coming to rest on a group of people a decade or so younger than she was. Their faces glowed with the warmth that comes from being in a densely packed room, with friends and food and wine, on a Friday night, in the greatest city on earth, with enough money in their pockets and nothing but the weekend ahead.

As she watched, a good-looking young man at the end of the table said something that made the others laugh, and the girl beside him smiled with a proprietorial brow-arch of amusement that marked her immediately as his partner. The ghost of dinner parties past came back to Jess. She and Matt had been that sort of double act, once upon a time. She could remember a particularly amusing set piece they'd performed, usually when someone in their wider circle had fallen victim to the perils of parenthood. Jess would say something about the demands of her job and Matt would concur, adding, with that droll smile of his, that besides – he wasn't the mothering sort. Cue: laughter.

But the last laugh had been on them. That is, it had been on her. For now, she had neither a job, a boyfriend, nor a child, while Matt had a new young wife, a delightful five-month-old daughter, and a sudden, born-again evangelism regarding the wonders of fatherhood. He also had a column in the *Daily Mail*, after the runaway success of a piece he'd written following the baby's birth. The column was called 'Dad About London', with the 'D' in Dad written atop a crossed-out 'L', suggesting that our one-time Lad had been reformed. Jess had heard through the grapevine that a book was forthcoming.

She took a larger sip of wine than she'd intended and cursed herself for not savouring it. The bearded man at the next table burst into laughter again, and as the sound reverberated off the low domed ceiling, Jess was of a sudden mind to slap him.

She was saved from the urge by Rachel, weaving her way back between tables. 'Speaking of editors,' Rachel said, sliding into place, 'did you hear anything about Well Walk?'

Jess didn't think she hesitated for long, but she must have, because Rachel followed up with: 'He passed? Bloody hell, what's the matter with him? Did he say why?'

'He doesn't want a series. He's looking for pieces that are more "immediate", less "historical".' The editor had telephoned soon after Mrs Robinson, while Jess had been in the process of trying to scrape together the taxi fare plus tip.

'I don't speak writer. What does "immediate" mean?'

'Personal. From my perspective.'

'Well, write about the history of *your* house, then. It's oldish – at least a hundred years.'

'Maybe. Though I got the impression that was one of the aspects he didn't like. He said people don't read the magazine for a history lesson. They want to see their own feelings and experiences reflected in the life of the writer. It must be "essential".'

'God – let's get you that drink.'

'No, I'm good.' Lately, it seemed like every conversation she and Rachel had was focused on some disappointment or failure in Jess's life. She wasn't sure when she'd become this person, so needful of reassurance. It made her feel like a stranger to herself.

'What are you talking about? My shout.'

Jess smiled in thanks. 'I really do have to go. I want to

ring the hospital early and catch the doctor before he starts rounds.'

Rachel nodded. 'I suppose I ought to be getting home, too. Responsibilities and all that. No matter how much I beg the nanny to move in with us, she insists on going back to the peace and quiet of her own home in the evenings.'

They paid the bill and then shrugged into their coats and scarves at the bottom of the stairs, pulling on woollen hats and gloves as they emerged onto the cold street. The forecast was for possible snow, but so far it had managed only icy sleet, visible as flecks in the streetlights. They hugged one another and Rachel looked at Jess seriously. 'Call me as soon as you hear about Nora. And if you're going back to Oz, let me know if there's anything I can do while you're away. Water plants, check your place, play your piano.' She grinned and kissed Jess on the cheek and then started making her way down Church Row in the direction of St John's.

Jess watched for a minute as her friend crossed the street and turned the corner into Holly Walk, hurrying towards the warm cottage halfway up the hill, filled with noise and toys and a cheerfully tired banker husband called Ben.

Jess walked between slow traffic on Heath Street and cut down Perrin's Lane. The Christmas lights were up, strings of tiny gold bulbs zigzagging across the narrow, cobbled alley. She always felt that the city came into its own at this time of year. Tonight, though, the beauty of the wonky houses and ivy-clad bricks, the lanterns on the cottages of the well-heeled, the hint of warm domesticity glowing yellow from behind the curtains, was acute. It pressed upon her sharply from all sides and where once she had felt part of it, now she felt as if she were outside, an observer looking in.

Her phone vibrated in her pocket as she was passing

Waterstones. She fumbled it out with a gloved hand and freed one cold finger to swipe.

The message was from Rachel: *I know what you should write!!* it exclaimed, followed by three dots presaging more to come.

Something everyone can relate to!

More dots, pulsing for long enough this time that the suspense took Jess across the zebra crossing and around the corner into the top of Flask Walk.

The message arrived as she was passing the fairy-lit window of Judy Green's Garden Store: *If you go back to Australia, write about that. Write about how it feels to go home after so long away.*

CHAPTER THREE

Heathrow Airport, 8 December 2018

The Qantas flight back to Australia departed late at night, and Jess had left Hampstead with hours to spare; partly because she was catching the train and you never knew what might happen, but also because, having packed and readied the house for her absence, she'd started to feel like a guest who'd overstayed her welcome and was now being tolerated by a well-mannered host. The train ride had been smooth, and she'd arrived well ahead of time, setting herself up in the Pret a Manger near security so she could have a bite to eat before going through the rigmarole. She preferred it on this side, where travellers and their families were still together. She liked to guess at their relationships and the purpose of travel, the destinations, and the length of time they'd be away.

She had been observing a group of three at the table beside her own and continued to watch them now as they made their way towards the security area. The young woman carrying a backpack was clearly the one leaving, walking faster than the older couple, with an eagerness and energy to her gait. A few metres out from the door she stopped and they all embraced; some further words were exchanged, the backpack was referenced, and a laugh was shared. Another round of hugs and the girl continued to the door alone. She gave her parents (presumably) a quick wave, flashed them a bright smile, and didn't look back again.

Jess had been that young girl once, twenty years before. She knew about the excitement on the other side of the gate: the first taste of real freedom, the thrilling sense of being, at last, in control of one's own destiny.

It was Nora who had seen her off at Sydney Airport, for what they'd both thought then would be a gap year. Jess had a new travel wallet – a gift from Nora – with her boarding pass inside, a set of traveller's cheques, the name of the schoolfriend's mother's aunt who'd agreed to let her stay in her attic room in Holborn, and a printed flight itinerary with a return date twelve months hence. She and Nora had waited together near the coffee shop at the International Departures gate, Jess too nervous and excited to drink more than a few sips of her cappuccino, Nora talking enough for both of them, happy chatter about various people they knew. Only when the departure board updated to show that Jess's flight to London via Singapore was being called did Nora run out of things to say.

Jess checked her documents for a final time and said: 'I guess I should get moving.'

'It wouldn't be an ideal start to your grand adventure if you were to miss your flight,' Nora agreed.

They went together to the gate and hugged, and in that moment Jess was seized by a sudden impulse to tell her grandmother it was a terrible mistake, that of course she didn't want to go all the way to London where she knew no one; she wanted to go home to Darling House instead, to sit together on the downstairs sofa with the BBC box set of *Pride and Prejudice*, and to take up Nora's friend's offer of a cadetship with the *Sydney Morning Herald*.

Perhaps her grandmother sensed by the tightness of the hug that Jess's excitement was balanced on a knife's edge, liable to tilt at any moment into trepidation, because she took both of Jess's hands and held them firmly between her own. 'Someone I used to know a long time ago told me once that fear is the doorway to opportunity. And I can assure you, my love, that every good thing that's happened to me since has come through acting *despite* my fears.' She wrapped Jess in a firm embrace. 'Just remember,' she said softly, 'no matter what happens, I'll be here, and you can always, always come home.'

From her vantage point in the Heathrow Pret, as a new group colonised the table beside her, Jess jotted the memory in her notebook. She was glad that it had come to her. It would give the article she was writing a nice circularity if she were to include Nora's advice from twenty years before. For all the trouble that she'd gone to and the angst she'd felt regarding her Well Walk idea, the 'Home to Sydney' pitch, dashed off after her phone call to the hospital the night before, had been approved with great alacrity, the editor requesting delivery at the end of the following week. With a return airfare still to find, Jess had hastily agreed.

Truth be told, it wasn't going to be difficult. Far from the heavily researched investigative reports she'd built her career on, this was a glorified travel piece about a place and person she knew well. She'd sketched out a rough outline on her way to the airport, asterisking a few spots where it would work to include some up-to-date colour and detail. Now, she made a brief note of an experience all too familiar from previous flights back to Australia: the befuddlement of long-haul travel; how it felt to lose a day from the calendar; the dizziness and sea legs on arrival and the irresistible pull towards sleep when one was least expecting it.

Jess capped her pen and eyed the departure board. Her flight had been assigned a gate and there was only an hour and a bit until it was due to depart. She tucked her notebook in her carry-on bag, checked that she had her laptop, phone, wallet and AirPods, and started making her way towards security. The man and woman from before were still there, she noticed, together and yet alone, each watching the empty departure door as if they expected their daughter to reappear at any moment. Perhaps they planned to stay until her flight had gone; maybe they didn't know quite what to do next. It was possible, Jess supposed, that after being responsible for another human being for so long, to be released was not to be set free so much as to be cut adrift.

As she took off her shoes and loaded them with her computer into a pair of security tubs, Jess wondered what Nora had done after she'd disappeared through the gates in Sydney. It must have been strange for her grandmother to return to Darling House. Jess had been living with her for a decade by then, and it was a very big house in which to find oneself alone. Jess was still struck every time she walked through her own front door in Hampstead by how inanimate the house had felt since Matt moved out; how quiet. Sometimes she found herself tiptoeing out of respect, at other times making noise to spite it. When she'd arrived home the night before, after her drink with Rachel, the air had settled slowly, silently, around her, and she'd quickly switched on the lights and the television to bring back some semblance of life.

She and Matt had rented the place when they moved to North London and been ecstatically happy; it sat in a quiet pocket by the small village green, in a street so short and

secluded it was easy to walk past with no idea of its existence. When the landlady put it on the market, though, the
open houses began to drive them mad. The idea that they
might buy it themselves, if only to put a stop to the process,
had been a joke between them at first. But the more they
made it, the less funny it seemed, until finally Matt decided
to cash in the shares his father had left him for a deposit and
they found themselves putting together a lengthy mortgage
application. 'You can't go wrong with London real estate,'
they'd told one another nervously, frowning at the eye-
watering figure on the loan forms.

Jess had taken over the mortgage repayments when Matt
left, and they'd come to a complicated agreement giving her
the option to buy him out in two years' time if she was able.
She had since lost her salary, gained a redundancy, and been
getting by for the most part on savings. Jess had always felt
lucky to live where she did; now she felt like a fraud, an
imposter, going through the motions of a beautiful life that
had once seemed strong and substantial, but had been
revealed as tissue-paper thin.

'Do you think your family would help?' Rachel had asked
one night, when Jess was agonising over whether she'd be
able to stay.

By 'family', she meant, of course, Nora, but Jess had shaken
her head so vehemently that Rachel had taken it no further.
The truth of the matter was that Nora would almost certainly
have been willing to help; she'd have been glad, even. She
loved houses – she'd built a business out of restoring them –
and had been delighted when Jess announced that she and
Matt were taking the plunge, demanding photographs and
descriptions and all sorts of specifics. But asking would have
meant admitting to the two things Jess was determined Nora

should not know: that she had lost both her job and her partner in remarkably quick succession. And so she'd committed herself to making the loan repayments herself.

Jess didn't like keeping secrets from Nora, but she was embarrassed by her current plight, and she didn't want her grandmother to think less of her. Besides, the situation wasn't permanent. Any day now she was going to turn the corner. In the meantime, she was doing everything she could to reduce her costs. A trip back to Australia wasn't something she'd factored into her budget, but she'd been left with no choice. When she'd called the hospital a second time and asked the doctor for an update, he told her Nora had been confused upon waking. 'It's not unexpected after suffering a trauma,' he explained. 'The MRI and CT showed some swelling.'

'I'm calling from London,' Jess said. 'I've held a flight, but I wasn't sure whether I should take it now or wait until Nora's back at home.'

The doctor's advice had been blunt. 'Your grandmother's eighty-nine years old,' he said. 'If you're thinking of coming home to see her, I wouldn't leave it any longer.'

While this might have seemed obvious to anyone else, it had struck Jess hard. She had always known there was a chance she'd receive a call in the night, the voice of a stranger delivering bad news. It was a reality of expat life. For some reason, though, she'd imagined that the message would pertain to her mother. It was far easier to picture Polly weakened by accident or illness than to accept that Nora was subject to the frailties that afflicted the rest of humanity.

But the doctor's meaning had been clear, and on ending the call Jess had gone straight to the Qantas website to confirm her seat on the next evening's flight.

*

With her shoes back on, and her laptop and other items gathered from the scanning machine, Jess emerged into the Terminal 3 departure hall. At the best of times, there was nothing remotely appealing or comforting about the place; in December, it was bedlam. Ordinarily, Jess operated outside school holiday rhythms, and it was always a mild surprise to head out the door and find children in her usual spaces. But on a Saturday this close to Christmas, naturally enough, they were everywhere, dragging miniature suitcases into the paths of unwitting adults, sporting light-up Santa hats and novelty sunglasses – even a blow-up swimming ring with a Rudolph nose in one instance.

She eventually joined the line at the final passport check for her flight, and then made her way into the glass-walled waiting room. She preferred it here. Unlike the departure hall, which was no-man's-land masquerading as your local shopping mall – shops and restaurants as a way of stopping people from realising they were now officially nowhere, between customs zones, on the edge of terrestrial existence – the boarding gate didn't pretend to be anything other than what it was: a holding room for human beings who were only going in one direction from here.

Jess found a spare seat overlooking the tarmac. On the other side of the window, in the dark London evening, she could see the big white bird that was going to fly them through the night back to Sydney. A fog had come in and the ground crew were using orange torches to signal as they carried out their routine tasks.

Four years ago, almost to the day, she'd taken Matt back with her to spend Christmas with Nora. Nora had liked Matt, and he'd *loved* Nora. He had also adored Darling House. 'It looks like it should be standing on the banks of the Mississippi,' he'd said one day. They'd been sitting together at the wrought-iron outdoor setting in the shade of an enormous jacaranda, sipping mint juleps and looking back across the garden towards the tall, weatherboard house.

'You're practically in the subtropics,' Nora reminded him. 'My grandfather built Darling House five years after he'd arrived from Scotland. He knew by then that the climate was going to require something different from what he'd been used to as a boy.'

'She's a grand old lady,' Matt said of the house. 'Dressed up in an iron-lace shawl, looking out over her harbour.'

Nora smiled. 'That's exactly what she is. It's the reason she and I get on so well together. We're two of a kind.'

Nora had lived in Darling House all her life and was as much a part of the building as the pair of lions guarding its entrance gate and the brick chimneys punctuating the sparkling blue sky. It was almost impossible to imagine her anywhere else. Jess had only to close her eyes now to invoke a vivid picture of her grandmother standing on the wide concrete steps that led to the front door, both arms lifted in welcome.

Countless people had tried to buy the house from her over the years: celebrities, socialites and developers. She'd been offered a small fortune, but Nora had remained resolute. 'I'm going to die in this house,' she'd said, time and again. 'What do I care for money? Far more important to me are the memories in these walls.'

Not that all of Nora's memories were good ones. Her childhood had been less than idyllic, Jess knew; her parents had been away much of the time, and she'd been left behind with a series of nannies and governesses – some of them intent, it seemed, on making the small girl's life a misery. But Nora had been blessed with a powerful imagination and a gift for make-believe and had created a whole world for herself in the garden and the hidden places of the house. It occurred to Jess that her grandmother would have been an excellent writer, had she not parlayed her love for stories into rescuing and restoring houses.

Nora had explained her passion for buildings to Matt in the same terms Jess had heard her use when she was interviewed for a Women in Business story on local radio some years before: 'People who grow up in old houses come to understand that buildings have characters. That they have memories and secrets to tell. One must merely learn to listen, and then to comprehend, as with any language. The language of houses is my mother tongue. This house taught it to me when I was a very small child.'

Jess wondered sometimes whether the house had meant so much to Nora because it was solid and reliable where her absent parents were not. Jess could certainly relate to that.

'Well, I think it's the most beautiful house I've ever seen,' Matt said, and given that loving Darling House was the key to Nora's heart, she'd given him her stamp of approval. Privately to Jess, though, she confessed she was confused as to why two successful people with enough money would choose not to have children. 'The world's overpopulated, Nora,' Jess answered, only half joking.

Nora had let the subject go, but only temporarily. With each year that passed, as Jess crept closer to forty, her grandmother grew more perplexed. 'Is it Matthew? Is he putting up opposition? Because it's different for men, you know. They can afford to wait. If you were simply to get pregnant, he'd change his mind soon enough. And if he didn't? Well, you'd have your baby, and I'll promise you something – you won't much care for anything else once you do.'

This advice had been delivered over the phone, so Nora wasn't able to see Jess roll her eyes. Jess didn't argue, though; she knew better than that. Nora was a person of great certainty, and on this subject she was intractable. She'd only had one child, Jess's mother, Polly, and had told Jess more than once that it was the greatest sorrow of her life that she hadn't been able to have more. 'I always imagined myself the matriarch of a large family,' she said, 'with cousins and in-laws and babies everywhere. But it wasn't to be. Just your mother, and thank God for her, because through her came you.'

Jess found it impossibly sad that someone with as much to give as Nora should find herself with so few doting family members. Many times, she'd wondered how her own mother could have been so selfish as to abandon Nora – and Jess, too, for that matter, when she was ten years old. But she'd learned not to make the point out loud. Nora was not a wallower and she'd refused to let Jess wallow, either. 'We can't allow ourselves to be the victims of our childhoods,' she said. 'One can't blame one's parents – or indeed one's children – for everything. Most people do the best they can and sometimes, sadly, it's not enough.'

Whether or not Jess's mother had done her best was arguable. She had left her daughter behind when she went north to Queensland to start a new life. 'It wasn't that she didn't love you,' Nora insisted, loyal to a fault and always ready to defend her errant daughter. 'Polly just couldn't cope. She wasn't ready to be a mother. She was very young, and she fell pregnant so easily. It's different when one has to wait and long and dream.'

'Easy come, easy go,' Jess said.

'Now, Jess dear, cynicism is very coarse, and it wasn't like that. She couldn't be the mother you needed – and it was big of her, when you think about it, to realise the fact. Besides, things turned out for the best, wouldn't you say? We've done okay together, you and me.'

They had done better than okay.

The plane had started boarding and Jess showed her ticket to the smiling flight attendant at the gate. 'Welcome back, Ms Turner-Bridges,' said the woman, her accent creating an instant bond. 'Travelling all the way through to Sydney with us tonight?'

'I am.'

'Enjoy your flight home.'

Stepping onto the air bridge, Jess experienced a sudden wave of vertigo. The cold air from outside had crept through the metal cracks and she was acutely aware of being in a liminal space: between terminal and plane, between countries, even between acts of her own life. The sensation reminded her of when she was a child, still living with her mother, and they had used to go to the park on the top of the peninsula. There was a seesaw that Jess would run to use. She liked to stand in the middle of it, shifting her weight back and forth in minute increments until she achieved perfect balance.

She glanced up at the large HSBC ad as she reached the end of the tunnel. On it was an enormous photograph of Piccadilly Circus. She thought of her house in Hampstead, the tapas bar, Rachel, and the houses along Well Walk, Judy Green's, Waterstones and the Heath. It was her neighbourhood, her life, all of it vitally real only hours before, and yet somehow tenuous now, little more than an illusion – a lovely dream dissolving behind her as she stepped onto the plane.

Where everything was bright and busy, and smelled like travel, and existed outside the regular rules of time, and Jess was focused again, because at the end of this journey, still a whole twenty-four hours and several oceans and continents away, Nora was waiting for her. And the pull towards home was physical and Jess was impatient to be on solid ground again, on the other side.

CHAPTER FOUR

Adelaide Hills, 24 December 1959

'Tell us again, Mr Summers, what you were doing at the waterhole?'

Percy had already answered all of their questions, but he understood they had a job to do, so he swallowed a sigh and told them again what had happened. He'd been at the police station on West Road for hours now. Over the course of time since he'd made the grim discovery, shock had given way to numbness and he found that he could now recount the details with some degree of separation – why he was there, what he'd found, the terrible hours that had followed as first one official and then another arrived at the God-awful scene.

He was distracted, though; bone-tired. The early rise, the long ride from the Station, the heat; his thoughts flitted and slipped like insects at dusk. As he reached the point in his telling that described his decision to walk up to the picnic rather than turn and head back into town, a low rumble of thunder sounded. Here, then, was the weather they'd been warned about.

'So, you went up to the Turner family's picnic to what . . . to say hello?'

'That's right.'

'Did you know the deceased personally, Mr Summers?'

A flash of sheet lightning illuminated the world outside the window and Percy flinched.

'Did you know Mrs Turner and her children personally?' the policeman repeated.

'My wife and I – Meg . . .' Percy began, before trailing off. Meg would be wondering where he was. He'd telephoned from the McNamara Station the night before, a lifetime ago it now seemed, and told her he'd be leaving first thing. *Don't be late*, she'd said. *And don't even think about stopping on the way home if you know what's good for you*. Percy had caught her meaning clear enough. He'd gathered that she was planning something; one of the boys had mentioned a birthday cake. 'My wife—'

'Thing is, sergeant' – this was Hugo Doyle, one of the local mounted constables, interjecting from where he stood against the wall by the open window – 'here in Tambilla there aren't many of us who don't know one another.'

Across the desk from Percy, the policeman who'd asked the question – Sergeant Peter Duke was how he'd introduced himself when he turned up at the waterhole at the Wentworth place – leaned back in the wooden spring chair. Not his own chair, mind; this wasn't his station. Sergeant Duke had come from Adelaide that afternoon. Evidently someone on high had decided this was a situation requiring out-of-town help.

Percy wondered how Sergeant Kelly, whose desk it was, felt about that. Kelly was new to Tambilla himself, having only recently arrived from the Mount Barker station. He had a large pair of boots to fill. Until recently, this had been Ernie Staffsmith's turf. Ernie had dominated the town for decades, as far back as when Percy was a boy. He'd been a big man, both in stature and reputation. Fair but tough, with a chest the size of a boulder and lines on his face as deep as the creases in an old saddle. As kids, they'd all lived in fear of Sergeant Staffsmith's looming shadow.

A sudden wave of missing the older man came over Percy. Never mind the hidings he'd received, the stern warnings and reports made to his parents. This loss of a childhood institution suddenly felt like a metaphor for the impermanence of it all – sunny afternoons, happiness, a human being's life. It was all so fleeting.

'You did know Mrs Turner personally then, Mr Summers?' Ernie Staffsmith certainly wouldn't have taken kindly to being usurped by a counterpart from the city.

'My wife and I run the grocery shop,' said Percy. 'We've been supplying food and sundries up the hill for as long as the Turners have lived on Willner Road.'

'And how long is that?'

'Fourteen years or so. They arrived after the war.'

'Your wife was a friend to Mrs Turner?'

'Meg is a friend to everyone.'

Sergeant Duke made a note and then drew a slow, straight line across the page. His shirtsleeves had been rolled up to his elbows, a concession to the heat and the storm humidity, revealing a pale, twisted scar running the length of his left forearm. 'So, you saw the family, the picnic laid out under the tree, and you went to say hello.'

Percy nodded. 'It seemed rude not to, particularly as I'd brought Blaze onto their land for a swim.'

'Was that unusual?'

He had already explained all of this. He'd already said that now and then he took Blaze along the creek when he was returning from a delivery down south. Percy was a patient man, but he felt a surge of frustration. When they left the Wentworth place, he'd heard Sergeant Kelly talking about rounding up some of the local men. He wanted to be out there with them, helping to search before the weather broke. Not here, in this small, stifling interview room.

'Mr Summers?'

'No. It wasn't unusual. But I didn't often see anyone else while I was there.'

'You said earlier that you could tell from the start things weren't right.' Sergeant Duke leaned forward. 'A "sixth sense" is how you put it.'

Even now, Percy's skin crawled as he remembered that walk up the hill towards the gathering. 'I got a strange feeling. I've had it once or twice before. Out in the bush. Everything was so still. Lifeless, you know?'

Sergeant Duke's face remained neutral. 'Was there anything in particular out of order? Anything specific?'

'Not that I can remember.'

'You didn't see any evidence that the picnic had been disturbed?'

'How do you mean?'

'Was there any sign that someone else had been there?'

Percy considered the scene, picking over his memory of it. 'I don't think so.'

'Did you notice any prints?'

Some of the men at the Wentworth place had been talking about dogs, Percy remembered. At the time, their words had drifted and dissipated. Any relevance to the horrific event by the waterhole had been lost on him. Now, though, he thought of the recent attacks in town, hens taken right from their coops – even a lamb one night, over at the McKenzie place. He thought, too, of the men out searching. The implication of why, precisely, the sergeant was asking was suddenly clear, and Percy felt sick. 'I can't remember. I didn't notice, I'm sorry.'

'That's all right, Mr Summers. If you remember something later, you can always come back to us. Talk me through your movements once you reached the family. You said you went immediately to Mrs Turner and ascertained she wasn't breathing.'

Percy's left hand brushed the fingers of his right. Strange the way the absence of something could leave an imprint. 'Yes.'

'Did you check any of the children?'

'No.'

'What about the baby's basket? A woven thing, hanging in the tree?'

'No.'

'What's that, Mr Summers?'

'I didn't go near the tree.'

He would curse that oversight for the rest of his life. Percy had been standing on the edge of the scene when they'd made the discovery. He'd been watching the police photographer, a thin young man with dark-rimmed glasses and a tan suit, sent from Adelaide to record images of the picnic: a wide view of the setting, a close-up of the crumbs left on plates. This wrist, that ankle, each kicked-off shoe. He'd been waiting to wake up and learn he'd dreamed the whole thing, when from beneath the willow there'd come a frantic call: *It's empty! The baby's gone!*

'You noticed the crib, though, Mr Summers?'

'I saw a hanging basket, but I didn't think – it didn't occur to me to look inside.' Percy's throat was dry. 'Once I realised what had happened, I couldn't think of anything but getting help.'

'So you went straight to the Hughes house?'

Once again, they had been through this. 'I knew Alastair – Mr Hughes – had a car and a telephone and that he and Esther were likely to be home.'

'Alastair Hughes is the local solicitor, I think you said?'

'That's right.'

'So you rode down Willner Road to number' – Sergeant Duke checked his notes – 'one hundred and six, and found both Mr and Mrs Hughes at home.'

Percy had knocked frantically on the door. When Esther Hughes answered, peering at him through her cat's-eye glasses, she'd guessed immediately that something was terribly wrong. She'd gestured that he should join her inside and called for her husband to come quickly. Alastair had appeared from a room off the hallway, still holding a pen. He'd been wearing odd socks, Percy remembered.

'Can you tell me again what you said to Mr and Mrs Hughes?' asked Sergeant Duke.

'I told them what I'd seen.'

'The words you used, if you don't mind, Mr Summers. Can you tell me the exact words you said to Mr and Mrs Hughes?'

Percy closed his eyes, concentrating. 'I told them that Mrs Turner and her children were by the waterhole. That there'd been some sort of accident. That Mrs Turner wasn't breathing.'

'An accident.' Sergeant Duke tapped the pen against his chin. 'I wonder.' He leaned back in the chair, his gaze shifting to rest on the elaborate plaster cornice that joined wall to ceiling. At length, he seemed to remember that he was mid-interview, glanced at the face of his wristwatch, and said, 'Go on, Mr Summers. You were at the Hughes house.'

'And then Alastair – Mr Hughes – telephoned immediately to the police station for help.'

'And you both returned to the scene?'

'Alastair drove us back, and we arrived in time to meet up with Sergeants Kelly and Doyle.'

Hugo Doyle nodded grave encouragement from where he stood against the wall as the sergeant turned back a few pages of his spiral pad. 'Bear with me,' he said.

Behind Sergeant Duke, on the other side of the window, the world was almost dark. The light bulb above the desk reflected yellow in one of the four mottled panes of glass. In the gap at the bottom of the sash, where the window was partly open, Mount Lofty's ridge line appeared at intervals as flutters of lightning flared against the deep-navy sky.

The range had been a compass all his life; Percy could have drawn the outline of its scarp in his sleep. The Kaurna people of the plains believed that once upon a time a great ancestral giant had been killed, his body collapsing to form the ridge, his ears becoming the twin summits of Mount Lofty and Mount Bonython. Jimmy Riley had told him that a long time ago, when the two of them were camping out near Cleland. His face, lit by the flickering campfire, had worn an expression on it of loss and pride.

Jimmy would be with the search party. He was the best tracker this side of Alice Springs. Young Eric Jerosch had some fine skills, too. Only a few years older than Percy's eldest and still a probationary constable, but he volunteered as scout master for the Piccadilly Valley group and knew the Hills almost as well as Percy had as a lad.

The wind outside had picked up and Percy could hear the scritching noise of fine twiggy branches scraping against the iron roof. A warm gust brought with it the smell of fresh rain hitting parched earth. Somewhere, not too far off, it was already coming down. Percy was impatient. His time would be better spent helping to find the baby than it was sitting in this stuffy room.

A clutch of cockatoos took flight, screeching on the wing as they soared across the dark sky to shelter, and as if receiving a signal Sergeant Duke closed his notepad. 'That's enough for tonight, Mr Summers,' he said. 'I'm sure you're ready to get home. I know my wife will be wondering where I am.'

Percy eased himself out of the chair. His muscles were tight from the ride and the heat and the day's tension, the distress of what he'd found. He stumbled a bit as he gathered his saddlebag from where he'd put it by the base of the desk.

'And Mr Summers – leave a note of your boot type and size at the front, if you wouldn't mind,' Sergeant Duke said with a final nod.

'I'll walk you out.' Hugo Doyle placed a solid hand on Percy's back as they left the interview room and headed down the narrow hall.

Neither man spoke a word until they reached the front office, where Doyle said in a low voice, 'Sorry, Perce. They've sent the top brass up from Adelaide for this one.'

Percy nodded that he understood. 'Anything I can do to help.'

'Hell of a thing. All of them just lying there like that. Last thing a man expects to find.'

Lucy Finkleton was sitting behind the office desk. Above her, a piece of twine had been strung from one nail to another displaying a cheerful assortment of Christmas cards. She stood stiffly and gave a smile that tried for comfort but fell short. 'Hello, Perce.'

'Luce.' They had been at school together when they were kids. Percy could still remember her announcing a wobbly tooth to the class and then crying because she'd swallowed it with her lunch.

'Lucy,' said Doyle, 'would you mind making a note of Percy's boots?' He turned to Percy as she felt about for a pad of paper on the desk. 'Just so we can check no one turned up after you left.'

Percy gave Lucy the details and she copied them down with a careful hand before coming out from behind the desk to trace an outline. When her head was bent over the paper he noticed there were grey strands in her brown hair.

'Give my love to Meg, won't you?' she said when she had finished. 'I telephoned earlier to say you'd be late, and Alastair Hughes called to let us know he had Blaze stabled over at his place. No hurry to collect her. Just when you're ready.' There was a momentary pause and then she said quickly, her voice so quiet it was almost a whisper, 'Such a wicked thing, Perce. Such a *wicked* thing to happen, here in our town.'

Percy was about to agree when he heard his name – 'Mr Summers?' – and looked over his shoulder to see Sergeant Duke standing at the end of the hallway.

For the first time, Percy realised how tall the other man was. The hems of his pale trousers were dirt-stained, and his city shoes were covered in dust. 'One more thing before you go. Did you say your son was involved with the eldest Turner girl?' He glanced at his spiral notebook and then over the top of his glasses at Percy. 'Matilda Turner?'

'They were friends. They went to school together. You know how kids are.'

Sergeant Duke gave no indication whether he knew that or not. He made a note and said, 'His name?'

Percy's attention was caught by the collection of Christmas drawings made by kids from the local school and stuck up on the wall. Maud McKendry had started the tradition years before, as a way to show some community spirit and fundraise for those less fortunate. He could remember his own boys taking part when they were younger, the two of them at the kitchen table with all their coloured pencils and funny ideas. It felt like yesterday; it felt like a hundred years ago.

'Mr Summers?' A drumming of light rain sifted across the iron roof.

'Kurt,' said Percy. The pointed edges of the name stuck in his throat. Only four letters long, and yet weighted with all possible love and hope and dreams. Setting it out there felt like blasphemy. Percy wanted to reach up and catch it in his hands; keep it for himself and away from the gaze of this policeman from the city.

'Thank you, Mr Summers,' said Sergeant Peter Duke, a mild, unreadable expression on his straight-featured face. 'That'll be all for now.'

CHAPTER FIVE

Rain fell in the glow of the streetlights as Percy made his way along the main street of Tambilla. His trousers were wet and fat drops pitted the brim of his leather hat. When he'd stepped out of the police station, he'd stood for a moment in the dark, face to the heavens, and Doyle must've been watching, because he'd come out onto the covered stoop. 'Give ya a lift, Perce?' he'd called over the rain. 'No trouble, mate. Car's round the back.'

Percy had thanked him, but told him no. He preferred to walk. His house wasn't too far and he needed time, before he arrived home, to put some space between himself and what he'd seen that afternoon.

The street was deserted. There was a light on in the kitchen of Betty Diamond's tearoom and a couple of people in the bar of the Tambilla Hotel across the street. Nowhere near as many as usual. A safe bet half the population was still out with the search. Tambilla was that sort of town. People liked to help one another, regardless of their differences. Percy had noticed Reverend Lawson gathered with the others down on Willner Road when he went with Doyle and the sergeant back to the police station. Word travelled fast. This wasn't an easy place in which to have a secret.

Christmas candles flickered in some of the windows along the main street. It was becoming something of a tradition in the Hills, started a few years back in Lobethal. Most of the shops over there – and some of the houses, too – put lights up now to mark the season. People liked that sort of thing. Some, he'd been told, took an evening meal when they went to have a look; a basket packed in the back of their cars with picnic blankets so they could make an occasion of it. Kurt had been talking about inviting Matilda Turner to go with him this year. The day before Percy left for the Station, his son had asked if he could borrow the ute. He'd tried to sound casual, but Percy had always been able to tell from the set of his firstborn's mouth when he was excited. He and Matilda Turner had been friendly since they were knee-high, part of the same group of kids who mucked around on the walk to school and on weekends at the waterhole or down by the old mine. But in recent months, Percy had sensed things were more serious between them. Hard to say how, exactly; an air they carried when they were together, as if they were surrounded by an invisible barrier, so intent on one another that they couldn't help but exclude everyone else. Then he'd seen the necklace on Kurt's desk, sitting in its box among the schoolbooks and careful study notes. 'That's a pretty piece,' he'd said, and if the intended recipient hadn't been obvious to him from the first, the flush that spread across Kurt's cheeks told a clear story.

That had been last week. Today, he'd seen the necklace again, fastened around Matilda Turner's throat, the dainty locket resting in the dip of her décolletage. For a split second he'd thought, *Well, how about that, the lad has done it!* before the shock and other worries pushed it away.

Christ! Percy's hand went out to steady himself against the trunk of the large old oak he was passing. What he'd seen – the horror of what had happened up there by the waterhole. He reached into his shirt pocket for a cigarette.

He'd kicked the habit some years ago, but Esther Hughes had offered him one when he turned up on their doorstep; he'd taken it so hungrily, she'd sent him away with more.

Under the shelter of the tree, he struck a match and drew deeply on the cigarette. What, he wondered, had Sergeant Duke been driving at with his final questions? He'd pushed Doyle for an answer when the two of them were standing out the front. 'What was that all about?' Percy had said, gesturing back towards the building. 'What's any of this got to do with Kurt?'

'Kurt?' Doyle had frowned, a look of genuine confusion on his face. 'Nothing to worry about there, Perce. Just the big city brass, crossing all the t's and dotting the i's.'

But something about the way Sergeant Duke had stood there in the hall writing Kurt's name in his notebook had made Percy's heart freeze in his chest. He kept returning to the pause during the interview as the sergeant considered the word 'accident' in relation to the scene at the Wentworth place. 'I wonder,' he'd said, as if the thought had never occurred to him.

But if not a terrible accident, then what? And why? And how could it have anything to do with Kurt?

A black cat abruptly materialised in the glow of the nearby lamp before disappearing again in a streak across the street. Percy stubbed the last of the cigarette out against the tree's trunk and started to walk again. It couldn't have anything to do with Kurt. It didn't. Like Doyle said, the out-of-town policeman had just been getting his bearings.

One thing Percy knew for certain: his son would be shattered by the news. He was a private person, Kurt – sincere and thoughtful. Marcus was their firebrand, reacting fast and hot whether he was happy or cross. Kurt, though, played things close to his chest; always had, even as a young kid. He would know by now, Percy realised. News travelled fast in small towns, bad news at the speed of light. He felt a pang of exquisite pain, a tactile memory of the fragility of the tiny baby – born six weeks too early – whom he'd held against his chest.

Just beyond the streetlight, Percy caught sight of the shop, and the sign above the awning that read:

Summers & Sons
Grocers

The 's' at the end of 'Sons' was glossier than the rest, a distinction that was less visible in the daytime, but which the nearby light brought to the fore, the white paint gleaming where the rest had faded to matt. It was Meg who'd suggested the recent modification. 'The boys are getting older now, Perce,' she'd said. 'Helping more, doing their bit. Won't be much longer and they'll be finished school. Might as well make it official.'

Percy hadn't agreed exactly – he had his own views about what the boys might do with themselves next – but he hadn't disagreed either, and because Meg had always been the more dynamic of the pair – quicker to action, quicker to anger, quicker to everything – it wasn't long before they'd received a visit from old Ted Holmes, the sign-writer. 'Seems like only yesterday I was climbing this very awning,' he'd said with a tobacco-dry laugh. 'Have a feeling my joints will tell me it's been longer than that, though.'

It had, in fact, been over twenty-five years since the last alteration was made. Percy could remember it well. He'd been seventeen or so, returning from a delivery near Nairne, when he found his mum and dad standing with Mr Holmes on the footpath outside the shop, right about where Percy was now. His father had called him over, regarding him with unusual focus, almost like he was making an appraisal, before telling him there'd been 'a few changes' while he was gone. Percy had looked up to where the old man gestured, at the half-moon panel that sat above the building's awning, and seen that the shop's long-time name – Summers Grocer – now read: Summers & Son Grocers.

'It's our family business,' his dad said. 'Only right that you should be up there on the sign beside me.'

Harry Summers was a man who'd spent a lifetime working hard to feel nothing, so to glimpse emotion on his face was stunning. It took Percy a moment to recognise the expression as pride. The realisation had caught him off guard, and at first he couldn't find coherent words to speak.

His father filled the gap. 'What? Not to your liking?'

'Nah, it's great, Dad.' Percy managed a grin. 'Looks terrific.'

His father, Percy could tell, considered that the alteration bestowed upon his son a great honour. But the change was more than a symbolic gesture. Something that had previously been murky and submerged was lifted into the light: Percy's parents expected him to take over the shop when it became too much for them. He was to step seamlessly into their shoes and walk the path they had laid out for him. His life was mapped, its borders drawn.

Standing on the footpath, his mother smiling at him with satisfaction, Percy experienced panic followed by a heavy sinking sensation. But he didn't have the heart, or the words at his disposal, to tell his parents that he wasn't sure he wanted to stay in Tambilla and become the town's next shopkeeper; that there were things he wanted to learn and places he wanted to see. His dad would never have understood.

In the moment, Percy figured there was no need to say anything. It wasn't like he had a travel plan mapped out, or a clear idea of what he wanted to do with his life. He had a notebook that he kept in his pocket, where he collected ideas and information about the pyramids of Giza and the canals of Venice, the giant sequoia trees in North America and the hot springs near Reykjavik. He kept a list there, too, of the places from his favourite novels. Villages in England, Jane Austen's Bath, the city streets of London and Paris. But all of that was still a dream. He couldn't afford to go anywhere now; he needed a job. Why upset his parents before he had to? He would wait and find a way to break it to them gently.

He didn't realise that by the time he had enough money in his account there'd be Meg to think of, too. They'd been going steady for a few years when his dad started to ask around his pipe of an evening when Percy was going to 'make an honest woman of her'. Percy brushed the questions off initially. It wasn't that he didn't want to marry Meg; he just had a lot of other things to do first. He'd always assumed Meg would want the same.

One night, as he drove the pair of them home from a trip to the pictures to see *The Hound of the Baskervilles*, Percy told her about the money he'd saved and floated the idea that they might spend it on two tickets to England. He'd read in the newspaper about the tensions in Europe, but he was confident Adolf Hitler would see reason: nobody wanted another war – even him, surely.

Meg had looked at Percy as if he were mad, and then

she'd laughed and said, 'I thought you were serious for half a second.' She'd tightened her hold on his hand and smiled contentedly as she leaned back in the passenger seat of the car. 'But it's wonderful news about the money,' she continued dreamily. 'After we're married, we'll be able to build a little place just for us.'

She waited a few more weeks before telling him her own news, which went a fair way to explaining why she'd refused even to consider an adventure on the other side of the world. The two of them were married soon after, when Percy was twenty-two and Meg was eighteen, and just before she started to show. They moved into the coach house at the back of the block, behind the shop and his parents' house.

Percy had dreamed of seeing the Eiffel Tower and walking the coastal paths of Cornwall, but now, he realised, it was time to become a man and put away childish things. He'd been showered with good fortune. These weakened, wonky legs of his could have held him back, but here he was, married to a woman like Meg, with the promise of a solid income and a good home in a fine town where everyone knew his name. And now he was going to be a father.

If his will ever weakened, and he found himself staring out of the window, lost in dreams of other places, his mother's words came back to him, spoken on a hot day at the edge of his convalescent bed when he was just a boy: 'There's other ways to travel.'

She was right. He had books, and there was no barrier to the places he could visit in his own mind.

Percy started across the street towards the shop. He let himself in through the gate that accessed the path running alongside the stone building. It was eerily quiet. For the past fifteen years he wouldn't have been able to make this walk without Buddy-dog racing out to greet him. He felt a wave of sorrow for the loss of the loyal old friend.

The house where they lived – where he had once lived with his mother and father – was behind the shop, in the middle of the narrow, rectangular allotment. There was a light on inside, golden and not too bright. Percy hesitated, wanting to observe the tranquillity of his home before breaching the threshold, the home where he and Meg had raised their boys, where scrapes had been patched and birth-days celebrated, scolding and praise dished out in turn.

He moved closer to the window. There was no one in the room, but the Christmas tree stood in the corner, Meg's treasured decorations hanging at the ends of the branches. The boys had made so many ornaments at school over the years, and Meg had kept them all, wrapping each one on Twelfth Night as carefully as if she'd paid a fortune for it in one of the expensive shops in Adelaide.

Percy pressed his hand against the rough stone wall. The scene on the other side of the window was so homely and warm. He felt a sense of profound isolation. It was as if the world he had known, all the safety he had imagined, had disintegrated and dispersed. He felt soiled. By the day, by the years of his life that had led to this point, by the things that he had seen that afternoon, the sight of them all there on that picnic rug. The stillness, that awful moment. Lord, he would never get it out of his head for as long as he lived.

But there could be no turning back. He would go inside, take off his boots, and line them up against the wall where he always did. He would fetch the gifts he'd hidden before he left for the Station and place them under the Christmas tree for his family to open in the morning. He would find his eldest son and do what he could to support him, and then he would wash himself and climb into bed and wait for the sun to rise on the holiest day of them all.

Percy turned the doorhandle, and as he stepped into the entry room, his hand went to his pocket where he'd put the little wooden bird he'd bought in Hahndorf, back before the world tilted on its axis.

But his pocket was empty.

Somewhere, somehow, in the space of the afternoon, along with so much else, he had lost the little carving.

PART TWO

PART TWO

CHAPTER SIX

Sydney, 10 December 2018

Jess watched as the taxi pulled away and then glanced once more at the morning sky. It was always a shock, after London's dense, mist-filled dome, to see how bright and blue the sky was in Sydney, and how far away. A plane was coming in across the ocean, she noticed, a distant speck of white drawing nearer.

That had been her, three hours before. The flight had been long; she hadn't slept out of London, her thoughts too noisy, but she'd put the time to good use, working on the draft of her article. She'd watched a couple of movies and dragged herself around the time-defying, lit-up mecca of Changi Airport, and then fallen asleep on the second leg, somewhere over Indonesia, waking only when a flight attendant leaned across her to raise the shade on the window.

It had been startling, after the artificial dark of the cabin, to see the rising sun like liquid gold on the horizon. Down below, silver shards flecked the surface of the rippling ocean, and as Jess squinted through the glass at the expanse of deep blue, she'd felt a pull within her chest of sudden yearning. The Pacific: ocean of her childhood. As she watched, rays of light had reached the distant coastline, visible first as a haze, then as a scribble, until eventually, as the plane drew closer, it had resolved into the familiar landscape of coastal suburbs. Streets and parks and buildings, among them the very place where she now stood: Darling House, tucked within its lush garden on the cliff-edged promontory of Vaucluse.

Jess typed her grandmother's security code into the keypad, hoping it was unchanged, and breathed a sigh of relief when the gates swung open. She pulled her suitcase behind her, following the agapanthus-lined driveway through the palm grove, and a memory came of the first ever time she'd dragged a small piece of luggage through this copse of trees. Her mother had been walking beside her that day. Jess had thought she was coming for a visit, but it ended up being the start of a new life.

As she rounded the last bend, Nora's house appeared at the other side of the gravel turning circle, arresting as ever. It was an irony – and perhaps, even, a foreshadowing – that she had been struck especially by the majesty of the house that long-ago day. It had looked to ten-year-old Jess like something from a fairy tale, standing tall with its gleaming weatherboards and elaborate tangle of wisteria branches. The longest boughs of the tallest trees arched together to form a proscenium around the house at centre stage, the sweep of green lawn fell away on all sides, and the round pond was just visible on the western slope, with its glossy lily pads and graceful stone statue. The effect was of a place set apart from the rest of the big wide world.

And at the heart of it, always, Nora.

Jess's gaze went directly to the wide concrete steps that led to the large front porch, as it did each time, but there was no Nora standing there today to meet her.

Mrs Robinson had said she'd left a spare key beneath the doormat, but Jess didn't need it. She still had the one she'd carried with her in high school and then at university; she'd kept it on her keyring after she'd moved to London, even though it was a large Victorian number with a series of loops at one end and big brass teeth at the other. Nora had been pleased to hear that. 'Good girl,' she'd said. 'Keep it close always. A person should never have to knock to come home.'

Jess had received an inordinate number of such small homilies when she was growing up. Her grandmother was unwavering in her convictions. There was a portrait of young Nora hanging above the downstairs sofa, in the sitting room that adjoined the kitchen, and Jess had gazed up at it sometimes when she was doing her homework at the bench, wondering whether the wide-eyed girl with the shock of thick woolly hair and toss of pale freckles across her nose had been just as clear-minded then as she was now.

After she'd come to live at Darling House, Jess had tried to match Nora's certitude. Even as a ten-year-old, she'd recognised it immediately as one of the starkest differences between her mother and grandmother. Where Polly wore a constant frown of concern, examining each proposal – even the most insignificant – from all angles and then agonising incessantly that she'd made the wrong choice, Nora had an answer for everything, waving away doubts. 'I'm ninety-nine per cent right, ninety-nine per cent of the time.' Once a decision was made, she was unflappable. 'There's no point looking backwards,' she'd say. 'Just make a choice and then trust yourself to have chosen correctly.'

It was advice that Jess tried to live by. Lately, though, she'd found herself seeing more and more shades of grey. And while it was her job, as a journalist, to keep an open mind, to take a nuanced approach and to report what she saw and heard, not what she thought and felt at the outset, the tendency to question had been creeping into her personal life, too. She'd developed a habit of weighing decisions so carefully that the scales never tipped, and she often lay awake relitigating those she'd already made. It was a worry: ability to self-critique was one thing, but the analysis-paralysis of overthinking was quite another.

From somewhere in the garden came the sound of a magpie singing, and a thousand days of childhood arrived with it. Jess glanced to her right and spotted the black-and-white bird perched atop the statue in the middle of the pond. There were magpies in England, too – Jess had seen them often on the Heath – but although they shared a name, they were different from their antipodean cousins: smaller, neater, prettier, and without the eerily sublime song. This magpie was looking directly at her. Jess tilted her head, watching the bird as he watched her. Suddenly, he spread his wings and flew away.

She crossed the turning circle towards the lawn. The grass was still damp with dew, even though the sun was rising fast, and cool shadows stretched towards the harbour. Jess reached the edge of the pond and followed the line of its curved rim until the elegant stone lady was directly before her, kneeling as she always had, arms folded above her head, face bowed to gaze down at the goldfish and lilies.

This was the same spot she'd been drawn to on the day her mother left her with Nora. It had been August, late winter, but still warm enough for Jess to have been sent out into the garden 'to play'. She hadn't had much heart for playing and had instead sat on the edge of the pond watching the fish swim through her reflection, breaking small twigs into pieces and setting them to float on the surface, keeping her hands busy while her thoughts ranged across recent events and conversations. She'd known that Polly was planning a move, that there was a new house and a new job up north, but somehow Jess had got it into her head that they would be leaving Sydney together. She'd even convinced herself, with a childlike love of conspiracy, that she and her mother were planning a cloak-and-dagger escape. As the day drew nearer, though, her mother had explained to Jess that she needed a bit more time to get things organised; she – Jess – would be happy staying with her grandmother, wouldn't she, in that lovely big house? It was nice and close to school, so she'd be with her friends each day, and she wouldn't miss any of her lessons. Jess had agreed cautiously that she'd be okay, and Polly had promised it would only be for a little while. But when they said goodbye, Jess could sense something was happening that she didn't understand. It was a familiar, unsettling feeling of adults keeping secrets while they pretended everything was fine.

Nora had come outside to find Jess that afternoon. There was an evening chill in the air, and she'd wrapped a woollen shawl around her shoulders. She hadn't spoken right away but had sat beside Jess on the pond's stone rim. Eventually, she said, 'Did your mother ever tell you that you were born in this house?'

Jess had shaken her head.

'It's true. You both lived here with me for the first three years of your life.' There was a pause and then, in a slightly puzzled voice: 'Have you really never seen any photographs or heard any stories of back then?'

A glance at her grandmother's expression told Jess that Nora's feelings were hurt, even though she was trying not to show it.

'You used to love this fountain even then,' Nora said. 'I used to bring you out here on the hottest days, and you would splish and splash and dangle your little legs over the edge and laugh when the goldfish came to nibble at your toes. I don't suppose you remember, but you gave our lovely lady here a name.'

Jess glanced up at the statue. 'Grace,' she said suddenly, the word coming from nowhere.

Nora smiled. 'That's right. Grace. I'm not sure where you got it. Divine inspiration, I've always thought, because of course that is her name. What else could it be?'

Jess had looked up at the statue then, taking in her features as if for the first time. Lichen had grown along the coils of her hair and across her face and down her naked torso, but no matter her exposure to the elements, there was something transcendent about her expression and her pose.

'You know,' Jess's grandmother said, 'my mother and father used to go away a lot when I was young. I hated being alone, until I realised that this was more than a house.'

Jess looked sideways at her.

'You'll see what I mean. It's a house that rewards the curious. Have you explored the nook under the east stairs yet? I used to love playing in there. I dare say it's been lonely all these years, just waiting for a child to claim it as her own.'

'Mum said she's going to send for me,' said Jess.

'Well,' said Nora, 'until we hear from her, you have free run of the house. Aside from the attic, of course – the stairs are steep and quite unsafe.'

Her grandmother was being very kind to her, which had the effect, as kindness often does, of making Jess feel terribly sad and lonely. She nodded, because she didn't trust herself to speak, and then her thoughts leapt away from the net she was trying to keep them in and she realised that she couldn't remember being without Polly, not even for a night, and her bottom lip began to tremble, and then: 'I miss my mum.' The awful, naked words tumbled out in a single gulp and Jess began to cry.

'I know you do,' said Nora, putting her shawl around Jess's shoulders. 'Do you know what I do when I feel sad? I remind myself that Grace stands out here in the wind and the rain and never complains, and I feel better at once. Bad things happen to the best of people, and we cannot let them overwhelm us. Life doesn't always work out the way we plan, but it does work out in the end.'

Jess made her way towards the house, the sun warm now on her shoulders. Understandable, she supposed, that the memories of back then were waiting for her here. She rarely thought about it all in London. It seemed irrelevant there. A couple of times over the years, when the subject came up in conversation, Rachel had shaken her head and said something along the lines of: 'But how could she leave you? She's your mother.' Jess had merely shrugged. She'd worked hard over the years not to feel animosity towards Polly. It wasn't as if she'd been a *terrible* parent. She hadn't been cruel or abusive, not as a habit anyway – and by leaving, she'd given Jess the gift of Nora.

Because Polly hadn't come back for Jess. She lived in Brisbane still, in a suburb called Paddington, not far from the city, where ramshackle wooden houses balanced on stilts across a rippling run of terrace-topped valleys. It had taken Jess a while to realise that the arrangement, their separation, was to be permanent. It had never really been announced. The 'little bit longer' turned into 'until the end of the school year', and by the time the September school holidays came around and Nora put Jess on a plane so she could fly up to Queensland as an unaccompanied minor, there was no more talk about staying or moving. Instead, Polly kept referring to Jess's being there as a 'holiday', saying how much she'd been looking forward to the 'visit', that she'd been counting down the days. This had troubled Jess, who even then paid close attention to the words people used, but she hadn't wanted to spoil their time together by asking awkward questions.

She and Polly had gone to stay on the Gold Coast for a week, a short walk from Main Beach. Polly had splurged on a little holiday apartment a few streets back from the water and found a boogie board at a second-hand shop. They played together in the surf each day, and ran along the sand, and ate hot chips with tomato sauce as the sun went down and the cooling night air brushed their burnt shoulders.

On the last day, while they were sitting on opposite sides of a splintery wooden table on the grass verge by the beach, Jess glanced at her mother, whose hair was wound into a bun at the nape of her neck and who was backlit by the sun so that the fine strands around her face were lifted by the sea breeze, glinting golden. Her skin crinkled near her eyes as she gazed out to sea and Jess felt something in the moment that was almost religious; her heart was full to exploding with happiness and she said, 'I want to stay here.'

Polly didn't answer at first. Her attention was still on the horizon and for a moment Jess thought she hadn't heard. The only sign that she was thinking was the slight movement of her jaw. Eventually, she said, 'You're better off down there with your grandmother.'

'But I want to stay here. I want to be with you.'

'You've seen my tiny place in Brisbane. One of us would be sleeping on a roll-out bed.'

'I will. I'll sleep on the roll-out bed.'

Polly smiled, but Jess could see that the smile didn't reach her eyes, and she knew then that her mother didn't feel the same way she did. She knew, even before her mother spoke, that the answer wasn't going to be yes.

'We'll have fun together when you come and visit,' Polly said, turning at last to meet her daughter's gaze.

Jess felt like crying then, but she didn't. She gathered the angry, sad, burning feelings and pushed them all together in a hot little knot inside her chest. And when her mother took her to the airport and gave her a big hug goodbye and told her that she loved her and would think of her every day and see her as soon as possible, Jess returned the hug and screwed her eyes tightly shut, but she didn't say anything back, because she was too busy concentrating her attention on that knot, forcing more of her feelings into it, rolling it up as tight as it would go.

Jess climbed the few stairs to the landing. There was a stoneware pot with an assortment of umbrellas in it and, she noticed, a walking stick. Nora's, she supposed, with mild surprise; her grandmother hadn't mentioned that she'd been using a stick. It had been a bone of some contention between them last time Jess was at Darling House: Nora had insisted that she didn't need one. Perhaps Patrick, in his capacity as her nurse, had actually managed to convince her there was no shame in making her daily stroll around the gardens a little easier on herself.

Jess picked up the spare set of keys from beneath the mat and pocketed them, digging into her handbag to find her own. She wondered sometimes in which ways her life might have turned out differently had her mother not left her behind with Nora, but only abstractly, and with a keen sense that right had prevailed. She could hardly remember the time before. It shocked Jess sometimes, how little detail she recalled from the first decade of her life. She had gleaned enough from Nora to know that the period had been marked by uncertainty and change and a lack of money, though she had no memory of feeling insecure at the time.

'Children forget, thank goodness,' Nora said when Jess admitted as much. 'There were a few times when I really did worry.' Jess had caught something in her grandmother's tone when she said that and pushed for more; even then, she'd had a journalist's instinct for secrets. But Nora demurred. It was some years before she finally told Jess about the incident she'd witnessed when Polly was just a new mum. In the meantime, Nora took great care to make sure Jess knew she was not the same as her mother. Where Polly had been a nervous child and an anxious teenager, prone to disorganisation and indecision, 'You're the complete opposite,' Nora said. 'You're far more like my side of the family.' Once, when Nora accidentally let slip that Polly had suffered something like a breakdown when she was finishing high school, she went on to explain: 'She never did well with stress. She was all right if everything was managed very carefully around her, but life can't always be controlled like that. You know what Peyton School is like. There's an expectation that girls will take advantage of the opportunities on offer. Polly couldn't handle it. I was deeply worried for a time. Thank God I knew a fine doctor who specialised in anxiety. I try never to let myself wonder what might have happened if not for Dr Westerby.'

Jess had met Dr Westerby at one of her grandmother's many parties. Nora was always fundraising for this charity or that, lending her name and the wonderful setting of Darling House to 'help make a difference'. She valued connection and community, and had the gift of making everyone she met feel that they were singularly important to her. That was the power of her personality. It was what had enabled a young, divorced woman with a small baby not only to survive the 1960s, but to build an empire. Because although she'd been born to a wealthy family, Nora's parents had died with empty bank accounts and several mortgages on Darling House.

'I'd lost so much by then,' Nora said, whenever the story was told. 'My whole family was gone, and I was all alone. But there was no way I was going to let the bank take my home. I'd made myself a new family – tiny though it was – and I decided then and there that I would do whatever it took to keep my daughter safe and to secure her future.'

Nora's firm ideas were never firmer than when describing what it meant to be a good parent: the sacrifices required, the elevation of one's child's needs above one's own. As far as Jess knew, it was the only subject that could bring her grandmother reliably to tears. She refused to read books that featured instances of child abuse and would change the channel on the television if a news story even skirted the subject. 'Some people aren't meant to be parents – I accept that,' she'd said more than once. 'What I can never forgive, and will always fail utterly to comprehend, is how a person could ever bring herself to harm her own children.'

It struck Jess now, as she turned her key in the lock, that it was the one act of human behaviour for which her grandmother did not have a ready explanation. Nora had tried to understand, especially where her own daughter was concerned, and certainly in relation to the incident, but the best she could come up with was: 'Stress.' She'd lift her hands up hopelessly whenever she said it: 'Stress can make even the most loving mother lose control.'

CHAPTER SEVEN

Darling House seemed to know itself unoccupied. It was the opposite of a haunted house; without Nora it was a house without a spirit. Morning sun streamed through the stained-glass fanlight above the door to land on the dark flagstones of the hallway, the beams thick with listless dust.

Although the house was empty, Jess couldn't help but send a tentative call of 'Hello?' up the elegant curved staircase. When she received no answer, she left her luggage by the door and made her way across the hall. Now that she had finally arrived, a wave of intense tiredness washed over her. The Florence Broadhurst floral wallpaper appeared to swim.

Nora's antique blue-and-white plate collection covered most of the kitchen wall, and this year's *Art Gallery of New South Wales* calendar was hanging on its hook by the pantry, open to December. There was a fresh arrangement in the majolica vase on the sideboard, Christmas bush and silver gum from the garden, and Jess could picture Nora in her wide-brimmed straw hat, secateurs in hand, carrying in the annual haul. She loved to 'dress' the house and observed all the festive points throughout the year ('What have we left if we don't honour our traditions?'), but made an extra effort in December because Polly's birthday fell at Christmas. The evidence that routines of twenty years before were still being followed was reassuring. It was also briefly crushing: a reminder for Jess that it had all been going on without her.

In the middle of the pine table was a welcome message from Mrs Robinson, its corner tucked beneath the fruit bowl. Evidently, the housekeeper had also remembered the customary return breakfast, noting that she'd left supplies on the bench.

Jess went to the sink to wash her hands and then filled the kettle. She dropped a couple of pieces of bread into the toaster but didn't start them browning. Tea and toast were the rule after long-haul flying. It was one of the great mysteries of the universe, that a person could be fed continuously over the course of a twenty-four-hour transit only to arrive at her destination ravenous. Science was also yet to explain the unique humanising properties of strawberry jam and butter on warm toast.

As she waited for the kettle to boil, Jess's attention drifted to the wall of the adjoining sitting room. The portrait of young Nora looked down on her from the centre, surrounded by an assortment of framed photographs. Polly as a little girl, wearing a smocked pinafore and a serious expression, as if she were counting down the seconds until the shutter closed around her image and she was free to slip out of frame, and a number of Jess – including one, she noticed, that she'd emailed from London a couple of years ago, she and Matt with their heads through the cut-out holes in the Fenton House Apple Weekend welcome sign.

There were also several photos of The Family: Edwardian tennis parties of women in long dresses and men with boater hats; garden lunches and cricket games; children with wooden hoops and toy engines. It had taken Jess some years to realise that her grandmother's use of the term 'The Family' denoted a schism in time. The Family had lived Before, the stories about them were historical, even those in which Nora herself featured. These were tales viewed through a lens of loss; Nora was the last surviving member of this large, robust clan. She was forever trying to bridge the gap with anecdotes, determined to foster a sense of continuity for Jess, whose experience of family was limited to Nora and Polly. 'You remind me of my Scottish grandmother,' she would say firmly. 'She was curious about the world and stubborn when she had to be. She'd have loved to be a writer – her journals were quite scandalous.' And then: 'Did I ever tell you about your great-great-aunt Beatrice? She was a live wire, like you, but quite naughty with it. She used to throw her crusts beneath the chair where her cousin Jamie sat. The poor little boy would cry and cry when his mother scolded, but he never did say who'd done it. They used to dress him up in a bonnet and drag him around the garden in a pony trap. How I wish you'd met them.'

One of Jess's favourite family photos was of Nora as a young woman, sitting on a wrought-iron bench in the garden of Darling House with a man in a jauntily cocked trilby hat, the two of them looking at one another, caught in a moment of laughter. This photo was not on the wall with the others, but in a quaint bronze frame in Nora's room. When she first saw it, Jess had assumed that this was 'Mr Bridges', the man to whom Nora had briefly been married, who was hardly ever mentioned, and always in inverted commas. It was only later, after she learned that Nora had once had an older brother, that Jess realised the laughing man beneath the hat wasn't Mr Bridges at all but Thomas Turner, soon after he returned to Australia from the Second World War.

The kettle began to shrill, and Jess poured boiling water over the teabag, watching as it began to steep. She started the bread toasting. There were no photographs of Mr

Bridges at Darling House. Early on, Jess had figured that the marriage must have been so terribly unhappy that Nora had banished every image of her former husband, but when she finally gained the courage to ask, her grandmother had only laughed. 'Oh, darling, you're dramatic! The truth is far less exciting. We married young and the marriage didn't last. It happens sometimes. To be honest, I barely remember the man. Why on earth would I hang his picture on my wall?'

'Because he was Polly's father,' Jess had ventured. (*And my grandfather*, she'd thought.)

But Nora had been unmoved, meeting the statement with a shrug. Yes and no, the gesture said: 'Parenthood is more than the supply of a bit of DNA.'

How quintessentially Nora it was to claim her daughter as hers alone. Jess had wondered what Polly thought about the erasure of her father from her heritage, before reminding herself that not knowing much about fathers was something of a family tradition. Polly had told Jess very little about her own. She'd said certain things when Jess was a little girl – that he was kind and clever and good – but by the time Jess was old enough to recognise such assurances as fairy tales for the young, her relationship with Polly was no longer of the sort to encourage intimacies and confessions.

Jess had turned instead, as ever, to Nora, who'd asked what Polly had told her and then said plainly, 'I'm sure your mother's right. He had to be kind and clever and good, because look at you. Though of course,' she couldn't help adding, 'it's just as likely that you got those traits from my side of the family.'

Determined not to be put off, Jess had pushed – 'But you must be able to tell me more' – and eventually Nora sighed and gestured to the seat beside her. 'I'm afraid I simply didn't know him. Your mother was barely out of school and young for her age, very unworldly. I've told you, I think, that she suffered with low self-esteem. She all but starved herself for a year or so during high school. We were starting to make headway – she managed to graduate with her classmates and even won a place at university – but she was vulnerable. This fellow, this young man, showed her a little attention and she mistook it for something else entirely.'

The toast popped and Jess gave both pieces a thick coat of butter before spooning lavish lumps of strawberry jam on top. She carried the plate and her tea to the sofa in the sitting room, meeting The Family's gaze as she sat down. Her roving attention landed on the framed school portrait of her mother in year twelve, in which Polly was wearing the same deep green tunic and blazer that Nora had worn before her and Jess after. Here was the serious, vulnerable young woman, barely finished being a girl, who had mistaken lust for love and found herself pregnant at eighteen.

Jess had sat with the information for a few moments after Nora told her, her thoughts shifting from her mother to the young man who had shown Polly 'a little attention'. Who was he, Jess wondered, and how had he felt when he found out she was on the way? Perhaps her grandmother had intuited Jess's next line of questioning, or perhaps she'd just been down the same path with Polly in the past, because she continued without prompting: 'It's not that he didn't want you. He didn't even know that you existed. He was visiting from overseas, and by the time your mother realised what was happening, he was gone.'

Rachel thought that Jess should join ancestry.com – 'I read about a woman who discovered her father wasn't actually her father and she had fifteen surprise cousins, one of whom worked in the office on the floor below!' – and Jess had considered it. But she baulked at the idea of sending a sample of her DNA to a mysterious address in the States. She'd written a series of investigative reports about online privacy and wouldn't even share her thumbprint with her phone anymore. When Jess mentioned it to Nora, her grandmother had concurred: 'A *ghastly* idea! And to what end? You're you, a Turner through and through.'

Jess took a big gulp of tea. She was aware of being alone in the house. She could hear the ticking of the metal roof expanding as the sun warmed it. She tried to calculate what time it was in London. One, perhaps? On Monday morning? She was uncomfortably aware that she was still wearing the same jeans and T-shirt that she'd dressed in on Saturday. Her head swirled and she felt an urge to curl up on the couch just for a minute. The sun had crept across the floor to reach the far cushion and she could just imagine the warmth upon her feet . . .

But she knew from experience how dangerous that would be. Jess made herself stand up, return her plate and cup to the kitchen, and collect her suitcase from the hall. She started up the stairs. She needed to shower, to wash the travel off her, and then she planned to get to St Vincent's for afternoon visiting hours. First, though, she was going to reacquaint herself with the house. Once she started moving around, she was sure the rooms would no longer feel so deathly still.

Small pleasant moments of recognition were everywhere. The smooth oak banister of the staircase was familiar beneath her hand, its satin lustre hinting at recent waxing. On the hallstand at the top, an antique washstand jug held another of Nora's Christmas bush and flowering gum arrangements. The jug was Nora's favourite, despite the chip in its spout. 'I've always found perfection tiresome.'

Jess stopped in the open doorway of the library, the first room off the landing. Aside from Nora's bedroom, this was the place in the house she associated most closely with her grandmother. No matter how long Jess had been away, no matter the season she returned, Nora's library always smelled the same – of furniture polish, mock-orange blossoms and, despite Mrs Robinson's best efforts, legacy dust. The northern and southern walls were lined with floor-to-ceiling bookshelves and Nora's wingback reading chair was angled to face the window, a large fern in a brass pot balanced on the wooden stand beside it. The leather chesterfield sofa had faded, but Mrs Robinson was keeping it in good condition. The housekeeper was almost as much a feature of Darling House as Nora herself; she'd been there for as long as Jess could remember, having started as a young woman before Polly was born. The room bore the look of a recent visit – the cushions had been plumped and straightened, and the curtains neatly gathered.

In the middle of the library stood one of Nora's most prized possessions. Her parents had sold off all of the heirlooms when they hit financial strife, and as soon as Nora's business started turning a profit she'd made a point of tracing and reclaiming every piece she could. 'History is important,' she'd said on the morning the movers negotiated the hefty mahogany gentleman's desk back into place before the bay window. 'My great-grandfather loaded this very desk onto the ship in Edinburgh when he set sail for the colony of New South Wales. He had no idea whether he was going to find fortune or ruination at the other end of the voyage. Imagine the optimism it must have taken to transport a desk like that across the seas. He wrote every letter home on that blotter and kept his papers in those file drawers.'

The surface of the desk, Jess noticed, was this morning covered with papers. Such untidiness was highly unusual for Nora, who made a point of returning everything to its place at the end of the day. Patrick had left her grandmother sitting at the desk on the afternoon she fell: Nora had either left in a hurry or intended to come back. Possibly both. But why on earth had she gone from here to the attic stairs?

Despite her grandmother's rule, Jess had spent half of her adolescence in the attic and couldn't for the life of her think of anything Nora might have wished to retrieve so urgently: an assortment of shabby once-treasured toys, plastic tubs of remnant fabrics and blankets and curtains, some of Jess's and Polly's old schoolbooks, and a beaten-up steamer trunk that had belonged to Nora's brother, long rid of any personal effects. Jess had been at Darling House the day the trunk arrived from London. 'Isn't it extraordinary,' Nora had said, 'that a human being's entire life can be reduced to a container this size.'

Jess didn't have many thoughts back then about life and death and the melancholy progress of physical artefacts. She'd nodded agreement, aware that it was required, but her thoughts were instead with the travel label on the side of the trunk. London. Jess was already well-acquainted with the city through her favourite books, but here was an object that had been recently in the very place.

'Did you ever visit him in London?' she asked, eager to hear more about the city and her grandmother's exotic, faraway brother.

But Nora shook her head. 'I would have loved to go,' she said. 'He was my best friend when I was growing up. He had a wife over there and a lovely house, I'm told. But I have a morbid fear of flying; I could never have made it that far.'

The idea of an old person being frightened of something – especially Nora, who was otherwise larger than life – astonished Jess. 'Have you never been on a plane?'

'Only a couple of flights within Australia, a very long time ago. That was enough for me. I had a horrific journey back to Sydney once when your mother was just a tiny baby. There was severe turbulence, and she was crying, really screaming, and I was convinced that the plane was going to crash. I looked down at her precious little face and made a deal with God that if I made it home, I would never, ever leave again. And I haven't.'

The seriousness with which Nora said it, the unexpected religiosity, and the high stakes of her promise, all impressed themselves on Jess. She was awed, although she couldn't then have found the words to explain what she was feeling, by the perfect paradox of the proposition: that only by remaining separate from her beloved brother, her favourite person in the world, could Nora keep her longed-for daughter safe.

Nora had held true to the deal she'd struck with God. She didn't see her brother again in all the years that passed between that day on the plane and the morning the steamer trunk of personal effects arrived from London in the wake of his death. The effects themselves had been removed and dealt with at some point, for by the time Jess came upon the trunk in the attic, it was just a storage container for clothing that was no longer needed or wanted but was too good to discard. Even now, the strong nostril-cooling smell of mothballs brought back warm feelings, the legacy of countless illicit hours spent beneath the A-framed roof, trying on fancy dresses and high-heeled shoes . . .

Jess was confident that Nora hadn't risked the attic stairs to play dress-ups, but perhaps the answer to what *had* driven her up there lay among the papers and notes on her desk. Jess went to have a closer look. A large stack of torn envelopes sat in a pile at the back and several open letters, invitations and résumés were spread across the blotter. Nora was a renowned mentor, frequently in demand to speak at women's events and girls' schools, and a little over a decade ago she had started a scholarship programme offering support to businesses run by young women, often mothers, with big ideas. It had taken off in recent years and she was now inundated with requests for assistance.

'Our Nora was never one to walk past a stray,' Mrs Robinson had said, when Jess made delicate inquiries as to whether it was all becoming too demanding. 'You know how much she likes having young people around. She misses you dearly; there was a huge absence in her daily life when you left. The silver lining is that your decision to stay over there has helped a lot of other women.'

At the back of the desk, Jess recognised the distinctive pale blue pages of her grandmother's current Smythson. 'My little gift to myself,' Nora said of the leather-bound diary she ordered annually from London's Bond Street. 'If a woman doesn't take herself seriously, she'll have a difficult time convincing anyone else to bother.' Jess moved the papers that were obscuring the week-to-view and scanned Nora's cursive script. Nothing leapt out at her. Friday's entry, in common with every other weekday, contained a list of people her grandmother had intended to telephone, a box to tick beside each indicating whether the call had been made.

Nora was a telephone person. 'With all due respect to the written word, if people would only pick up the phone more often, we'd save ourselves an awful lot of time and misunder-standings.' Even when Jess was in London, Nora had refused to keep in touch by email, preferring a lengthy telephone conversation every Sunday to catch up on the week gone by.

Last Friday's call list included a solicitor in Rose Bay; the initials 'M.S.', which likely noted a charity event Nora was involved with; and someone named Professor H. Goddard. None had been ticked off, and it was impossible to tell from sight alone whether they were important. There was nothing else on Friday's diary page except a note to pay for the Christmas turkey and a reminder that Patrick would be finishing early.

Jess knew Patrick a little because she'd helped to engage him last time she was back in Australia. Nora had been characteristically indignant at the idea. 'I don't want some bossy woman glowering at me and telling me what I'm not allowed to do,' she said, to which Jess answered, 'Think of a carer less as a nurse and more like a PA.' After that, Nora had consented to meet with a shortlist of candidates – 'although I'm not promising anything,' she warned.

Her ultimate acceptance of the idea had everything to do with Patrick himself. With his six-foot-four-inch frame, long blond hair and dazzling smile, he confounded any preconceptions Nora (and Jess, for that matter) might have had. 'He's a delight,' Nora still said each week when they had their phone catch-up. 'Such a zest for life, so many amusing stories – he makes me laugh and he's teaching me a tremendous amount about house plants. He has a very green thumb.'

Bit by bit, he'd filled the rooms of Darling House with baskets of devil's ivy and pots of ridiculously healthy fiddle-leaf figs. Jess had been shocked to hear that her grandmother had allowed him to grow philodendra up the Broadhurst in the dining room, but Nora only laughed and said that he amused her.

Jess pulled her phone from her pocket and scrolled until she found his number. Patrick picked up on the third ring.

'Jess!' he said. 'How is she?'

'I haven't seen her yet; I only just got in this morning. But I'll be heading to the hospital soon.'

'I'm so sorry, Jess. My sister was in town for a wedding-dress fitting and I'd promised to go with her, so I took the afternoon off. I feel dreadful about it now.'

'It's not your fault. No one expects you to work seven days a week.'

'*I* expect better of myself. One of my special talents is paying attention, really listening to how my people are doing. Nora had been a bit out of sorts lately. I should have guessed something like this might happen.'

Jess frowned. 'In what way, out of sorts?' This was the first she'd heard of it.

A pause as he considered. 'Talking about the past,' he said. 'I know that's not unusual with old folk – some I've cared for are living back there – but it wasn't Nora's style. She always seemed much younger than she really is. I'd arrive for work, and she'd look at me with those bright clear eyes of hers and start talking to me about the news of the day – Brexit, Trump, climate change, whatever.'

Jess smiled at that.

'Lately, though, she seemed distracted. As if her mind was on other things.'

'What things?'

'Closer to home. She talked a bit about when she was a girl, about her brother and how close they'd been, about how tough it was when he went to war and her parents were travelling and she was here all by herself, how excited she was when he came back. And just this week, I went to fetch her from the garden seat and she had a worried look on her face, almost defensive, and when she saw me, she said, "I'm not going to let him take my baby."'

'Which baby? Polly?'

'I don't know, and I might've misheard, because when I asked her to repeat it, she looked at me as if *I'd* said something strange, and then just smiled and said we should be getting inside.'

'That *is* odd. Has she said anything else along those lines?'

'Just a lot of talk about the old days. I mean, it's not as if she's never mentioned the past before, but Nora doesn't usually dwell.'

'No.'

'She'd become a bit secretive, too. A couple of times she was reading in that chair of hers in the library, the one in the bay window –'

Jess glanced at the wingback, picturing Nora.

'– and when I came near to bring her a cup of tea, she quickly pulled the book against her, as if she didn't want me to see it. I knocked it off the table the other day by accident when I was clearing away her teacup, and it was just an old detective novel.'

'Why would she care if you saw that?'

'No clue. That's what made it so weird.'

'And what about the attic stairs – any idea what she might have been doing up there?'

'I'm sorry, Jess. I only wish she'd told me. I'd have happily gone up for her if there was something she wanted.'

Jess ended the call, promising to update Patrick when she'd seen Nora. As she left the library, she considered what he'd said. He was right. Nora must have known that he'd have willingly retrieved anything she needed from the attic, and yet she hadn't asked.

The whole thing felt off, but by the time Jess reached her bedroom she'd decided she was creating mysteries where there were only gaps in her knowledge. She didn't need to guess at her grandmother's behaviour, after all – as soon as she saw Nora, she would simply ask her what on earth she'd been thinking.

There were other priorities right now: true to her word, Mrs Robinson had made up Jess's bed, and the crisp sheets, with their neat folds, were enough to make her swoon. She found her toiletry bag within the suitcase and went to have a shower. Hot water on her skin, the lemon myrtle smell of soap, shampoo in her hair and, at last, some clarity of mind.

CHAPTER EIGHT

It was half-past one by the time Jess arrived at the hospital in Darlinghurst. She was eager to see Nora, and rushing, and when she caught a glimpse of her own reflection in a dark glass window, she was taken aback. Despite the hot shower and the fresh set of clothes, she appeared tired beyond the ability of a good night's sleep to fix. With a jolt, she realised she resembled Polly when she was worrying over something.

'I'm here to see Nora Turner-Bridges,' she told the woman on the front desk, who typed something into her computer and then directed Jess down a corridor: 'Ask again at the intensive care desk. They'll give you her room number.'

Intensive care was a surprise; Jess had presumed Nora would be in an ordinary ward.

The IC nurse looked at Jess with a pleasant, distant smile when she gave her grandmother's name. 'Are you a relative?' she asked.

'I'm her granddaughter, Jessica Turner-Bridges.'

'You'll find your grandmother in room nineteen, halfway down the corridor on the left. Don't be concerned by the heart monitor – some people find it a bit confronting, but it's just so we can keep a close eye on her.'

'I didn't expect she'd be in the ICU,' Jess said.

'She was moved this morning. Next of kin will have been notified.'

'I'm her next of kin.'

'That's strange. Let me check.' She stabbed at her keyboard and squinted at the monitor. 'Jessica, did you say?'

'Yes.'

'We have a number here, but . . . no, that doesn't look right.'

'It's a UK mobile,' Jess explained.

'Ah, that's the problem, then. Our system can't make international calls. Is there a local number I can add to her file?'

Jess gave the number at Darling House and made a mental note to check that the answering machine was still plugged in and working. 'Why was she moved? Did something happen?'

'I'll ask Dr Martin to come and have a talk with you when he's finished his rounds. It shouldn't be long. He tries to see family during visiting hours.'

'Is Nora okay?'

'She's stable now. And if anything should happen, she's in the best place she could be.' The nurse smiled apologetically at the flowers in Jess's arms. 'I'm afraid you'll have to leave those here. They're not allowed in the ICU.'

Jess handed over the bunch of red-blossomed Christmas bush from Nora's garden and started down the corridor, keeping a note of the room numbers. Catching glimpses through the open doorways of small, lonely scenes she thought, redundantly and with unforgivable obviousness, how much she hated hospitals. The balancing thought presented itself instantly: how fortunate it was that there were people, incredible people, who chose to work among and care for the very ill. Jess felt a wave of gratitude that made her unexpectedly tearful. She blamed jet lag – it always brought emotions closer to the surface. And coming home. And Nora being unwell.

As she neared room nineteen, Jess stopped to collect herself. She wanted to appear bright. Nora hated sympathy and would be aghast to see concern writ large on Jess's face. When she turned the corner and entered the room, though, the thoughts of an instant ago seemed trivial.

The person in the bed was lying completely still beneath a white hospital sheet, her eyes closed. She was dwarfed by an alien machine – the heart monitor the woman at reception had mentioned, Jess realised – and any sense of tranquillity was shattered by the electronic noises it emitted.

Jess's first reaction was embarrassment at having entered the wrong room. This frail old woman with skin so thin it was transparent could not be Nora. Nora was full of life; when she entered a room, people turned to see what had just happened. This person, this imposter, took up no space at all; her body was so tiny, her face in repose so old. Jess wanted to bundle up her grandmother and take her home, back to Darling House, where she would sleep and mend and wake up and be herself again.

Nora's bedroom, with its Pimpernel wallpaper and wrought-iron bed beneath the window, was a sanctuary of carefully curated textiles, paintings and patterns. Although one of the smaller rooms at Darling House, Nora was adamant that she preferred it over the larger options, even the master bedroom on the other side of the hall, with its views across the harbour. 'That's always felt like my parents' room,' she said once, with a shiver of distaste. 'I'm happy enough here, thank you very much.' Mrs Robinson said Nora had moved into the room after Polly was born – 'It adjoined the little nursery, you see' – and had just never got around to moving back into her old, more spacious room.

Jess dragged the vinyl visitor's chair closer to the bed. She was mindful not to knock the heart monitor as she arranged herself, glancing at the moving graph on its screen and drawing hope from the fact that the line seemed to be displaying a pattern of repetitive, evenly spaced squiggles. The metronomic beeping was regular, too, which she also took as a positive sign. She reached out and clasped her grandmother's hand. It was colder than she'd expected, the knuckles hard and smooth beneath Nora's tissue-paper skin.

'Ms Turner-Bridges?'

Jess looked up to see a neat man with short brown hair and thin-rimmed glasses at the door, holding a file in one arm.

'I'm Dr Martin. I'm looking after your grandmother while she's in the ICU.'

Jess experienced a rush of pent-up tension. 'Why is she in intensive care? What's happened?'

'She had an episode of atrial fibrillation – rapid heartbeat – earlier this morning. Of itself that's not necessarily a concern, and we can medicate to bring it back into rhythm, but considering her age, and the CT and MRIs we took, she needs to be monitored closely.'

The doctor's tone was measured, and it made Jess wary. 'What do you mean about the scans? What did they show?'

'A colleague of mine spoke to you on the phone a couple of days ago, I believe. There was some swelling. Not unexpected after the impact she suffered when she fell.'

'He said she was confused – is that why?'

'The swelling could certainly account for some of it. But we've been giving her morphine for pain, and she's almost ninety years old; a lack of clarity isn't surprising.'

'Is it too early to ask when she'll be coming home?'

Dr Martin smiled patiently. 'Ms Turner-Bridges—'

'Nora will want to be at home as soon as possible.'

'I appreciate that, and I'm sure most people would share the sentiment. But it's premature to be talking about moving her.' His voice softened. 'I understand that you are your grandmother's next of kin? While we're doing everything we can to help her, and she clearly has a strong constitution, if there's an advance care directive, now would be a good time for you to consult it.'

Jess felt light-headed as she tried to absorb this information.

The doctor consulted his file and then, pushing his glasses back to the top of his nose, reminded Jess that she should let the nurses know if there was anything she or her grandmother needed.

His words and their grim connotation hung around in the room after he left, and Jess sat very still, holding Nora's hand as she slept and the machine beeped, waiting to see if they would sink in.

. . . *if there's an advance care directive, now would be a good time for you to consult it . . .*

They did not. They stayed where they were, an ugly dark cloud near the ceiling. It was one man's view, Jess told herself; the opinion of a doctor who might have been used to reading scans and was no doubt accustomed to treading carefully where the elderly were concerned, but who did not know Nora.

Jess leaned back in the chair and closed her eyes. She could hear the regular pulsing of the monitor, the efficient tick of the clock above the door. Her own breathing fell into line with the rhythms of the room. Her eyelids were heavy. Her thoughts were being pulled into a funnel, down, down, down, falling fast through black spaces and folds of time and electrical storms of memory until, at last, she found herself on a beach . . .

She was three years old and wearing new swimmers, down on her hands and knees digging. She was conscious of the sun on her shoulders and the small of her back, the white lines of drying salt on her arms, the collapse of wet sand beneath her fingers. Waves crashed in the distance, right out there beyond the calm inner lagoon that had formed within a sandbar closer to the shore. She was very busy, concentrating on the castle she was building, and everything else was a blur of summery, holiday bustle.

Time stretched and bent around her until, suddenly, something caught her attention. Someone laughed loudly, a siren began to sound, a bird flew overhead with a shrill call – Jess looked up and was shocked to see that the tide had crept away from her. The patch of sand she'd waded to when it was just a little island in the middle of the warm pool had been exposed and expanded on all sides as the water withdrew.

She stood up, her fingertips grainy, and looked back towards the shoreline, but it was so far away now she could barely see it.

She was all alone.

The hazy, warm swirl of seaside noise and motion was gone. Everything was in sharp focus and Jess was aware that the ground was moving all around her. Only, it wasn't the ground pulsating; it was hundreds of crabs, appearing at once from small holes in the sand, round bodies bobbing, legs click-clacking along the hard surface of the wet sand, all skittering towards her at once.

The raw scratch of pure terror spread across her skin, and she opened her lungs to cry out—

*

Jess woke with a start.

The room was light, the air was warm and still, the ceiling above her was a low grid of white panels.

It took three long seconds to remember where she was and what she was doing here.

Sydney.

Hospital.

Nora.

She straightened in the chair. Her head swirled and her lower back ached. The hands of the clock were almost at four.

The dream was a familiar one; she'd been having it on and off for most of her life. More than just a dream, it was a memory. Only in real life, as the crabs made their approach, Nora had stepped in and scooped her up, wrapping her in the comfort of an embrace that had felt enormous.

Jess blinked and her vision sharpened.

Nora was awake. Her expression was perplexed, almost fearful, searching Jess's face as if trying to remember who she was.

Jess leaned forward. 'Hello, Nora,' she said, taking her grandmother's hand.

'You.' Little more than a whisper, yet heavy with relief.

Her grandmother's gratitude made Jess feel wonderful and ashamed at the same time. 'Here' – she took up the plastic cup on the side table – 'let's get you some water.'

Nora's eyes were pale and clouded, the skin around them red. She continued to study Jess's face as she took a small sip from the straw. Her voice, when she spoke again, was barely there. 'I've missed you.'

'I've missed you, too, but please don't talk now. We can catch up properly later, when you're on the mend.'

'I've been waiting.'

'I came as quickly as I could. England is a long way away.'

There were tears on her grandmother's face that seemed to have sprung from nowhere. The thought came to Jess that they were old tears, though she couldn't have explained exactly what that meant. 'You came from England.'

'But I'm here now. I'm here in Sydney and I'm not going anywhere. I'm staying at the house, at Darling House, and everything is perfect, just as you like it.'

'I've looked after her.'

'I know you have. The Christmas arrangements are marvellous and the garden is thriving. Everything is waiting for you to get better and come home.'

Nora closed her eyes. Her cheeks were damp and glistening, and Jess reached to wipe them gently with her thumb. Nora's breathing was growing deeper, but her face muscles flickered every so often, as if a wayward thought had crossed her mind and caused her trouble.

The doctor might think Nora wasn't ready to leave the hospital, but Jess knew otherwise. Nora needed to be back in her Pimpernel-papered room with its bed beneath the window. She liked to say that the view from her bedroom was all the religion she needed. 'I cannot tell you the satisfaction one gets from having planted and loved a garden,' she'd declare. 'To be able to leave even a small patch of this earth more beautiful and bountiful than it was when one arrived.'

The north-western escarpment at Darling House had been a formal and rather staid series of rose beds originally, but after her parents died and the property came to her, Nora had committed herself to making it something new. She'd envisaged a very different sort of garden – wilder, more profuse and tangled, with natives and introduced species combined – and had planted and tended it over decades with the utmost love and care. The result was a place of utter joy and wonder. It had even been featured in a segment on *Gardening Australia* some years before.

Jess had seen the old episode a number of times because Nora had videotaped it when it aired on TV and still took it out periodically to watch. She loved to narrate as she and the host walked through the clematis-and-jasmine-entwined arbour and into the native-bee haven, where he commented with genuine awe at the vision she must have had, the awesome scope of the undertaking. Nora was less fond of the end of the episode, when she and the host were sitting in the wisteria-clad rotunda, and he produced a series of black-and-white 'before' photos that he'd unearthed.

'Oh, turn it off now,' she always said when the episode reached that point. 'I look such a fool.'

But Jess would never oblige. 'You do not!' she'd say. 'I love this bit. You were perfectly imperious.'

And Nora would shake her head and sometimes even cover her eyes with a hand, but she'd allow the tape to keep rolling, as the camera zoomed in closer on the pair of them in the rotunda and the host said, with a grin, 'I have a bit of a surprise,' before flourishing the photos; and Nora, who most emphatically did not like surprises, appeared to shudder.

'I've never been a lover of roses,' she told him, recovering herself. 'The fragrance, the blooms, the godforsaken thorns. It was the one rule I had when I set out to redesign my garden: there wasn't to be a rose in sight.'

'But they're the flower of love.'

'So people say,' Nora answered, before bestowing on the young host a flirtatious smile. 'But I've certainly never suffered a lack in that regard.'

The monitor began to beep, and Jess looked up sharply.

The jagged lines were moving faster, and a new light was flashing on the screen.

She noticed that Nora's lips were trembling. Her breathing was laboured.

The beeping noise was getting faster, louder.

Jess found the call button on the end of the bed and pressed it.

Nora's eyes opened and she reached out, her fingernails scratching Jess's wrist. She was trying to say something.

'I'm here,' said Jess. 'I'm here, Nora.'

'The pages.'

Jess couldn't be sure that she'd heard the words correctly. 'Which pages?' She looked up sharply as the monitor began to sound an intermittent alarm. She could feel panic rising in her chest. 'Please, Nora, it's okay. Everything's okay.'

A nurse hurried around the corner, and Jess let go of her grandmother's hand. She took a few steps back, closer to the window, trying to stay out of the way. 'Is she all right?'

The nurse didn't answer. She was reading the machine, checking Nora's drip, counting the pulse in her wrist.

'Please . . .' Nora's voice was a rasp. 'Jessy, help me.'

'We're going to help you,' said the nurse. 'Never mind about that.'

'He's going to take her from me . . .'

'No one's going to do any such thing,' said the nurse matter-of-factly. 'You can rest assured of that.'

Jess watched uneasily as her grandmother closed her eyes. The nurse was working quickly, and a change was coming over Nora's face already. She was drifting to another place – whether of peace or oblivion, it was difficult to say.

'There you are now,' said the nurse at last, as the beeps began to slow. 'That's better.'

Jess moved to retake her grandmother's hand. She held it tighter than she should, the only way she had of expressing all the worry and love that she was feeling.

'She'll sleep now,' said the nurse. 'Visiting hours are over and she'll be able to have a nice long rest.'

The last thing Jess wanted to do was leave Nora alone, but she could take the hint. 'Sleep well, Nora,' she said softly. 'I'm not going far. Rest, and get better, and then we'll spend Christmas together at the house.'

'Halcyon.' The word on Nora's lips was no more than a mutter from the very rim of consciousness. 'Christmas together . . . halcyon.'

CHAPTER NINE

The afternoon was clear and hot, and Jess craved movement after being in the hospital. She asked the taxi driver to leave her at the intersection at the top of the promontory so she could walk back along the cliffs towards Darling House. The fresh, salty air was the balm she needed. She was rattled. Dr Martin might have been able to list several perfectly valid reasons to explain Nora's confusion, but Jess had a creeping sense that there was more to it.

Jessy, help me. The diminutive was not one Nora used, and while Jess had been touched, it had been disconcerting.

Jess crossed the playground and made a brief detour past the apartment complex where she and Polly had lived before her mother left for Queensland. The sight of the Art Deco building on this bright, sunny day almost three decades later made her wistful. She used to balance along the fence at the front, she remembered. Her mother had picked posies of lavender from the garden and put them in jam jars on the windowsill.

Jess turned away and headed towards Nora's place.

Patrick said that Nora had been out of sorts *before* she fell, and Jess felt certain now that whatever had sent her grandmother to the attic was related to that earlier disquiet. She refused to believe that Nora was in a state of general mental decline. Jess had spoken to her on the phone every week and she'd been fine. Far more likely she'd been upset by something specific. If Jess could figure out what the something was, she might be able to help.

Mrs Robinson's note said that she intended to drop by Darling House later that afternoon; Jess would see whether she could shed any light on Nora's state of mind. Also: Patrick had reported hearing Nora say, 'I'm not going to let him take my baby', and just now Nora had repeated, 'He's going to take her from me'. It spoke to Nora's centrality in all of their lives that it had never occurred to Jess to wonder about the custody arrangements put in place when Polly was a baby. She had just assumed that her grandmother would have been granted full custody. Now, though, she wondered if there was more to it; perhaps there'd been greater animosity between her grandmother and Mr Bridges than Nora let on.

And there was something else, too. Deep within Jess's memory, a bell was ringing. Halcyon. She let the soft word slip from her lips, and felt somehow that she was small; sensed heat on her bare arms and saw the glinting blue glare of the harbour, her grandmother's anguished face . . . But the memory was elusive, darting away like a slim shimmering fish in an ocean pool.

Jess reached Nora's place and keyed in the gate code, then made her way along the shaded driveway. The house rose into view, but she didn't cross the gravel turning circle to reach the front door. Two decades of London living had cured her of the Australian nonchalance towards good weather. This was an afternoon too glorious to waste indoors.

She followed the narrow path towards the ferns and busy lizzies that grew in a grove beneath the palm trees. This was the oldest part of the garden and had been her favourite place to read when she was a child. On the hottest days it was reliably cooler. She had eschewed the nearby summer house, preferring to burrow down deep into the dark spaces between the leaves where she could smell the rich soil and—

Halcyon. Jess smiled to herself. She remembered now precisely where and when she'd first heard that word . . .

It was a special party called a wake, which seemed odd to Jess because the guest of honour was decidedly unawake. She'd asked her mother about the discrepancy before they left home that morning, but Polly had only shaken her head, given a slightly anxious smile, and said she wasn't sure. Jess had sighed and her mother, who never could stand to be a disappointment, had promised to find out; and then she'd pressed her hands together the way she always did when she was worried and said that it was not the sort of thing Jess should be asking her grandmother, and certainly not today. Jess had sighed again (to herself, this time) and said, 'Of course I won't.' She knew the rules.

The funeral itself was her first. Jess watched wide-eyed as the shiny coffin disappeared and the curtains closed behind it. It reminded her of a magic show she'd seen down at The Rocks during the previous Christmas holidays: the pastor's serious ministrations, the incantating lines, the involvement of the congregation before the portentous puff of smoke. Just as she had then, Jess tried very hard not to blink as the coffin slid away on its rails. She couldn't shake the feeling that something important was going to happen. She sat right on the edge of the pew so she couldn't possibly miss the magical moment, but alas there was nothing of note. Just the curtains jerking shut, followed by a hymn and the distraction of her grandmother's perfume tickling her nose as they sang.

Her grandmother, she noticed, was not crying, though from where she was sitting Jess could make out the hint of a linen handkerchief in the closed palm of her hand. Nora's face had the look of someone who was far away with her own thoughts. It was a proper mask to her feelings, Jess decided approvingly; at least, that's how she'd have described it if this were a story and her grandmother a character in it. She looked the picture of a dignified older lady of meticulous manners, attending a funeral on the occasion of her only brother's death.

For that's who was in the coffin: her grandmother's mysterious, secret-until-recently older brother. Jess liked the look of the man in the black-and-white photograph that sat atop the casket during the service. He didn't resemble her grandmother, not exactly, but there was something familiar about him nonetheless. She had never met her actual grandfather, and she didn't have a dad of her own, so she was often curious about what it might be like to have a kindly older gentleman in her life.

Sometimes Jess pretended that the man who gave the finance news on TV was her father. He seemed sensible and informed, his voice was good-humoured, and he had a twinkle in his eye that made her feel he would be kind. She had nominated Charles Dickens as her grandfather. She'd collected all of his novels – except *Martin Chuzzlewit*, a copy of which she was yet to find – and had decided, after finishing *David Copperfield*, that they'd have got on very well. He enjoyed walking, as did she; he was curious about people, ditto; and he had a very well-developed sense of justice. This, Jess knew, was also true of her: she had heard her mother say so the last time she was called to school to see the principal. (It was on the same afternoon she learned that charges of 'impertinent' (Mrs Taylor) and 'perspicacious' (her mother) were in the eye of the beholder.)

Interestingly, Jess's benign, pleasant feelings about the man in the photograph were not shared by all. Before the funeral began, when people were still arriving, a smooth-faced woman had commented quietly to her companion, 'The prodigal brother returns,' to which the other woman replied, 'No sign of the English rose,' causing the original speaker to add, 'He certainly could pick them.' Jess had wondered what she meant, and why the statement had merited such an arch, knowing tone.

Someone had brought the photograph from the funeral home to the wake, and it was propped now in the middle of the mahogany chiffonier at the end of the long entrance hall of Darling House, taking pride of place among other black-and-white photographs of The Family. Jess spent a while examining it, her nose almost touching the rim of the chiffonier as the other attendees passed back and forth behind her, trailing wafts of hushed conversation. The man's wide smile and jaunty hat, his trousers and knee-skimming coat, his long stride along an unfamiliar city street. There were ruined buildings and the great white dome of a cathedral in the background. The photograph had been trimmed to fit the frame and the hint of another person crept in on one side: the edge of a darker sleeve, the hem of a coat or skirt.

By chance, Jess and her mother had been visiting Darling House on the afternoon that Nora took the phone call informing her of her brother's death. The unexpected news had caused her to drop her teaspoon.

Jess had felt a thousand unknowns bubbling up inside her: 'Where?' she asked. 'Where did he live?'

'A place called London,' said Jess's grandmother. 'Beside an ancient river called the Thames.'

'Why did he live so far away?'

'He was born with wanderlust.'

Jess turned the unfamiliar term over in her mind. What-ever it meant, she liked the way it felt.

'He loved to travel and was never one to settle,' her grandmother explained. 'Not for long, anyway. When he was a young man, our mother used to despair: "My only son," she would say. "What will become of the family line?"'

'Didn't he want a family?'

Jess's mother, sitting on the sofa by the curtain, made a throat-clearing noise then, and Jess didn't need to glance her way to know that she was signalling a warning. When they visited Darling House, Polly insisted that Jess wasn't to pry and should speak only when spoken to. Jess found this con-fusing, as her grandmother enjoyed supplying answers and didn't seem to find her questions tiresome at all. Sometimes, it seemed to Jess that the rules were more for Polly's sake than Nora's.

'Didn't he want a family?' she repeated disloyally.

Nora had been sitting on the wingback chair that looked through the bay window towards the harbour, and the after-noon light thrown off the water was so bright that her blue eyes flinched against its glare. 'What one wants is rarely the point.'

'Jessica,' her mother said then, her voice surprisingly stern, 'why don't you go outside and enjoy the garden before the rain sets in?'

Jess frowned and cursed herself silently, because she knew she was being got out of the way, and that it was her own fault for pushing too hard, too fast. She did as she was told but took longer than was strictly necessary to leave the room, which was how she was able to hear her grandmother say: 'She's my granddaughter, Polly. We deserve to know each other.'

Jess stopped where she was on the other side of the door and held her breath, wondering what her mother would say to that. But without so much as a pause, her mother said only, 'What about the funeral?'

And her grandmother, deflated, returned to the topic at hand. 'It will be held here, of course, in Sydney. He's a Turner and this is his home.'

The sun was beating in through the fan-shaped window above the front door now, perfumes and voices were mingling, and the hallway where Jess was standing was stifling. A lot of people had attended the wake. Another surprise, for how could a man who'd spent his life on the other side of the world have so many friends in Australia? 'They're your grandmother's friends,' Jess's mum had said when she asked.

'She's very popular,' Jess observed.

'She certainly is.'

Jess wondered where her mother was now. Corralled into conversation somewhere, she supposed, or else hiding out in the kitchen with Mrs Robinson and the two young waitresses who'd been paid to hand around plates of sandwiches and cake. She closed her eyes and listened. Polly had a sound. It came from the necklace she always wore: a long silver chain, from which she'd hung two pendants – one fine and shaped like a jacaranda tree, the other a sterling silver cat. The jacaranda tree had been a gift and the cat had come from a second-hand shop; it had once been the top of a baby's rattle, Polly said, back in the olden days, a 'hey diddle diddle' cat with a ball inside that made a soft tinkle whenever she walked. Jess loved that sound. It always made her feel safe and warm and happy.

But she couldn't hear it now. She opened her eyes again, taken with a sudden urge to be away from all these people. The day's formalities were over and the wake, for all that its unexpected name had promised, had turned out to be nothing more than another tedious adult excuse to socialise. She had liked the velvet dress she wore very much when her grandmother gave it to her, but now the elastic in the puff sleeves was beginning to scratch and the seam across the velvet bodice made her feel sweaty and uncomfortable.

In other circumstances, she might have enjoyed exploring Darling House further while her mother was distracted. The house stood high on the peninsula of Vaucluse, three storeys tall with a turret on one side. It had been built in the middle of the nineteenth century, when Jess's great-great-great-grandfather arrived in the colony of New South Wales, and had been featured in several glossy books about architecture that her grandmother kept open on the display tables in the library. Inside it was entirely unpredictable: unexpected doorways led to hidden staircases that wound around brick chimneys and allowed a person to arrive in a vastly different part of the house from that which they'd left.

Jess wasn't supposed to like the house. 'Don't you find it draughty?' her mother would ask, if Jess ever ventured to say after a visit that the halls were grand or the ceilings high. 'Don't you prefer our cosy little home?' And because the lovely, familiar face seemed crestfallen, Jess always quickly agreed that of course she far preferred their small apartment.

Today the house was too full, big as it was, and so she went outside to the garden, a place with which she was far more familiar, having been sent out by her mother 'to play' almost every time they visited. The most prominent garden at Darling House had been designed and planted by Jess's grandmother, but on the other side of the property, if one followed the path that led past the flagpole and the fountain, was a much older, more overgrown place of ferns and busy lizzies that formed a primordial mass around a mould-speckled summer house. Jess made her way through the greenery until she found a spot beneath the curving tendrils of a hulking great tree fern. Far from view of the house and surrounded by a curtain of foliage, she unzipped her fancy velvet dress and lifted it off, laying it down flat on the ground. She unbuckled the new patent leather shoes and stripped off her socks. Sitting cross-legged in her white singlet and knickers, Jess breathed freely for the first time in hours.

She wished she'd brought a book. Ordinarily, she didn't go anywhere without one. She'd read through the entire children's collection at the local library and, at ten years of age, had recently been granted special permission to borrow from the high school shelves, though many of the books there were of little interest to her. They seemed to focus on friendships and bras and boyfriends, all of which Jess found exceedingly dull. Recently, her favourite books were those she chose herself when her mother took her to second-hand shops on weekends. In a particularly grimy garage, in a part of Sydney she'd never heard of before, Jess had found *David Copperfield*; she'd sat cross-legged on the floor with it, and when it was time to go there was no way she could leave the story behind. Since then, she always managed to discover at least one more treasure to add to her stack – unlike her mother, who, for all her love of looking, never managed to find what she was searching for.

Now, though, without a book between whose covers she could disappear, Jess fell to exploring her surroundings instead. She followed a line of ants making their way through the undergrowth, noticed a curled leaf that hid the white-webbed nest of a caterpillar, made a teepee of lichen-coated twigs. She was observing the surprisingly tight coil of a tree fern frond, examining it between her fingers, prodding the little black hairs, when she realised she was no longer alone.

She could hear voices: her grandmother, she realised, in conversation with a man. Their footsteps on a hard surface informed her that they'd entered the summer house. She tried to hear their words so she could decide whether their conversation was going to be of interest.

'I take it the paddocks will be sold?' This was the man.

'I can hardly tend them myself. Thomas was the one with all the dreams . . .'

'And Halcyon?'

There came then a terrible sound, a guttural, groaning noise, that caused a tightness to form instantly in Jess's stomach. She was so surprised and intrigued that she risked lifting her eyes above the top of the ferns. She couldn't see inside the summer house from where she was, and so, as quiet as a mouse, she crept closer.

Her grandmother was seated on the bench, but something about the looseness of her posture, the curve of her shoulders, made Jess think she'd collapsed onto it rather than chosen to sit. She was trying to hide her face from the man with her hand, but Jess could see from where she was crouched that her grandmother's mouth was open in a silent wail. To witness an adult in such distress was shocking. A word came into Jess's mind and the word was *bereft*.

Nora stayed like that for what seemed an interminable length of time, the man making an awkward pretence at not seeing her anguish, until at last she spoke. She was trying to sound calm and collected, Jess could tell, but her voice was strained to the point of threadbare. 'Please, Mr Friedman,' she said, holding her fine hand up against the possibility of further hurt. 'I cannot bear to hear that name. Of course, it must be sold at once. He should have sold it himself years ago. It is nothing to me now but an awful, awful millstone.'

CHAPTER TEN

The death of Nora's brother in 1988 had represented a demarcation in Jess's own life. Before his death, Jess had lived with her mother in a small first-floor apartment with a narrow, tiled patio and no back garden; afterwards, she had lived with her grandmother at Darling House. There was no clear corollary between the two events, it was just a matter of coincidence and timing, and yet the first and firmest human addiction is to narrative. People seek always to identify cause and effect and then arrive at meaning, and so it was for Jess: Thomas Turner's death was linked forever after with her own change in circumstances.

At the time, though, the day of his wake was notable for a smaller, more specific reason. Ten-year-old Jess liked words. She collected them. In her favourite books, it was always in words that true power lurked, whether the enchantments and curses of the fairy tales she'd devoured when she was small, or the wills and deeds and legal loopholes she'd discovered in Dickens. The day of the wake had thrown up multiple new treasures. First there'd been the 'wake' itself, and its chilling premise that a party for the dead might be known by such an emphatically active name. Then came 'prodigal', a term previously heard only during Religious Instruction classes at school, but applied now, most intriguingly, to a mysterious man from her own family. And what of 'halcyon', a warm, honey-coloured word that met her ears like an incantation, but whose warmth was almost immediately doused by the bleak deployment of 'millstone'.

Back in the shade of the tree fern frond, in the aftermath of the eavesdropped conversation, Jess pondered what she'd heard. It presented quite a predicament. 'Millstone' was a word with which she'd thought herself familiar, courtesy of Thomas Hardy, but why would her grandmother be in possession of a circular stone used to grind corn? More to the point, why would she describe the stone as 'awful' and be so insistent about the need to sell it 'at once'? Jess decided it could only mean one thing. A homonym! Clearly 'millstone' had another meaning. Words, Jess had observed, could be as tricky as people: seeming to say one thing, when all the while another, secret meaning lay beneath the surface.

As soon as the coast was clear, Jess shimmied into her dress and ran barefooted back to the house. She slipped between the groups of adults in the shadowy hall and hurried upstairs into the dark library where the cool, still air enveloped her. Walls of books lined each end of the room, but Jess knew where she was going. She'd glimpsed the old blue leather-covered *Oxford English Dictionary* set on previous visits with her mum. She took down the 'L–M' volume and located the entry for 'Millstone', skimming past the familiar, literal meaning until she came to 2. *Fig. A heavy burden; an oppressive force.*

Jess was at once deeply satisfied and further intrigued. Her grandmother's behaviour in the summer house had certainly accorded with that of a person shouldering a heavy burden, but what sort of burden was a 'halcyon'? She replaced the 'L–M' volume of the dictionary and pulled out 'H–K', leafing through the pages until she found the entry she was after. According to the *OED*, the word 'halcyon' could be both a noun and an adjective, the former describing a type of king-fisher bird, the latter meaning 'calm, peaceful; happy, pros-perous, idyllic'. But neither suggested itself as particularly burdensome. The latter, in fact, seemed to connote the op-posite.

She and Polly walked home together after the wake. Their apartment wasn't far from Darling House, but they went on foot because they didn't have a car. This was an ongoing bone of contention between Jess's mother and grandmother. Nora wanted to buy them a 'nice little runabout' and said it was perverse to go without the necessities of life, but Polly claimed to prefer public transport. The truth, Jess knew, was that driv-ing made her nervous. A lot of things made her mother nervous.

They walked along the foreshore, even though it took longer than going via the streets. Jess liked to walk with her mother. Polly was shy with other adults, but not when it was just the two of them. She knew a lot about nature, and although she wasn't one for volunteering information or lec-turing her daughter, she could always be counted on to notice and share small instances of beauty. The curled side of a grey-green gum leaf, a delicate discarded nest, the way an Illawarra flame tree in flower was a firework against a deep blue sky. They never managed a trip down to the beach with-out amassing a collection of seaweed and shells and elegant pieces of driftwood that would then be carted home and displayed on windowsills or turned, by Polly, into a striking mobile; even, on one occasion, a spidery dreamcatcher for Jess. Polly had nailed the delicate creation into the ceiling directly above Jess's bed. 'Don't tell the landlady,' she'd said. 'I don't think she'd approve.' And then they'd smiled at one another, because the apartment was owned by Jess's grandmother and not by a 'landlady' at all. Moments like that were Jess's favourite. Her mother didn't make many jokes. She had a face that always managed to look slightly sad, even when its owner was not.

On this walk, however, Jess's mum was quieter than usual. She was thinking about the funeral, Jess supposed, as they emerged from the trail, removed their shoes, and walked down onto the white sand of Queens Beach. Jess's mum hadn't known her English uncle, but she was the sort of person who felt other people's unhappiness as if it were her own. Once, Jess had told her about a girl at school bullied by the other children. They called her names, rushing to jump off the monkey bars if she tried to use them, yelling excitedly to one another that they'd 'catch' something if they didn't move quickly. Polly's eyes had welled with tears as she listened, and ever since she made a point of chatting with the girl at the school gate if they happened to cross paths.

Now, Jess's mum went all the way down to the shoreline, but she wasn't hunting for shells or sticks or the pale, faded skins of sea creatures. She was standing, looking out across the water, her arms by her side, a finger through the straps of her good sandals. Jess went to stand beside her. She had a feeling they were thinking the same thing. It would be sad to leave the ocean when they moved to Brisbane, but her mother said there'd be a river there instead, and lots of sunshine, and in the summertime big storms that would end as quickly as they arrived, leaving the air behind them clean and fresh. Polly had a new job. She'd told Jess over dinner one night and the ends of her sad mouth had flickered when she said it so that Jess could see that the prospect made her happy. They were going to live in a place called Paddington, in their own house, which would be made of a type of timber called chamfer boards, and have a roof not of tiles but of shiny corrugated iron.

Jess had liked that word – corrugated – and her mother had smiled when she said so and found a picture in a magazine to show her what it was. The reality had been very satisfactory, the word a perfect fit for the undulating waves of iron sheeting. She – Jess – would have to start at a new school, Polly cautioned, which wouldn't be as fancy as the one she was due to attend in Sydney, and she would have to make new friends, but Jess said that was fine with her. The truth was, she didn't have many good friends to leave behind, though she never would have told her mother, who'd only have seen it as another thing to worry about.

'Did you tell Nora about Brisbane?' Jess asked.

'Not yet. Not today.'

'When?'

'Soon. When she's not so sad about her brother.'

Jess considered this. It made sense, but she couldn't help noticing that her mum always seemed to have a reason to put off speaking to Nora about the move. Ordinarily, Jess might have pushed harder, but today she had other matters on her mind.

They were holding hands now, and the air smelled of salt and brine and a sailboat was balancing on the very edge of the horizon, and Jess decided there was no time like the present. 'What is halcyon?' she asked.

Her mother's grip on Jess's hand tightened. 'I don't . . .' she began, the sentence catching in her throat. 'Where did you hear that word?'

'I heard Nora say it today. I looked it up in the dictionary, but it didn't sound like a good thing when she said it.'

Jess wondered whether her truthful answer was going to lead to further questions as to how she happened to overhear her grandmother's private conversation, so it was a pleasant surprise when her mother said simply, 'It's a house.'

She'd spun on her heel and was walking back towards the grass.

A house. Jess turned the answer over in her mind as she ran after her mother. It was difficult to understand how a house could be a millstone, particularly to her grandmother, who collected houses as keenly as Jess collected words. 'Where is it? Where is Halcyon?'

'In the middle of nowhere. Far away from here.'

And then Jess understood. 'Halcyon' was the name of her grandmother's brother's house – a burden, she supposed, because it was so very far away. All the way across the sea in England. 'That's why Nora wants to sell it.'

Jess's mother glanced at her and the little frown line appeared between her eyes. 'What do you mean?'

'She wants to sell it *at once*.'

'How do you know?'

Jess hesitated. To say more risked inviting admonishment for eavesdropping. But Polly really did look worried, even more so than usual, and so Jess said, 'I heard her today. She was talking to a man. She said that Halcyon was a millstone and must be sold *at once*. Was it her brother's house?'

Jess's mum nodded.

'Maybe it makes her sad to think of her brother's house sitting all alone in the middle of nowhere?'

'I'm sure that's what it is,' said Polly, and then they'd reached the winding set of concrete steps that led back up to the road, and Jess had started running to the top the way they always did, turning to call over her shoulder for her mum to hurry up because she was being unusually slow.

'Hello, stranger!'

Jess looked to where someone was standing now at the top of the Darling House driveway. It took her a moment to reposition herself in the present and let the ghost of an afternoon thirty years before recede. Mrs Robinson had one hand lifted against the glare of the setting sun and was waving the other.

Jess returned the greeting: 'Hello!'

'I bring offerings,' the housekeeper called, pointing towards the basket on the ground as Jess started making her way up the grass hill. 'Some mail for your grandmother and a lasagne for you.'

'You're a sight for sore eyes,' said Jess, as she reached Mrs Robinson's side.

They embraced, and Jess was surprised by how easy it was and by the depth of fondness she felt for the other woman. 'Come inside for a cuppa?' she suggested.

'That'd be lovely.'

Jess unlocked the front door and they went together into the kitchen, where Jess moved quickly to the kettle, putting it on to boil.

Mrs Robinson sat on a stool at the bench. 'You've been to see your grandmother?'

'This afternoon.'

'You'll have noticed she's gone downhill a bit.'

'I wish you'd warned me.' Jess hadn't meant to sound so accusatory. It was a reaction to the shock of Nora's state. She had been completely unprepared. 'I suppose she made you promise not to.'

'You know what she's like. She wouldn't admit that she was having any trouble.'

'She's lost weight.'

'And height,' Mrs Robinson agreed.

'We're going to need to feed her up again when she gets home.'

Mrs Robinson raised an eyebrow. 'Did the hospital say anything about that?'

'They were a bit vague. I guess they have to be; they don't know who they're dealing with.'

The kettle whistled. Jess poured boiling water over the tea bags and swirled them as they steeped. She asked after Mrs Robinson's family and smiled at the antics of her four cheeky grandsons and single, doted-on granddaughter. 'I sometimes think she's the rowdiest of the lot of them,' said Mrs Robinson. 'Not that I disapprove. On the contrary. More power to her.'

'The future is female,' said Jess, bringing over their teas. 'Isn't that what they say?'

'You sound exactly like your grandmother.'

Jess sat on the kitchen side of the bench, opposite Mrs Robinson. She could just reach Nora's biscuit tin and plucked it down from the shelf, pulling off the lid and proffering the open container. Mrs Robinson helped herself to a shortbread and Jess took one, too, setting it on the bench beside her cup of tea. 'May I ask you something?'

'You can ask. I can't promise to know the answer.'

'You were here when Nora and her husband separated?'

Mrs Robinson nodded. Did Jess imagine the caution? 'I began working for your grandmother a couple of years before that. I was only sixteen when I started.'

'I didn't know that.'

'No reason you should. I was well and truly part of the furniture by the time you came along!'

'A very fine piece of furniture.'

Mrs Robinson laughed. 'Your grandmother and I met quite by chance. I'd only recently arrived in Sydney, having left behind an unhappy past. I was heading down a bad path and Nora threw me a lifeline. She gave me a few odd jobs to start with, paid me enough to keep me in food and shelter, but the best thing she did was to put her faith in me. It was the first time anyone had trusted me with real responsibilities.' The older woman had relaxed into the telling and was enjoying the memory.

Jess prompted gently: 'I was wondering about the custody arrangements for Polly when they divorced.'

Mrs Robinson glanced at her, momentary confusion clearing quickly as she remembered the question that had sparked her recollection. 'I'm afraid I don't know the details. As I said, I hadn't been working here for long. Your grandmother wasn't in the habit of taking me into her confidence back then. Why do you ask?'

'I think there's something playing on Nora's mind. Patrick mentioned that she'd said a few strange things recently – that she was worried about someone taking her baby – and I wondered whether it might be a concern from her past that she's reliving.'

Mrs Robinson smiled sympathetically. 'Your grandmother hasn't seemed quite herself lately. She's been a bit confused. But whatever it was she said to Patrick, there's every chance it didn't mean a thing.'

'But it might have,' Jess countered. 'And if it did, and we can work out what it was, we might be able to offer her some relief.'

'I'm sorry, Jessica,' the housekeeper said, 'but nothing comes to mind. And I have to say, even if she were remembering a past event, it could be one of any number of minor fears. She was a very protective parent of a much longed-for baby. I dare say there were many times when Polly was tiny that your grandmother worried she'd somehow lose her. It's every parent's nightmare.'

But Jess was not prepared to let go that easily. 'It seems strange to me that she and her husband went their separate ways and he never got in touch again. They can't have parted on good terms.'

'It seemed to me at the time that they were both ready to call it quits.'

'Maybe he wanted to take Polly with him?'

'No.' Mrs Robinson was shaking her head. 'I really don't think so.'

'How can you be sure?'

'Things had been difficult between them for several years, starting before your grandmother fell pregnant. Most men don't understand how hard it can be on a woman, particularly someone like your grandmother, when those things don't happen easily. She suffered a few losses before your mum, and he thought they should give up, that they could lead a happy life without children. But that wasn't the life she'd envisaged. She used to say that she wanted her very own cricket team. She saw every doctor, guru, and faith healer this side of the Blue Mountains, and eventually her persistence paid off. I was here when she got the good news; you've never seen a woman glow like your grandmother did that day, and all the days thereafter. She had terrible morning sickness, the poor thing, but she was so damned grateful that she never, ever complained.'

Jess smiled. The description sounded exactly like Nora. Tough, determined, and relentlessly positive. She was never one to take no for an answer, seeing it as a form of failure. It made Jess wonder sometimes how she'd *really* felt about the breakdown of her marriage. Whenever the subject came up, Nora had just shrugged breezily and characterised it as a pragmatic decision to correct a minor mistake of youth: '*C'est la vie.*'

But Jess only had to think of her own break-up with Matt to know that parting from someone with whom one had shared a portion of life couldn't help but throw up feelings of loss. And Nora's husband had been the father of her baby. Surely that carried extra weight. 'I can understand tensions when they were trying to conceive, but if he was amenable to having a baby, why separate right when they'd finally succeeded?'

'I suspect he wanted their life to return to the way it had been before your mother was born,' Mrs Robinson said. 'He considered that he'd been patient and now he wanted his wife back. But motherhood changes some people. The world was different for your grandmother once Polly was on the scene. Understandable when you know what she went through to have her. She doted on her, would hardly let her out of her arms, and he became jealous.'

'Of the baby?'

Mrs Robinson nodded. 'Sad, isn't it, to think of a grown man being jealous of a baby? It became untenable. It broke Nora's heart in a way. Of course, being Nora, she committed herself to making the best of things. If she couldn't have a big family of her own, she would surround herself with people who needed her help and devote herself to being the very best mother she could be to Polly. And she was. You've never seen a parent as involved as Nora. Well, I don't need to tell you how caring she is.'

Jess met the other woman's fond smile. She was certainly familiar with Nora's dedication. After she came to live with her grandmother, Nora had never missed a single school debate, drama performance or netball game. Eventually, Jess had been forced to insist that she start taking time for herself. 'You're making the other parents look bad,' she'd joked, but Nora had been hurt and the conversation had become awkward. They'd got there in the end, though.

Now, at the kitchen bench, Jess yawned broadly. 'Oh,' she said, unable to stifle it. 'Excuse me.'

Mrs Robinson laughed. 'Not at all. You must be exhausted. What time is it for you?'

'God only knows.'

'I should let you get some sleep. Shall I heat up a slice of lasagne before I go?'

Jess said that she'd do it herself and thanked Mrs Robinson again for bringing it. She walked her to the front door. It was seven o'clock but still light, a drowsy early evening on a warm summer's day, the sky starting to soften into the pink, purple, and gold folds of dusk, and the lower reaches of the garden just beginning to darken and cool. The colours and smells, the quality of the light, were visceral. Jess could feel them in the rhythm of her heartbeat, deep in her lungs, in the cells of her skin. She knew them as one can't help but know the cadence of their mother tongue.

An ibis cut across the sky, followed by another three in formation, and Jess's daze was broken. She yawned again and turned to go inside for dinner. If she could just make it to eight, she had a chance of sleeping the whole night through and maybe getting on top of her jet lag.

Her mobile rang as she was closing the front door.

'Patrick!' She had forgotten to call him. 'I'm so sorry.'

'How was she?'

'She's getting rest and I'm going to make sure she's back to her old self as soon as possible.'

'Were you able to speak with her?'

'A little. Not properly.'

'Are you going back tomorrow?'

'Every day, until they let me bring her home.'

'Good. That's good.' He paused, and something about the quality of his silence made Jess feel he had more to say.

'Was there something else?'

'Maybe. You asked me earlier whether I knew why Nora was so distracted lately.'

Jess's pulse began to quicken. 'Yes?'

'I was collecting my mail this afternoon and I remembered that Nora received a letter a week or so ago that seemed to upset her.'

'What did it say?'

'Well, I didn't read it.'

'No, no, of course not.'

'And even if I had, I'm not in the habit of breaking the confidence of the people I care for.'

'I'm sure that's true.'

'It's only that I was so worried about her.'

'I understand. What did you see?'

'I noticed it because the envelope had an official look about it. I always open and sort Nora's mail for her, so I've come to know what's usual. This letter was from a law firm.'

Jess tried not to sigh too loudly into the phone. It was kind of him to want to help, but Nora had a lot of business interests and received mountains of mail; a lawyer's letter was nothing out of the ordinary. 'Do you remember the name of the firm?'

'No. But as far as I'm aware, all of Nora's business is in New South Wales. Isn't that right?'

'I think so, yes.'

'This solicitor, the one whose letter upset her, was writing from South Australia.'

CHAPTER ELEVEN

Adelaide Hills, 25 December 1959

Meg and the boys were asleep at last, and Percy was alone. He was halfway through the last of Esther Hughes's mercy cigarettes and his wristwatch said that it was ten past two. The worst of the storm had passed for now, but rain was still falling. In rare moments, the three-quarter moon appeared between leaden clouds, illuminating the tops of the hundred-year-old oaks that lined the main street. Percy could never look at those oaks without thinking of his mother. She'd talked often about their planting, especially when there was something going on in town that, to her mind, smacked of short-sightedness; worse, self-interest. 'My grandmother was a girl when they planted those trees. None of the adults there that day lived to see them grow to full height. People were wiser back then, and less selfish. They understood that they were part of a line, not the beginning, middle, and end of it.'

From where he was standing, Percy could glimpse only the leafy tops. This spot, on the narrow verandah that ran along the back of the small wattle-and-daub building in the rear corner of their lot, had been his special place when he was a boy and needed somewhere to hide from his parents. The coach house, as they'd called it, had been a general-use storage building back then, home to snakes, spiders, and an odd assortment of possessions deemed too good to be thrown away. In the years since, it had been repurposed as accommodation. He and Meg had fixed it up, back when they were first married.

It had been a good solution, far enough from the main house and shopfront, with a vegetable garden laid out in between, and they'd soon settled into a rhythm. Meg got on well with Percy's parents, even his dad. She'd been one of the few people who did and, in a funny way, it had brought him closer to his father. It took years for Percy to understand that Meg and his father were alike in certain ways. They'd both survived hardship as kids and the concealed scars, carried into adulthood, made them wary of change and inclined to grip tightly to the things they had.

Percy started. He'd heard a noise nearby. Above the rain and the water gurgling through the downpipes had come the crying of a small animal craving shelter and warmth. He strained, listening, but the sound didn't come again. His nerves were shot. Little wonder, with the evening he'd had. He leaned back against the post of the coach house, glad to have something firm behind him. He could remember painting the posts and rails out here, he and Meg together, spending every spare hour getting it ready. They'd been young and excited, all of it ahead. Things had felt so solid then.

The plan had been to stay just until they could afford something for themselves, but life had a way of upending the plans of those foolish enough to make them. They lost the baby. A little girl, born perfect in every way but for her failure to draw breath. Then the war started, and his dad died, and it made sense to stay close enough to help his mum. Truth be told, she and Meg were a support to each other. When the boys came along, and the family started to outgrow the small building at the back of the lot, they'd moved into the main house, and Susan Summers, glad to be somewhere more snug, had taken up residency in the coach house.

It had lain dormant since she passed. Lately, though, there'd been some talk from Kurt, keen to claim the space for himself. It hadn't come to anything yet, but Percy wasn't opposed to the idea. Anything to keep the boy happy at home; make things easier financially so he could take up a spot at the university when the time came.

He and Kurt had gone down to Adelaide together to see the campus some months ago. A beautiful spring day and Percy had parked the car on North Terrace, near the gallery. The grand stone university building next door was like something out of a Victorian novel and he'd felt like Jude the Obscure, circling his way around the edge of academic life with all his private reading and thinking. He'd fumbled the keys hopping out of the car and dropped them into the gutter. His own deficiency had struck him like a brick. But not Kurt. 'Come on, Dad,' he'd said, with a wink. 'Let's go see if it's up to scratch.'

Percy had been awed at the way his son walked into the place like he hadn't a care in the world, as if he already belonged within those hallowed halls. A few years back, a lad from Adelaide had been awarded a Rhodes Scholarship to study at Oxford University. Kurt's teacher at the Tambilla and District High School had said that Kurt, too, had the potential to go all the way. The key would be getting him to focus. His easygoing nature was his greatest gift; it was also his biggest hurdle. Calm and caring, inclined to see the best in people and places, he was predisposed to expect the same in return. It was as if, having fought to survive his premature birth, he'd arrived sure of his place on earth. Even as a baby, he'd been a breeze.

Chalk and cheese, in that respect, their boys. They'd joked after Marcus was born that just when you thought you'd got the hang of the game, another one came along and changed the rules. Marcus had been two years old before he slept through the night and there were times when nothing seemed to placate him. It wasn't until he grew old enough to speak that they'd understood he was a small person with big emotions. 'He's passionate,' they'd told one another. He'd had firm ideas about fairness, too. 'A bit black and white at times,' they'd said with weary smiles, 'but he means well.' Then, somewhat hopefully, 'He'll come good in the end.' And he had. He'd blossomed into a real fine kid, loyal as could be, and kind, too, always advocating for others, collecting strays and standing up for lost causes. Moody lately, but that was part and parcel of being fourteen.

Percy looked across the night-black garden towards the rear of the main house, the dark upstairs windows of his sons' bedrooms. If either boy were to glance through the glass, he might notice the tiny orange tip of a cigarette in the far back corner. But Percy was confident they wouldn't. They were asleep and he knew he was alone. For as long as he could remember, he'd had an almost animal instinct for such things. Senses honed over the long period of bed-bound confinement he'd endured as a lad.

If he and Meg agreed on one thing, it was their fierce determination to protect their sons. The search party had stayed out long after the rain started to fall heavily. Both boys had returned home together, drenched and muddy, around ten o'clock. Neither had volunteered much, each as quiet as he'd seen them. But Percy had been able to glean that Jimmy had told them any tracks left by dogs – or humans – were long gone, washed away by the rain. There was talk of starting up again the next morning, but no one held out much hope.

Marcus had kicked off his boots and gone straight to his room, shrinking from Percy's attempt at comfort. The door upstairs closed loudly behind him and moments later strains of Buddy Holly began drifting through the floorboards. Meg, who'd come rushing in to see that they'd arrived safely, towels at the ready so they wouldn't catch their deaths, disappeared again quickly, leaving him alone with Kurt.

She was intuitive like that. She knew what he wanted, even if he'd decided against mentioning to her Sergeant Duke's interest in their boy. She'd been distressed when he came in from the police station. Along with the rest of the town, she'd already heard what had happened. Percy could tell how upset she was by the glass of sherry she'd poured: Meg was a teetotaller, having suffered at the hands of her old man's drink-fuelled rages, and although she hadn't touched it, the mere fact of the small glass of deep burgundy liquor was proof of how shocked she'd been by the afternoon's events. She listened carefully as Percy filled her in on the interview at the police station, raising her eyebrows slightly when he mentioned the sergeant from Adelaide. Then she took a deep breath and told him how the afternoon had run from her end.

The boys were still out with the search at that point, and he and Meg talked together about the Turner baby, trying to understand what had happened, wondering what was unfolding out there in the dark, stormy night.

'Will they find her, Perce?' Meg said at last, her voice weak with worry. 'Will they figure out what happened?'

Percy didn't know what to say. He wanted to reassure her, to tell her what she needed to hear – that the baby would be fine, that everything would turn out for the best. But he decided to stick with what he knew for sure. 'There's no finer tracker out there than Jimmy. Young Eric Jerosch is no slouch, either. But this weather will make things difficult. That's serious rain and it looks like setting in.'

'Perhaps someone saw something?'

'Perhaps. Though you have to think they'd have come forward by now.'

Meg considered his words. 'I'm so worried, Perce,' she said at length. 'I'm so very frightened. What's going to happen to that dear little child?'

Percy finished his cigarette and stubbed it out. He'd done the right thing keeping his concern about Kurt to himself. Meg had enough on her mind; there'd been no need to burden her further. Their son had done nothing wrong. The policeman's interest would come to nothing. He was simply being thorough, just as one would expect when faced with a scene like that.

Percy only wished he'd been able to get more from Kurt himself. Meg had told him on the cusp of sleep that she was worried their boy would take the deaths extra hard because he and Matilda had argued recently. He'd come home very glum a day or two before, she said. But when Percy tried to talk to Kurt, the boy had looked at him with the weary countenance of someone twice his age and said that he wasn't ready yet. His sons had been lucky, Percy realised. They'd grown up in the wake of the war; their lives to date had been led in a period of peaceful prosperity in a sleepy country stranded between oceans on the far side of the globe. They'd been upset to lose their granny, Percy's mother, but she'd been an ancient figure to them, and it had been the natural order of things. Their first taste of anything like grief had been Buddy's death a couple of months before, after a weekend camping.

But where the death of the family dog was gutting, what had happened at the Wentworth place, to the Turner family, was very different. There was the shock of the situation for starters, the enormity of it, the horror, a whole family gone like that; but then there was the loss of each human being individually. The future, their hopes and dreams – each one was a tragic loss. The death of children especially was hard to bear. It was a sacrilege. For a boy – a man – who thought himself in love . . . well, it was crushing.

Percy had wanted to console his son, to tell him that he understood, but he knew the words would fall hollow. 'She's dead, Dad,' Kurt would say. 'I loved her, and she's gone. How can you ever understand?' And what on earth could Percy possibly have said to that?

His chest ached, as if a great pair of hands had closed around his rib cage and started squeezing. He realised suddenly that he needed to get away from this plot of land, this house that had contained him all his life. On many occasions Percy had felt trapped by it. Tonight, though, he felt exposed. His limbs were filled with nerves that needed settling. He craved to move, to walk, to be somewhere else for a time.

Percy left the verandah of the coach house and crossed the yard, letting himself in through the back door of the house. He crept along the hallway until he reached the small room at the entrance. A lamp with a fringed shade glowed yellow on the table by the Christmas tree. He shrugged into his raincoat and took a flashlight from the shelf by the door, aiming it towards the ground to check that it was working. Its beam illuminated a row of work boots lined up against the wall. When Percy couldn't get his boys to talk, after Marcus had stormed off and Kurt had retreated to his bedroom, he'd set himself to work cleaning their muddy boots. He'd needed to keep busy, to find some sort of purpose. It had been the only way he could think of to care for them in the moment. A small act of love, in place of the comfort he was unable to provide.

Satisfied that the battery would hold, he switched off the torch, tucked it inside his deep coat pocket, and, careful not to make a sound, slipped outside, closing the door silently behind him.

CHAPTER TWELVE

Percy had been walking for an hour by the time he entered the wooded grove at the edge of Merlin Stamp's property. He hadn't planned to go the back way out of town, but it had suited him to be in the dark, away from streetlights and other people. It struck him that he was acting like a man with something to hide.

The trees were dense here, in this higher, damper part of the Hills, a blend of ghostly candle bark gums and stringybarks, with silver banksias growing thick beneath them. Percy had the torch, but he didn't need it. He knew the way.

Rain dripped through the canopy, hitting the lower foliage and trickling to the ground. Small nocturnal animals, swamp rats and bandicoots, slipped among the underbrush unseen. This was a natural place, untouched by humans; one of the few truly wild patches left. Percy knew Stamp a bit, and something of his troubles, but he hadn't seen the man himself up close in decades. He was aware that people talked. Over the years, he'd heard his boys and their mates scaring one another with tales of bodies buried in the cellar and disappeared children. But kids could be ghoulish like that, and Percy had never had an issue with Merlin Stamp himself, nor his dogs.

His thoughts were on Isabel Turner as he made his way through the trees on the border of Stamp's land. He'd seen her here once before, she and her husband, about five or six years ago. Percy had been assessing the place for risk ahead of the fire season when he'd become distracted by what he swore to this day was a platypus. The duck-billed, egg-laying mammal had been thought extinct in these parts for most of the century, but he was sure he'd seen one glide from the bank and into the water. He'd hurried his notebook from his pocket and was eagerly recording the position when the sound of twigs breaking underfoot on the other side of the gorge arrested his attention.

He'd known at once that they were arguing, even if he couldn't hear the words they were saying. Mrs Turner, walking ahead of her husband, had stopped abruptly, her body rigid, her gaze lifted to the treetops. Even from a distance he could read the anger emanating from her stiff posture. She stood like that, her husband's words washing over her, until finally she turned and responded, her hands moving like a pair of birds.

Percy had been transfixed. He didn't usually stare, but the whole situation was utterly unfamiliar to him. He and Meg didn't have that sort of argument. They didn't fight at all, really. He could vaguely remember that, once upon a time, they'd held different views on things; over the years, though, their disparities had mostly softened and merged.

'What's that?'

Percy had jumped at the voice beside him. A child of around five had materialised, as if from a crevice between the great grey-speckled rocks that loomed this side of the gorge. She was pointing at the sketch he'd made.

'A map,' he said, his heart still racing with surprise. 'I drew it.'

'Why?'

'I want to remember this spot.'

'Why?'

The child was Evie Turner, he realised. He'd heard Meg talking about the Turners' youngest daughter: 'She's an odd little bird, that one. Bright, but so many questions!' He explained about the platypus.

'The platypus is a monotreme,' she said.

'That's right. Same as the echidna.'

Her face was a study in implacability. 'I draw, too,' she said eventually. She took her own sketchbook from a bag strapped diagonally across her body, opening it to a page that featured several proficient nature sketches. 'I notice things. I'm going to be a scientist when I grow up.'

'Very good. We need more of them.'

He saw then that her gaze had dropped, and her focus sharpened. She was studying a nearby bush covered with vibrant yellow pompom flowers.

'Wattle,' he said.

'Golden wattle,' she corrected.

'You're right.'

'Did you know,' she began, 'that the seedlings from a golden wattle can live for up to fifty years?'

'That so?'

'That's a long time.'

'It is.'

'How old are you?'

'Younger than fifty.' He was thirty-six, in fact.

'Wattle seeds are germinated by bush fires.' Evie Turner nodded with vague disdain towards her parents, still engaged in heated discussion in the distance. '*She's* frightened of bush fires. That's because she's English. But I'm not. I'm Australian and golden wattles are my favourite flower and I'm not going to live in England no matter what *she* thinks.'

With that, before Percy had a chance to tell her that golden wattles were his favourite, too, she'd run off to join the adults, sun-browned legs leaping over fallen logs with the expertise of one who seemed more familiar with this lonely place than she ought to be.

Percy shook the memory away. It was replaced, despite his best efforts, with an image of the same child lying still and silent as the grave on a picnic rug that very afternoon, a line of ants crawling over her skinny wrist. A surge of sickness overwhelmed him, and he planted his palm against the smooth wet trunk of a gum, retching hard.

The fertile smell of rain and earth mingled with other rich, secretive bushland scents. With a swipe at his chin, Percy pressed on, eager now to get away from this place, away from the memories of that little girl and the warring couple and the nagging sense of disquiet he carried about Merlin Stamp. Finally, he reached the edge of the woods and emerged where the Onkaparinga Valley Road made its narrowest bend. On the other side was the beginning of Willner Road. Percy came to a standstill, deliberating for a moment, and then he crossed over.

He didn't follow the road, choosing instead to slip beneath the fence and onto Turner land. The route was longer, but more concealed. He knew now why he was walking. He knew what he was doing out, what he was looking for. He was retracing his steps in the hope that he might find the little wooden wren. After so much loss today, the need to possess it again was imperative. It was a gift, chosen with love, and it was out there in the darkness somewhere. He imagined that he could hear the rapid quiver of small wings, its tiny heart. Most likely he had lost it at the spot where he had knelt, stumbled backwards; where his thoughts had begun to multiply and collide and break.

The ground was wet and the grass long, but Percy moved swiftly. The wind had died down now; the storm had settled into a lull. He skirted around the edge of the foothills, sticking to the hard-beaten cow paths that cut across the undulating slopes. To his right, the land rose steeply, sweeping up to the plateau at the top. Old Mr Wentworth had come from a family of seamen; it was no surprise that he'd chosen the highest ground on which to build his home.

Percy stopped walking and looked back towards the town. There was very little to see: here and there the faint glow of a solitary light. He hoped that Meg was still asleep. She'd been exhausted, having spent most of the night fussing and worrying. He didn't want her to wake and wonder where he was. He didn't want her to know that he'd been out. He just wanted to find the carved wren and take it home.

Meg would have liked six kids. She'd loved their boys as babies, she'd been a natural, even during the difficulties with Marcus. Sitting up at night when they were ill, nursing them when they were struggling to sleep. She'd had a knack, a real baby charmer. Many times, Percy had frowned with fearful incomprehension at the irate mewling face of the tiny creature in his arms, refusing to settle no matter how he rocked or patted, only to hand the little one to Meg and have the crying ease at once.

Once Marcus had settled into himself, she announced that she was ready for another. Percy wasn't in the habit of denying her the things she desired, though privately he'd worried. It was a daughter she wanted, he knew, even though she never would've said it out loud. 'Happy with whatever God sees fit to give me,' she always insisted, 'so long as the baby's healthy.' But he'd seen the way she watched the little girls at church, a fond smile on her face as she admired their hair and their manners, shooting a glance sideways at their boys and laying a careful, warning hand on the nearest one's knee, lest he forget where he was and start brawling.

He'd noticed, too, the way she kept adding to that glory box of hers. The hand-carved wooden chest, with its smell of ancient European forests, was the only thing she'd insisted on keeping from the shack by the river that passed for a family home when she was growing up. That, and the old book of family recipes. Both had come from Germany with the Lutheran ancestors on her mother's side, when they boarded a boat alongside the other sick, broke and hungry willing to roll the dice and gamble on a better life in an unknown country on the opposite side of the world.

Inside the chest, Meg had amassed a trove of treasured items. The boys' best articles of clothing, once outgrown; a bisque doll with an exquisite painted face; a miniature Blue Willow tea set; a guilloche hairbrush and hand mirror. Her prize possession, though, and one she took out to inspect when she thought he wasn't watching, was a collection of soft pink cashmere balls of yarn, purchased at great expense when they made their trip to Sydney some months after they'd lost their little girl. 'I've got a feeling, Perce,' Meg had said earnestly, as she clutched the bag from the haberdasher's. 'One of these days we'll be glad we bought them; you'll see.'

Alas, they had not been blessed with another child after Marcus, boy or girl. Percy felt guilty about this. Even though he knew it was superstitious rubbish, he felt as if the fates, God, whoever it was that decided such things, had known that his heart wasn't in it. Sometimes he even wondered whether it was his fault, with his hankering to live a different life, that they'd lost the first. Meg had taken it stoically. Each year that passed, she'd softened her language around the subject, until Marcus turned ten and she put the matter to rest. That's when she started saying, 'Never let yourself get outnumbered!' as cheerfully and as often as she could. 'Children are God's gift, but two's my limit.'

Funny enough, it was around that time, as Marcus came good and Meg let go, that Percy started to feel the lack of another. As the boys got older, he began to glimpse how brief the window was before they drifted away and family life as he knew it – the fishing trips, the laughter and ribbing around the dinner table, the line of boots he was always tripping over by the door – would be over.

Lightning whitened the sky and a long, low howl, like a dingo's call, reverberated across the foothills. It was as if the two had conspired to jolt him from his introspection, reminding him that he was out here for a reason, with limited time remaining before the skies re-opened and rain began bucketing down.

He started walking again, his torch lighting the way ahead. A second howl came, desperate and raw, matched this time by a rumble of thunder that rolled around the hills. He quickened his pace as another flash of lightning illuminated a great dark shape before him: the hollow tree, a local landmark known by all the kids. The ancient gum had a trunk so wide you could walk right through the centre, a clearing large enough for a group of eight – nine or ten at a squeeze – to shelter from the rain. A travelling bush poet had written a poem about it once, which, in Tambilla's great claim to fame, had wound up in the *Sydney Morning Herald*. Meg kept a yellowed copy of the poem, trimmed from the newspaper, on the wall behind the register, because it mentioned the 'sturdy shoulder of the good shopkeep of Tam-billa' – a moniker she wore like a badge of honour, even though the poem had been written about another shopkeeper, a century before.

Meg was exactly the sort of person the poet had described. After those six children she'd expected failed to show, she became mother to the town, always busy in the evenings knitting a pair of bootees for this new baby, or a jumper for that scrappy child she reckoned could use it. A couple of winters before, Percy had glanced around the congregation at church one Sunday and counted no fewer than nine children wearing Meg's creations.

It wasn't just the children, either: people were always dropping into the shop to tell her their problems. She'd listen with that kind, focused expression of hers, never leaping to talk over the other person, and then she'd call Percy, or one of the boys, to take over at the counter. 'I'm just going out back to have a cuppa with my friend here,' she'd say, before disappearing with whichever local woman had come in need that day.

Even Isabel Turner had sat across the flimsy card table in the back room of the shop, sharing a pot of tea with Meg. That must have been around the time Percy had seen her in the woods near Merlin Stamp's. Meg hadn't mentioned what they'd talked about, other than to offer the general observation that she was 'homesick, poor thing'. His wife never divulged a confidence; she was a secret keeper, all right, the good shopkeep of Tambilla. But he'd noticed Isabel Turner dabbing at her eyes with a handkerchief and nodding as Meg spoke to her in a quiet voice.

*

By the time Percy reached the picnic site, his vision had adjusted to the dark and he could make out the shape of the willow tree by the waterhole. He couldn't help turning to look down the hill to where he and Blaze had been walking earlier, when he'd chanced to spot the Turner family.

Even without the torch, Percy could tell that the place where the Turners had been was a mess. He switched on the feeble light and surveyed the area. There was no sign of the wren. The storm had been heavy, the sort of rain he'd heard about them having up in the tropical north of the country. Where policemen and photographers had walked back and forth earlier was now a mudslide, with not a single footstep visible. The picnic items had been removed by someone, the Turners taken away. The morgue, Percy knew, was down in Adelaide, in the middle of the city, and the thought of them all down there, cold bodies waiting in the dark, made him retch again. It was a nightmare.

His torchlight grazed the base of the willow and he noticed that the crib was also gone. Someone had taken it down. Returned it to the house, he supposed. The earth was churned up beneath the tree, but less rain-affected than elsewhere. If only he'd gone to look inside the basket that afternoon. If he'd looked then, he might have seen the baby still sleeping and taken her down to the Hughes house with him, kept her safe until the police could be told and arrangements made for her care. He hated to think of the search that had yielded nothing, the party out so long once the rain had started falling, a child without her mother.

Thea Turner had been the newest baby in Tambilla. Meg had knitted a pair of yellow bootees ahead of the birth, just as she did for all the newborns, but she'd taken a particular shine to Isabel Turner's babe. A few weeks after the child was born, she'd even pulled out the rolls of pink yarn. 'What? I like to have a project,' she said when she noticed Percy's surprise. 'Better a matinee jacket for that sweet baby than a nest for the mice.' Young Becky Baker, whom Mrs Turner had hired as a nursemaid, couldn't walk that hulking great perambulator past the shop without Meg finding a reason to join her outside. 'Such a pretty little thing,' she would say when she came back in at last. 'A real neat little face – and those rosebud lips! She's an absolute doll.'

Percy had cursed the Baker lass for passing their door so often. This, he knew, was utterly unfair. From what he heard she was a good worker and a kind soul; she was just doing her job. All the same, he wished she'd keep the baby out of Meg's way. He'd known his wife long enough to detect the hidden note of longing underlying her comments. One afternoon, a few weeks ago, she'd even said: 'If Kurt and Matilda were to have a baby, she'd look a bit like that, don't you think?'

Marcus had been stacking flour onto the shelves in the corner of the shop at the time and had tossed a bag down in disgust, sending white dust pluming into the air. Typical fourteen-year-old behaviour, Percy had told himself, nothing to get too concerned about; he'd reprimanded the boy later. Secretly, though, he'd had some sympathy. The last thing he wanted was for Kurt to settle down to the business of having babies. Plenty of time for all that later, after he'd studied and learned and travelled, made the most of himself and everything that the world had to offer a young man with a fine brain and legs that did what they were told.

Percy felt a stab of terror as an image of Sergeant Duke making a note of Kurt's name came to mind. There was nothing to fear, he told himself. His son hadn't played a role in what happened to the Turners. He just needed to keep Kurt safe as the policemen carried out their work – their real work – of finding out how a family had wound up dead on Christmas Eve as they ate their picnic lunch by the creek.

It was raining again now. Lightning lit up the sky beyond the mountain ridge. The sound of dingoes came like a scream. This place felt haunted, changed.

Percy knelt to touch the earth where they had lain. Tears fell, as away from his family, his other concerns, he was able to feel the full weight of what he'd discovered that afternoon.

He stayed like that for a time, until something crept up on him, drew his attention.

A noise? An instinct? Percy wasn't sure. All he knew was he was nursing a vague new sense of dread.

He switched off the torchlight. Waited.

Slowly, he stood.

He couldn't shake the feeling that he was not alone.

Was that movement in the shadows?

He stood very still and listened. There was a rustling. The hairs on the back of his neck stood up. Percy knew that he was being watched. Something – someone? – was there with him.

PART THREE

CHAPTER THIRTEEN

Sydney, 11 December 2018

In her single bed, in her childhood room, Jess slept fitfully. She'd left the window open and the smell, the sounds, the touch of Nora's sheets against her skin, conspired to form a time machine. Her dreams were shot through with people from her past, forgotten versions of herself. She was a girl at school, a child visiting Darling House with her mother, a teenager at the beach . . . and then, with a surge of panic, she was awake again, wondering where and when and who on earth she was.

It was pitch-black. The clock told her it was 3 a.m.

Jess stayed very still, waiting, hoping, trying to fall back into slumber. Just an hour or two more, and she could get up and start the day.

But sleep was elusive. Lying in the dark, she felt divided, dissolvable, displaced. She pictured her bed in London and it seemed like make-believe. But this place was not right or real either. *I want to go home.* The thought came to her in a flash and immediately she pushed it away. The sentiment was childish, but also meaningless. It wasn't that she wanted to *go* anywhere; rather, she wanted to *feel* at home, settled. This was jet lag, she told herself. The discombobulation, the separation of mind and body, the struggle of each to reclaim the other and together resume circadian rhythms.

Whatever the case, she was now wide awake. Jess switched on the bedside lamp and the circle of warm yellow light chased shadows into the corners. The world began to make sense again. She pulled out her laptop and waited while it booted up and connected to Nora's wi-fi. A list of new emails scrolled into place. She scanned the sender names in case of anything urgent but saw only subscription emails and discount offers.

Jess considered writing to Rachel, decided against it, and opened Word instead. Work had always been her safe harbour and so would it be now. She opened the article about coming home and picked over the outline she'd drafted on the plane. When she got to the end, she let out a long, slow exhalation. It was dreadful. Thin and flimsy. Worse, and strangely, it was like someone else had written it. It didn't speak to Jess's reality or with any authenticity to the greater human experience. It was advertising copy with a bit of trite humour thrown in.

None of this, she suspected, would be a barrier to publication. But reading it here, in the same bedroom where she'd sat to fill in her application for university more than twenty years before, Jess felt exposed. She was well-acquainted with the demands and stresses of adult life – bills to be paid, compromises to be made – but there were moments that highlighted the distance she'd travelled from the idealism of her youth, and they never failed to make her feel ashamed.

Jess minimised the document and opened her search engine to the BBC page. For all that the twenty-four-hour news cycle had distorted journalism, politics and possibly democracy itself, it was a gift to the lonely insomniac. She started with the headlines before finding her way, somewhat inevitably, to Matt's weekend column about the etiquette of baby music classes, and then following a link that led to another, through the current events forest of Meghan Markle presenting a fashion award, NASA discovering signs of water on a nearby asteroid, and Theresa May facing a leadership challenge over Brexit. The accompanying photograph of Number 10 and its oversized Christmas tree, the familiar slick of the wet London road, brought on a pang of homesickness. Jess glanced at the open window and wished the sun would rise.

It was too easy in the dark to glimpse the things she preferred not to see: the depth of Rachel's sympathy when she learned of Nora's fall; Dr Martin's advice in the hospital; the unutterable suggestion that Nora might not get better.

Jess closed her eyes against an outcome she didn't want to contemplate. The air was muggy, and she could smell gardenia and a hint of salt. Night-time smells, so familiar after years of sleeping in this room, and before that in her tiny bedroom in the apartment further along the peninsula.

On the night of Thomas Turner's funeral, Polly had told Jess, 'I found out why it's called a wake.' They were in Jess's room together. This was their usual routine, Jess lying in her narrow single bed beneath the window, the dreamcatcher dangling from the ceiling above; Polly sitting beside her on the chair she'd bought second-hand and that they'd stained together on the balcony with shellac. ('Resin from the lac bug of India,' Polly had said, stirring the rich syrupy mixture. 'Isn't that something?')

So much had happened since they'd left that morning that Jess had forgotten she'd started off by puzzling over the word, and that her mother had promised to find out its derivation.

'It's an ancient Anglo-Saxon tradition,' Polly began, 'the

mixing of two ideas – one from earliest Christian times, the other from long before. The first Christians used to follow the custom of "waking" a new church by singing, feasting and praying in it.'

Jess, disappointed: 'But that's got nothing to do with a dead body.'

'I'm not finished yet.'

Jess mimed zipping her lips.

'The other tradition I mentioned is much older. Long before the Christians came to Britain, an all-night vigil would be held over the body of the recently dead. Loved ones would mourn and chant and share stories of the person's life. It was called "waking the dead".'

Jess felt her eyes widen involuntarily as her thoughts went to Dr Frankenstein and his monster, to Cathy's ghost haunting Wuthering Heights. 'You mean they brought them back to life?'

'Well, no.'

'But you said—'

'Back then, the word "wake" didn't mean to become alert; it meant "to watch" or "to guard".'

'But what were they guarding against?'

'There were those who believed the newly dead soul was at risk of theft by evil spirits.'

Soul theft at the hands of evil spirits had been almost as exciting as bringing the dead back to life. Which probably explained why the idea had stayed front of mind, while Halcyon, a dull old house in England where her grandmother's elderly brother had lived for a time, slipped deep into a crevice of her memory.

It had never occurred to Jess to ask more questions about the house or to look further herself. Now, though, with time to kill and eager for distraction, she typed the word 'Halcyon' into her search engine. The responding entries included a link to the word's definition, a retirement village in California, and an organic skin-care range. Jess shook her head at the random list and cleared the field. This time, she added 'Thomas Turner' to the search terms.

The first few links were ads for hotels and wotif.com, but further down she spotted an archived article from *Esquire* magazine that piqued her interest. The date was January 1960, and the summary mentioned a house called Halcyon and a man with a passion for it.

A Lucky Man

THE HOUSE ON THE HILL, in the middle of the steep-rising fields at the end of Willner Road, belonged to Mr Thomas Turner, a farmer neither by birth nor inclination. Mr Turner was a man whose currency through life was not the gathering and application of expertise, but rather an unbridled enthusiasm for whatever it was on which he chose to shine his full attention. 'Could've sold snow to the Eskimos,' came the considered opinion from beneath the hat of one old-timer on the bench in the Tambilla Centenary Garden; from the other: 'Never knew a man to tell a story so well you could've sworn it happened to you.'

Business-wise, he was a speculator; more charitably, an entrepreneur. In a different country, at a different time, he could've made a fortune traveling town-to-town selling snake oil – or religion. But Mr Turner was born in Sydney, Australia, in 1919, to parents whose wealth and class rendered them distant and disapproving. He was raised by a series of nannies in the company of a sister ten years his junior, whose adoration made him bold and charming. Like most children whose parents deny them attention in their early years, he learned to recognize and make the most of their limited shifting focus, to woo and cajole his child-weary carers, and to enlist the alliance of his devoted younger sibling.

To nobody's surprise, he grew into a self-assured young man, hungry for adventure and keen to make his mark. What marvelous timing, then, that just as he was taking his first steps into adulthood, the faraway cogs of old empires turned, and the world found itself on a precipice. War was declared, and whatever frustrations Turner suffered initially – when it looked unlikely that the Australian Imperial Forces would be sent overseas – were quickly swept aside by the establishment of the Empire Air Training Scheme. He was among the first to sign up and was sent to England to fly with the RAF.

And no matter that his new-fashioned farming ideas and shiny city shoes raised eyebrows among the good people of Tambilla; no one could argue that he wasn't a genuine war hero. 'He had the Victoria Cross,' Mrs Betty Diamond, the proprietress of Diamond's Tearoom, confirmed. 'He wore it on his breast pocket every Anzac Day.' A lean woman with sun-weathered skin and shrewd eyes, Mrs Diamond was generally more inclined to listen than to speak, but having lost her young husband in the Great War, military conflict was a subject to which she warmed.

'Shot down over France, but he managed to get himself back to England to fly another four years until Germany surrendered. Rescued an English officer into the bargain, I'm told. Not that you ever heard him brag about it. He was a humble sort of fellow, not one to chase praise. But it wasn't false modesty, either. "I'm a lucky man, Mrs Diamond," was what he said to me. "A very lucky man."'

Mr Boris Braun, a teacher at the local school and spare-time history aficionado, was glad to supply more detail. He had invited Mr Turner to speak to his year six class and still lit up with the glow of a starstruck child when called upon to recount the visit.

'He came down near the Channel but was able to free himself from the wreckage and make contact with members of the Resistance. With their help, he traveled south, reaching almost as far as the Free Zone before the Germans caught and imprisoned him in Saint-Hippolyte. They didn't count on an Australian, though – that's what he said, and you can imagine how the children loved to hear that! Australia was a nation founded on men who knew how to break free of prison, he told the class, and in the spirit of his forebears he managed to escape – with a British officer in tow – over the Pyrenees and into Spain. The pair of them arrived back in England aboard the HMS *Sheffield* and went on to win the war!'

A photograph that some of the local newspapers chose to run when reporting the deaths shows Mr Turner some weeks after VE Day, striding down a damaged city street with his pregnant young wife, wearing a pale, tailored suit, his fedora angled over one eye. And wasn't it just like Thomas Turner, people said from behind their schooners at the bar of the Tambilla Hotel, an unmistakable glint of admiration in their exchanged glances, to somehow find himself both a well-fitting suit *and* a family in bomb-ravaged London? 'And all while he was waiting to be sent back home.'

The man in the photograph is handsome by any measure, but Mr Turner's appeal was about more than his sharp jawline and devil-may-care smile. He was the sort of person to whom criticism did not stick; a man

whom people longed to know, whose honor they leapt
to defend, and whose innate charisma could no more
be explained than it could be resisted.

'I'm a lucky man,' he said over and over, with the
cheerful ease of an upstanding citizen stating his name
for the record. 'I can't explain it, I almost certainly
don't deserve it, but it's God's own truth.' And thus, he
learned what all truly charming people know: others
would make allowances for any foibles he had. They
wanted to.

His decision to purchase the Wentworth place on
the outskirts of Tambilla, a house he'd never seen in a
town to which he'd never been, was a case in point. He
caught his first glimpse of the property, or so the story
went, after his Spitfire was shot down in July 1941.
On his way south, he slept here and there in the farm
buildings of dissenters, and it was in the loft of one
such barn, on the back of a piece of newspaper he'd
been using to wrap his tobacco, that his imagination
was captured by the black-and-white image and
loquacious description of a property for sale in South
Australia. An element of homesickness recalled the
faraway land of red earth and olive-green trees and
shimmering azure-blue skies, and an idea lodged at the
back of his mind. He nurtured that idea and, over time,
it turned into a dream, and the dream kept him warm
at night. When he suddenly came into money ('quite
by chance', as he was to say whenever the tale was
told) – more on that later – he knew exactly what to do
with it.

All change and happenings are notable in small
towns, but Mr Turner's purchase of the Wentworth
place attracted particularly avid comment in and
around Tambilla. Outsiders did not often buy into the
town – not because it wasn't a pleasant place to live,
but for the practical reason that there were limited
employment opportunities. More to the point, there

were next to no available dwellings. The same families
had owned the same houses for as long as anyone
could remember, passing them down, parent to child,
generation by generation. Occupation was so settled
that no one bothered with street addresses. Instructions
were given to 'the Landry residence' or 'the Misses
Edwards at the mill', and sometimes simply 'Old
Stamp's, out beyond the railway line'.

The Wentworth place, though both unoccupied
and available, had been that way for so long folks had
forgotten it existed. To some extent, it was a matter
of being out of sight, out of mind. Mr Wentworth's
garden of imported European specimens had come
to envelop the house, and the overgrown property
acquired an air of mythology. A few small parcels of
land had been sold off around the edges, but local
planning laws prevented the property being subdivided
further, and not a lot of people were willing (or able)
to pay the asking price.

The sale itself took place in February 1942, the
same week the Japanese dropped bombs on Darwin,
and may it stand as evidence of the importance of the
transaction to the townspeople that the bombing to the
north was only the second-most-talked-about event in
Tambilla that week. News that the Wentworth place
had sold traveled like bushfire through the Hills. *Who
was the buyer?* residents wanted to know. There were
only so many people in South Australia who could
afford to make such a purchase. Confirmation that the
new owner was from out of state pushed speculation to
a fever pitch.

When Mr and Mrs Turner finally arrived in the
autumn of 1945, fresh from London by way of
Sydney, and affixed a sign on the gate that read
HALCYON, the local grapevine was alight. Mrs Marian
Green at the telephone exchange reported that until
the Turner tragedy, the reopening of the Wentworth

place spurred the greatest switchboard 'frenzy' she had ever seen.

'Having that house sit empty up there, well, it was like a bad omen,' she was to tell police, when she was interviewed after the deaths. 'Houses are for living in, and a nice young couple like that, their little Matilda just a babe in arms – we were all of us so pleased to welcome them into the community.'

By all accounts, they *were* well received; at least, they were for the most part. Farmer McKenzie, next door, put on a show of holding a grudge about the sale, grumbling about the indignity of a 'Johnny-come-lately' snatching the opportunity from a local, but that was 'just his way'. As police would hear more than once, 'He's a prickly old dog, Hamish McKenzie, but he's all bark.'

Thomas Turner had fallen in love with the romance of growing grapes and making wine when he was hiding on the property of a vintner in the French countryside on his way toward the Free Zone and, once home, threw himself into the task with formidable energy. His knowledge might have been lacking, but his enthusiasm was unrivalled. He didn't always take the advice he sought, and he certainly set other fruit growers' tongues wagging with some of the unorthodox decisions he made – 'He'd read some book when he was abroad,' reported Mr Walter Hansen of the co-op, 'by a fellow called Steiner who had ideas about "biodynamics"' – but he overcame early setbacks and was starting to make real progress.

There was a degree of consternation in the community when he suddenly pulled out every vine and put cattle on his land instead. Whether farming or weaving, sausage or cheese making, brewing or blacksmithing, there was a 'way of doing things' in Tambilla. The proprietress at the local grocery shop, Mrs Meg Summers, still held the book of recipes that

accompanied her maternal forebears aboard the *Zebra*
when it set sail under the stewardship of Captain
Hahn, and it was said, with more than passing
solemnity, that no one in Tambilla baked a *Roggenbrot*
loaf as well as she.

Mr Hansen scratched his head as he pondered the
matter of Thomas Turner's abrupt change of heart.
'Winemaking can be a fiddly business,' he said at
length. 'More of an art than a science. And his ideas
were strange to say the least. But he was turning things
around. He'd have got there in the end. No, I couldn't
understand him altering tack like that. I thought he was
committed.'

Mr Hansen was not mistaken. Thomas Turner *had*
been wholly devoted to his ambition of making wine –
right up until he wasn't. Like so many men of his type,
Turner suffered the dreamer's curse: the moment one
grand plan came close to fruition, another bright light
started flickering on the horizon. By 1959 his interest
in a life on the land was waning.

Indeed, in the weeks leading up to Christmas that
year, Thomas Turner was on the other side of the globe,
chasing a new dream. As the summer sun began to rise
over the line of gums on the highest ridge of his fields
on Willner Road, the wintry evening darkness of the day
before was drawing around London and Mr Turner,
having enjoyed a long, hot bath in the hotel's gleaming
tub, was now polishing his silver cuff links and
straightening his three-piece suit, taking one last
approving look at himself in the Dorchester mirror
before trotting downstairs and across the lobby, out
through the big glass doors onto Park Lane, on his way
to dine with a pair of investors whose support he hoped
to gain for a new scheme of 'boundless possibility'.

And lucky it was, too, the townspeople were all
quick to agree, when they gathered in the Tambilla
Hotel and Diamond's Tearoom in the days and weeks

that followed, for not only was he spared the
immediate horror of the discovery, but he was also
shielded from the hot flares of speculation and
suspicion that fired up afterward. Everybody knew that
the first person police looked to when a woman and
her children turned up dead was the husband and
father. So it was that, even as his family lay dead in the
West Terrace morgue, the assessment of the townsfolk,
when talk turned to Thomas Turner, was how lucky he
was, the poor, poor man; how lucky that he hadn't
been home.

Daniel Miller, January 1960

Jess let out the breath she'd been holding. What had she just read? She scrolled quickly back to the top and skimmed the article again. The name of the man, the name of the house – both of those were right. Thomas Turner had been born in Sydney and he'd had a doting younger sister. Nora had mentioned something about him being a war hero. But the rest of it was wrong: weirdly, specifically, intricately wrong. Nora's brother had lived in London, he'd had a house there and a wife, but he hadn't had any children – let alone children in a morgue.

Maybe this was a piece of fiction, the biographical similarities some sort of strange coincidence, or a psychedelic sixties mash-up of fact and fiction?

Jess added the word 'Tambilla' to her search and then, for good measure, 'murder', and watched as a new page of responses appeared. She scanned their titles, bracing herself against the impact of words like 'infamous' and 'secret' and 'tragedy'.

Spoiled for choice, she opened the first entry: a brief post on a blog called *Australian Historical Crime Chronicles*.

Turner Family Tragedy

ON CHRISTMAS EVE 1959, one of the hottest days of the summer, the Turner family of South Australia left their grand Georgian house 'Halycon' and carried the makings of a picnic across their paddocks and down to a creek that ran through the property. Isabel Turner and her four children – the youngest, Thea, still an infant – were well-known within the Adelaide Hills village of Tambilla, and it was not unusual for them to be spotted outdoors enjoying the beautiful natural surroundings. On this summery day, they had set up camp beneath the shade of an old willow that grew on the edge of the bank where the creek widened to form a waterhole. The bodies of Mrs Turner and her three eldest children were found late in the afternoon by a passer-by who raised the alarm. Baby Thea was missing from her crib.

A high-profile detective from Adelaide, Sergeant Peter Duke, who had previously worked on the notorious Somerton Body case, was called out to assist local officers with their inquiries, and an extensive investigation was launched. Despite local fears that a murderer was on the loose, police were able to determine that the crime's perpetrator was closer to home. A coronial inquest was held in July 1960, seven months after the deaths, at which testimony was given by numerous witnesses. The South Australian coroner, Mr T.R. Sterling, found that the family had died from poisoning, though the type and source could not be determined. The case was ruled a murder-suicide, the coroner satisfied, after hearing evidence, that the poison had been administered by Mrs Turner herself.

The infant's remains were discovered in 1979, only a mile or so away from where the bodies of her mother and siblings had been found. Animal prints had been

detected at the picnic site, and the coroner heard
evidence that a pack of wild dogs had been active in
the area during the spring and summer of 1959.
Expert evidence was mixed, but the coroner accepted
that dingoes, coming upon an unprotected infant, were
capable of removing the small body from the scene,
and indeed were likely to have done so. It was a
scenario that was to gain attention in Australia after
the death of baby Azaria Chamberlain during a
family camping trip at Uluru in 1980.

Greedy now for more information, Jess clicked on the
next link, and then the next, reading each page faster than
the one before. Aside from minor differences, the information was the same. A woman named Isabel Turner was found
to have killed herself and her children. Her husband, who
was travelling in the UK for business at the time, never
returned to Australia. His name was Thomas Turner and his
house in the Hills, known locally and historically as 'the
Wentworth place', had been rechristened 'Halcyon' by the
Turners. He had died in London in 1988, and only after his
death was his body returned home to be buried in the family
plot in Sydney.

It was Nora's brother. His name, his house, his residence
in London and the year of his death: every detail matched.
The house named Halcyon had been in South Australia, not
England, and there had been another wife, daughters and a
son, too, before he moved to London and began his new life
there.

Jess clicked through to Google Images. A single photograph circulated on the internet, released at the time of the
tragedy presumably. She wondered who had handed it over,
and what they'd have thought had they known it would still

be floating around in cyberspace sixty years later, giving the family an uncanny virtual life after death. It had been taken in 1955, four years prior to their deaths and some time before the youngest child was born, so there were only three children pictured. The image was black and white, and the resolution wasn't great, but it was clear enough to make out their faces. The family was on holiday in Sydney. If the background of the Harbour Bridge hadn't made that obvious, the caption beneath the photo said as much.

Thomas and Isabel Turner were standing together, his arm around her back, hers in turn resting on the shoulders of their eldest child, a girl named Matilda, who wore black Mary Janes with white ankle socks and clutched a small purse. Two younger children stood in front of their parents, the boy sporting a peaked cap, the girl with ribbons tied at the ends of two long plaits. John Turner had his hands pushed casually into his trouser pockets and flashed a broad gap-toothed smile, whereas Evelyn Turner, while dressed as finely as her siblings, had not yet learned to pose prettily for the camera. She held her hands together, playing with her fingers, and had tucked her right shoulder behind her brother's. It seemed she had been caught on the edge of a thought; she was frowning distractedly at something beyond the camera lens.

Jess could see flashes of Nora in their faces. There was no doubting that these were her nieces and nephew. Matilda, John and Evelyn. It was sobering to witness this family in a shared, happy moment, each member unaware of what the future had in store.

She shifted her focus away from the children and onto their mother. During the investigation and after the coroner returned his findings, Isabel had become something of a cause célèbre: the latest in a list of that most scandalising of figures, the beautiful female killer. Like her youngest daughter, Mrs Turner had glanced sideways at the moment the photo was taken, but Jess nonetheless took in the attractive features of her profile, the tilt of the chin and the intelligent-seeming gaze.

A kookaburra somewhere outside in the breaking dawn threw his cackle across the sky and Jess felt a sudden frisson. Never in her wildest imaginings had she suspected that a scandal of this type lurked within her family. Nora had never said anything to suggest the possibility – not a word. In fact, it now seemed clear to Jess that her grandmother had gone out of her way to keep the terrible tragedy hidden.

But it must have impacted her life significantly, even if it had happened far away from Darling House. Nora had adored her brother. Had she been close to his wife, to Isabel Turner, as well? Jess was impatient to know, and she could feel other questions rising inside her, too. Every investigative instinct she had honed during the last two decades as a journalist was alert. She needed to find out more about Isabel Turner, the woman in the photo, and precisely what had led up to that afternoon by the creek.

Her very next thought, and one that she had been having in various forms for the better part of her life, was that Nora would know.

She had to speak to her grandmother.

CHAPTER FOURTEEN

But Nora was still asleep when Jess arrived at the hospital. She tried to get a sense from the nurse as to when her grandmother might be expected to wake, but the other woman only noted that Nora had passed the night without disturbance. An element of restraint in her manner gave Jess pause. 'That's an improvement, right?' she asked.

'It's better than the alternative,' said the nurse.

Despite the cryptic reply, Jess could see for herself that her grandmother was looking better. She was still impossibly small and pale, tucked neatly beneath the white hospital sheet, but her expression was easier than it had been, and the heart monitor was counting out a steady beat.

Jess pulled the visitor's chair closer to the bed and slid her notebook from her bag. 'No evil spirits on my watch, Nora,' she said softly.

As she sat in silence, Jess kept circling back to her grandmother's secrecy. Nora was never one to shy away from past sorrow. She'd been forthcoming on subjects like her failed marriage, the loneliness she'd suffered as a child, a number of professional setbacks. She knew that history was cumulative. That the past was not something to be escaped from, but a fundamental part of who one was.

Even more confusingly, after her brother's funeral Nora had spoken about him to Jess often and at length. She'd start by saying, 'I recognise myself in you, Jessica,' and then,

'More than that, I see my brother.' This, Jess understood, even then, to be the highest praise. 'He was determined, decisive, and he didn't sit around and let opportunities pass him by. He was brave, too. He saved a man's life in the war. That's how he made his first fortune.'

'By saving a man?'

'An important man.'

'How?'

'It's a long story. I'll tell it to you someday.' And then she'd shake away the sadness that inevitably crept across her face and force a cheerful tone: 'Have I ever told you about the time he and I found a convict tunnel at the bottom of our garden?'

But she'd never come close to revealing any of this particular story. In fact, Jess realised now that Nora had rarely spoken about Thomas Turner as an adult. This omission had not seemed odd to Jess at the time – brother and sister had been close when they were growing up, but in adulthood their paths had diverged. He'd moved overseas before the internet and routine air travel made connection easy, and Jess was aware of her grandmother's fear of flying.

'We wrote letters,' Nora said, 'but it's not really the same as seeing someone.'

'He should have visited you.'

'He'd have liked to come back.'

'Then why didn't he?'

Nora had considered the question carefully before saying, 'It's a hard thing to explain to a young person. Sometimes coming home isn't as simple as you think.'

Now Jess understood. Grief had driven him away. Australia, his home country, must have been layered with traumatic memories.

But was grief enough to keep Nora quiet for so long?

'Why didn't you tell me?' Jess said quietly, tapping the nib of her pen gently on the lined page of her notebook. 'Why didn't you tell me about Halcyon?'

And why had her grandmother started to think about the place now?

As if she knew she were being watched, Nora's sleeping face animated into a mild half-smile. Jess reached out to take a small, bird-like hand in her own. The past often came back to the minds of the elderly, just as Patrick had said – perhaps that's all it was. But – she thought of Patrick's revelation that Nora had been upset recently by a letter from a South Australian solicitor . . . Thomas Turner's house had been in the Adelaide Hills.

Jess gave her grandmother's hand a gentle stroke then lowered it carefully onto the sheet. Opening her notebook, she added a reminder to look for the South Australian lawyer's letter to her to-do list, then stood and went to the refreshment machine at the end of the hallway and made herself a cup of tea. The result had a dishwater-grey tinge, but it was hot, and it would do. She took it back to Nora's room and typed 'Turner Family Tragedy' into her phone's search bar, scrolling through the results until she reached entries that she hadn't yet read. Most contained the same information, but every so often there was a new snippet.

After a couple of hours, with her internet browser full of open tabs and her vision swimming, Jess sat back and closed her eyes. Some of the blog posts contained quotes that had been taken from newspaper articles of the time, and one journalist's name had come up a lot. The name rang a bell, and Jess had to think for a moment as to why that might be.

Then she remembered: the essay about Thomas Turner that had sent her down this rabbit hole in the first place.

She typed the journalist's name into the search bar and opened his Wikipedia page. Daniel Miller was an American reporter born in 1930; his black-and-white portrait, an unposed photograph in suit and hat, had something of a *Mad Men* look about it. He had written for *The Atlantic*, *Esquire* and *The New Yorker*, among other publications, and was an early adopter of New Journalism, as practised by the likes of Truman Capote and Joan Didion – a more intimate style of reporting, where fiction techniques were applied to non-fiction topics with the aim of bringing readers emotionally closer to the story.

Daniel Miller had stationed himself in South Australia for the duration of the police investigation and inquest into the Turner deaths, producing a series of essays that developed into a book. *As If They Were Asleep* had been lauded at the time for its fresh approach and was a *New York Times* bestseller in 1961. An updated edition was published in 1980 after the discovery of the infant Thea Turner's remains, but in the years since the writer had disappeared from public view.

Jess typed the title and author name into her search. The book wasn't in print anymore and she couldn't find any mention of an Australian edition. There were, however, copies showing up on various online second-hand book sites. Jess browsed some of the options at AbeBooks before selecting one that looked to be in good condition.

She fished her credit card out of her handbag but stalled when she saw that delivery to Australia was estimated to take twenty-one to thirty-six days. Jess doubted she would still be in Sydney in a month's time. For an extra seven dollars, priority shipping could have it to her in five to eight days. Jess selected the faster shipping option and finalised the transaction just as Nora's nurse came in to check the monitor and let her know that visiting hours were ending.

A very young woman at the nurses' station caught Jess on her way to the lift. 'Excuse me – you're Mrs Turner-Bridges' granddaughter, aren't you?'

Jess nodded a confirmation.

'We had a phone call before. Someone wanting information about Mrs Turner-Bridges. I didn't give it out, as we're not allowed to do that. No personal information unless to the next of kin.'

Nora was well-connected in the local community, but her friends would have contacted Mrs Robinson or the office. 'Did the caller give a name?'

The nurse searched the desk, cluttered with papers, before finding the message. 'She said her name was Polly Turner, that she'd only just heard about her mother and wondered how she was . . .'

The young woman trailed off. Jess understood her awkwardness. Naturally it was difficult to comprehend a situation in which the daughter of the patient wasn't the next of kin. Jess realised, too, that she hadn't called Polly herself to report on Nora. Worse, that it hadn't even occurred to her to do so. She wasn't in the habit of contacting her mother with family updates. 'Thank you,' she said, with what she intended to be a reassuring smile. 'It's fine to bring her up to date if she rings again. In the meantime, I'll give her a call and let her know where things are at.'

'Do you need the number?' asked the nurse uncertainly, holding the piece of paper towards her.

'No, no, of course not,' said Jess. 'I've got it.'

And then she took the lift to the ground floor, struggling to remember the last time she had spoken with her mother.

In the end, Jess didn't speak with Polly that afternoon, either. She rang from the back of the taxi, but her mother's voicemail picked up, so she left a brief message explaining that she'd only just arrived in Sydney, that Nora's condition was improving and they hoped to have her home soon. She said she was staying at Darling House and then left the phone number before hanging up. Immediately she chided herself, because of course Polly had the number; she'd lived at Darling House for longer than Jess. It was only that she'd removed herself so completely from Nora's world in the intervening years that it was easy to forget.

Back at Nora's place, Jess held her breath as the taxi driver took payment from her debit card. The card was attached to an account she hadn't touched in years – ever, really – liberated that morning from an unopened envelope in the dressing table drawer in her childhood bedroom. Nora had established the 'Birthday Account' when Jess turned ten, making a deposit each year so it would be there 'in the future' if the need arose. What constituted a 'need' had never been spelled out, but having had to rebuild her own life once, Nora was adamant that Jess should have something saved for a rainy day. 'It might not put a roof over your head, but it'll buy you a nice umbrella.' It had long been a point of pride for Jess that she hadn't had reason to access the account. The driver handed back the card with a receipt, and Jess thanked him for the ride.

Inside, she made herself toast with avocado and sat at the kitchen bench, notebook and laptop both open before her. She read through her article for the travel magazine, shifting the cursor from line to line, paragraph to paragraph, looking for a spot to break in, to add clarity – perhaps even (dare she hope?) some panache – but every sentence she added just made things worse.

She couldn't concentrate. The business of coming home was interfering with the task of writing about it. Things were rather more complicated than she'd expected.

Jess was still pondering Nora's secrecy, wondering about her relationship with Isabel Turner. Her plan to ask her grandmother about the other woman hadn't worked out, but she was eager to know more. They would have been of a similar age; Nora had adored Thomas . . . Had her affection extended to his wife?

Jess drummed her fingers on the bench top and then, with the nudge of an idea, picked up her phone.

Mrs Robinson answered on the second ring. 'Hello?' She must have had the Darling House number programmed into her phone, for she continued: 'Is that you, Jess? Is everything all right?'

'Yes, yes, it's fine. I've just been to see Nora; she's doing well.' Jess took a deep breath and decided that the direct approach was best. She explained briefly what she'd discovered and why she was calling and said at last, 'I'm wondering if the memories are part of what's upsetting her. But there are so many things I don't know. I hoped you might be able to tell me about Nora's relationship with Isabel?'

There was absolute silence at the other end of the line and Jess began to wonder whether the connection had dropped out. 'Hello?'

'I'm not at home, Jess, I'm at the shops. I can't talk about this now, not over the phone.'

'Could we speak later, then? It doesn't have to be by phone – I could meet you somewhere. I'll be back at the hospital between three and five, so any time after that?' When Mrs Robinson didn't reply, she added, 'I'm only asking because I think it might help Nora.'

Mrs Robinson sighed heavily and named the park with the playground further along the peninsula. 'I'm going to be taking my afternoon walk at six. I can meet you there at half past.'

Once lunch was cleared away, Jess settled in for a spot of time travelling. Through the State Library of South Australia's Trove portal she could access and explore the newspapers of the period, starting with the earliest reports on Christmas morning 1959.

She read the first few articles before sending them to the printer, relishing, as she always did, the ability of the written word to transport. The period typesetting, the formality of the style and the voices of the people quoted caused time to collapse in upon itself so that Jess could see and feel and smell the scenes described. She could picture the readers of the day opening their newspapers at the breakfast table or on the tram home from work, straightening their horn-rimmed glasses and pouring their evening Scotch over ice as they settled down to read the latest news. She felt a sentimental pang for a time in which the press had occupied an unassailable position as the conduit between current events and a well-informed citizenry.

Over the years, many news reports had been written relating to the Turner family, but Jess was short on time. Reluctantly, she started hitting print without reading first. The majority had been published in the seven months between

December 1959 and July 1960, when the coroner's inquest had been held, but the story had made regular resurgences in the popular imagination, with a flurry of articles at the one-year, five-year and ten-year anniversaries, culminating in a huge amount of coverage at the twenty-year mark, coinciding as it did with the discovery of baby Thea's remains. Thereafter, the Turner Tragedy seemed to have been largely forgotten, mentioned only occasionally in lists of other cases whose notoriety had earned them capital letter status – the Somerton Body, the Pyjama Girl, the Beaumont Children.

It took almost two hours to reach the last article, and Jess was pleased when she collected the pages from the printer to find that a large pile awaited. Later, she would read it all thoroughly and draw up a timeline of the police case. She felt enlivened at the prospect. It had been a long time since she'd worked on a proper investigative assignment, and she'd missed it. The possibility of uncovering the source of Nora's recent upset lent the enterprise an even greater sense of purpose.

Jess had a quick look around the office in case the letter from the South Australian lawyer was there; Nora received a lot of correspondence and her bookkeeper, Anita, came in once a month to pay bills and sort mail. But Anita kept a very tidy system, and it didn't take long for Jess to ascertain that the letter had not been filed with other business paperwork.

The library was a personal domain, and thus the more likely repository. Jess went upstairs to check. She turned up nothing of note on the desk or in any of its drawers. She looked among the pile of books on the coffee table and between the pages of the display book on the sideboard in the entrance. Nothing. Maybe, she thought, Nora had taken the letter to her bedroom.

Jess felt a pang of nostalgia as she entered the fruity green haven of the Pimpernel-papered room. She half-expected to see Nora propped up in the bed, cup of tea in hand as she read the news of the day: 'Listen to this, Jessica, you won't believe what those clowns in Canberra have done this time.' Jess checked inside the colonial cedar chest and the drawers of the small writing bureau but found nothing. The surface of the bureau was empty, too, but for the framed photo of Thomas Turner that Jess had first seen at his funeral. He was striding through the City of London (as she now recognised it), the dome of St Paul's rising above the Blitz rubble behind him. She wondered whether the hint of someone else's coat on the left of the frame, the suggestion of a hand, were evidence of Isabel, and whether the photo had been cropped before or after the events of 1959.

Jess turned slowly to take in the rest of the room. She was running out of places to look. Her gaze came to rest on the door to Nora's dressing-room, modelled from a small adjoining anteroom after Polly outgrew it as a nursery. Without much hope of success, Jess took a cursory look inside. She felt mildly uncomfortable, going through her grandmother's things, but told herself the ends justified the means. She checked the pockets of the larger coats and had a peek inside each of the polaroid-labelled shoeboxes. No letter.

Out of ideas, Jess sat on the edge of the bed and glanced through the leadlight window. Nora's attachment to this room was easy to understand. The view over the garden she'd created was beautiful. Jess leaned forward to unlatch the casement and was met by a wash of warm air and the soporific hum of bees in the flowering wall-climber. A wave of dizziness overcame her. She was very much aware that she'd been awake since three.

There was still an hour or so until she was due back at the hospital for afternoon visiting hours. Jess slipped off her shoes and lay down on Nora's bedspread. She would close her eyes, just for a minute. She felt herself dissolving. The smell of the linen was so familiar she ached. She rolled onto her side, balling the down-filled pillow to fit beneath her head . . .

There was something hard and sharp-edged inside the pillowcase. Jess fished it out. It wasn't the letter she'd been searching for; it was a book. A small, worn hardcover with blunted corners and a tattered jacket, yellow with a pale pink banner for the title and author name.

Jess let out a long, steady breath. *As If They Were Asleep*. Daniel Miller's book.

She scrambled to a sitting position. A brief introduction provided the history of Tambilla, including an account of the house that Mr Wentworth had built. His love story, albeit tragic, Jess skimmed. Similarly, the first chapter of Part One, which she realised she'd already met in the form of Daniel Miller's essay.

When she reached Chapter Two, though, a shiver crept up her spine, for here, at last, was Isabel Turner.

As If They Were Asleep

DANIEL MILLER

2

On what would be her last day on this earth, Mrs Isabel Turner woke early. She preferred to sleep with the bedroom curtains open and did not draw them when her husband was away. She liked the way first light spread across the bedroom floor, suffusing the room with a filmy, unreal quality, as outside in the camellia bushes the dawn birds alerted one another to the indisputable fact that morning had once again broken.

Like so many mothers before her, Mrs Turner had come to cherish the pale, early hour before the rest of the household stirred. Since the baby was born, she'd prized it even more. On the morning of December 24, 1959, she crept around the upstairs balcony, passing each child's bedroom door in turn, picturing them asleep on the other side, dolls in a dollhouse awaiting animation, before moving silently downstairs, careful to avoid the creaky floorboards.

In the kitchen, with the door latched safely behind her, she was free to begin her morning routine. Her habit was to fill the kettle the night before because the pipes were noisy when cold and ran a direct path through the walls in her only son John's bedroom. Now, she lit a flame in the gas range and started the water boiling atop the rings. The

Wedgwood teapot was already in position in the center of the wooden bench, alongside her favorite teacup, which had come with her from England. A small silver spoon, part of the gift from her husband's family on the occasion of their wedding, lay beside it.

A number of townspeople were to comment later that Mrs Turner was 'always just so', and one of the elderly Misses Edwards, both of whom still lived in the flour mill their father had operated until the yeast virus of 1938 shut it down, expounded thus: 'She had high standards where those children were concerned. Whenever I went to teach piano at the house, she made sure they were ready with their music books in their hands and clean shoes on their feet.' The latter report was offered approvingly, and one could not help but infer that such fastidious preparation was not always the case among the budding pianists of Tambilla. 'She was English, of course,' Miss Enid Edwards (the older of the pair 'by at least half a minute') added by way of explanation. 'A proper English lady.'

Mrs Turner *was* English, but she wasn't a 'Lady' and would have been surprised to hear herself described as such. Her father had been a scientist of natural history, her mother an artist whose lithographic plates of flora and fauna had been included in several published works. The three had lived a rich and varied family life, traveling together throughout the remote regions of the United Kingdom, observing diminishing numbers of sparrows, counting otters, and tracking the migration of wild bees. However, this bucolic childhood was not to last. Orphaned at seven years of age, Isabel spent the next ten years in residence as a pupil at the Woodford Dormitory School in Sussex.

It is perhaps the latter fact that best explains her

attachment to protocol, an adherence that, in concert with her received-pronunciation accent, conveyed an impression of heightened civility. If a decade of boarding school had not been enough, four years spent in undisclosed wartime service had cemented a view that tried-and-tested procedures, whether familial or individual, large or small, were in place for a reason. Furthermore, that proper thought and planning were required to succeed at any tough assignment.

She was a woman of habit, then, and it was her wont to drink her first cup of the day, preferably before having uttered a word to anyone, while seated at the wicker table and chair on the north-facing verandah of the house. It was not the prettiest outlook afforded by Mr Wentworth's garden, but it was the place where the driveway met the house and therefore, in Mrs Turner's judgment, an apt vantage point from which to take stock. She always brought her journal with her. Some days she wrote reams; other mornings she simply sat, listening as the wind moved through the treetops and the rainbow lorikeets shrieked and swooped in the upper branches of the bottlebrush.

With an instinct for these things, Barnaby, the family's beloved arthritic retriever, would appear soon after she did, padding patiently along the verandah to take up position on the concrete at her feet. He had been brought home for the children as a pup – another 'surprise' with which Mrs Turner had been presented by her husband (whose penchant for decisions of a unilateral nature was a source of some friction between them) – but Matilda and John had been young at the time and the dog's upkeep had fallen to her. An additional duty, though one she did not mind. Barnaby's company had proved agreeable, particularly as Mr

Turner's absences from home grew in both frequency and duration. He was in London now, or so she was given to believe. She had stopped listening, truth be told, when he enthused about his newest fancy.

And so, on the morning of December 24, 1959, nothing marked the day out as different from those that had come before, nor did anything allude to the terrible events that the afternoon would bring. There was no sign that the lives of every soul still slumbering within the house, all of the men, women, and children down in the township, their countrymen and women in cities and towns dotted around the coastal hem of this island nation, would by day's end be altered. For few would forget where they were when they heard what had happened on the grounds of the big old Gothic house in South Australia that Christmas Eve. The news was to ignite every kitchen table conversation across the country, the name 'Tambilla' becoming synonymous, for a time, with tragedy, shorthand for the unthinkable specter of children and death on a hot, festive afternoon.

When Mrs Turner, wrapped in her robe of pearl satin, pulled on her field-muddy boots and sat with her tea and her journal on the wicker chair on the north side of the house, though, all of that was yet to come. Her children were still asleep inside, the Christmas gifts were wrapped and tagged beneath the tree. The outlook from the verandah, as Mrs Turner opened her journal to a fresh page and recorded the date in her precise hand, was the same as ever: directly ahead, on the other side of the driveway, the summertime foliage of the enormous oak was so dense that she could barely see the children's tree house in its middle branches. An old tire swing dangled from a bough of the nearby plum, and beyond that, behind the lattice, the newfangled rotary clothesline that Thomas had ordered from a local factory down at Edwardstown struck its elbowed pose.

Much would be made, over the following days and weeks, of what she wrote in her journal that morning – and of what she didn't. In recent months, Mrs Turner had leaned more heavily than usual on her journal, and it would prove a useful voice from beyond the grave. She had been introduced to the practice as a child. Her parents, through their work, had been observation makers and record keepers, filling copious leather-covered books with sketches, both textual and pictorial. Their influence had been long-lasting, cemented when young Isabel Turner found herself cast into the strange new world of boarding school. She had clung then to her routine of confiding thoughts on paper, and the habit never left her.

Throughout 1959, Mrs Turner had been grappling with an all-consuming problem and her entries had often been lengthy and tortured. But by Christmas Eve morning, a decision had been made, and her uncertainty of tone and content was replaced by serenity. She made no mention of her previous dilemma; nor, explicitly at least, of any plans she might have held for the afternoon. Indeed, Mrs Turner wrote only a few perfunctory lines, a record of the day's weather conditions:

Fog in the valley again, but the sun rises on the hill. The mist will clear soon, and the day will be hot. The threat of fire lurks, as it ever does this time of year. The sun-bleached fields crackle and shimmer, but a storm is forecast for tonight. Hard to imagine that the change will come, but the man on the wireless says that it is so and who am I to argue? It is of no concern to me. I know as well as any that change, like solution, often comes suddenly.

Police would later speculate as to whether the entry contained a coded message. 'The bit about the mist clearing, solutions coming suddenly . . .' Mounted Constable Hugo Doyle would muse past his chewed pencil in the Tambilla police station. 'Maybe she was talking about her own plans?'

But Sergeant Liam Kelly, who had been around the block a few more times, remained dubious. 'Sometimes when a person says there's fog down in the valley, they just mean there's fog down in the valley. What was the weather like Christmas Eve morning, MC Doyle?'

'It was hot, sir.'

'Earlier than that. Was it clear?'

'No, sir.'

'No?'

'There was a fog, sir.'

'There was a fog down in the valley.'

There was indeed fog in the valleys surrounding Tambilla as the sun rose on December 24, 1959. In the Adelaide Hills, it is possible to wake to a world shrouded in mist at any time of the year. In winter, when the temperature dips below zero most nights and the days are wet and bitter, but in the summertime, too, when despite the blistering heat of early afternoon, the evenings tilt cool and crisp and one cannot help but sense the desert plains to the north as darkness deepens into night.

Mrs Turner had often sought to explain her conviction that the fog was different here in her adopted country than it was back home. Glancing through her bedroom window, having woken to find the natural world shrouded, never failed to make her shiver. To describe the effect as 'menacing', was too melodramatic for her tastes, but there was something undeniably charged about it – secretive, even. It was the ghostly gums, she had decided, their smooth silver limbs like ladies' naked bodies in the mist.

There were eerie sites in England – the haunted cliffs and caves of Tintagel, the ruins of Ludlow Castle, Hadrian's Wall, and Stonehenge – but their mysteriousness stemmed from their role in the human story, the crumbling vestiges of people from the past. In Australia, the strangeness came from the land itself. Its mystery and meaning existed outside language – or outside her own language, at any rate. It told its story in far more ancient ways and only to those who knew how to hear it.

Her children had brought home a tale once, from wherever children learned the things they knew, about a bunyip. 'A what?' she'd asked. 'A bunyip,' they'd said, appraising her with wide, direct gazes that implied *of course*. Mrs Turner found it a somewhat unsettling proposition to raise children in a land other than the one in which she'd been a child herself. Their points of reference were different from her own and they sometimes felt quite foreign. On such occasions, they were her husband's children: alien creatures whom she had birthed but could never really know.

The bunyip, according to their telling, was a shifting, nebulous, amorphic entity with feathers and scales and ill-fitting ears: 'A hideous, monstrous thing.'

'Like a swimming dog.'

'Or a seal.'

'But with a really long neck.'

'And fins.'

'But also a snout.'

'That hides in the swamp—'

'– and *grabs* children if they come too near.'

The story had given her chills, but of recognition rather than fear. Mythical though the creature might have been, inherent in her children's description was a recognizable truth about this place: the uncomfortable but certain sense that danger, the unknown, was always lurking in the dark spaces 'out there'. This continent was one where beauty and terror were inextricably linked. People died here from thirst if they took a wrong turn. A single spark of fire could grow to consume an entire town. Children who wandered beyond the back fence disappeared into thin air.

3

As the morning lightened and the fog began to thin, Mrs Turner set her journal on the wicker table. She scratched Barnaby's golden head and he stirred to attention. Taking her teacup with her, she gathered the kitchen scrap bucket from the spot near the eastern door where young Becky Baker had left it the day before. Two lines of plane trees stretched up the rise from the house, rounding a bend to arrive at the farm sheds near the bore tank. Halfway along, beside a small sunny garden bed, was the chicken coop. The Hen Hilton, Mr Turner had christened it, having stayed at the new Hilton hotel in West Berlin the year before.

Barnaby lolloped ahead, looping back to rejoin his mistress, who was walking with less haste than usual, stopping every so often to inspect the garden. She had never gardened in England and had taken to it at Halcyon with a zeal that surprised her. Glossy agapanthus spears lined the gravel driveway, their purple spangles erupting with exultant cheer, and on the other side of the fence, beyond the greenhouse with its broken pane (care of John's ongoing obsession with Australia's homegrown cricket champion, Donald Bradman), fields of yellow grass shimmered in the morning light. It was still a shock to see them empty. She had loved the optimism and purpose of the vines, but her husband, immovable once his mind was made up, had insisted on the change.

She wondered sometimes what Mr Drumming thought of the new direction – it was he, after all, who had poured his energies as farm manager into the vines for the past decade. But for all the private frustration she felt toward her husband, Mrs Turner would never have asked the manager outright, and Mr Drumming was not one to offer an opinion unsought.

He was a well-liked fellow, with a reputation in the village for keeping his business to himself. No need to share it, of course; in a place the size of Tambilla there was a good chance one's business was already known. But Henrik Drumming's reserve went beyond the constitutional. His habit of silence was philosophical. He carried in the serious lines of his face and the enduring set of his shoulders a history of personal grief.

Mrs Turner had gleaned the story of his wife via the same system of community osmosis by which she knew that Miss Marian Green at the telephone exchange had been sent away for a month the summer she turned seventeen, only to return with a picture of her new baby 'niece' in a locket around her neck. More than mere gossip, this was a vital underground flow of information that strengthened the community by letting its members know when and to whom they ought to be extending extra understanding and assistance. So Mrs Turner had come to recognize the dates each year on which Mr Drumming requested a late start, and to anticipate his drawn and sober mood when he arrived for work.

Only once had she breached their tacit agreement not to admit the matter. She had come across him accidentally in the manager's office at the back of the house, a terrible sight, his back turned, his lean shoulders visible through the thin cotton of his shirt, shaking as he wept. She'd failed to close the door without drawing attention; he'd stumbled in providing an explanation, and she'd said, very quickly, with the wave of a hand, 'Please, Mr Drumming. My mother suffered from a similar affliction to your wife. You have my deepest sympathies.'

Mrs Turner followed the narrow herringbone-brick path that ran behind the yew hedge and finished at the gate. The henhouse was almost obscured by the rich green leaves of a Virginia creeper, interwoven in places with a thorny deep-red rose. Sensing her proximity, Dickens the rooster let out a rousing crow. He was a relatively new addition, and his proud, demanding nature had been the cause of some un-settlement lately in the coop. He'd taken to foisting his attentions on the smaller of the Araucana hens when she was least expecting to receive them.

Mrs Turner had a great affection for her girls and a deep antipathy toward the aggressive overtures of the cock, but she couldn't deny he'd kept his harem safe. There'd been wild dogs skulking for the last few months, and one dreadful night, before the arrival of the rooster, they'd managed to breach the wire fence and help themselves to two of the hens. One had been carried away, never to be found, while the other – Evie's favorite – had been left behind in a ghastly state. Mrs Turner and the children had buried the discarded body in the garden, performing a short ceremony before planting a delicate pink-and-white floribunda over the top of the small hen's corpse. Evie, stoic in grief, had read a poem she'd written about 'Henny' in honor of the occasion, and Becky Baker had served tea afterward, along with ribbon sandwiches – cucumber and, in an acknowledgment of the gravity of the situation, Meg Summers's famous fish paste, the latter allowed by special permission from Mrs Turner's very own supply.

Now, Mrs Turner balanced her teacup on the corner of the garden bed, where the wooden railway sleepers met. She unlatched the henhouse gate and scattered yesterday's kitchen scraps in the yard. The hens, released from their overnight roosting boxes, clucked and tumbled their way toward the bounty, pecking determinedly through the spoils as Dickens strutted the perimeter, ruffling his feathers. They were all present and accounted for this morning, thank goodness.

Locking the gate behind her, Mrs Turner collected her teacup and started back along the path. The fog had lifted now, and the day was warming. Sunlight glowed orange through the lacework of slender eucalyptus trees that lined the ridge to the east, and in the vegetable garden, directly across the driveway, pale purple garlic flowers swayed at the top of their stems. The sweet scent of basil reached her with the breeze and, on a whim, Mrs Turner crossed the driveway to inspect the beds. The four square planters were set like windowpanes and divided by truncating brick paths, each box overflowing with carefully-tended strawberries, tomatoes, and spinach, as well as copious herbs. A row of bay trees lined the back wall of the garden, either side of a wooden arch trailing white wisteria flowers.

A sundial marked the middle of the garden, standing where the paths crisscrossed, and in the far back corner a wooden bench beneath the shade of a crab-apple tree was home to the whimsical flowerpot man.

'Mrs Turner came up with the design,' Mr Drumming was to tell police in the days that followed. He had been deeply affected by her death, and though a private man by nature, not given to speaking out of turn, was determined that she should be remembered well. 'I had to work out how to thread the terracotta pots onto the metal rods to make limbs and then solder it all together, but it was her idea. Mrs Turner thought it would amuse the children. She was always thinking of them. They were well loved, those kids. I tell you: they were well loved.'

As Mrs Turner took what would be her last walk around the vegetable garden, Smarty, the ginger tabby, materialized to sit beside the flowerpot man, a position that afforded him a bird's-eye view of the *petit* fishpond. There was a larger, more formal water feature on the western side of the house, a rectangular pool with a leafy canopy above it and marble tiles around the rim, well-fed goldfish gleaming beneath glistening lily pads, but this little pond was far more cheerful: small and shallow, with fallen petals floating on its surface. The cat's focus was absolute as he watched for flickers of rose gold in the water, paw at the ready.

But Mrs Turner was paying no notice to the cat. From where she stood, at the highest corner of the vegetable garden, she was able to see through a break in the yew hedge to the eastern wall of the house. The rising sun had flooded the white render, giving it the temporary sheen she'd sometimes likened to the iced edge of a wedding cake. The cake her husband's parents had organized for their wedding reception in the gardens of Darling House in Sydney had been similarly grand and glossy. There'd been much tense discussion in preceding weeks as to how many tiers the cake should have, one view being that three layers was traditional. But the groom's mother had been set on four: 'If it's good enough for the Queen of England,' she'd said, 'then it's good enough for me.' With Isabel disinclined to argue over cake, the older woman had prevailed.

It had occurred to Isabel Turner, at certain times over the course of her marriage, that antipodeans were more concerned with tradition and its observation than any of the so-called aristocrats she'd known in England. She had written letters home to old school friends in which she'd said she thought she was coming to a country where she'd be free from the weight of her past; she'd been eager, after the war, for something new and different. It had surprised her to hear so much talk when she arrived about the way things were done 'back home', particularly from people who'd never left Australia. The romance around stately houses struck her similarly. Her husband was far more impressed than she was by the history of their home.

It was a not-altogether-comfortable thing to live in a house built to woo another woman. Mrs Turner thought about the ill-fated Miss Stevenson sometimes. A young bride-to-be who had never made it to Australia, let alone this house, and yet whose doomed presence seemed to animate every corner. Mrs Turner had wondered whether the reason she'd never felt completely at home was because the home had never really belonged to her. How could it, when every stone and cornice had been put in place with another woman in mind?

The Turners had called the house 'Halcyon' in an attempt to 'make it their own'. The name had been Mr Turner's idea, and one to which he'd become very attached. Indeed, he had already placed his order with Galloway Bros. Signwriters in Double Bay when he presented the name to his wife for her consideration. She had agreed without debate – as with the number of tiers on the wedding cake, she cared little what they called the house, and a great deal, at the time, for him. The suggestion had seemed to her romantic, very much in keeping with his nature; it was this nature, after all, that had attracted her in the first place, shining as it had, like a rare and precious gem, in the grime of wartime London.

He had proclaimed his grand plan to her during the first supper they shared, on the very night they'd met by chance in October 1944 in the middle of Blackfriars Bridge. She had been walking, he had asked directions, and somehow she'd found herself some hours later sitting across from him at a table in an underground club, the likes of which she hadn't known existed anymore. He was Australian, on leave and eager for the war to end so he could go back home. She'd asked what his plans were when he got there.

Without the merest hint of a gloat, he'd told her about the fortune he'd come into in the early years of the war. Imprisoned in France, he'd found himself in the same cell as a wounded English officer; when he decided it was time to break out, he'd taken the other man with him. 'It would have been rude not to,' he said modestly, by way of explanation. He hadn't realized that 'old mate' was the 'Duke of something-or-other' until he was back in England, recuperating at the RAF hospital in Ely. A gray-haired woman 'draped in furs and strings of pearls' had appeared at his bedside one day and said, 'Is this him?' to someone over his shoulder. 'Apparently, I was,' he said. 'Turned out old mate was her eldest son and his father's heir. What are the chances of that?'

Thomas Turner had been rewarded with a small fortune and somehow, in his telling, it made perfect sense that he should have used this newfound wealth to buy a manor house and plant a vineyard on the outskirts of a town in South Australia that he was still yet to visit.

And so, Halcyon it was. But a name is just a name, wishing does not make it so, and the township of Tambilla was home to many people with prodigious memories. Thus, it had not taken long after their arrival for Mrs Turner to learn the sad tale of Miss Arabella Stevenson. Wherever Isabel went in those early months, to church or to a meeting of the local Country Women's Association, someone was eager to tell the tragic tale of the house into which she had moved. The locals enjoyed what they saw as a kinship between the two women. Both English, each having left her homeland with the intention of living in the grand house on the edge of their town. It didn't matter how profusely Mrs Turner denied feeling any such tie to the stranger who had died at sea before she herself had even been born; the community had spoken.

Fourteen years later, in the aftermath of 'that Christmas Eve', the evergreen idea that the fates of the two women were entwined was to gain new currency.

'I'm not saying there was any link between the two events,' the postmistress of Tambilla, Mrs Edith Pigott, was heard to say to Mrs Betty Diamond (who, as proprietress of the tearoom, was the recipient of most town 'reckonology'), 'but as you know, and I said it at the time, they were tempting fate to put that shiny new sign on the road gate.

Halcyon indeed! It wasn't a halcyon place for Mr Wentworth, and neither was it, as things turned out, for them.'

Others drew an even more direct link between the house and the fate of those who lived within its walls.

'I tried to warn her,' said Mrs Marjorie Fisher, recently widowed and even more pious than usual in grief. 'Soon after they moved in, I told her there are some houses that bring ill fortune. All to do with the land itself. Blood spilled, old curses. Things from the past.'

Mrs Turner had, indeed, received such news and advice, and had accepted both with typical equanimity. Sad things happened; people died. No one who had lost both parents in quick succession only to graduate from boarding school and launch herself alone into the world on the eve of a five-year war could have thought any differently.

'But don't you ever get a strange feeling when you're alone up there in that big house?' she had been asked more than once.

'Not at all,' she always answered.

'You're not even the tiniest bit nervous?'

'Only that I might leave a door open and find a brown snake waiting for me in the loo.'

Mrs Turner had little time for superstition. She was her father's daughter, a scientist, governed by the twin principles of logic and reason. At the Woodford Dormitory School, she had won the prize for chemistry and been awarded a place at Somerville College. She would have gone up to Oxford had the war not intervened.

That said, there had been one matter relating to the house on which she had allowed emotion to overrule reason. When they first arrived, much of the original furniture had remained in place, under sheets, with still more in storage in the shed at the top of the driveway. Books and personal items had filled the shelves; art had hung on the walls. Above the sweeping central staircase, surveying the balcony that ran around the second floor and glaring down into the entrance hall, had been a large gilt-framed portrait of Mr Wentworth.

Mrs Turner had taken an immediate, strong dislike to the painting. It was the eyes, she had decided: angry eyes that followed one across the room, furious that people should be living in his house, that children should laugh and run down the stairs and tear around the balcony. She'd have gladly got rid of it for good, had even made noises about burning 'the horrid thing', but Mr Turner, made reverent by signs of provenance, had been aghast. 'The father of this house! Has the poor man not suffered enough?'

With the patience of a newlywed, Mrs Turner had agreed that it could stay – 'So long as I don't have to look at it,' she'd added, according to Mr Drumming, who had been called upon to move the offending portrait.

For a time, they'd just turned old Mr Wentworth to face the wall, until finally a place was found for him in a room on the southern side of the entrance hall. They'd already taken to calling it Mr Wentworth's Parlor on account of the large collection of hunting trophies and pilfered colonial spoils that lined its shelves. The arrangement had satisfied Mrs Turner. She had no plans ever to cross the threshold.

'She hated that room – she found it cold and stuffy,' Mrs Esme Pike, the longtime housekeeper at Halcyon, was to recount in the week following the deaths. 'And she wasn't wrong. Even on the hottest day of summer, it could bring on a chill. She didn't like the wallpaper, either.

Called it "demoralizing" and said that it reminded her of a room she'd sat in a long time ago, after the death of her mother, when she was waiting to learn what would become of her.'

Mrs Turner was seven years old when her mother died – a shocking thing to happen to a child at any time, but especially traumatic coming only five weeks after the death of her father in a fall from the Clo Mor Cliffs while count-ing puffins. Mother and child had repaired to Inverness after the accident, where they were taken in by one of her father's scientific colleagues, the wife of whom, with a per-durable Protestant faith in the stiff upper lip, promptly outfitted young Isabel in 'appropriate attire' and sent her along to school with the children of the household. It was from the chilly Inverness classroom, with its wall-length chalkboard and rows of wooden desks, that she had been collected unexpectedly by an unfamiliar woman with a ser-ious face and taken to the austere library, whereupon the crushing news of her mother's death was delivered.

Miss Bathsheba Stern, headmistress at the Sussex board-ing school to which young Isabel was then sent, did not consider it appropriate to discuss the particulars of her students' personal circumstances, even twenty years after a girl's graduation and in the face of a police investigation into her untimely death. However, Miss Stern was willing to concede that the 'child in question' had been 'unlucky' to suffer two such terrible losses in quick succession. Reports sent from Miss Stern to the girl's guardian – a dis-tant great-uncle on her mother's side, who lived in a stone farmhouse in the Bourgogne region of France – describe 'a resilient child, not afraid of hard work, unshakable once her mind is set. Gifted in the sciences.' One letter, referring to previous correspondence that has since disappeared, provided the only suggestion that young Isabel had suffered in adjusting to her new circumstances. 'You will be glad to hear that there has been some improvement with respect to her sleep habits. She no longer pines with quite the same zeal, and I predict that she will, in time, overcome her hardships.'

On the face of it, Mrs Turner *had* overcome the hardships of her childhood. With her enduring marriage to a charming man, her brood of spirited and handsome children, her grand house and glorious garden, there were few among the locals of Tambilla who could fathom that she might have been anything other than exceedingly happy. Indeed, the most common question conducted back and forth between the main street shoppers and customers in Betty Diamond's tearoom during the early weeks of 1960, when suspicions began to spin and dart in new directions, was, 'But she had everything, didn't she?'

'There's always more to a person's situation than meets the eye, though, isn't there?' Mrs Pike was to comment in her interview at the Tambilla police station. 'And it's the peaceful-looking water holes that hide the sharpest rocks. Mrs Turner was a discreet person – we were alike in that, I think. We each respected the other's privacy. She didn't much talk about herself, her past. I suppose that's what made it so odd when she mentioned Mr Wentworth's parlor and how it reminded her of being a child after her mother died. In fact . . .'

'Mrs Pike?'

The poor woman had adopted a most anguished expression and begun twisting her hands together in her lap. She glanced up at the young policeman. 'It's only that, well, she'd been doing quite a bit of reminiscing lately. It struck me as somewhat unusual at the time, but I didn't *do* anything. Now, though, considering all that's happened, I just can't help thinking that I should have seen it coming.'

4

An unseen bird, cutting from one treetop to another, dragged its shadow across the garden, causing Mrs Turner to startle. The teacup she'd been balancing on its saucer slipped from her hand and fell to the bricks, shattering into a hundred small and smaller fragments. Years later, residents at the house would still be finding shards of fine French porcelain in the paving cracks.

Mrs Turner knelt to pick up the larger pieces. She had not always been a nervy person – quite the opposite. She had received an award for valor at the end of the war; she had done brave and dangerous things. Not only had she learned to perceive risk and act anyway, but she had also enjoyed it.

'Issy was ever resolute,' explained Miss Gemma Hancock, a schoolfriend with whom Mrs Turner had gradually lost contact after she moved to Australia. 'The sort of person who needed to feel vital, like she was working to a higher purpose. Some of us resented putting our lives on hold during the war, but she wasn't like that. She was furious when she found out she was pregnant and had to wind back her efforts before it ended.'

Smarty, the cat, meowed disdainfully and executed a

graceful exit as Mrs Turner sat on the end of his garden
bench. She turned the pieces over in her lap. The cup was
one of the few items in her possession that had come with
her from her past. Limoges, with hand-painted purple vio-
lets on each side and decorative gilding along the rim and
handle. In one of the rare moments of disclosure that had so
struck Mrs Pike, Mrs Turner had told the housekeeper she
could remember her mother drinking from the teacup in the
evening, after supper, while finishing the day's sketches. Her
family had moved a lot back then, 'home' determined by the
demands of her father's work, but no matter where they'd
been stationed the cup had accompanied them, carefully
wrapped in tissue at the end of each assignment and carried
to the next.

It had come to Isabel some years after their deaths,
according to Mrs Pike. Her parents' immediate legacy had
been a stipend allowing for the payment of school fees,
accounts to be administered by the maternal great-uncle in
France. On her graduation, which coincided with her
eighteenth birthday, she'd inherited a bank account with a
none-too-shabby balance, along with a leather steamer
trunk containing various items that had, according to the
accompanying note, belonged to her mother.

'Issy' had been a serious eighteen-year-old, remembered
by school friends as 'determined', 'capable,' and 'jolly intelligent'. When she completed school, she said goodbye to
her teachers and the indomitable Miss Stern and headed to
London for the summer. There, she'd taken a cheap-but-
cheerful bedsit in Bloomsbury, convincing the landlady – a
fastidious widow with mauve curls and a hutch of rabbits in
the back garden – that she was a worthy tenant by paying
two months in advance. There hadn't been much to the

room, but it had been sufficient. Boarding school had conditioned her to straitened circumstances, and she was grateful for the view of checkerboard gardens from the small rear window of the terrace.

The trunk, which had been sent by sea from France, had arrived during her second week in her new home. The men from the shipping company deposited it, as instructed, on the floorboards in the middle of the bedsit, and for three days she left it there, unopened, observing it from all angles, walking as wide a circle around it as the small space would allow. Her mother's maiden name, *Mlle Amélie F. Pinot*, was stenciled in faded gold ink along one side of the tan leather lid.

Much like that adventurous young woman who had followed her heart from France to England, Isabel Turner had arrived at a crossroad in her own life's journey. She had sat the entrance exams for Oxford, but a part of her craved travel. 'She spoke about going as far north as Orkney,' her friend, Miss Hancock, remembered. 'She wanted to see things she'd never seen before, and I suppose she did by going to Australia. You can't get much further than that.'

On the fourth day, Isabel opened the trunk and started removing items from its compartments and drawers, setting them on the floor around her one by one, until the room was awash with heirlooms and trinkets, unrelated but for the fact that they had once belonged to her mother. Her mother's married name, Amélie Fleur Hart, appeared here and there, embroidered on a set of linen handkerchiefs, and written in dark blue ink on the face of a bundle of envelopes bearing French stamps. A card saved among the letters – a child's sketch of a kingfisher – brought a pang of remembrance. Isabel could vividly recollect the careful observation she'd made of the bird, the race to sketch an outline in pencil, to observe the color of each feather. *For Maman*, she had written at the top, *with love on your thirty-fifth birthday, Issy.*

Although the trunk had not contained the answer to her life's big question, she had at least recovered the teacup. She rinsed it at the small sink in her kitchenette, boiled the kettle, and selected Darjeeling, her mother's favorite, over English breakfast. She was saved from making any more consequential choice about her life by the war, which began mere weeks later. She signed up at Whitehall and was put to work typing, delivering and filing memoranda. The Phony War, the Battle of Britain, the Dunkirk Evacuation, and then the Fall of France: each phase rolled into the next, generating copious paperwork and terse instructions.

Mid-July 1940, on a warm, clear night, she was dragged to a soirée by a girlfriend from her typing pool and found herself trapped in conversation with a group of red-faced older men, pontificating loudly on the subject of capitulation.

'That's our French friends done,' one of them puffed around his cigar.

'I hear they all but gift-wrapped Paris,' growled another. 'The Germans simply walked in while the Parisians were buying bread.'

'Pétain says it himself: France is defeated and must give up the war. It's just a shame we sacrificed so many of our finest in the process.'

'Not to mention the machinery,' added a thin man with a gloomy pallor.

Isabel's head ached, and her girlfriend's shoes were pinching her toes. Her voice was sharper than she intended. 'Pétain is a pandering fool. He doesn't speak for the French any more than you do. The people have been betrayed, but they are not slaves, and they won't capitulate.'

Silence met her pronouncement. And then: 'Won't capitulate?' The first man's face had reddened further. He planted a thumb in his stretched waistband and ashed his cigar. 'My dear, it's a bit too late for that.'

'The Nazi flag flies over the Eiffel Tower,' said the second. 'The only thing for it now is to leave them to it, and focus all our might on defending our own bloody borders.'

Smoke had made the room hazy, but Isabel's thoughts were clear. 'France will fight back, and she will win. When she does, it will be with no thanks to "friends" like you.'

Her companions had not expected, nor did they appreciate, such sentiments, at least not from the likes of her. Little by little, they turned their backs, closing ranks before drifting away in search of more agreeable female companionship.

Isabel drained the last of her whisky and was deciding whether to have one more for the road when she became aware of an older woman she hadn't noticed before standing by her side. Barely reaching Isabel's shoulders, the newcomer was of perfectly plain appearance. Indeed, Mrs Turner was to think back many times over the years that followed to their meeting in the stuffy room on Bedford Place, and although she could remember very well the worn leather of the chesterfield and the ticking of the clock, the heady fragrance of perfume coming from a giggling fawner near the cocktail trolley, she could not recall the details of the woman's face. She did, however, remember what she'd said, her tone even, her volume low: 'Were you in earnest before, about the situation on the Continent? Or was that just a clever girl's clever talk?'

'I'm always in earnest.' Isabel realized as she said it that it was true.

'You have a connection to the Continent?'

'My mother was French.'

'Was?'

A short nod.

'And your father?'

'English.'

'Is?'

'Was.'

A small rectangular card was drawn from a pocket and proffered. 'Ring this number,' the woman with the remarkably unremarkable face said. 'We might be able to use you.'

Down in the house a door slammed shut, shattering the early morning stillness. Barnaby straightened, ears alert, as a sprinkling of fairy wrens dispersed from the top of the crabapple. Mrs Turner glanced through the hedge. Someone was awake.

John. Enthusiasm had always made him effervescent, ever since he was a small child. He had been rising early all week, excited about something in the way only a thirteen-year-old boy could be. There was Christmas, of course, but she suspected there was more to it than that. He had been *lurking* and had posed a number of pointed questions recently about films and cameras. He had also struck up a friendship with a boy called Matthew McKenzie, the grandson of their neighbors, recently arrived from Adelaide.

Mrs Turner stood, listening for further signs of life. From over at the McKenzie place came the distant drone of farm machinery. The Turners' own shed, higher up the rise, remained quiet. Ordinarily, Mr Drumming would have appeared by now to start his work, but this Christmas Eve the farm manager had arranged a day off. As he was to tell police early the next week, 'I had some other business to take care of that morning, business of a private nature. I'd asked Mrs Turner if it was all right for me to start late and she said there was no need to come in at all, that I could no doubt use the time off.' Pressed further, he answered that no, he wouldn't say that she'd *discouraged* him from coming to the property, it was more that she'd wanted to give him 'a bit of a break', and no, he hadn't seen it as odd – he had worked for the Turners for as long as they'd lived at the Wentworth place and they 'had an understanding'. Not himself and Mrs Turner, he clarified, a hint of color burnishing his face; he had an understanding 'with the pair of them'. He would, he told police, his voice snagging on the sentiment, regret not turning up for work that day 'as long as I live'.

It was Mrs Turner's practice, each morning, to follow the perimeter of the inner paddocks before the children woke up. She valued walking highly and had recorded in the front of her current journal two quotes, the first from Rousseau:

There is something in walking that stimulates and enlivens my ideas. I can hardly think at all if I stay still. My body has to be on the move to set my mind going.

The second was a line from Wordsworth's 'In a Carriage, Upon the Banks of the Rhine':

To muse, to creep, to halt at will, to gaze.

Although not in the business of composing poetry, Mrs Turner nonetheless had thoughts to order, plans and preparations to make. She had written numerous times about 'the little coil of tension' in her chest that needed frequent easing. Walking had long been her habit, but motherhood, with its constant interruptions, had tested her, and the hobby had become a salve.

Her own mother had also been a keen walker. Mrs Turner had remembered her to Mrs Pike 'pulling on her boots and heading out alone each day, come rain, hail or shine'. She had called it her 'daily constitutional'; Isabel's father had called it 'your mother's medicine'. Only on the rarest of occasions had Isabel been permitted to go with her, and she had soon learned that it was not a time for idle conversation. Her mother had walked with purpose, striding across the moors or hills or clifftops (depending on where they were stationed) as if she were hastening toward something. Or else, as Isabel had later considered, away from it.

Mrs Turner had adopted the habit herself devotedly in the dwindling months of the war after D-Day. Returned to her Bloomsbury bedsit in autumn 1944 – spared, miraculously, by the bombs that fell around it – she had struggled. Four years had passed, Paris had been liberated, she was back where she had started, but everything was altered. As she would record in her journal, the view from the window had changed. There were rows of vegetables in the back gardens, and mounded air-raid shelters. Her landlady's rabbits were gone. People were leaner and meaner than when she'd left, and a curious form of cultural amnesia gripped everyone. They had all seen and done things in order to survive. Everyone had secrets now.

She was changed, too. She had stilted conversations with people in the streets and at the greengrocer's in which she heard herself say mundane things about ration cards and the likelihood of German surrender, as all the while a voice inside her head was screaming, *Run!* At night, her mind raced as she tried to sort through events of the past, sought to envisage a future. Rather than lie in bed as the minute hand dragged itself around the clock face, she had begun to walk instead, street by street in the dark as the gasping city lay in shambles around her. Her mother had been right: to walk was to think, to think was to breathe, to breathe was to stay alive.

If not for her walking habit, Mrs Turner might never have met and married her husband; she might never have set eyes on Mr Wentworth's big house at the end of Willner Road nor given birth to her brood of bonny Australian children with loud voices and freckles across their noses. For it was on such an evening, in October of 1944, that she encountered Thomas Turner on Blackfriars Bridge. It was a foggy night and Isabel had already walked from Bloomsbury through Holborn and around St Paul's.

She was to describe the meeting to Mrs Maud McKendry, the wife of Tambilla's only doctor, at a CWA Saint Valentine's Day cake stall.

'She told me she'd been standing in the middle of the bridge when she heard a voice behind her. He asked her for directions, and by and by she offered to walk him where he was going. She said she couldn't for the life of her remember why she'd made such an offer to a stranger in the dark. We laughed about that. If you knew Mr Turner, you'd understand why. He's not an easy person to say no to.'

During his interview with London officers, carried out on behalf of the South Australia Police Force, Mr Turner was to confess that for many years he had forgotten the circumstances of the night he met his wife. He had spent the better part of an hour answering questions as to whether she had any enemies and if he thought there was anyone who, for whatsoever reason, might have wanted to hurt his family – or, indeed, in doing so, hurt him.

'No,' he had answered to each and all, repeatedly. Mr Turner was not the sort of man to brook suggestion that anyone would wish to do him harm. He loved the world and expected it to love him in return.

Toward the end of the session, DI Harris, who had drawn the short straw to be working Christmas Day, leaned back in his chair, folded his arms across his chest and asked if there was 'anything in your wife's past that might have led you to suspect that she could commit such a heinous act herself?'

Mr Turner was so thrown by the question that he found himself at first unable to reply. 'Opened and closed his mouth like a goldfish,' DI Harris was to type in his report to the South Australian police later that evening.

'Your wife, Mr Turner,' the police officer prompted. 'Has she ever, to your knowledge, fallen victim to depressive thoughts?'

At which point, Mr Turner's mind went unbidden to his farm manager, Mr Drumming, whose wife was known to be resident in an institution down in Adelaide. He had heard talk about Mrs Eliza Drumming and her 'episodes' and felt great sympathy for his farm manager, as, he knew, had his own wife. Henrik Drumming was a good man who did a good job. In Mr Turner's world, bad things happening to good people was an assault on natural law and the essential doctrine of fairness to which he held firm.

Sitting in the cold interview room of Charing Cross police station, Mr Turner's inclination was to deny the association of his wife with any such condition. She became frustrated with him sometimes, certainly, her tension obviously by the grim set of her features, the close-lipped smile that he saw more often lately than any other kind. But depressive thoughts? Hardly! She was happy. She had a wonderful life, didn't she? A beautiful house, healthy children. The new baby. What more could a woman want?

But then he recalled their meeting on the bridge. The image came to him, he was to say later, 'like a vision – spiritual, almost like a message'. That foggy night in '44, he had been too stunned by her beauty in the filtered moonlight to wonder what she was doing there. Afterward, he had been too distracted by the thrill of the chase to ask – a month after they met, they were married. Now, under the scrutinizing gaze of DI Harris of the Metropolitan Police, he remembered the way she'd been gripping the rail, standing right there on the edge, and he realized, with a certain element of bewilderment, that yes, he supposed he might have seen evidence of his wife's propensity to depressive behavior.

Moreover, he remembered something else he'd forgotten, because he did not, as a rule, dwell on unhappy matters. 'Her mother,' he said, surprising even himself.

'Her mother?'

'Her mother suffered with depression and, in the end, she shot herself.'

The last hint of fog in the valley was gone now, and down in the township of Tambilla folks were waking. Mrs Pigott at the post office was already cursing in her back room as she sorted last-minute Christmas parcels, and Mrs Diamond, in the kitchen of her tearoom, was mixing curried eggs in the large ceramic bowl her grandmother had brought to South Australia from Staffordshire. Mrs Diamond was expecting a big day, what with people bustling about in town chasing the final provisions they needed for Christmas. Along with the usual trade, she had assured Reverend Lawson at St George's that she could supply ten trays of sandwiches to be shared after the Christmas Eve service.

Some fourteen miles away as the crow flies, Mr Percy Summers was also on the move. As he loaded up his old horse, Blaze, and prepared to leave the McNamara farm, known locally as 'the Station', he had little idea that by the end of the day he would be inextricably linked to a tragedy on the cusp of unfolding at the big stone house at the end of Willner Road.

Percy's wife, Meg, of *Roggenbrot* fame, had started her day, too. As the proprietress of Summers & Sons, the only grocery shop in Tambilla, this would be her busiest morning of the year. She had a number of orders ready to go and was waiting on her two strapping lads, Kurt and Marcus (acknowledged by all in town to be 'her pride and joy'), to finish breakfast so they could start making deliveries. On top of her already heavy workload, Mrs Summers had a cake to get in the oven. Her husband's forty-first birthday had passed while he was down at the Station, and she was determined to surprise him when he got home that evening, before Christmas rolled into town and swept everything else aside.

Of all this, Mrs Turner, still standing in her vegetable garden with fragments of porcelain in her palm, was unaware. A hot wind swept up the driveway at the Wentworth place, sending a flock of dry leaves skimming across the gravel. A metal gate creaked in the distance. Mrs

Turner glanced down at the shards. Remarkably, the painted violet was still intact. Mrs Pike would later tell police that she was shocked to see the broken pieces on the kitchen bench when she arrived for work that morning.

'It was one of the first things I noticed. I gasped out loud when I realized what it was. I knew how important that cup was to her, and it's not just retrospect that makes me say I felt a deep sense of foreboding when I saw it.'

But Mrs Pike's arrival was still a couple of hours off yet. It would be eight o'clock before she rode her bicycle along Willner Road, alighting at the bottom of the driveway to walk the steep ascent. She would appear, as she always did, just in time to help clear up the mayhem of the Turner family's breakfast. The first 'outside' person to arrive at the Wentworth place that day would be Becky Baker, who, at eighteen years of age, was the eldest of the five flaxen-haired children belonging to Mr Cliff Baker at the brewery.

Miss Baker had been engaged initially to help Mrs Pike with household tasks. Truth be told, Mrs Turner had been uncertain that they needed a 'housemaid', but she'd taken the girl on because Mrs Pike had made a case. It was envisaged that Miss Baker would come in at noon each day to help with the housework and the dinner preparations, but after the baby was born she'd proved herself such a capable nursemaid that by the end of her trial period Mrs Turner had declared her indispensable.

'It came as no surprise to me,' Mrs Pike was to inform police in her first interview. 'Becky's been looking after those younger brothers and sisters of hers all her life. Slow she might be, but she's not lacking in good sense. Loyal, too, and caring. Why, the way she took to that baby! She doted . . .'

The piano started up inside the house and Mrs Turner all but jumped out of her skin – those nerves again. Certainly, that was John. She had often remarked (and sometimes lamented) that he took after his father in almost every way. It didn't seem to matter how many times she reminded him there were other people in the house (including a small baby who had kept her mother up half the night), and that societies functioned best when their members considered one another; he only offered a good-natured apology and a broad, genuine smile and stopped what he was doing. Until the next time.

It wasn't just that he was playing the piano in the library so early, it was the *way* he was playing it. Loudly, merrily, with so much *vigor*! Leaping up the octave to play the same cheerful round of 'Long, Long Ago' yet again. Like her husband, his tastes ran from sea shanties to Russian folk songs to rousing military marches. The jaunty tune's notes and spirit spread out in reels across the early morning garden. It was exhausting, all of it, the never-ending burden of being in charge, the repeated disciplinary conversations, the wearying explanations, but it fell to her to stop him – hopefully before he woke them all.

With a last regretful glance at the gums on the ridge – there was no choice but to skip her walk today – Mrs Turner closed her hand around the broken pieces of her teacup and headed back toward the house. The black cockatoos were in the walnut tree again. They traveled as a group, swooping down in pairs, their black quiffs cocked, to strip the tree of fruit, and as she crossed the rose garden lawn, the dew-damp ground was littered already with shell remnants as sharp as glass.

PART FOUR

CHAPTER FIFTEEN

Sydney, 11 December 2018

Jess was late to the hospital that afternoon and she still had Daniel Miller's voice in her head when she arrived. The town of Tambilla, its surrounding area and the people who lived there, would not leave her. The landscape, as described by Miller – the silver-trunked gums and hidden congress of water through bush that ticked and teemed with insects, the corrugated-iron roofs and caramel stone settlers' dwellings – was an Australia she recognised from childhood books and films, and yet it was unknown to her. Despite having travelled extensively through Europe, she'd never ventured further west than the Blue Mountains.

Sitting in a taxi as the driver battled his way along Oxford Street, she'd typed 'Adelaide Hills' into her phone's search engine and scrolled through the images presented. The pictures she'd formed in her mind as she read Daniel Miller's book overlay the photographs of vineyards and misty green hills and autumnal trees with startling red and yellow leaves. The effect was disquieting. She felt a frisson: the strange dissonance, as she looked at the pictures, that the world of Isabel and Thomas Turner, Mr Drumming, Mrs Pike, Betty Diamond and Meg Summers was something she'd experienced, rather than a place she'd read about. As if, were she to lean near enough to the images and close her eyes, she might suddenly hear the Onkaparinga River trickling through the bush.

This was not an entirely unfamiliar sensation. It was, Jess suspected, the common preserve of all true readers. This was the magic of books, the curious alchemy that allowed a human mind to turn black ink on white pages into a whole other world. Nonetheless, the hold that Tambilla had assumed over her went beyond the usual. She was overcome with an impatient feeling, agitated, an emotion almost like hunger or envy. As if she needed to know everything there was to know, to possess the place; as if she felt she had some *right* to possess it.

As twenty-first century Bondi Junction passed by outside the taxi window, Jess viewed it distantly: bumper-to-bumper traffic, shopping centres, apartment towers. She wondered what the Turner family from the holiday snap of 1955 would have made of it all. Jess had saved the image on her phone and sat studying Isabel Turner as they approached the hospital. No longer a stranger, she was a woman with a favourite teacup. A transplant to a different country, something Jess well understood: belonging, but never quite fully, while another place, far, far away, maintained a stubborn claim as 'home'.

But was homesickness enough to explain what she'd done? Jess thought of some of the more difficult times she'd faced; to feel alone in a far-off land could be extremely isolating and must have been even more acute back then. But Jess was willing to bet that there was more to it. A few of the articles she'd read online had mentioned testimony given at the inquiry that the coroner had suppressed. It seemed likely that whatever it was that had encouraged him to find Isabel

Turner culpable for the murder of her children was contained within that evidence.

When they finally pulled over at the entrance to the hospital, Jess paid the driver and hurried through the glass doors. A glance at the clock above the nurses' station confirmed that she'd missed forty-five minutes of visiting time.

She arrived at Nora's room just in time to cross paths with a nurse she hadn't seen before. Her name tag read *Aimee,* and she smiled kindly at Jess.

'How is she?' Jess asked, moving quickly to set her bag down on the visitor's chair by Nora's bedside.

'A bit unsettled, but we gave her something to help her sleep.'

Jess mustn't have managed to hide her disappointment, because Aimee's voice carried a hint of consolation as she continued: 'It really is the best thing for her at this stage.'

'I'm just so eager to speak with her,' explained Jess, taking Nora's hand. Her grandmother's face was relaxed to the point of slackness, and it made Jess realise how animated it usually was and how much she yearned to have the old Nora back.

'You can still speak to her, you know,' the nurse said, as she updated Nora's chart. 'People often feel they need to keep a reverent silence, but I've always thought it must be lonely, this strange, artificial setting. We do our best, but it's far better to fill the room with the voices of loved ones.'

'Can she hear me?'

'I'm sure of it.'

'It won't disturb her?'

The nurse tucked the chart back over the end of Nora's bed and offered a reassuring smile. 'How could your presence ever disturb her?'

The room was noticeably still and hushed in the nurse's wake. Jess thought about what Aimee had said. It felt self-indulgent to speak to her sleeping grandmother, but she was willing to give it a try. After a moment's hesitation she said tentatively, 'Hello, Nora, it's me, Jess.' She thought at once of Judy Blume and ardent teenage Margaret, and couldn't help but laugh. It was an unexpected, jittery noise, but it loosened her up. 'Hello, Nora,' she repeated. 'I'm here. I wanted to let you know that I've been thinking about Isabel.'

Nora did not move a muscle.

Jess tried again: 'I've been thinking about *Issy.*' She watched her grandmother closely, because that's what Nora had been saying in the hospital the day before, she realised now; not Jessy, but, Issy – *Issy, help me* – right before she mentioned Halcyon.

'I found your book about the Turner family,' Jess continued, '*As If They Were Asleep.* I've been reading it.'

Still no reaction. The quiet when Jess stopped talking stretched all the way to the stale, sun-warmed corner by the window. Outside the distant sound of construction droned, machinery and loud male interjections.

She gave it one more try: 'I've been reading about Thomas.'

Nothing. Jess dragged the visitor's chair closer and sat down. If mention of her brother couldn't raise a sign from Nora, it seemed unlikely that anything would. Deflated, she resigned herself to watching her grandmother sleep.

What, she wondered, as the hospital clock slunk sullenly from second to second, had Nora made of Daniel Miller's book? What had she thought of his depiction of Thomas Turner, the beloved older brother whose absence had been a tremendous grief in her life? Every story Nora told Jess had made Thomas Turner seem a heroic figure, and Jess had never questioned the portrayal. Now, viewed through the lens of Daniel Miller's essay and book, Thomas Turner appeared more complex. Charming, but mercurial. Well-liked, but flawed, capable of being selfish and thoughtless, of letting his ego override his better angles.

Of course, Daniel Miller's portrait was just one writer's opinion. He was not the arbiter of truth any more than Nora was. It was a fact of human existence that no two people could ever see a set of facts in precisely the same way; furthermore, that each would swear – and probably believe – they spoke 'the truth'.

'What is the truth anyway?' Jess had once been asked by a curious friend.

'It's what happened.'

'According to whom?'

In this case, according to Daniel Miller. Jess enjoyed and admired Miller's careful world-building, his close observation of his subjects. That he had cared for them, she didn't doubt; beyond his meticulous attention to detail, Jess perceived a genuine desire to imbue them with humanity. But while any journalist might aspire to do the same, Miller had taken it a step further, crossing the line from observer into animator when he entered their heads, described their imagined thoughts, turned them from subjects into characters.

No doubt this was what had made the book so much more compelling than a straight reportage might have been. But *how* had he done it? How did he claim to know what Isabel felt about her life in Australia, or her husband's increasingly frequent trips abroad? How did he know that Isabel struggled with being an outsider, distanced from her children, unnerved by the sparseness of the landscape?

The first chapter she'd read that morning depicted Mrs

Turner sitting on the verandah of the house writing in her journal – a habit, the reader is informed, that she followed each day. Jess suspected that this inclusion was Miller's effort to embed aspects of his own research in the text; a way of getting ahead of any pesky reader questions as to how he could possibly be privy to the things he claimed to know. The scene suggested that he had gained access to the journal during his research; that he could describe Isabel's thoughts because he'd read them from her own pen.

But Jess found herself wondering whether Miller's own encounter with the continent, his emotional response, whatever it might have been, had also coloured his depiction of his subject. To an extent, all writers of non-fiction relied upon a palette of personal experience to animate their subjects; at what point was the line crossed and too much liberty taken?

'How are we?' Aimee was back, moving towards the bed to make another hourly note of Nora's vital signs.

'She's still sleeping,' said Jess.

'Good for her. She looks peaceful, doesn't she?'

Jess supposed that she did.

'I'm afraid visiting hours are over,' said the nurse with a smile of apology. 'But I'll take good care of her while you're gone.'

Jess gave Nora a gentle kiss on the forehead and promised she'd be back soon.

She found a taxi waiting outside the hospital and gave the driver the address for the playground where she was meeting Mrs Robinson. As the cabbie executed a U-turn and started weaving his way amongst the other traffic, Jess watched unseeing through the window. She was still thinking about

Miller and the ethics of his project; how he'd approached the task of turning the lives of real people – including some who were no longer available for interview – into a book. How, for that matter, an American journalist had happened to be in South Australia to write about the crime first-hand. What was it about the Turner family story that had drawn him, and then kept him in the one spot long enough to make their tragic deaths the subject of a book? All journalists hoped for a lucky break. Had he simply found himself in the right place at the right time?

She whipped out her phone and googled 'Daniel Miller' and 'As If They Were Asleep'. She'd hoped to find some interviews with him, but there was little of use and – weirdly – nothing at all relating to the 1980 edition. Miller appeared to be the sort of reporter who was more comfortable asking questions than answering them. It was possible that, if she were to read his other essays, she'd find the clues necessary to glean his approach, but it was going to take some time to track them down . . .

Jess brightened as a new idea occurred. *As If They Were Asleep* had been published by Quill Press. She typed the name into her phone's search engine, and it returned a number of results, none of them a direct link to a website. The imprint appeared to have been absorbed over time into Crown Publishing, which was a division of Penguin Random House. If all else failed, she could send an email to their general contact address, but Jess wanted information quickly and was concerned that her request would disappear into the black hole of unsolicited correspondence.

She typed 'Daniel Miller website' into the search bar and found links to Wikipedia, an entry on Britannica.com, and a website that raised her hopes but turned out to be a single page, written by a fan, containing little more than a short biography and some reader messages. What she really wanted was to locate someone who had known Daniel Miller personally. She deleted 'website' and replaced the word with 'estate'. The results contained links to a few pages referencing a Daniel Miller Literary Trust. Jess followed one to the Foundation Directory Online, where she learned that a charitable trust had been established after Daniel Miller's death, offering scholarships to young writers. There was a street address in Los Angeles, but nothing more direct.

Jess searched for 'Daniel Miller Trust'. The first return was a news article referencing Columbia University, announcing the proposed establishment of a journalism lectureship. It named the administrator of the trust as Daniel Miller's long-time lawyer, Ben Schultz. At the bottom of the article was an email link inviting 'Media Inquiries'. Jess drafted an email, explaining her interest in learning more about Daniel Miller's time in Australia. After a moment spent debating whether it was best to avoid seeming *too* interested – she'd dealt with lawyers before and knew them to be expert in deflecting attention from their clients' affairs – Jess decided that she didn't have time to be coy. She added a sentence outlining her connection to the Turner family and saved the email draft just as she arrived at the playground to meet Mrs Robinson.

A group of teenagers with bikes and phones lolled on the grass near the drinking fountain while a harried mum in lycra trailed a deliriously exuberant toddler from one potential danger to the next. Her grandmother's housekeeper, Jess saw as the taxi pulled away, was standing near the swing set.

Jess waved in greeting, and they both moved, by tacit

agreement, to sit at the picnic table beneath a large gum on the eastern edge of the playground.

'Thank you for coming,' said Jess, as a yellow-eyed currawong on the rim of a nearby bin spread its wings and flew away.

'I came out of concern for Nora,' Mrs Robinson replied crisply. Her arms were wrapped tightly across her middle. She was nervous, Jess realised. 'I'm not one to talk out of turn,' she continued. 'Your grandmother's more than an employer to me, she's a loyal friend, and I don't want to feel that I'm gossiping when her back's turned.'

'Of course not.'

'If she hasn't spoken to you about these things, she has her reasons.'

Jess knew she was on shaky ground. She drew on every bit of experience she'd gained coaxing wary subjects to engage with the interview process and, betraying only mild curiosity, asked, 'Why do *you* think she didn't tell me about the Turner family?'

'I expect she felt there was no reason you should be blighted by such a terrible happening in your family's past.'

'She wanted to protect me?'

'That's just the sort of thing your grandmother would do. As I think I've said before, I've never known a mother – or grandmother – to be so protective, so focused on making sure nothing could hurt the ones she loves.'

Perhaps this explained why she'd kept the secret from Jess when she was a child, but Jess was an adult now. She'd been an adult for over two decades. She didn't feel personally tarnished by the actions of a great-aunt (by marriage) sixty years before. 'Well,' she said lightly, 'it's too late for any of that now. It's all over the internet.'

'Bloody internet. It's got a lot to answer for.' Mrs Robinson's tone was brusque, but she allowed the hint of a helpless smile to pull at the edges of her mouth.

It was enough for Jess to see that her grandmother's housekeeper's resolve was crumbling, and she followed up with a nice, gentle question. 'Was Nora close to Isabel Turner?'

Mrs Robinson glanced away, watching as the toddler squealed past, plane-wing arms out wide. Jess waited. This, she knew, was the moment of decision. Often the reluctant subjects had the most to say, once you got them started. And then, 'They were very good friends,' said her grandmother's housekeeper, and Jess knew they were away.

CHAPTER SIXTEEN

'Your grandmother was only sixteen when they met,' Mrs Robinson began. 'Her brother had come back from the war and told her he was bringing a surprise with him. She used to joke that she'd expected a dress from Liberty, not a new sister-in-law. She told me once that she was all set to hate this other woman who'd stolen her brother's heart, but then she met Isabel and lost her own heart in the process. She was devastated when they told her they were moving to South Australia, taking baby Matilda away. It was even harder when the other children started arriving. She had to take two suitcases whenever she went to visit, one filled only with the toys and gifts she'd been collecting for them. She adored those children. "Such little Turners," she used to say.'

Jess smiled, recognising this as Nora's highest praise.

'They were good kids,' said Mrs Robinson. 'Very spirited. Country kids, you know, but they scrubbed up nicely.'

'I saw a photo.'

Mrs Robinson looked surprised before raising her eyes skywards. 'Let me guess: the internet?'

'They must have used it in the press at the time. It was taken here in Sydney.'

'I remember. It was in all the papers back then. They came on holiday. Stayed at Darling House with your grandmother.'

'They looked a lot like Nora. The young girl especially – Evelyn – was a dead ringer.'

Mrs Robinson nodded agreement. 'That was one of the saddest things about the whole sorry affair. Among the terrible losses was the death of your grandmother's dreams of a big, bustling, extended family. She'd been so excited that your mother was going to be born into a ready-made clan with an aunt and uncle and cousins. But in one fell swoop, it was gone. By the time your mother was born, they were dead, all of those beautiful children. Then her husband left her, and her brother – her very favourite person in the world – disappeared out of her life.'

The mention of Mr Bridges' absence reminded Jess that she'd wondered about the custody arrangement. 'Do you know why Nora's husband disappeared so entirely out of Polly's life? Was that unusual for the time?'

Mrs Robinson sighed. 'You know what Nora's like. She's stubborn. Once she's made a commitment, she doesn't easily let it go. When things started going awry in their marriage, she was determined to make it work. Not just make it work; to be in love, to be a happy family. But men can be vain creatures. Needy. He was jealous of the time she was spending with your mum, but Nora was devoted to her baby. I think, ultimately, it was too much for him. It was easier to leave altogether. He married again soon after they parted – a young girl from the office. Someone Nora had hired.'

A picture of Matt and his new wife and their baby came into Jess's head. She pushed it aside. 'Did he go on to have other kids?'

'I believe they had three or four. With indecent haste, I might add.'

So: a new family and an ex-wife unwilling to share her precious baby. Jess supposed that explained why he hadn't bothered fighting Nora for custody. Not, though, why Nora would be worrying about the whole thing now.

'The end of a marriage is sad, of course,' Mrs Robinson continued, 'but even worse for Nora was losing her brother. It hurt her terribly when he didn't come home from London. She hardly spoke of him after that. I imagine she felt betrayed. She'd loved his children so much, and he didn't even bother to travel back to meet your mother.'

Husband and brother gone; sister-in-law, nieces and nephew dead. No wonder Nora had held on so tightly. 'Polly was all she had left.'

'That's certainly how your grandmother saw it,' Mrs Robinson agreed. 'More than once she referred to the two of them as an unbreakable pair. She felt they'd been bonded, above and beyond the usual, through their shared trauma.'

Jess raised her eyebrows; she'd heard this before. One of Nora's evergreen adages was that a child born of trauma bore the scars forever. She'd said it often during conversations about Jess's mother, usually when she was trying to explain her daughter's nervousness, her thoughtlessness, the incident when Jess was just a baby. Whenever her grandmother made such comments, they'd seemed to be coloured with a tinge of guilt – personal responsibility, at the very least. Jess had taken the explanation at face value when she was young; as she'd got older, though, it had struck her as an overly dramatic way to describe a relatively common experience. Melodrama was not usually Nora's style. 'But Polly wouldn't have remembered much of the divorce, would she? She was tiny at the time.'

'Not the divorce,' said Mrs Robinson, meeting Jess's gaze, surprised. 'Your grandmother was talking about the tragedy in South Australia.'

'Why would that be a trauma for Polly? She wasn't even born when it happened.'

'That's what I'm saying. It's what started Nora's labour. It was unexpected. She wasn't due until the new year, but hearing what happened by that waterhole brought it on.'

'Nora went into labour after she took the phone call?'

It was Mrs Robinson's turn to frown in confusion until suddenly realisation dawned. 'Oh, I'm sorry, I didn't realise you didn't know – your grandmother was there. She went down to South Australia for Christmas that year. She'd suffered badly with morning sickness throughout her pregnancy, and she wanted to be with family. There was no phone call. She was at the house when the policemen came to tell her the news. She'd stayed behind when the others went on their picnic.'

Jess's thoughts were spinning. She couldn't sort through them quickly enough to figure out what to ask next. As it happened, she didn't have to say anything. For all that Mrs Robinson had been reticent to meet, she'd warmed to the telling of her story.

'I think there was a part of her that felt at fault,' she continued. 'That her dearest friend – her sister, that's how she thought of Isabel – could do such a terrible thing, that she'd planned it and carried it out, all while Nora was there . . . I think she spent a lot of time reproaching herself for failing to see the signs, wondering what she could or should have done. She couldn't have done anything, of course. Most women are familiar with the baby blues, but what happened in that house was a different kettle of fish.'

'Is that what it was? Postnatal depression?'

'What else could explain a mother doing such a thing? She was all alone in that big house on that big property, three children and a new baby, no family to speak of nearby. Strange things happen in the human mind.'

Jess, trying to remember what she'd read: 'Was that the coroner's official finding?'

'I don't know all the details. I was more concerned with supporting Nora. But I know there was evidence: things Mrs Turner had written that suggested a depressive state of mind, loneliness, a desire to be free of it all, that sort of thing. From memory, there was a consequential tip-off to police; someone testified – a priest, maybe? – that she'd asked him whether it was ever justified for a parent to leave her children behind. Her own mother had killed herself, as I understand it, leaving her alone in the world. Evidently, she decided it was better for all concerned to take her kids with her.'

It was difficult to know what to say after that blunt assessment. Jess's gaze fell upon the toddler, who was growing fractious, less stable on his feet as he capered wildly away from his weary mother.

'I'm sorry, I know I sound unkind,' Mrs Robinson said, without a lick of contrition in her voice. 'But as a mother, it's impossible to accept that a woman could do such a thing. It changes you, motherhood. Gives you a whole new range of feelings.'

Jess smiled with stiff politeness. She refrained from pointing out that being childless did not mean she was incapable of finding filicide abhorrent.

Mrs Robinson remained blissfully unaware that she had caused offence. 'And then, after Nora had finally put all of that behind her, twenty years later the little one's remains were found, bringing it all back home again. Thea – such a pretty name. Police were confident from early on that she'd been taken by dogs, but it was still a shock for your grand-mother to have it confirmed.' Mrs Robinson watched as the group of teenagers gathered up their bikes and backpacks, ready to head for home. 'The bones turned up in a garden bed near the house, Mrs Turner's rose garden. Nora could never stand roses after that. No way she could have known, but she'd heard those dogs in the night. There was a brutal storm, she said, and in the break between bouts of rain they were howling to one another.'

Over by the swings, the toddler's good luck had worn out and he tripped to fall forehead first against the steel support. Jess winced as she watched, but the boy's mother didn't panic, sweeping him into a cuddle and hushing him as she bore him back to the stroller, where he was strapped into place for the walk home.

'It's horrible, isn't it?' said Mrs Robinson, who had also been observing the scene. 'To think of that little baby, all those years alone in the garden. So many people looking for her and she'd been right there, close to the house, all along. I know it haunted your grandmother.'

Jess felt a shadow of melancholy fall across her. The thought that her grandmother had withheld so much on a subject so intrinsic to her inner life was deeply upsetting. She wished Nora had trusted her. She wanted to tell her grand-mother that she shared her grief and understood what she'd lost.

The playground had emptied, the teenagers having disap-peared over the crest of the hill, and the conversation seemed to have reached its natural conclusion. Jess walked with Mrs Robinson back towards the street. As they reached the edge of the playground, Mrs Robinson said, 'How are things at the house? Does it need a clean? I usually call on Fridays, but I didn't get a chance to finish things last week.'

Jess told her there was no need. 'It's only me there. Wait and come before Nora gets home. That way it will all be perfect for her return.'

They shared an awkward embrace. 'Thank you for agreeing to meet,' Jess said. 'I really do appreciate it.'

'I'm glad I did.' Mrs Robinson hesitated, as if choosing her next words carefully. 'It feels right to have told you. In certain ways, I've often thought all of that business explained why your grandmother was so close to you.'

'How do you mean?'

'When they found that poor little baby's remains, you were a tiny new thing yourself, only just a year old. You and your mother were still living at Darling House, and I'd find your grandmother standing in the open doorway to your room, just watching, reassuring herself that you were okay. I sometimes think she felt that by keeping you safe, she could somehow make up for what she saw as her failure to save that little baby.'

Jess smiled; she didn't mention to Mrs Robinson that Nora had confided once that she'd had good reason for worrying about her safety when she was a baby.

'She adored you. Near broke her heart when your mother moved you both out. You didn't go far, but Polly was never one for visiting. Poor Nora was so alone, there were times I thought it was more than she could bear. Even after everything she'd suffered, I think that was her lowest point.'

'But I came back in the end.'

Mrs Robinson's eyes had glazed with tears, but now she smiled. 'You did. And my goodness, that made her happy. It was like a second chance, she said. Those were her very words. And she was determined to take it.'

By the time Jess arrived back at Darling House, it was nearly half-past eight. Dusk was falling across the garden and the last of the day's sun had turned the western horizon a luminous pink. The Opera House sails were in silhouette, and she was struck by a memory of Isabel Turner's black cockatoos, their feathered quiffs raised as they wreaked havoc in the walnut tree at Halcyon.

Jess had never been to Isabel Turner's garden in South Australia, and yet she saw it in her mind's eye with the clarity of a childhood place, buried deep within the visceral part of memory: the gracious sweeping driveway, the line of gum trees on the highest ridge, the kitchen garden with its small fishpond and greedy cat . . .

She was still processing everything Mrs Robinson had told her as she let herself into the entrance hall of Darling House. That her grandmother had been at Halcyon when the bodies of Isabel Turner and her children were found by the side of the creek was a shock – even more of a shock that she'd been pregnant then with Polly.

Jess was doubtful that the Turner tragedy would have had any direct impact on a newborn baby, but it had certainly been traumatic for her grandmother. The distress, as Mrs Robinson said, had been enough to send her into labour . . . No wonder Nora had felt herself so tightly bonded to her baby.

Jess heated up a slice of Mrs Robinson's lasagne and ate standing at the bench. When she was finished, she stacked her plate in the dishwasher and headed upstairs. She took a shower but cut it short when she found herself leaning against the tiles with her eyes closed, drifting off to sleep while the warm water rained over her.

Exhaustion always made her senses raw, and the smooth, cool sheets were a delight as she climbed into bed. The window was ajar, and Jess was aware of every sound outside: the boughs of the great oak creaking, an eastern koel making its 'coo-ee' call, an ambulance siren wailing across town. She opened her phone to have a last scroll and found the news sites full of ads offering Christmas suggestions. A list promising 'the perfect gift for Mum' brought a crashing reminder: she had meant to try Polly again before the day was done.

Jess considered ringing now, but decided she was too tired to face it. She promised herself, sternly, that she would call first thing the next morning and programmed a reminder in her phone to be sure.

There were no new emails to read before bed. No surprise there – it had only just gone 9 a.m. in London – but the email she'd tapped out to Daniel Miller's trust, she noticed, was still sitting in her drafts folder.

Jess read it over, her finger hovering above the send arrow. Finally, satisfied with what she'd written, she sent it into cyberspace. The whooshing sound caused a small current of excitement to zip along her spine.

With a broad yawn, Jess plugged her phone in to charge and nestled back against the pillows. Picking up Daniel Miller's book, she opened to the next chapter. She smoothed the page, enjoying its powdery age against her fingertips, and paused just for a single anticipatory instant before letting her gaze find the first words.

Jess had expected the new chapter to lead her back to Christmas Eve morning in Tambilla, where a family was just waking up to the happy chaos of a festive morning, no idea yet of the horrifying events awaiting them.

What she hadn't anticipated, bringing with it an immediate, incandescent sense of something very much like déjà vu, was finding her grandmother's name at the start of the first sentence.

As If They Were Asleep

DANIEL MILLER

5

Nora Turner-Bridges had been aware since she arrived in Tambilla that her sister-in-law was suffering with insomnia. It was Nora's habit to take a dawn walk around the rose beds, which was how she knew Isabel was spending the wee hours pacing the house or escaping into the garden. At first, she reasoned that Isabel was merely busy. It was a lot to manage – a new baby and three older children, all of them underfoot as the summer school holidays stretched interminably ahead – but something had niggled. More than once, Nora had come across her sister-in-law in a state of distraction, a distant unhappy expression on her face, as if she were thinking very deeply about something knotty.

Isabel had been unusually forgetful, too. They'd laughed together the day she put the milk in the cupboard and the sugar in the fridge, but there'd been other occasions that were less benign. One afternoon, she'd nodded off with the baby on her lap and a fresh cup of tea in her hand. It was only a momentary lapse – she'd blinked herself awake, embarrassed and apologetic, before any harm could be done – but for Nora, sitting on the facing chair, the episode had been disturbing.

Another time, Isabel had left the baby asleep in her crib

beneath the walnut tree while she ducked inside to answer the telephone, only to forget completely to return. It had been simple good luck that Nora spotted the cockatoos assembling on the branch above and rescued the baby before they had a chance to swoop. 'They might not have bothered,' she told police, 'but they're such big birds, it was unlike Isabel to take the risk.'

'Any idea what had been troubling her?' Sergeant Duke was to say, leaning back in the chair inside the interview room of the West Road police station, fan whirring on top of the filing cabinet. 'Did she tell you?'

'Not in so many words.' Mrs Turner-Bridges had concluded that her sister-in-law was missing her husband, perhaps even harboring some small resentment that he'd left on business so soon after baby Thea's birth.

Thomas Turner was a man whose personality occupied an enormous amount of space; Nora knew firsthand how large and silent the hole left by his absence could be. When he'd gone to fight in the war, she'd been marooned in their family's big house on Sydney's eastern rim. Still but a child, she'd thought the loneliness would kill her. It didn't matter how idyllic her life appeared, Nora could well imagine how Isabel – who had, after all, left her homeland behind – must suffer bouts of loneliness when her husband was away.

The policeman taking Mrs Turner-Bridges's statement had perked up at this. 'Had Mrs Turner said she felt lonely? Homesick? Did she talk to you about a desire to go back to England?'

Mrs Turner-Bridges was adamant that she had not. 'My brother often said that he could never live in England. He was Australian, that's who he was. No, Isabel was under no misapprehension that they would ever be moving the family over there. And she wouldn't have wanted to; she loved it here. We were her family. There is a difference between a romantic nostalgia and one's real life.'

Although not yet overly concerned, Nora had nonetheless determined that the two women should spend some time together away from the children, away from the house. A nice day out, she reasoned, might be just the thing her sister-in-law needed to 'pep her up'. Nora wasn't sure that she, herself, was up to the hot, summery drive down the steep and winding Greenhill Road, with its hairpin bends and dramatic cliff-edge drops, to visit a restaurant in Adelaide, but there was a neat little tearoom in Tambilla, and she'd spoken with the owner, Mrs Diamond, to reserve a table beneath the window. They would get through Christmas – all of the family noise and hubbub – and then she'd sit Isabel down and have a good long talk.

In the days, weeks, and months that followed, Nora would reproach herself for putting off that conversation. 'If only had I spoken to her sooner,' she was to say a couple of weeks later, pressing her hands together in her lap as her baby slept peacefully beside her in the parlor of her brother's empty house, 'might I have made a difference? Might I have grasped how low she'd sunk?'

On Christmas Eve morning, though, as the sun dawned pink behind the row of gum trees on the ridge to the east, Nora had no way of guessing that by the end of the day her family would be gone. Her biggest concern in that moment was the heat. The thick air presaged rain and induced her, at last, to ease out of bed and move to the window, and it was from this vantage point that she noticed Isabel in the vegetable garden at the top of the driveway.

Nora experienced a strange, unsettled feeling as she

watched. Her sister-in-law wore a pensive expression, and there was no verve or purpose to her bearing. She was standing as still as a statue until suddenly she flinched, as if in shock, and the teacup she'd been holding dropped to the ground, shattering. When she knelt to gather the broken pieces, the scene, bathed in morning light, was so pretty and deliberate, so much communicated by the actor's delicate, curved shoulders, that Nora had the oddest sense that she was viewing a stage tableau.

A hissed admonishment disrupted the quiet inside the house then, coming from the landing outside her bedroom door where the telephone sat on its smart new laminate table. 'Stop it, you little creep!'

Nora placed her hands against her swollen belly, as if she might that way block her little one's ears from the sibling animosity of the older cousins.

The voice belonged to her eldest niece, Matilda. 'If I've told you once,' the girl continued, 'I've told you a thousand times: leave me alone.'

There followed a delighted boyish laugh and a scattering of footsteps that then slapped down the stairs. At last, the door to one of the ground-floor rooms slammed shut.

Nora eased the window open a crack and a breath of warm air took the opportunity to sneak inside the sleeping house. The merry, thumping strains of 'Long, Long Ago' started up on the piano downstairs, and she closed her eyes briefly before lowering the window again. She kept forgetting that she wasn't by the coast. To open the window at Darling House, her home in the eastern suburbs of Sydney, was to admit whatever sea breeze happened to be skimming by. Here, though, she was landlocked in the heat.

Movement on the other side of the glass caught her

attention. Isabel was coming toward the house, the scrap bucket in one hand, shards of white porcelain in the other.

Nora would later recall noticing what she took for a pleasing resurgence of purpose to her sister-in-law's gait. Perhaps, she thought, the requirements of the festive season would be all the medicine Isabel needed. It was Christmas Eve, after all, and there was much to do.

Afterward, she was to view the moment differently. A switch had indeed been flicked, but the new vigor she observed in her sister-in-law's advance heralded an ominous shift. For with it, the day's progress had been set on its awful path.

While Mrs Turner was returning to the waking house, Becky Baker was making her way along the main street of Tambilla. Every morning, she set out on foot from her home at the brewery and followed the river until she reached the narrow path leading through the bush to the back of the shops. She liked to pass beneath the tunnel of towering oaks and elms that grew in the town center before veering off the road again and moving across the paddocks toward Willner Road.

If she was on time, which she almost always was, she would see Mrs Summers bringing in the newspapers and milk bottles to sell in the grocery shop. Becky found Mrs Summers easier company than some of the other ladies in town, who made her feel embarrassed or clumsy. They would exchange cheerful greetings and Mrs Summers would duck inside for an apple to send with Becky as she walked. Sometimes Becky ate the apple, but other mornings she kept it in her pocket for when she reached the fields at the end of

Willner Road where Mr Hughes, the local solicitor, kept his horses.

Today, she was earlier than usual. She wasn't expected at the Turner house until eight, but she didn't want to waste a minute. Mrs Turner had insisted that Becky take a break over Christmas. 'You've worked so hard for my family this year,' she'd said firmly, when Becky ventured that she'd rather keep up her duties. 'You ought to spend some time with your own.'

Becky had been crushed. Working for the Turners up at Halcyon – she refused to call it 'the Wentworth place' when Mr and Mrs Turner had given it such a pretty name – was a dream come true. She had been engaged in the beginning to help Mrs Pike with the cleaning, but when the baby came, and Mrs Turner seemed so worn out with it all, Becky had stepped in. She had four younger siblings and knew a thing or two about minding wee ones, and baby Thea was just the sweetest little child, content to watch the leaves blowing on the trees with a look of utter wonder on her small, perfect face.

Becky had started to think she might not have any babies of her own. There was only one boy she could imagine wanting to marry and do that with, and he had never looked twice at her. Why would he? Half the girls in Tambilla carried a torch for Kurt Summers. He was the sort of boy who ought to be lifesaving down at Glenelg Beach on the weekends. Strong German build, blond hair, but a kind nature that showed on his face. He was smart, too, one of the smartest boys in class. Far too smart for her.

'Morning, Becky,' Meg Summers called from across the street. 'Happy Christmas Eve.'

Becky crossed to the front door of Summers & Sons Grocers, where Mrs Summers was sweeping the walkway.

'You're early today,' she said as she swept. 'So am I. So much to get finished – I'm like a headless chook! Come inside and choose an apple?'

At the counter, Mrs Summers checked her order book. 'I've a delivery to go up to the house. I won't send it with you now, it'll be too heavy. Besides, it's not quite ready. Time has got away from me this week, I'm afraid, with Perce down at the Station taking care of the grasses. I'll send one of the lads up with it later. Just let Mrs Turner know that if she thinks of anything else, she's to give us a bell and I'll make sure it finds its way up the hill.'

Becky nodded that she understood. Eager to get to Halcyon, she had turned to leave when Mrs Summers called her back.

'I do have a little something you can take with you now. Something I've been working on.'

Mrs Summers produced a tiny pink knitted matinee jacket from beneath the counter, holding it up so Becky could see.

'That's going to be just darling on the baby!' Becky exclaimed.

'Isn't it? I've been saving the wool for something special. Now, let me just check on that delivery while you're here, so you can let Mrs Turner know for sure about the time.'

Mrs Summers called for Kurt, and Becky Baker's cheeks blushed as rosy as one of the ripe peaches in the fruit boxes at the front of the shop.

But Kurt Summers did not appear from the room behind the counter. Instead, his younger brother, Marcus, poked his head around the doorway and said, 'He's on the telephone.'

'So early?' Mrs Summers raised her eyebrows. 'I suppose I don't need to ask who's at the other end.'

Kurt was on the telephone to Matilda Turner, Becky knew, and this was what she told Sergeant Kelly in her interview the following week.

The policeman seemed interested in this. 'Did someone tell you that's who he was speaking to?'

No, Becky replied. She had been able to guess because of the look that passed between Mrs Summers and her younger son, which was frustrated but also fond. Also, Becky had seen Kurt and Matilda together near the hollow tree one afternoon when she was walking home, so she knew they were in love. Becky was proud of herself when she told the policeman that. She had put two and two together and reached four. This was something Mrs Pike said to her when Becky was worried that she wouldn't be able to perform a work task well enough. 'Just take your time, Becky,' she would say, 'and you'll see that two and two usually make four.'

Sergeant Kelly was pleased, too. 'That's very good, Becky,' he told her. 'You're a clever girl.'

Becky knew that wasn't true, but she also knew the policeman wasn't poking fun. She recognized his comment as one of the things people said when they were trying to be kind.

Becky wasn't clever. She wasn't stupid, either, no matter what some people said. It was only that she had to think about questions for longer than most. Mrs Pike said that thinking more was no bad thing: it meant that by the time she found her answer, she could be surer than not that it was right.

School learning was different. Becky had left when she

was twelve years old. Her daddy had sat her down one night and told her there was a special job for her at the brewery and would she like to come and work with him instead? Becky had been glad enough to leave school. She had missed the singing they'd done in the afternoons with Miss Brickell at the piano, and renditions of 'God Save the Queen' at assembly each morning, but she hadn't missed the other songs. There was one that the other children had especially enjoyed:

> Becky Baker, the brewer's daughter,
> Fell in the well and no one caught her,
> Hit her head and banged her brain,
> And never could think straight again.

When Becky was younger, she'd sung along heartily. Her little sister, Fay, was the one who'd told her she ought to quit joining in. Old habits weren't easy to break, though, and Becky still caught herself humming the rhyme under her breath sometimes, especially when she knew she'd made a silly mistake, like the other week, when she broke Mrs Turner's best gravy boat.

Becky might not have been clever like Fay, but she did know that two plus two equaled four, and she was confident that Kurt Summers had been on the phone to Matilda Turner that morning. She knew, too, that Kurt and Matilda had argued, though she did not tell the policeman that as he did not think to ask. Becky had seen Kurt as she was leaving the shop. She'd glanced down the alley beside the building and he'd been standing with his hands on the fence, his head bowed. Becky had spent a lot of time watching Kurt and she could read his mannerisms better than she could ever hope to read a book. She saw the tension in his shoulders, and the way his jaw had stiffened like his teeth were clenched, and she knew that Kurt Summers had just heard something that made him very, very unhappy.

Becky Baker was not wrong. Kurt Summers had indeed been speaking to Matilda Turner early on Christmas Eve morning. This fact was confirmed to police by Marian Green at the telephone exchange during her interview late on the afternoon of Monday, December 28. The call had come through from the Turner residence just after 7:00 a.m. on the twenty-fourth: 'I'd been up early,' she told police, 'because I knew how hectic the day would be.'

Miss Green was adamant that she did not know what the pair had discussed – 'Contrary to what people might think, I don't make a habit of listening in on conversations' – but, when pressed, suggested that she *might* have heard Matilda Turner say something along the lines of, 'I have to see you,' and, 'It can't wait until Christmas,' and possibly even the words 'meet you there'. She wouldn't swear it, she warned the young probationary constable, who was taking notes on his small, lined pad: 'I just caught a few words while I was replacing the earpiece.'

She was more certain as to the duration of the telephone call, which she informed police had not lasted more than a few minutes. She was so busy all day that she hadn't given that particular call another thought. 'It was one connection after another, only to get worse in the evening after what happened. You can imagine how the phones started running hot after that.'

Kurt Summers was interviewed by police on Tuesday, December 29. Having been established as Matilda Turner's boyfriend, he had already been included on the list of close associates; in the end, though, he surprised Sergeant Kelly and Mounted Constable Doyle by turning up at the station of his own accord, first thing in the morning. His father, Percy Summers, was by his side, explaining to the officers that the lad was still in a state of shock, but that he understood it was his duty to render whatever assistance he could.

Kurt nodded when Sergeant Kelly asked him about the phone call, agreeing that Matilda had telephoned him early that morning.

'She wanted to meet,' he said. 'She said there was something she wanted to talk to me about in person, but she didn't know when she'd be able to get away. Her mother had been in a bad mood lately, unusually strict, wanting them to spend time together as a family.' At this his eyes closed involuntarily, and the struggle to retain his composure made his lips press tight. Finally, he managed to continue, his voice reedy with the effort not to cry. 'I loved her. I wanted to marry her. I never would have wanted anything to harm her.'

The telephone at the Turner house was situated in a small nook on the side of the landing farthest from the stairs. Mrs Turner had been known to say that it was like having their very own 'whispering gallery', such that a word spoken at normal volume into the telephone bounced off the far wall and could easily be heard on the landing.

On this occasion, it was Mrs Turner-Bridges, still ensconced in the guest bedroom, who heard Matilda mutter (soon after her brother whooped down the stairs): 'I have to go. I'll see you later,' before returning the receiver to the cradle with a force that made the bell rattle.

Once again, Nora's hands went to her belly as if to shield the baby from the domestic strife. She was beginning to think there was something going on at the house. Like her mother, Matilda was in an unusually fractious mood. Nora had put it down to hormones at first, and the delicate business of being fifteen years old, but she was starting to wonder whether there might not be something deeper to her niece's irritation. Matilda had been eating like a bird, moving food around her plate as she glowered at the table, and snapping at whomever had the misfortune to draw her ire.

Nora was still wondering about her niece's odd behavior when, through the window, she noticed the village girl, Becky Baker, appear in the garden. She glanced at her fine wristwatch, saw that it was too early for Becky to start, and felt a quiver of irritation. The girl was a relatively new addition to the household staff and Nora had been observing her closely in the weeks she'd been at Halcyon. She seemed proficient enough (although there had been the breakage last week of the heirloom gravy boat, a gift from Mrs Turner-Bridges's own parents on Thomas and Isabel's wedding), and she was certainly very confident with the baby.

A little *too* confident, Mrs Turner-Bridges thought, as Becky disappeared under the eaves. Isabel had ceded all responsibility to the girl; in fact, she appeared to be quite capable of continuing with her journaling, or gardening, or even frowning into space, when the baby cried. If Nora drew attention to the needy child, Isabel would say, almost as an afterthought, 'Oh, Becky will see to it.'

It wasn't that Becky Baker's treatment of the baby was troubling per se – the girl seemed to be a natural carer – rather that for Nora, whose own baby's birth was imminent, it seemed unthinkable that a mother might so willingly let her child out of her sight. But then, Thea wasn't Isabel's first baby. She was the fourth in a series of regular, easy pregnancies and healthy, bonny babes. Little wonder Isabel was more relaxed than another woman might have been.

Nora put her niggling concerns aside. Only later did she allow herself to voice the observation she had been too loyal then to countenance. Quietly, reluctantly: Isabel did not appear to have bonded with the baby. Not as she had with the others, and not as one might expect a mother to bond with a beautiful little girl like Thea.

6

Mrs Turner was serving eggs when Becky Baker entered the dining room at Halcyon. The longcase grandfather clock that Mr Wentworth had ordered from Dorset to please the young wife-to-be who would never arrive had just chimed half past seven, and its admonition still lingered in the sunlit air of the domed entrance hall. The atmosphere in the breakfast room, by contrast, was dense with the smoke of burnt toast and sibling rancor. John and Matilda sat on opposite sides of the large square breakfast table, the former shoveling lumps of scramble into his mouth, the latter watching him with a practiced moue of distaste.

'Where's Evie?' Mrs Turner paused as she reached the empty place, a scoop of egg held aloft on a large silver spoon. 'Morning, Nora,' she said to Mrs Turner-Bridges, who had just come into the room via the doorway on the far side. 'Would you like some eggs?'

'Oh, dearest, I don't think I could,' Nora replied. The heat of the day had caught up with her on the walk from bedroom to breakfast. Her head was aching and although she'd tied her hair up on her head, fine strands at the nape of her neck had coiled as tight as springs. Her flushed cheeks were at odds with her pale (but freckled, to her eternal regret) complexion.

Matilda, too, was unexcited by the prospect of scramble, needling curdles of egg with the tines of her fork. John, however, waited for his mother to deposit the pot and began helping himself to a heaped mound of seconds. Mrs Turner did not serve herself, sitting instead before her empty plate at the head of the table. She lifted her cup of tea and took a sip before frowning at the lukewarm liquid.

Into this scene of domestic activity stepped Becky Baker. Such was the nature of her overwhelming shyness in the face of the good-looking, well-heeled Turner family that she did not announce herself, lingering instead near the wall to the side of the door, where no one – except Nora, as she was later to report to police – noticed her. The Turners were not self-centered people, but as a family they were so complete, their loyalties and grievances so tightly interwoven, that they did not easily admit outsiders. There simply wasn't room.

'Where are you off to, John?' asked Mrs Turner, as the boy leapt to his feet, pushing his chair with cheerful approximation toward the table.

'I have to give something to Matthew.'

'Be back in time for lunch.'

'If Matthew asks me to go and eat lunch with them, can I?'

'*May* I.'

'Please do,' said Matilda. 'In fact, do us all a favor and stay forever.'

'Matilda—'

'Mother?' John pressed.

Upstairs, in the distant nursery, the baby began to cry. Mrs Turner laid a fine hand against her forehead.

'Mother!'

'No, not today.'

'Why not?'

'It's Christmas Eve.'

'And?'

'We're going to do something as a family.'

'Like what?'

Whether or not it did in the moment, Mrs Turner's brief pause gained weight in later retellings: 'A picnic,' she said. 'We're going to have a picnic.'

'Can't we do it another day?'

'No, I have everything planned. We're all going together.'

'Aunt Nora, too?'

Nora enjoyed picnics and was unfeasibly gratified by her nephew's thought to include her, but she was suffering terribly with swollen ankles and light-headedness and didn't know that she could face a day in the elements – all that direct sunlight. She was considering how best to demur politely when Isabel saved her the effort. 'No, not Aunt Nora,' she said, a fresh firmness in her voice. As if realizing that she might have caused offense, Isabel sent a half smile of apology in Nora's direction. 'She's in no condition to walk anywhere in this heat.'

Matilda, who had been crumbling small morsels of toast into tinier pieces between her fingers and letting them rain onto the white rim of her plate, looked up. 'What time do you expect us to be finished?'

'Why?' said John knowingly – a parting shot as he left the room. 'Got something else planned?'

'Little worm!' Matilda tossed a corner of toast across the

table after him, causing excitable peals of laughter to erupt from her victorious brother.

'Oh, Matilda.'

'Well, Mother?'

'Well?'

'How long will this picnic take?'

'For goodness' sake! It will be over when it's over.'

'I have to be back in time for choir rehearsal.' This was Evie, who had appeared from nowhere and was standing now behind her chair. 'Kitty and her mum are stopping by for me.'

With her long, straight, fair hair and wide, all-seeing blue eyes, there was something of the Midwich cuckoo about Evie Turner. Mr Simon Ackroyd, the visiting science teacher, was to say of her later that he'd 'rarely met a girl so eager to ask intelligent questions and so apt to make one feel a fool when seeking to give a satisfactory answer'.

'There you are,' said Mrs Turner. 'I'm afraid your brother didn't leave much breakfast. You're going to have to make do with the scraps. I'm not able to prepare more now – there's just too much else for me to do. I need to have things in order.'

'Have things in order?' Sergeant Duke was later to stop Mrs Turner-Bridges as she recounted the morning's conversation, leaning forward across the desk to fix her with a curious frown. 'What do you think she meant by that?'

'At the time, I thought she meant the picnic. Isabel always did things perfectly. I remember thinking she seemed rather stressed about an activity that should have been a pleasure.'

'And now?'

'Now? Well, I suppose I wonder whether there wasn't something different on her mind.'

Whatever it was that Mrs Turner intended by the comment, Evie said only: 'Mrs Landry is picking me up at five.'

Before Isabel could reply, Becky Baker, who had slipped out of the room unnoticed, returned with baby Thea in her arms.

'You're early this morning, Becky,' said Mrs Turner.

Becky was smiling down at the baby's face, a tiny star-shaped hand visible above the hem of the blanket, but dragged her attention away from the child and adopted the manner of a student repeating a lesson learned by rote: 'Mrs Summers said that if you think of anything else you need for Christmas, to give her a bell and let her know. She's going to send one of the boys up with the grocery delivery at eleven-thirty.'

At the mention of the Summers boys, Matilda glanced at her round-faced wristwatch and then brushed a non-existent crumb from her bottom lip. She appeared to be deep in thought. And then, 'Please excuse me,' she said, 'I've had enough.'

'You haven't eaten a bite!'

'And Mrs Summers sent you this,' Becky continued, handing over a small tissue-wrapped item.

Mrs Turner's face tensed with the discomfort familiar to all who have been the recipient of a gift without having thought to send one in return.

'It's for the baby,' Becky added, which improved things somewhat, gifts for new children belonging to a category unto themselves.

Mrs Turner nodded at the bundle in Becky's arms and

her attitude seemed to shift from uncertainty to decision. 'Is she ready for her crib?'

'Yes, ma'am, she's all settled.'

'Then put her down in the basket, will you, and come with me. There's something I need to speak to you about before the day gets away from me.'

What passed between Mrs Turner and Becky Baker in the good parlor after breakfast would become a matter of some interest to investigating officers in the immediate aftermath of the Turner family tragedy – specifically, the provenance of a small ornament that was found in Becky's possession in the days following.

The ornament in question was a miniature Japanese carving, known as a netsuke. Mrs Turner had a modest but valuable collection, which had come to her in the trunk after her mother's death. The antique ivory pieces were kept in a petite mirrored display cabinet in the good parlor, from which they were taken out only once a week, on Wednesday mornings, when Mrs Pike dusted the glass shelves. The cabinet was not locked (Evie had lost the key when, as a two-year-old, she'd developed a fascination for shiny pointed objects), but it didn't need to be. Everybody who lived within the Turner house knew the rules when it came to the netsukes.

The netsuke in question had been Mrs Turner's favorite. Although not as elaborate as the others, there was something beautiful about the white rabbit. Human beings are drawn to symmetry, and the small figure crouched on all four haunches was a deeply satisfying creation. 'She used to say it fit perfectly in one's palm,' Mrs Pike remembered to police. 'She got me to hold it once, very gently, and wrap my fingers around its smooth back, and I'll be darned if she wasn't right.'

Evidently, Becky Baker found a similar satisfaction in holding the rabbit, for that is precisely what she was doing on the Monday after Christmas, when young Matthew McKenzie spotted her sitting on a stool in the outbuilding behind Betty Diamond's tea shop. Matthew, who had moved only recently to live with his grandparents on their farm next door to the Turners, mentioned the sighting during his interview with Mounted Constable Doyle, who was going door to door along Willner Road in the days following the tragedy.

Since becoming friendly with John Turner, Matthew had spent a fair bit of time inside the Turner house, and he'd recognized the glass cabinet in the good parlor immediately as a repository for small treasures, the way a certain type of eagle-eyed thirteen-year-old boy is wont to do. Street smart, with a good memory and a young person's innate fascination with miniature items, he had familiarized himself with the contents of the cabinet almost by osmosis and had known at once, therefore, what it was in Becky Baker's hand.

'I saw her by her aunt's teahouse,' he was to tell police. 'She didn't know I was watching, because I was all the way across the street using my new binoculars. My mum sent them to me for Christmas. She lives in Sydney now. The binoculars are from West Germany, Carl Zeiss. Mum thought I'd like to have them for birdwatching.' He had the good grace to look sheepish at that point, but only briefly. 'That's when I noticed the rabbit. I saw her passing it from one hand to the other, and I saw her tuck it in her pocket, really quickly, when someone called for her to come inside.'

'Are you sure it was Mrs Turner's rabbit?'

'Positive.'

After Mrs Pike confirmed that there had indeed been a white rabbit netsuke in the cabinet and Sergeant Kelly verified that there was no longer any such object among the small carved figures in the good parlor of the Turner house, a pair of officers turned up at the old brewery to have a word with Becky Baker. Her father and younger sister, Fay, insisted on sitting with her, which was agreed because, although Becky was over eighteen and therefore an adult under the law, the Bakers were an old family and the rules of courtesy in a small community were clear.

Becky's cheeks flooded with color when she was asked about the rabbit and she stammered as she said, 'Mrs Turner g-g-gave it to me.'

She hesitated when requested to produce the item.

'Don't worry, love,' her father said, with gruff encouragement. 'They're not going to take it off you. They just want to have a look.'

'Mrs Turner gave it to me,' Becky repeated more confidently when she returned. She was rubbing her thumb against the smooth curved back of the ivory animal. 'She said it was a gift.'

'A gift? For Christmas, do you mean?' said the older policeman.

'And for all the work I've done since I started.'

'Did Mrs Turner often give you gifts, Becky?' The officer doing the questioning was Sergeant Liam Kelly, a large man with sun-reddened skin who was new to Tambilla, having transferred across from the larger Hills township of Mount Barker. His rugged, man-of-the-people exterior belied a fastidious nature and a penchant for puzzles, both in his work life and leisure. The weight of his focus made Becky nervous. She wasn't used to new people.

Kelly's offsider, Probationary Constable Eric Jerosch, had been known to Becky since they were both young children, however. He was a few years ahead of her at school and had once doubled her home on his bicycle after she'd fallen and twisted her ankle and was crying by the roadside. Now, when Becky glanced his way, he nodded reassurance. She returned her attention to Sergeant Kelly and shook her head.

'She'd never given you a gift before?'

'No.'

The older policeman made a note and then, without looking up from his writing pad: 'Did she say anything else?'

'She'd told me before that it was a family treasure. It came to her when her mother died.'

'A family treasure?'

Becky nodded.

'It must have been very important to her.'

'One of the most precious things she owned.'

Sergeant Kelly held out his hand. 'May I?'

Becky placed the rabbit in his wide, callused palm, and the policeman held the small carving up to the light, turning it this way and that as he took in its details. 'Well, there's some fine work in that. My wife's father and his before him were woodturners, and I can tell you this is a very elegant piece indeed.' He set the rabbit down on the table between them and regarded it for a little while longer before turning his gaze back to the girl.

'You like your job up at the house, don't you, Becky?'

'Yes, sir.'

'It's hard work, though, a lot of things to learn?'

'Mrs Pike teaches me what to do. She shows me when I don't know how.'

'She's a nice lady, Mrs Pike. It's good to have someone like that to work with, isn't it?'

'Yes.'

'And what about Mrs Turner? Was she a nice lady, too?'

Becky answered quietly. 'Yes, sir.'

'What's that, Becky?'

'Yes, sir.'

'Was Mrs Turner ever stern with you, Becky?'

Becky lowered her gaze. It had been a shock when Mrs Turner shouted at her. She hadn't meant to break the gravy boat the other week. It had fallen out of her hands somehow. She'd tried to catch it, but her fingers had been all thumbs and it had slipped through, landing on the floor with an almighty smash.

'Becky?'

'I broke something.'

'Something precious?'

'I don't usually break things.'

'Was Mrs Turner angry with you, Becky?'

'She got cross.'

'Had Mrs Turner been crosser than usual lately?'

Becky glanced over at her sister's perpetually protective face, as if she might find there a way to end the interview. She was uncomfortable with its turn toward the mishap with the gravy boat and Mrs Turner's mood.

'Becky?'

She'd been embarrassed when Mrs Turner saw her drop the gravy boat; she'd felt like a clumsy oaf, and the song the children used to sing to her in the playground had come back into her head.

'Miss Baker?'

And then Mrs Turner had started shouting at her, and Becky had felt her face go red and hot, and she'd run out of the house, all the way to the back of the rose garden, where she'd finally allowed herself to let go and cry.

'She doesn't mean to be cross,' Becky said at last, her words coming in a rush. 'It isn't easy being up there by herself. And she's had all of that extra paperwork to be sorting through lately. That's why she needs me to help with the baby. She knows I can be trusted to care for the baby as if she's my own.'

Nora Turner-Bridges was unable to shed any further light on how the netsuke rabbit came to be in Becky Baker's possession. 'Well, of course, I wasn't in the room,' she was to say, when police put Becky's version of events to her. 'But . . .'

'But?'

'When Isabel asked Becky to join her, I thought she meant to fire the girl, not reward her.'

'Fire her?' Sergeant Kelly pressed. 'Why would you have thought that?'

'Her voice was very serious – determined, even – and I thought immediately of the gravy boat. It was an heirloom piece and had meant a lot to Isabel.'

Mrs Pike, however, scoffed at the notion that Mrs Turner was planning to fire Becky. 'I was the one that recommended the girl to Mrs Turner, and I stand by that judgment. She's a good girl. Not the brightest penny, but there isn't a bad bone in her body, and always willing to learn.'

'Was she prone to making mistakes?' the police officer asked.

'We all make mistakes, Sergeant Kelly. Mrs Turner was pleased with Becky's work. She wouldn't have dreamed of letting her go, and certainly not without mentioning it to me first.'

'Becky had worried about being fired, though, hadn't she, Mrs Pike? After she broke the gravy boat?'

'She got upset when Mrs Turner snapped at her, yes, but the matter soon blew over.'

'She ran off, didn't she?'

'Not far and not for long. She was frightened, that's all. It was nothing more than a young girl's silly overreaction.'

'You believe, then, that Mrs Turner gave her the rabbit as a gift?'

'If that's what Becky says, then yes, I believe it. Considering what happened next, it seems to me Mrs Turner had good reason to give Becky a little something to remember them by.'

But Mrs Turner-Bridges frowned when this possibility was put to her. 'If that were the case, it seems strange that the only person Isabel thought to leave with a farewell token was a clumsy eighteen-year-old girl from the village.'

'You think it's likelier that Becky was fired and took the rabbit to spite Mrs Turner?'

'I know how upset being fired would have made her. She was very attached to baby Thea.'

'Too attached?'

Mrs Turner-Bridges paused very briefly. 'In my view, yes. It concerned me.' She broke off then and her hand leapt to cover her mouth. 'You don't think the girl had anything to do with what happened to them, do you? If she was upset

over being fired, it would be one thing to seek revenge
through the theft of a precious ornament. But surely –
surely – she wouldn't have done anything so wicked as to
harm them?'

'Complete poppycock!' Mrs Pike said to this. 'No. Not
ever. She wouldn't have dreamed of such a thing, let alone
known how to do it. Why, even the suggestion makes me
sick to the stomach. She loved Mrs Turner, and the feeling
was mutual. In fact, now I think of it, I *do* remember seeing
the two of them together that morning. I'd just arrived, it
was eight o'clock, and I glanced through the door into the
good parlor on my way to the kitchen. It was a lovely sight.
Lovely. Mrs Turner had her hand on the top of Becky's arm,
and Becky was smiling down at something in her hands.
Something white, yes, I remember now. It was right before
I went into the kitchen and saw Mrs Turner's favorite
teacup on the bench, broken into pieces. "Now, that's a bad
omen," I remember saying to myself. "Nothing good can
come of that." And I was right, because look at everything
that came after and all that's happened since.'

7

Whatever it was that Mrs Turner and Becky were discussing in the good parlor, John Turner took the opportunity of his mother's preoccupation to put some distance between himself and the house. He had been disgruntled by her insistence that the family spend the middle of the day together and had a sneaking suspicion that if she caught him 'lurking' (her pet word), she was just as likely to decide that he was 'bored' (her pet hate) and assign him 'things to do'. And while he didn't mind helping – was constitutionally glad, in fact, to be considered useful – at thirteen years of age, John was a very busy person with other ideas about how best to spend the coming hours. He had, in fact, arranged to meet his friend Matthew McKenzie by the fence that ran between their fields.

John's friendship with Matthew was only a new one. They had met early in 1959, at a session of the scouts at Woodhouse over near Piccadilly, and it is fair to say that the two had not hit it off at once. Indeed, John had been troubled enough, when he came upon the other boy using a magnifying glass to fry ants by the old water tank behind the scout house, to mention the issue to Henrik Drumming as he helped chop wood one afternoon. 'John was a soft-hearted lad,' Mr Drumming was to tell police officers during his interview in the week after Christmas. 'One of those boys that presents all happy-go-lucky – a big smile on his face, a willingness to give things a go – but whose trust and loyalty leave him vulnerable to the wrong elements.'

'Was Matthew McKenzie a "wrong element"?'

'He was a different sort of boy; harder, sneakier. Not his fault – life works like that sometimes. But if I'd been young John's father, I'd have been steering him in a different direction.'

But John's father had been away from home a lot during 1959 and Matthew lived next door and enjoyed a long rope for a boy his age. His residence at Farmer McKenzie's was fairly recent, after his mother, Mrs Eileen McKenzie, formerly a secretary at a doctor's surgery in Norwood, relocated to Sydney with her new fiancé, and his father, a dentist with a busy slate of patients and a 'hands-off' approach to child-rearing, deposited the boy with his own parents at their farm in Tambilla. Farmer McKenzie and his wife had been stern disciplinarians with their own children, but the bafflement and bewilderment of having their grandson arrive on their doorstep in their golden years had found them unprepared.

Until recently, had John been asked to rate his friends and allies, he'd have topped the list with his sister Matilda, followed closely by his best mate, Marcus Summers. But John had really started to dislike Matilda lately. When he looked at her, he could hardly recognize his partner in so many games and adventures. She had once been as skinny as he was: knobbly knees, strong ropy legs, scabbed elbows. They'd been the same height, and she'd often pulled on his trousers when the two of them were heading outside. But over the previous summer she'd grown inches taller than him. She'd changed her hair, so that rather than tie it out of the way she was leaving it to hang loose, and even doing some secret thing overnight that made it curly the next day. A horrid odor had started coming from her room, too, of rosewater and talcum and concerning, womanly things. Smells like that were fine for Mother – lovely, in fact – but from Matilda's room were a betrayal. John did not like it when things changed unexpectedly, and his response to this development was to behave with as little maturity as possible. For Matilda's part, when she deigned to look at him, it was with one of two attitudes: as if he were invisible, or else a smudge of cow dung that she'd walked onto the rug.

Things with Marcus weren't much better. They had met as five-year-olds on the first day of school and been as tight as could be for the next seven years, even sharing the role of sports equipment monitor in year six. But Mr Braun, teacher of the years six and seven composite class at Tambilla Primary School, told police that he had observed a fresh tension between the boys this year.

'Young Marcus came back after the last summer holidays with a different attitude. It's not uncommon with that year level. Hormones have a lot to answer for. He was more sullen in general, but he seemed to have set against John especially. A shame, as they were always such good mates.'

John was no more certain of the cause when he spoke to Mr Drumming of the rift.

'He was real sad about it,' the farm manager was to lament in the days after the Turner deaths. 'I know it's not a big thing, the friendship between a couple of lads, after everything that's happened, but I keep thinking of the boy. He was lonely, I reckon, with his dad gone so much. I came across him one afternoon, up in the shed where I keep the machinery, sitting alone there in the dark. I could tell he'd been having a bit of a cry, but I didn't know what was troubling him. I just planted my hand on his shoulder. "He's my best mate," he said then, and, "What have I done to make him hate me? He won't even come near my house anymore."'

Police, during their investigation, were to learn the source of Marcus Summers's ill mood. As it turns out, it had nothing to do with John Turner, although John was not wrong when he observed that his friend was avoiding his house. It was Reverend Ned Lawson from St George's Anglican church who was able to shed some light on the matter.

'Marcus Summers came to me one afternoon and told me that he'd caught someone close to him in a compromising position, up at the hollow tree on the Turner property.'

Sergeant Kelly, though respectful by nature, was the sort of man who'd been calling a spade a spade for as long as he'd been able to speak. He spent a few seconds trying to decode the implications behind the reverend's evidence before deciding he simply didn't have time for such delicacy. 'Can you tell me who and what we're talking about, Reverend Lawson?'

'His older brother had been courting young Matilda Turner.'

'And he saw them together?'

'From what he described it made for a rather shocking sight. To be confronted like that was confusing, the last thing he expected. It's a difficult age for a boy, all of those new feelings, and seeing the pair of them in flagrante delicto, so to speak, made him angry.'

'Angry?'

'I have often found, Sergeant Kelly, that anger is a convenient stand-in when men – or boys – aren't ready to name their true feeling.'

As the sergeant was new to town and therefore not aware of the ins and outs of local family relationships, the reverend went on to explain that of course Marcus Summers had felt betrayed by his brother, and hurt. It had been the two of them for as long as he could remember – a duo, a pair, a team. But now his brother had joined the adult world and left Marcus behind. And although the barrier between them had nothing to do with John Turner, in Marcus's view, his friend was guilty by association.

'It was John's sister,' Reverend Lawson explained, 'and his great big house, the wonderful, wealthy world of the Turners, that had seduced Marcus's brother away. And so he did the only thing he could think of to exert some form of control: he cut his friend out of his life.'

All of which is to say that when Matthew McKenzie began appearing on the driveway of the Turner house, John was more willing than he might otherwise have been to overlook his new neighbor's foibles. It certainly didn't hurt that Matthew seemed to sport another shiny piece of kit each time they met. While Mrs Eileen McKenzie's departure created a minor scandal in Adelaide medical circles, it had proved an unexpected boon to her son, in that Mrs Edith Pigott reported a significant increase in the number of packages arriving at the post office from Sydney marked FRAGILE and HANDLE WITH CARE.

'You're so lucky,' John had said enviously, inspecting the new Carl Zeiss binoculars, the Gibson guitar, and, most excitingly of all, the Kodak Brownie camera. 'I'd give anything for one like that.'

His new friend had laughed. 'It's 'cause of the guilt,' he'd said, and for a split second John had caught himself fantasizing about what his own mother might send him if she were to run off to Sydney, too.

But John didn't really want his mother to leave. He wanted his whole family to stay together forever. Indeed, it was this very fact that ended up tying him to Matthew McKenzie and sent him to meet his new friend at the fence line that Christmas Eve. The last time his father was home, John had heard his parents arguing. John was good at hearing things he shouldn't and had started keeping note of them in the little leather-bound book his mother had bought him so he could write down his big ideas and thoughts.

'It seems I can't do anything to keep you happy,' his father had said. 'I've given you all of this. What more could you want?'

'You know what I want.'

Their voices had got low then, too low even for the old glass-against-the-door trick to work, until finally John's father's exclamation cut through: 'They're my children, too.'

At thirteen, the vagaries of adulthood were still a mystery to John. He had been shocked to hear his parents using hard voices, but when he tried to tell Matilda about it, she refused to listen. John had carried the conversation around with him for days, and then Matthew had come along with the brand-new camera, and he'd forgotten his troubles for a time. Until one afternoon, when the two of them were sharing a round of ham sandwiches in the shade of the hollow tree, John had found himself telling his new friend what he'd heard.

Matthew considered the information. 'Has your dad been staying away from home a lot lately?'

John agreed that his father's business had been taking him abroad more often than usual.

Matthew batted a fly from his nose and finished chewing a mouthful of bread. 'Sounds like your dad is planning to split. My mum had a lot of sudden "work trips," too.'

John had been shocked at the suggestion that his father might ever want to leave them. He didn't, couldn't, believe it was possible – but he did start paying closer attention to Thomas Turner's actions. He also took the opportunity to look through his father's briefcase when it was left in his study one evening, and that's where he'd found the letter from 'Rose'.

Matthew was the one to inform police officers, shaking his head and adopting a world-weary tone: 'The letter was a shock, poor kid. He idolized his dad.'

Thomas Turner, when questioned in London, was to confess that yes, he had met a woman named Rose in the course of his business in England, and she had developed an infatuation for him.

'It was all a bit embarrassing,' he told the Met officer, when asked why he hadn't volunteered the information sooner. 'It didn't seem remotely important. My wife didn't know about it. There was nothing to know. I returned to Australia soon after the woman wrote the letter. I certainly hadn't meant to keep it – I'd forgotten it was there.'

John began thinking solemnly about ways he could convince his father not to leave. And that's when he remembered the trip the two of them had taken to see the documentary film *The Back of Beyond* when it was playing at the cinema on Hindley Street down in Adelaide.

Thomas Turner had been thrilled by the experience. 'Do you see how the filmmaker manages to make us think and feel new things, all while telling a story? What a skill.'

Mr Turner had always praised his son for enterprise. 'He takes after me' was the proudest comment John could hope to hear. Faced with the new camera, remembering *The Back of Beyond* and his father's reaction to it, John had known exactly what he had to do. He was going to tell a story that would make his father think and feel and realize just what he'd be giving up if he were ever to leave this place – this was John's new and most important mission.

He just needed to convince Matthew to let him borrow the camera.

As John scanned Farmer McKenzie's field waiting to catch sight of Matthew, back at the house Evie Turner was completing a mission of a different nature. Unbeknownst to her mother, Evie had also been up since before the dawn. She'd woken in the dark and crept very quietly around the landing and down the stairs, escaping the house via the heavy front door rather than the kitchen, so as not to alert Charles Dickens and set him off crowing for his morning scraps.

In and of itself, this was not unusual. Evie often sneaked out while the rest of the house was asleep. At ten years of age, she enjoyed a great deal more freedom than her peers, independence that was not by parental consent so much as an acceptance by Mr and Mrs Turner that their third-born child was, and had always been, utterly ungovernable.

'She is a true libertarian,' Mrs Turner had said to others, her tone one of description rather than apology, when called upon to explain her daughter's refusal to comply. 'Happy to follow the spirit of the law, but with no compunction to be bound by its letter. She reminds me of my father. He was just the same.'

Whether Evie had heard this comparison or not, she had developed an affinity with the faraway, long-ago figure of her maternal grandfather. He had been a naturalist, just as she was, and while her mother did not speak often about her own childhood, Evie had gleaned enough to inform Mr Simon Ackroyd during science class that her grandfather had been a celebrated scientist – had even published a book called *Fungi of the British Isles*. This seemingly innocuous fact was to be of some interest to police officers in the weeks following the Turner tragedy.

It so happened that throughout 1959 Evie had been putting together her own study of plant and animal life around Tambilla. She was torn between whether she would be a scientist or an artist when she grew up, but either way had written, as part of an autobiography project at school, that she planned to surround herself with animals and plants and as few human beings as she could manage.

'Yes, she did strike me as a loner,' Mr Ackroyd told police. 'But not in an unhappy way. She seemed content – the sort who preferred her own company.'

One of the few children who did consider Evie Turner a friend was Kitty Landry, a fellow student in Miss Metcalfe's year four class at Tambilla Primary School, and the type of even-tempered ten-year-old who was already growing into the role she would someday occupy of community peacemaker. Kitty sat very close beside her mother in the police station on the Tuesday after Christmas when she told Sergeant Kelly, 'People used to say Evie was weird, but she didn't care. She said she liked weird things.'

This professed love of the weird might go some way to

explaining Evie's particular interests in the world of fauna and flora. Not for her the 'obvious' choices like koalas and kangaroos; her favorite animals were monotremes. And while she loved the smells and sights of gums and banksias and wattles, it was the primeval expanse of the forest floor that excited her. Evie was mystified when her classmates spoke of magic and make-believe, and by the stories Reverend Lawson told in church on Sundays of water turning to wine and angels appearing to men. Why, she puzzled, did people seek refuge in such fantasies, when the natural world offered endless wonder? She delighted in entering the cool, dark realm of the bush after rain, searching through sopping leaf muck to discover that a whole new variety of fungi had sprouted overnight, an array of unimaginable shapes and sizes and colors waiting to be explored and catalogued.

But in the early hours of Christmas Eve morning, when Evie Turner crossed the Onkaparinga Valley Road at the end of Willner Road and headed into the deep woods that grew on the other side, she was not seeking to explore. She knew precisely where she was going and what she was expecting to find.

The wildest, thickest patch of bush remaining in Tambilla was on land belonging to a man by the name of Merlin Stamp. Stamp, a lean, lanky fellow with dishwater hair somewhat longer than was usual, was the town hermit. His age was unknown, and for as long as anyone could remember he'd lived in a caravan on the sprawling bushland property that had once belonged to his parents.

Fictions love a gap in which to grow, and the lack of verified information surrounding Stamp was fertile ground. Some said he'd been damaged in the Great War. For them, he was a figure of pity, whose impressive mind ('I heard he used to be a scientist down at one of the universities') had been shattered by the unrelenting horror of it all. Others swore that in fact he was a former felon, whose connections, stretching right back to the founding of the colony, had kept him out of prison. 'He had a family of his own once,' went a common whisper, which then expanded to explain (in rather nebulous terms) that they'd been lost in 'suspicious circumstances'. There was a child, said some, who had drowned – but no, interjected others, it was his wife and she'd fallen . . . been pushed . . . been smothered in her bed . . .

Whether these rumors met young Evie's ears is unknown, but regardless, she was not afraid of Merlin Stamp. She spent a lot of time in his woods and knew the platypus gorge well. She knew, too, though police were unable to establish how, the shed that Mr Stamp kept nearby. Little more than a shack, really; when, in the aftermath of the Turner tragedy, the police searched it thoroughly, they found a panoply of exotic items: microscopes and saucepans, countless jars containing plant samples and strange animal parts bearing handwritten labels with indecipherable descriptions and the initials M.S. There were spiderwebs and curious wall charts and shelves of moldy books and countless piles of hessian sacks. Police didn't know what they were looking for exactly, not at that point, and they didn't find it.

This much, though, was known: early on December 24, Evie Turner located the hidden key to the shack and let herself into the dim room, sorting through the jars until she found what she had come for. Later, when he arrived at the shed to start his work, Merlin Stamp noticed that the key was not precisely where he'd put it, but it would be some days before, under police questioning, he realized why and who had been responsible and what had been taken. He would claim never to have shown Evie where he kept it; indeed, he professed to have spoken only a word or two to 'the girl', despite having glimpsed her in 'his woods' now and then.

In any respect, half an hour after she'd locked the shed door behind her, Evie was back at the house, picking over the breakfast table pans for scraps that John had left. No one questioned the fact that she was already dressed for the day, her customary leather satchel over her shoulder and dirty boots on her feet. Perhaps they assumed she was on her way outside? Perhaps they had long ago given up trying to discern the purpose of this very independent little girl? Perhaps, with everything else that was going on in each of their busy lives, they just did not notice?

Whatever the case, on the last morning of her life, after her aunt retired upstairs to rest, and her sister threw down her napkin and slipped away, and her mother left the room to speak with Becky in the parlor, Evie ate breakfast alone. The only person remaining in the room with her was the baby, sleeping peacefully in the woven basket that their mother liked to take outside on clear, warm days and suspend from a tree branch.

When Evie had eaten an elegant sufficiency, it was thus only to the walls and the sleeping baby that she excused herself, before leaving the table and making her way upstairs. She did not go immediately to her own room. Instead, on the far side of the landing, she knocked on her older sister's door and waited to be admitted.

8

When Evie knocked on the bedroom door, Matilda had been waiting for an excruciating fifteen minutes, pacing back and forth across the length of her small room, pausing every so often to rest her hands on the windowsill and glare out across the hills. All hint of dawn's soft light was gone, and the long grasses, dried by weeks of sunshine, shifted between silver and gold as the morning breeze moved between them. But Matilda was too tense to notice the scenery (or the distant figure of Matthew McKenzie approaching John by the far-off fence). She had left the breakfast table as soon as mention of Kurt threatened to send her anxiety spilling over. The last thing she'd needed was for Isabel to notice how jumpy she was that morning.

Matilda had recently stopped calling her mother 'Mum'. At fifteen, she was impatient to grow up and eager to shed the last vestiges of childhood. She was tall for her age and had a striking tendency to look people directly in the eye. She did not suffer fools gladly and lately found that more and more people could that way be described. Even her teachers, with whom she'd once shared pleasant and

collegial relationships, were now proving to be dis-
appointments.

Why, just the other day, Mr Collins, the neat, pencil-
thin head of mathematics, with whom she'd always got
along very well, had made a series of incorrect calculations
in the algebra problem on the blackboard. Matilda had
raised her hand to point them out and instead of rewarding
her perspicacity, he'd colored like a sun-ripened apple and
made her stay behind to clean the erasers after class. Writing about the event in her diary that evening, Matilda had
noted: *It isn't the first time he's frozen me out. Ever since The*
Episode, he's gone out of his way to treat me as if I'm
invisible.

The Episode, important enough to occupy a full page in
the diary, had involved Mr Collins surprising Matilda and
Kurt Summers behind the school gardener's shed during
lunch break. (Any awkwardness had evidently been forgotten by the time of the funeral, where Mr Desmond Collins
was to remember Matilda to other mourners as 'a terribly
bright girl. So much promise, in music as much as in
mathematics.')

With her father away so often that year, Matilda had
come to consider herself the second adult in the house, and
had thus been somewhat irked by the arrival of her aunt
Nora and what she saw as her own demotion to second-
class citizen. When she'd first heard the news of her aunt's
imminent arrival, she had imagined that they might be
three women together, retiring to the parlor in the evenings, analyzing world news and comparing opinions on art
and music and faraway places. But the moment Aunt Nora
arrived from Sydney, her swollen belly announcing her
presence long before the rest of her made it through the

door, it was clear that Matilda's fantasy was not going to be realized.

For one thing, the subjects raised for discussion were not at all what she had hoped. Matilda had fast become tired of pregnant bellies and exasperated by talk of babies and milk and sleeping times. As she listened to her mother and aunt, she had decided she was never going to have a child of her own. *I can't imagine anything more hateful than being tied down by a mewling, puking, helpless creature*, she had written on November 27. Worse than having to endure the drudgery itself was what babies did to otherwise intelligent women. Her own mother was almost unrecognizable. She had been distracted, and weakened, both physically and mentally, by the birth of baby Thea.

Matilda's bedroom, which she had occupied since she was a baby herself, was on the front corner of the house and looked toward the north. It had been decorated at great expense by Mr Wentworth's English designer and was at its bones a quintessential Victorian infant's nursery of the type that would once have been adjoined by a nanny's bedroom and a schoolroom. The wallpaper depicted a series of cheerless Victorian nursery rhyme characters, which Matilda had done her best to cover with posters of her favorite musicians – John Coltrane, Ella Fitzgerald, and Louis Armstrong. A steel music stand occupied the spot by the window, a saxophone balanced upright on a prop beside it.

Before Evie knocked, Matilda made two adjustments to her appearance: she fastened the fine necklace chain she'd received recently as a gift from Kurt Summers behind her hair, and she changed her blouse, choosing one that buttoned all the way to the collar. That evening, Dr. Larry Smythson, the chief medical examiner at the West Terrace morgue, who had stayed back late as a favor to his longtime colleague Sergeant Peter Duke, would notice, when he removed the piece of jewelery from Matilda's neck, that the clasp had been bent slightly, in a manner suggesting a hurried, possibly frustrated, fastening technique. Her aunt, during an interview with police, would say that she had noticed her niece was wearing a different outfit when she returned downstairs that morning, but that she'd thought little of it.

'Girls of that age are sensitive about their appearances – about almost everything – and Matilda had been especially changeable since I'd arrived.'

'In what way changeable?'

'She would sit with us in the evenings, agree to a cup of tea, and then just as we were pouring decide that she didn't want one after all. She didn't seem to know if she was coming or going.'

Matilda *had* been out of sorts in the weeks leading up to Christmas Eve, 1959. She'd spent a great deal of time alone in her bedroom with her diary open on her lap, counting the calendar dates again and again, all the way back to the day at the hollow tree. This date she had circled carefully. It had been seven weeks ago now, and she was still late. Matilda had always been like clockwork. She'd prided herself on the fact, even though she knew it was nothing more than a quirk of nature and biology.

For the past month or so, Matilda had waited and hoped and prayed and cried. And then, a week ago, she'd told Kurt. She'd debated whether to say anything. Her preference was to keep it to herself and deal with the situation in private. But she hadn't a driver's license or access to a car, and she needed to get to the city.

But Kurt had refused. He was in love with her, he said. He was also an optimistic young man whose perspective was yet untroubled by the ambivalence that would come with time. Life was sacred, he reminded her. 'We can do this. Together, we can do it. We'll get married.'

'Married! How would we afford that?'

'I'll get a job.'

'You're going to university when you finish school.'

'I don't have to.'

'But it's your dream.'

'It's my father's dream. I've got no idea what I want to do yet. I'll do something else. Something outside. I'll mow lawns.'

'The Misses Edwards aren't going to be able to pay you enough to support a wife and baby.'

'Then I'll run the shop with my mum. We can do this,' he said again. 'My parents did it.' And the next time they saw one another, he gave her the necklace, as if encompassed within the fine gold chain and the little garnet stone was all the potential and promise and sheer good luck they would need.

But Matilda didn't want to do it. He had told her about his parents, married due to a pregnancy (that didn't even eventuate) and as happy as could be, but Matilda didn't want to be a mother. She didn't want to be married. Not now. Perhaps not ever. She had big dreams for the future. She planned to travel, to live in New York City, to play jazz in nightclubs with their names spelled out in neon lights.

And so she'd come up with a new idea. The only catch had been the need to enlist her younger sister. Matilda, being a responsible person by nature, had debated the pros and cons of involving Evie, who was, after all, only ten years old. Eventually, she'd reasoned that it was acceptable on two conditions, written like the solution to a logic problem at the bottom of the diary entry on December 3.

1. *She mustn't be told the reason, that way she'll bear no moral burden.*
2. *She must be paid with something she values to a similar degree.*

When the soft knock came at last on the door, Matilda opened it within a matter of seconds. Her face was flushed. 'Did you get it?'

Her sister gave a short nod.

'Show me.'

Evie reached into her satchel.

'Not out here!' With a quick glance over her younger sister's shoulder, Matilda grabbed Evie by the wrist and pulled her into the room, where the microscope she'd managed to purloin from the school science room as payment was waiting.

Silence fell once more on the landing, as the sun, which had continued its slow arc across the sky, arrived high enough at last for rays of light to begin pouring through the glass dome in the ceiling, illuminating lazy motes of dust, suspended and unsuspecting of all that the day had yet in store.

John, meanwhile, had just discovered a problem. Securing the loan of the camera had not been an entirely straightforward matter. Never one to miss an opportunity, Matthew had recognized his new friend's eagerness and been quick to capitalize. He agreed to lend the Brownie on one condition.

A week or two earlier, when the two boys were executing a raid on John's mother's pantry in search of Mrs Pike's fresh batch of *Lebkuchen* Christmas biscuits, Matthew had caught sight of a stash of brown glass bottles hidden at the back of the bottom shelf. He knew immediately what they were, and his first thought was of the fun he could have baiting the wild dogs that had been howling in the valleys of an evening.

John, who for all his high spirits was an honest and dutiful boy, had agreed to the deal reluctantly, settling on two bottles (rather than the four requested) in exchange for a one-week loan of the camera. But by the time he managed to sneak into the pantry, only a single bottle remained on the shelf, with half of its contents gone. He had cursed himself for not having ventured sooner to secure the ill-gotten gains, but decided it would have to do, squirrelling the bottle away, ready to make the swap at the specified place and time.

So it was that, as Matilda inspected the jar Evie had brought her from Mr Stamp's shed, and Evie examined her new microscope, and Mrs Pike sorted through the pieces of broken cup in the kitchen, and Becky Baker slipped her hand into the pocket of her pinafore to stroke the smooth back of the ivory rabbit that had until recently occupied pride of place in Mrs Turner's cabinet, John handed over the half bottle of Thall-Rat to Matthew McKenzie.

'What's this?' said the boy. 'I was promised two!'

'It's all that was left.'

'But there were so many.'

'My mum hates rats,' said John with an unhappy shrug. 'She and Mrs Pike both. One of them must have used the rest already.'

Matthew considered the bottle, and then, with a grunt of deep dissatisfaction, took it from John and tucked it in his pocket. 'I'll still lend you my camera, but you can forget about the week,' he said, handing over the Brownie. 'I want it back on Boxing Day.'

John received the item as if it were worth its weight in gold. Two days didn't give him long, but if he started that very afternoon, he had a good shot at getting the footage he needed.

'Should mention,' said Matthew, almost an afterthought, as he turned back toward his grandparents' house, 'the film door jammed last time I used it. You'll have to fix it first.'

'I'll take it to Mr Drumming,' John called after him. 'He can fix anything.'

Matthew McKenzie continued toward home, a spring in his step and a whistle on his lips, and, with the clock ticking on his loan, John turned and ran like a hare back up the hill, disappearing over the crest in the direction of his family's shed.

9

Unfortunately for John, although it was true that Henrik Drumming possessed an unrivaled ability to fix almost any broken object put before him, Mr Drumming was not at the Turner house that day. He had asked for, and been granted, a rare morning off.

Later, during his interview with police, Mr Drumming would hesitate when asked how he'd spent December 24. 'I was down at Parkside,' he said at last, when it became clear he was going to have to answer.

None of the officers needed to ask what Parkside was. They looked from one to the other, avoiding Henrik's eyes, until finally Sergeant Duke, being the highest-ranking officer and the only non-local, was the one to ask, 'And what were you doing there, Mr Drumming?'

'I was taking my wife some flowers for Christmas.'

Mrs Eliza Drumming had been in and out of Parkside Mental Hospital, the grand Gothic building on Fullarton Road, for much of the past two decades, and it was at her usual spot within the dayroom, by the window with the best light and the view over the gardens, that Henrik Drumming found her. Along with flowers from their old school friend Maud McKendry's garden, he had brought his wife a

Christmas gift. Her beautiful face, once capable of more nuanced emotion than Henrik had ever seen on another human being, was expressionless, courtesy of the strong pills the doctors prescribed for her. The small paint set fell from its wrapping paper to land upside down on her lap, and she turned it over gently in her hands.

She had adored painting once, and Henrik had built her the studio himself at the back of their garden. She'd always needed time apart from others, even before she suffered the onset of whatever it was that had taken over her. Despite being well loved and loving others in return, she was happiest by herself. He'd used to watch her wandering through the garden, inspecting this leaf and that petal. It gave him pleasure to see her out there, the sun finding golden strands in her hair. She would stop sometimes and stare up at the topmost branches of the gums that grew along the fence line, her focus shifting to a comprehending frown. He'd asked her once what she was doing. 'Listening to the leaves,' she'd answered. Henrik had thought little of it at the time. He'd assumed she meant their rustling.

His dear wife was the one broken thing he had not been able to fix.

'I should have seen the signs,' he was to tell police after the Turner deaths. 'I should have realized.'

'Can you tell us about those signs, Mr Drumming? When you look back now, what was it that struck you about Mrs Turner's behavior in the weeks leading up to the tragedy?'

'She was preoccupied. I met with her every week about the farm records when Mr Turner was away. She was very bright and had an instinct for business. But lately, I could see her heart wasn't in it. She seemed indifferent.'

'Why do you think that was?'

He shook his head. 'I don't know.'

'But you knew Mrs Turner was having difficulty sleeping – isn't that right, Mr Drumming?'

Henrik looked up at that. He didn't answer at once.

Sergeant Peter Duke was a man in the happy situation of having found himself in the very occupation for which he knew himself to have been formed by God. His pleasant face was just what one might have conjured for the role of the ideal interviewer: interested but impassive, open and absent of judgment, disarming without resorting to trickery. He made a person want to help him solve his puzzle. 'Can you tell us your wife's name, Mr Drumming?'

'It's Eliza.'

'Eliza Drumming? Mrs . . .' He turned back several pages of his pad to find the note he'd made and then looked up again. 'Mrs E.W. Drumming?'

'That's right.'

Sergeant Duke nodded at the young probationary constable, Eric Jerosch, who glanced apologetically at Henrik, red to the tips of his ears. He was Maud McKendry's much younger brother and had spent a number of summers learning how to rewire radios and electric heaters in Henrik's shed when he was a boy. Now, at his superior's behest, the young officer turned to the cabinet behind him and retrieved from its top drawer a small amber bottle, placing it on the table between Henrik and Sergeant Duke.

'Do you recognize this item, Mr Drumming?' Sergeant Duke asked.

Henrik nodded. Later, he would say that although he hadn't thought of that bottle or its contents in months, he'd experienced a strange foreshadowing as young Eric's back was turned, and he wasn't so much surprised as sickened when he saw the amber glass, the faded label with his wife's name typed across it.

'What we need help understanding is how a bottle of pills prescribed to your wife wound up in Mrs Turner's bedside table drawer.'

Henrik's throat was dry when he answered. 'Like you said, she was having trouble sleeping.'

'What's that, Mr Drumming?'

'Mrs Turner was having trouble sleeping.'

'She told you that?'

Henrik gave a short confirming nod.

'Did you and Mrs Turner often discuss her sleeping habits?'

'No, sir.' His cheeks flushed at the question. It was true that he and Mrs Turner had seen more of one another while Mr Turner was away. Henrik had reported on the farm to her each week, told her what supplies they'd be needing, his plans for the various fields. That sort of ritual, while not a social event by any stretch of the imagination, had a way of lowering one's defenses. 'Only the once,' he said, remembering how she'd apologized that day, asking him to start his report again. *It doesn't matter what I do*, she'd said, *I can't get to sleep at night, and by day I find I'm sleepwalking.*

Sergeant Duke picked up the empty bottle and read the label. 'Barbital. That's a sleeping aid?'

'Yes, sir.' Henrik noticed that the bottle was empty, and the implication arrived like a stone in his stomach. 'You're not saying that these pills had anything to do with what happened to them?'

'We don't know that yet, Mr Drumming. The forensic results won't be back for some time.'

But all of that was still to come. As the blazing sun continued its passage across the sky that Christmas Eve, and as Henrik Drumming was leading his wife, Eliza, out of the women's ward to sit among the gracious ornamental trees and elaborate flower gardens of the Parkside grounds, back in Tambilla, Mrs Meg Summers was finalizing the Turner family's Christmas order. She had also taken advantage of a rare quiet moment between customers to get her sponge cake in the oven, and the smell of browning sugar was beginning to infuse the air, traveling all the way through to the shop from the kitchen.

Meg checked the grocery order one more time. She'd been surprised not to receive a last-minute call from Mrs Turner regarding forgotten items. Truth be told, she'd expected them to need a fair bit more up at the house to see them through the festive season, particularly with Mr Turner's sister adding to their numbers. Then again, perhaps that was the cause. Mrs Turner had a lot to think about, what with the new baby and a houseguest to entertain.

There was a bit of space left in the top of the Turners' box, and Meg added a few extra treats – she'd done the same for all of her best customers: some homemade strawberry jam, a jar of her fish paste, and a loaf of her much-loved *Roggenbrot*. Finally, with the box full to overbrimming, Meg called for Kurt. She experienced a fleck of impatience as she waited, provoked in part by the lingering effects of the pace at which she'd worked all day.

When Kurt didn't appear, she called again. It was unlike him to skip out when the day's work was yet to be finished.

'Turns out he was checking that the Misses Edwards' lawn was shipshape for Christmas,' she was to tell police in the coming week, when they inquired after his whereabouts. 'They're such fine and dainty ladies, the pair of them. They hark back to a different time and they like everything just so.'

'So when you called for him to take the Turner delivery, he was unavailable because he was out at the old mill?' asked Sergeant Duke.

'Yes, sir.'

'Asking the Misses Edwards whether they needed the lawn done before Christmas?'

'I don't think he spoke with them. They do very well, but they're nearing ninety. They take a long rest in the afternoon. No, he just went and had a look for himself. Did what needed doing.'

While Sergeant Duke was making a note, Mrs Summers hesitated, and seemed to judge that clarification was required. 'He'd been taking care of the lawn out at the old mill since he was knee-high to a grasshopper. He knew what to look for.'

'Can you tell me how long he was gone?'

'I wasn't paying attention – I had that much on my plate. Not long, though, I'm sure of it.'

With Kurt unavailable, Mrs Summers called instead for her younger son. She did so with some trepidation. He'd helped her at the counter all morning, but he was fourteen, and somewhat moody with it, and had been in his bedroom for the past hour cycling through his rock 'n' roll records. When he appeared at the back of the shop, though, Mrs Summers was pleasantly surprised.

'He could see how harried I was,' she explained to

Sergeant Duke. 'He's a good boy, my Marcus. Mood or not, he never could stand to see me troubled, bless him. I loaded the box into the canvas bag we use for bicycle deliveries and told him to get the order up there nice and quickly, so the cold items didn't perish – it was so hot that day – and he certainly was fast: he was back before I took my cake out of the oven.'

Indeed, sitting beside his father in the police station the following week, the day after his brother, Kurt, Marcus was to confirm, after a certain amount of probing, that his plan had been to get in and out of the Turner place as speedily as he could.

'You and John Turner weren't getting along?'

Marcus didn't answer at once, but he looked so dejected it took all of Sergeant Duke's mettle to hold the line. Interviewing kids, especially a boy who'd lost a good mate that he'd been bluing with, was one of the worst parts of his job.

'Just give me a nod or a no, mate,' he said, thinking of his own son, Pete Jr., whose stubborn little face could crumple in an instant when pressed too hard.

Marcus managed a nod. He *had* been out of sorts with his good friend, John. He'd agreed to make the delivery to help his mum, but in truth, Marcus Summers admitted, glancing up briefly at Sergeant Duke, he had hoped not to see *any* of the Turners if he could help it.

10

Unfortunately for Marcus, as so often happens when one is dead set on avoiding an encounter, the first person he'd seen as he rounded the final curve of the driveway and arrived at the house was John. His erstwhile friend was up in the top field, still some distance away in the long grass, a brown box-shaped object slung over his shoulder on a strap, and a long, straight stick in his hand that he was swinging first this way and then that like a sword. The grazing cows, their black backs silver in the sun, ignored him. He looked hot, and decidedly bothered. Marcus hurried around to the back of the house and made his way along the verandah.

Some distance ahead of him, Evie Turner was riding a red tricycle that had been antique long before she was born and was, anyway, far too small for her. She was pedaling slowly away from Marcus, her long plait snaking down her back, the wheels of the tricycle making a rusty squeak with every turn. Evie had been riding lazy laps around the verandah for at least thirty minutes. As the youngest (until baby Thea's recent arrival), she was often called upon to wait while the others got themselves organized.

As Evie disappeared around the far corner, Marcus

passed beneath the walnut tree and reached the back door that opened directly into the kitchen. He hoped to leave the groceries on the bench and then escape, as he had done many times before, but alas, both Mrs Turner and the visiting aunt from Sydney were standing right there in the center of the room. Mrs Turner was in the midst of lunch preparations, and the pine table was covered with buttered bread laid out in rows, as well as a rainbow cake, thickly iced, that had already been cut into slices. Four thermoses stood waiting to be filled, beside a very large stainless-steel teapot, the sort his dad kept for camping.

'What good timing,' said Mrs Turner when she saw him. Although she was preparing lunch, her dress was of the type he had seen in the glamour magazines in his mother's shop. 'I was just deciding what to put in these sandwiches.'

Surprise at having found the kitchen occupied made Marcus slow to respond. Being faced with Mrs Turner made him awkward. Finally, he found his voice, hating himself for stammering as he said, 'M-mum says she put in a few extra things. F-for Christmas.'

'How kind, and after sending a gift for the baby already. There really is no end to her generosity. Of course, I have a little something for her, too. I've been meaning to drop it down all week, but I've hardly stopped. There's always so much to do at this time of year, don't you find? I'm sure your mother's just the same, busy with the shop and everything else she does. I suppose she has a big Christmas planned for your family?'

Mrs Turner-Bridges, sitting in a cane chair in the coolest, dimmest corner of the kitchen, had been watching this exchange with no small amount of surprise. It was not like Isabel to be so garrulous. Her face had taken on an almost tortured expression when she commented on the other woman's kindness. Nora listened for a time, wondering what her sister-in-law could possibly be skittish about, before she realized. Isabel didn't have a gift for Mrs Summers. She had been caught out and was now stalling. 'Dearest,' Nora interjected gently, 'you're busy here. Shall I go and fetch the present for Mrs Summers?'

Isabel was confused at first, but quickly caught on. 'Yes, thank you,' she said, with perfect faith that Nora would be able to find something suitable. To Marcus: 'You don't mind waiting, do you?'

Whether he minded or not was beside the point. He had been asked to wait by a customer of his mother's, an older person in his community, and thus a lifetime of parental instruction made it impossible for him to do otherwise. Marcus glanced back toward the open door before giving a quick, agonized nod.

'And, Nora, will you ask Matilda to come and see me?' Isabel called after her sister-in-law. She smiled at Marcus, apologetic at having raised her voice, and started unloading groceries from the box. 'I'd best get these cold items away,' she continued. 'It's so hot today. So very hot. Fish paste – my favorite . . . However did your mother know?'

She was joking. Everyone knew that Mrs Turner had a penchant for his mother's fish paste. A fair portion of Tambilla felt the same way. It was one of the most-made recipes from Meg Summers's great-grandmother's heirloom cookbook. Along with the *Roggenbrot*, of course.

The wooden-framed wire-screen door slapped open and shut and John entered, the Brownie camera still slung across his shoulder, his face pink with heat and frustration. After searching for hours, traversing the property from one end to the other, he'd begun to despair of ever finding Mr Drumming. Frustration over the camera had put him in a bad mood, and in the habit of young boys everywhere, he'd come in search of food to assuage his tension. 'I'm starving,' he announced. Very briefly his gaze met Marcus's, before each boy looked away in an obstinate show of vexation.

'We're leaving soon for the picnic.'

'Mum, no, I can't.'

'Nonsense, we're all going.'

'But there's something I have to do, something important.'

'I thought you said you were starving.'

'I need to find Mr Drumming.'

'He's not here today.'

'What?' The panic in John's voice was such that under any normal circumstances, any normal mother (and certainly Mrs Turner) would have had her suspicions raised and set about Getting to the Bottom of Things, but at that precise moment, Mrs Turner-Bridges reappeared with Matilda close behind her.

'I'm not going on a picnic,' Matilda blurted. 'It's far too hot.'

'It's not.'

'I'm melting.'

'You're not.'

'I'm bilious!'

She *did* look rather green around the gills, and her eyes were bloodshot, as her aunt was later to confirm. 'I assumed it was the heat,' Mrs Turner-Bridges would tell the police. 'Lord knows, I was feeling peaky myself. But it turned out she'd been busy that morning.'

It was Mrs Pike who was able to shed light on Matilda's

actions, in her interview the week following the deaths. The housekeeper had just finished telling the police that Mrs Turner had insisted she and Becky Baker only work a half day on Christmas Eve ('I thought she might have wanted some help making lunch – she still hadn't started on dinner, and now there was a picnic to prepare – but she was adamant that she could manage on her own; she was very firm about it') when she paused and added, 'It was busier than Hindley Street that day. Becky and I passed Marcus Summers on his way to make a delivery, and when we parted ways at the bottom of the driveway – I had my bicycle, and she prefers to walk back to town across the paddocks – I almost rode straight into young Matilda. I'm not sure where she'd been, but she was stalking back toward the house, her face red and her expression anguished.'

Matthew McKenzie, who had been 'birdwatching' nearby, offered further information on Matilda's movements after breakfast.

'I saw them sitting together in the Summerses ute,' he told police. 'Where that dirt track breaks off from Willner Road. He was parked right up on the verge. I knew it was him. Even if I hadn't seen him, I'd have known, because he had his lawn mower in the back. They were arguing, him and Matilda. She was crying and he was angry with her.'

'How do you know he was angry? Did you hear what they were saying?'

'After she left, he watched her go, and then he slammed his hand down on the roof of the car and swore.'

Isabel, though, in the kitchen spreading fish paste onto *Roggenbrot*, knew none of what had passed. She was aware only that her fifteen-year-old daughter was behaving in a recalcitrant manner, and she was having none of it.

'It's Christmas Eve and we are going on a picnic together, as a family. Consider what you'd like to bring with you and gather it now. A book, some writing materials, a towel. That goes for you, too, John.'

'Why do I need a towel?' he asked.

The kitchen was becoming crowded, people and discord causing the atmosphere to roil. Mrs Turner-Bridges had brought with her a small, gift-wrapped parcel that Marcus longed to reach out and grab so that he could finally escape this room, this family. But alas, it sat on the far corner of the table, ignored by Mrs Turner, whose knife was moving ever faster, spreading lashings of strawberry jam onto the remaining slices of buttered bread. Unable to leave, Marcus Summers watched her, miserable but mesmerized, from his place near the door.

'Why do I need a towel?' John said again.

'I thought we'd go to the water hole,' Isabel replied. 'You can swim, and there's that lovely big willow to sit beneath. Lots of shade, and a bough that will be perfect for the baby's crib. Matilda, will you go and fetch your baby sister?'

'Isabel, please,' said Matilda, employing her best grown-up voice. 'I really do feel wretched. I need to lie down.'

'There's a small bag near the crib,' Isabel added. 'Bring that as well.'

Silence fell. A stalemate had seemingly been reached, and with no further shots fired, the room's thick ambience briefly settled. But there is nothing surer than that two siblings, each nursing a problem, will seek refuge in the familiar comforts of quarreling, and so it was with John and Matilda in that moment.

'What are you looking at?' said John, his face pink with heat.

'Have you been crying?' Matilda replied tartly. 'Your face is as red as a lobster.'

'Like looking in a mirror, I'll bet.'

'That's enough!' As an only child herself, the idiosyncrasies of sibling rancor were inexplicable to Isabel. 'I don't know what's got into the pair of you today. It's hot and I can see you're fractious, but I've made iced tea and I'm going to pack all four thermoses. There'll be plenty for everyone.'

'I hate iced tea.' This was Evie, rolling past the screen door on the squeaking tricycle.

'You won't hate this batch. I've added extra sugar, just for you.'

'And she had,' Mrs Turner-Bridges was to say to a close acquaintance in the weeks after. 'I can picture her now, as clear as the day, stirring and stirring, round and round. It was one of those stainless-steel teapots that you might use to cater a party. Very large. I didn't think anything of it at the time. The sun was beating down – there was no doubting they'd all be thirsty.'

Mrs Turner had finished making the sandwiches by now. Having sliced them into triangular quarters, she packed them and the cake into boxes and was about to start pouring the iced tea into thermoses when she noticed Marcus Summers still standing in the shadows by the doorway, looking for all the world like he was trying to make himself invisible.

'Oh my!' she exclaimed. 'I completely forgot. Your mother's present!'

Nora handed the gift to Isabel; she was very pleased with herself, having managed to find in her suitcase a small pot of Yardley Skin Food, bought in Sydney but not yet opened.

A little piece of tissue paper, and it looked for all the world as if it had been sitting under the tree all week, awaiting its recipient.

With a grateful smile for Nora, Isabel transferred the gift to Marcus. 'Give Mrs Summers my very best wishes, won't you?' she said to the lad. 'And have a lovely Christmas yourself, you and your family.'

Marcus gave the shortest of nods and slipped out through the door, letting it swing shut behind him. Pent-up energy, having been stalled for so long, had him cycling with the furies back down the hill and into town, so that his mother, who was just taking her cake out of the oven when he arrived, was moved to remark on how quick he'd been with the delivery.

Isabel, meanwhile, turned to Nora. 'You're a lifesaver,' she said. 'You really are. But how rude of me, and how forgetful! My mind has been all over the place lately.'

'Don't be so hard on yourself, Issy,' said Nora. 'You've a new baby, on top of everything else.'

At mention of the baby, perhaps, Isabel's attention fell to Nora's pregnant belly. 'But what about *your* lunch?' she exclaimed. 'Here I am, preparing all of these sandwiches, and not a thought for you.'

'Don't worry about me. With this enormous child making herself so comfortable, I don't know that I'll ever eat again.'

'But you might get peckish while we're gone.'

'If I do, there's ample in the refrigerator to keep me going.'

That was true enough. As anyone who has lived in a small town will attest, a feature of residency, whether desired or not, is the significant amount of neighborly generosity one can expect to receive during life's times of need. The arrival of a new baby (along with, as Mrs Turner-Bridges was soon to learn, the death of loved ones) tends to bring out the best in people. Every second day or so for the past six weeks, a knock had come at the door, usually in the afternoon, and Isabel had opened it to find one of the neighbors standing there with a cake or a casserole or a plate of biscuits for the family. The refrigerator and larder were overflowing.

'I'll be fine,' Nora said again.

'We're abandoning you,' said Isabel, her resolve suddenly wavering. 'And after you've come all this way to see us.'

'I'm sure I can manage being alone for a few hours. I heard on the wireless they're predicting rain for tomorrow, maybe even as soon as tonight. It would be a crime not to go out and enjoy the sun while it's shining.'

Isabel still looked doubtful.

'I'll rest,' came Nora's reassurance. 'I'm looking forward to it. I want to be at my best for Christmas.'

'Well . . . you've certainly got more chance of resting with my brood out of the way.'

As if on cue, the children reappeared. The act of gathering supplies had succeeded in brightening their spirits. They had found towels and books, even a flag and some decorations, and loaded all of it now into baskets.

Matilda had brought the baby as her mother asked, the little one still fast asleep in the crib. It was a lovely piece, that crib. Woven by Mr Bartel in the village to the same exacting standards his ancestors had applied in their furniture business in Muschten before emigrating to South Australia.

'Well then,' said Isabel, placing her hands on her hips, a

gesture of decision, all uncertainty now fled, 'I should say that's everything.' With one final check that Nora was all right, she called for Evie, and then ushered the rest of them out the back door and along the verandah. When they reached the corner of the house, Isabel turned to her sister-in-law, so very pregnant and pink-cheeked, and someone she had met as a girl of about Matilda's age, and after a moment's hesitation she embraced her. 'I'm glad you came to see us,' Isabel said. 'I'm so very glad we've had this time.'

11

Later, Nora was to wonder whether she'd really seen the flicker of doubt in her sister-in-law's eyes as she said goodbye that morning, but before she could even think to respond, to say that she, too, was delighted to be spending time with her family at Halcyon, Isabel had rallied the children and, with Matilda and Evie carrying a picnic basket each and John the baby's crib, they all waved farewell to Nora and left the garden, the sun beating down on them, so hot and blazing, heading in the direction of the water hole and the big willow tree.

What did they do when they reached the picnic site? Was there an argument as to where, precisely, they should put the tartan picnic blanket? Unlike Isabel, whose English skin remained as pale as paper, the Turner children were as brown as the quandong berries that grew on the bushes along the creek. Did they choose, just to rile their mother, to set themselves up in the sun? Hot from the walk, did John opt to swim before he ate? Did Matilda's queasiness recede? One can only speculate.

What is known is that the thermoses were empty, the sandwiches were gone, and all that remained of the cake was crumbs. Their shoes were off. They had been swimming. The baby's crib had been suspended from a large, strong branch of the willow. Reports from those first on the scene indicate that although lunch had been eaten, the provision boxes had not yet been packed away. There was no sign of illness or disruption. There had been no struggle. To all appearances, it seemed that at some point, whether because a great weariness had overcome them, or a feeling of dizziness, or perhaps just a strange unsettlement, they had lain down together, using rolled-up towels as pillows, and retreated into a sleep from which they would not wake.

Birds flew overhead. Lizards warmed themselves on the hot rocks nearby. Snakes moved in the long, dry grass of the paddock beyond. All around, the noises of Australian summer intensified to form a deeply soporific afternoon soundtrack of crickets purring, leaves whispering, birds chittering in the tops of giant gums. The birds knew, even if most human beings were yet to notice, that there had been a change in the atmosphere around Tambilla that afternoon. Clouds were gathering in the distance, the wind had shifted, a storm was coming.

Not far from the picnic blanket, a colony of ants continued to build their mound: diligent, resourceful, ever busy. They would realize, at some point, that a great boon of crumbs awaited them nearby, and set out to retrieve them. They were at once a vital part, and yet separate from, the human story unfolding on the blanket beside them, their quest for survival no more or less important in nature's eyes than that of any other creature on that blistering afternoon.

As the sun continued its crossing of the cerulean sky, and the shade thrown by the willow tree shifted across the field, down in the township of Tambilla the two local ministers, one Lutheran and the other Anglican, retired to the vestries of their respective churches on diagonal sides of the town's main intersection to finalize their Christmas Eve sermons.

Not too far away, Betty Diamond was busy in the kitchen of her tearoom, swatting flies away with one hand while working her knife deftly with the other: margarine and then curried egg, along a production line of bread, followed by a leaf of iceberg lettuce to each, a second slice of bread, and *voilà* – a tray of sandwiches wrapped in checked seersucker and ready for the reception at St George's that evening. The kitchen always got warm in the afternoons, its only window being on the western wall, but today it was unusually muggy. Betty wasn't sure if it was simply because she'd been working fast, or whether the storm her customers had been speculating about all day was actually going to hit.

Across the street, Meg Summers closed the grocery shop with the satisfaction of a ledger book filled with orders met and deliveries made. The sponge cake for Percy's birthday was finally cool, and she finished it carefully with a layer of fresh whipped cream and some of Maud McKendry's home-grown strawberries. They were Percy's favorite, and a sunnier-than-average spring had made them extra sweet this year.

Up at the old mill, the Misses Edwards were still fast asleep in their twin beds, being of the age and inclination to pass the hottest part of the day slumbering. When they woke and drew back the lace curtains, they would see that their lawn was as neat as could be, the edges trimmed just the way their father – a man of exacting standards – had always demanded.

Henrik Drumming, who had left his wife in the dayroom, where he'd found her, had driven back up Greenhill Road and stopped out the front of the Tambilla Hotel. He wasn't one of the regulars, but he'd felt like company without conversation, so he sat at the bar and ordered a club soda. It was always hard to return to an empty house on the days he'd been to see Eliza. (He was still sitting there, nursing his soda, forty-five minutes later, when a siren flared up over at the police station on West Road, and half an hour after that when the young schoolteacher, Boris Braun, came rushing into the bar to announce that a search party was being put together, shouting something about a baby and some dogs.)

At four o'clock, though, as Henrik cradled his first drink and reflected on his wife and the life they'd once dreamed about and how lonely he'd been without her, down the road Maud McKendry, whose garden was now in full beating sunshine, gathered the last flowers for the church service and arranged them into bunches for the pew ends. Four houses away, young Kitty Landry had already tried on three different dresses before settling on one she considered 'fancy' enough to wear to sing in the church choir that night. As Percy Summers guided his faithful mare Blaze through the gap in the fence at the edge of the Turner property, intending to make a brief stop for the animal to swim, Kitty climbed onto a kitchen chair so she could see most of herself in her mother's duchesse mirror, and was practicing the new hymn with a hairbrush for a microphone, swaying like Peggy Lee, who she'd seen singing 'Fever' on the new television set at her aunty's house in Sydney when they were visiting for Easter.

Up at the Turner house, its iron roof ticking in the heat,

Nora Turner-Bridges wondered when she could expect her family to return. Nora wasn't yet worried, but she was lonely. She had looked forward to having the house to herself; she'd been exhausted by the time they left. But she had failed to sleep. There'd been an ungodly squawking outside her bedroom window, and when she pulled back the curtains, she'd been met with the glassy eye of a colossal black cockatoo in the uppermost branches of the walnut tree. She hadn't liked the way it stared and had redrawn the curtains, allowing the room to darken; her efforts, though, had been in vain.

The warmth of the day was pooling now in the dim corners. The thick stone walls that had held it at bay had reached their limits, but to open the windows would be folly. Nora decided she would fix herself a cool drink and lie down again, just for a few minutes. No doubt that would do the trick – it was Murphy's Law, wasn't it? As soon as she made herself comfortable and started to drift off, she'd hear them coming up the driveway, chatting and laughing, bubbling over with stories of the day's adventure.

PART FIVE

CHAPTER SEVENTEEN

Sydney, 12 December 2018

Jess woke at four on Wednesday morning, thinking about Nora and summer and the scene by the creek. Of big stone houses and paddocks of pale grass and gum trees with tall silver trunks. She was also thinking about poison. The coroner had ruled the tragedy a murder-suicide but, as with the infamous Somerton Man case in 1948, he'd been unable to determine the type of poison used. It seemed to Jess that there'd been several contenders: the mushroom (for presumably that's what it was?) that Evie sourced for Matilda; the rat poison John and Matthew discovered in the pantry (all of that 'sugar' Isabel stirred into the iced tea?); the tranquillisers Henrik Drumming had given Isabel to help her sleep.

Jess didn't know a lot about poisons, but supposed there must be many in nature for which diagnostics hadn't existed in 1959. She could also think of a number of possibilities as to how Isabel might have known about them: her father had been a naturalist and she'd spent much of her childhood cataloguing plants; Miller had included a quote from a former headteacher to the effect that Isabel had excelled at science; and then there was her war work. The conversation with the nondescript woman at the London party around the time of the occupation of France suggested that Isabel had been engaged with the Resistance. Maybe she'd learned about lethal poisons there – how they worked and the best way to administer them without leaving a trace.

Jess googled the University of Sydney, found a professor in the School of Public Health who looked to have suitable research specialties, and then drafted an email explaining that she was a journalist working on a report for which she needed to know what types of poison might have been used lethally but without detection in 1959. Knowing how the murder had been committed wouldn't tell her anything about Nora's recent state of mind, but Jess was curious, and that was a huge improvement on the worry and discombobulation she'd been grappling with lately. Chasing down a lead made her feel more like herself.

It was still pitch-black outside the window, but occasional early birds were making themselves known, and the air had acquired the light thrum of promise that precedes the dawn. Jess was about to close her email and head to the kitchen to make a cup of tea when a new message dropped into her inbox. She didn't recognise the sender's name, Nancy Davis, but the subject, 'Your Request', piqued her interest.

Dear Ms Turner-Bridges,

Ben Schultz forwarded your request on to me. Daniel Miller was my uncle, and I am the executor of his estate. I would be more than happy to help with your inquiries. Please feel free to reach out to me via this email address, or, if you'd like to have a chat, send me a message on the cell phone number below to arrange.

Kind regards,

Nancy

There was a footer beneath the sign-off, with the business name Davis Genealogy Research and Consulting LLC, followed by Nancy's cell phone number, email, and an address in Vermont. Jess checked the world clock on her phone and, seeing that it was still only mid-afternoon in the eastern United States, typed the number into her text message app.

Hi Nancy, she wrote. *Thank you for getting in touch! It would be great to have a chat about your uncle. Please let me know a time that suits. Jess Turner-Bridges*

She read over the message and then, after removing her surname (too formal) and the exclamation point (too frivolous), pressed send and felt the fond, familiar stomach-turn of anticipation.

Her phone pinged almost immediately.

How about now?

Jess typed back quickly: *Great. Give me five minutes and I'll call you.*

She ran downstairs into the dark kitchen, boiled the kettle and dunked a tea bag, all the while sifting through her thoughts to set them in order. She still wanted to know more about how Daniel Miller came to be in South Australia, why he wrote about the Turner family, how he'd conducted his research. But now, having read more of his book, she was also interested in how well he'd known Nora, how often they had spoken.

Jess took her cup of steaming tea back up to her room and sat cross-legged on the floor. In her notebook, she wrote the date at the top of a fresh page, along with 'Interview – Nancy Davis', and underlined both.

Nancy answered on the third ring. 'Jess?'

'Nancy, it's lovely to speak with you. Thank you for getting in touch so quickly.'

'The pleasure is mine.' Her voice was warm, and her accent carried a trace of the South. 'I was surprised to get your message, but very glad. We're proud of my uncle's book in my family. I first read it when I was fourteen years old, and I felt as if the characters in the story – your family – became people I knew. They've been with me all my life and I'm over sixty now. Your email to Ben Schultz said that you were looking for background information. I hope I can help, though I suspect you know the book and its people every bit as well as I do.'

'Actually . . .' Jess hesitated – she was used to asking questions, not answering them – 'I only started reading it for the first time this week. I've just finished Part One.' There was silence at the other end of the line, in which Jess sensed considerable surprise; she felt compelled to explain. 'My grandmother never told me about Halcyon and what happened to her brother's family. She had an idea, I think, that it would be too great a burden to carry. That's why I'm getting in touch – I've got so many questions about the book, but Nora's not able to answer them at the moment. She's in the hospital.'

'I'm so sorry – I hope she's okay?'

'She had a fall, which is worrying at her age, of course, but she's receiving excellent care. She'd been re-reading your uncle's book – that's how I discovered it. I'm a journalist, too, and I was curious about how Daniel Miller – how your uncle – came to write the book. I couldn't find anything useful online.'

'There's very little. Uncle Dan was always modest, turning down publicity requests, saying the book could speak for itself, but I'm happy to help. As I said, we're very proud of him. What was it you wanted to know?'

'How he happened to be in Australia, for starters. How he came across the story in the first place.'

Nancy paused. 'You know,' she said thoughtfully, 'in a way, I've always felt it was because my dad died. I never knew him – my mom was seven months pregnant with me when it happened – but Uncle Dan took his death very hard. They were supposed to be going out of town together that weekend, but Dan had cancelled at the last minute. After Dad's death, he lost his faith; he almost lost his job. He'd been working as a scoop reporter in New York City, filing news stories at a punishing pace, but afterwards, he wanted – needed – his writing to do more. His editor kept hauling him into the office, telling him to pick up the speed and stop trying to find the meaning of life. He became very unhappy and he went off the rails a bit – all-night benders, that sort of thing. My grandparents were very worried about him; they thought they were going to lose a second son.'

Gently, Jess asked: 'How did your father die?'

'Suicide. He'd been a bit depressed, according to my mom, but there was no red flag; he left no note. Uncle Dan couldn't accept that. He searched for answers, tried to solve the mystery, and in the absence of a better option, he blamed himself. Then one morning, after a night of heavy drinking, his father's brother called from Australia. Mike said he'd heard things were a bit rough and that maybe Dan would like to come over for a while.'

'And Mike lived in Tambilla?'

'Near enough. He and his partner Nell – lovely woman – had a small place outside Hahndorf and a caravan at the back of the property that they used for travelling. They told Dan it was his for as long as he wanted it.'

'So he was in the right place at the right time.'

'Sort of. Once he got the idea to leave New York City, Dan moved quickly. He quit his job, sublet his apartment, and was all packed to go when Clay Felker at *Esquire* threw him a line. Have you heard of him?'

Jess had. Clay Felker was a legendary editor, long-time friend of Tom Wolfe and credited with giving Gloria Steinem her first big break as a writer.

'Dan had pitched him the idea of a regular column – dispatch from Down Under, reporter on the road, that sort of thing – and Felker offered him a gig filing two and a half thousand words every fortnight. Uncle Dan started in Sydney, worked his way north all the way to the Top End and then down to Alice Springs. Wrote about whatever struck him on his journey – the laid-back surf culture of Bondi Beach, the spectacular orange and red rock of Katherine Gorge at sunset, incidental things that happened along the way. He was out at Uluru that Christmas and put in a call to his uncle to wish him season's greetings. That's when Mike told him what had been going on in Tambilla. Dan got himself on a train south as quick as you can say "scoop".'

That made sense. Jess could well imagine how an event like the Turner tragedy – a whole family, Christmas Eve, a grand old estate – would have got her professional curiosity firing.

'Have you ever done that journey, the Ghan?' asked Nancy.

Jess admitted that she hadn't. When she added that she'd never seen Uluru, nor set foot in the Territory, she felt a flicker of shame.

'Ah, you must,' Nancy said. 'You haven't lived until you've seen a flock of luminous green-and-yellow budgerigars take off in the vast red outback. Magic.'

'I wondered,' Jess offered, 'when I was reading about Isabel and her feelings of homesickness – her sense that Australia was a beautiful place, but utterly foreign and desperately far away from her own home country – whether that was also your uncle speaking? It seemed to me to have an extra ring of truth to it.'

'I know he was deeply affected by his time there,' said Nancy, considering. 'He used to talk often about Uluru. He met a guy in Alice Springs called Tony whose family had been there since the start of time, who agreed to act as a guide. He took Dan out to the rock and explained it as a church, a holy place. Dan said it had a profound effect on him. Not just Uluru itself, but Tony's connection to his country. He said it was the first time he'd been aware of his own dislocation. He wrote about craving the other man's certainty, his knowledge that he truly belonged exactly where he was.'

Something in Jess, an absence that she hadn't realised was there but could suddenly feel, recognised this state; she thought of the pangs of unnameable melancholy she'd experienced during the years of coming and going, of late nights in airports, of living between landscapes, between cultures. She had considered herself a global citizen, her jet-setting a destination in itself, but what if it weren't? If she were honest, wasn't the love she felt for the sights and sounds of her life in London always experienced at a slight but unbridgeable distance? As if she knew on a cellular level that she didn't truly belong.

Jess shook off the feeling. She didn't have time for navel-gazing. The other woman's admission that Daniel Miller had used some of his own experiences to inform his writing gave her a convenient lead-in to the tricky question of truthfulness and authenticity. 'I'd been wondering how your uncle came to write the book; how he went from being a journalist to an author of . . . well, I suppose it's true crime?'

Nancy laughed. 'He called it a "non-fiction novel". He believed that the tools used by novelists should be available to journalists, too.'

'He fictionalised at times?'

'I wouldn't say that. His aim was to capture the truth, to tell the story, but he didn't much care if he was one hundred per cent accurate as to whether a bird flew overhead at a particular point in time. He couldn't know everything. The fact that Mrs Turner had observed her son John to become 'effervescent' when he was excited was more important to him than whether she reflected on it at the precise moment he records her having such a thought in his book, if you know what I mean.'

Jess considered this. Nancy's description chimed with everything she understood of New Journalism. That Miller was published in the early 1960s helped to explain how a book about the people of a small town in South Australia had reached the top of the *New York Times* bestseller list; it had been carried on a wave of literary fashion. Jess pushed a little harder. 'It sounds like he might have taken some licence?'

'Only of the poetic variety. His concern was to be truthful to the Turners and their story, and I believe that he was. He did an enormous amount of research – his notebooks are full of it – and there was evidence, whether in an interview or a diary entry or a letter, for every claim he made. In fact, he built up so much trust with his subjects that he was able to render important assistance to the police.'

'Really?' Jess put aside the tantalising mention of notebooks for a second to explore this claim. She remembered Mrs Robinson's comment that police had received a consequential tip-off as to Isabel's state of mind. Mrs Robinson had thought it came from a priest, but perhaps it had been delivered via Daniel Miller. 'Did he interview a priest, by any chance?'

'A reverend, yes – Reverend Lawson from the local Anglican church.'

'And Reverend Lawson had information about Isabel's mindset?'

'As you can imagine, in his position he was privy to all sorts of intimate thoughts and feelings; he also kept a fastidious record.'

'A written record?'

Nancy made a small noise of agreement. 'The reverend fancied himself a novelist, so he was extremely eager to talk to Dan, a real-life writer.'

'And your uncle passed what the reverend told him on to the police?'

'Dan came to know the sergeant who headed up the investigation quite well. He had a lucky break there. Sergeant Duke was married to an American woman. Her people came from Atlanta, Georgia – same as my grandparents. She'd been living away from home for the better part of two decades, and once she learned there was a newcomer up in the Hills hailing from her hometown, well, she did what any self-respecting Southern woman would do and insisted he come for dinner. You said you'd finished Part One, I think? Part Two is when the investigation begins. You're about to meet the reverend and Sergeant Duke.'

Jess was only half-listening; she'd been considering how to discern precisely what Daniel Miller had learned from the reverend, when it occurred to her there was a sure-fire way of discovering what he'd discussed with all of his subjects, including, presumably, Nora. 'You mentioned your uncle's notebooks,' she said. 'Are they still around?'

'They are,' Nancy replied. 'I inherited them after he died.' She laughed. 'Let's just say, my uncle was an excellent journalist, but his penmanship left much to be desired. I retired from nursing last year, and along with my genealogy work, I've been spending time going through his notes. You know, I loved my uncle's book when I first read it – was obsessed with it, really – but I can't tell you how much more vivid the world of Tambilla and Halcyon became to me after reading the notebooks – so many extra layers.'

'I'm really interested in how he worked. Can you give me an idea of the notebooks' contents? Are they interview transcripts? Detailed descriptions? Notes to himself?'

'All of the above, and some whole scenes, too – almost like drafts that didn't make the final cut. He seems to have had two ways of working: the first, as you'd probably expect, was formal, in that he would set up an interview and take his notebook with him, full of questions. But where he was most successful, I think, was his informal research. Dan was a humanist. He liked people and he was interested in them. He had the knack of making whomever he was speaking to feel as if he were really listening. More so, that he understood them. His favourite thing to do when he was working was what he called "finding the story". He would arrive without a preconceived notion of what he expected, or even hoped, to hear, and then just strike up a conversation. And for the book – well, he moved into his uncle's old caravan at the back of the block and became something of a local himself. People trusted him, and he grew genuinely fond of them. Mr Drumming, young

Becky Baker, Meg and Percy Summers – Percy was the one who found them, of course, poor man. He moved away in the end. He'd lost his wife by then. Terribly hard on him; he and dear Meg were childhood sweethearts.'

Not for the first time, Jess found herself noting the way Nancy spoke as if she'd known the residents of Tambilla in 1959 personally. She appeared to have an encyclopaedic knowledge of the people and place. How much extra information about Nora and the Turner family must be contained within the notebooks?

'As for Becky,' Nancy was saying, a certain 'memory lane' quality softening her voice, 'I always felt quite sorry for her. I don't know the truth of what happened with the netsuke, but you couldn't blame her for being hurt when Isabel scolded her. And I can only imagine what it must have been like for her to lose the Turner family. She idolised Isabel, and she loved little Thea as if she were her own. She cried and cried when she spoke to my uncle. Awful, loud sobbing. It was very hard to sit through.'

Jess was taken aback at first, and then she realised. 'They're on tape?' she said. 'The interviews were recorded?'

'Not in 1959 – that was a few years too early for him to have been carrying a portable tape recorder – but he went back to Tambilla twenty years later and spoke with some of the townsfolk again.'

'After Thea's remains were found,' Jess said softly.

'That's right. I'm not sure which edition you have there, but from 1980 onwards the book contained a final chapter. It was important to Uncle Dan that it was republished with an addendum, to bring closure to that little baby's story.'

'It must have given him great satisfaction, being able to tie off that thread.'

'You'd think so,' Nancy said musingly, 'but I seem to remember he came home from Australia unsettled. He wrote the final chapter, but he didn't promote the book again and he barely wanted to talk about it, even with family. I guess it brought the whole thing back to mind. Reminded him that he hadn't been able to find answers for the rest of them. No investigator likes to be left with mysteries.'

Jess could agree with that.

'He was glad to return, though,' Nancy said. 'He never forgot them. They were all bonded together. You have to remember, when he met them he was also trying to understand an inexplicable death in his own life. Like them, he was grappling with grief and guilt and the bitter, creeping sense that he might have been able to prevent my dad's death if he'd done things differently. It's devastating to lose someone so close, like losing a part of yourself.'

Jess thought of Nora. Mrs Robinson said she'd loved Isabel like a sister and had suffered her own guilt and grief at not having been able to save her. It struck Jess that Nora and Daniel Miller must have had rather a lot in common. Did that explain the familiar, almost tender way he wrote about her? The scene at the end of Part One, in which Nora was alone at the house, waiting for her family to return, had been very poignant. It seemed to bring the focus back once more to Nora as the human face of an unimaginable loss. The person left behind.

'Your uncle spoke with my grandmother.'

'She was one of his most important sources,' Nancy agreed. 'For all that Isabel had been a well-liked member of the community, Nora was the only person who knew the Turner family intimately and could offer a real insight into who Isabel was.'

'What did she say?'

'At first, she refused to accept that Isabel could have done it. She was convinced that she'd have seen the signs and implored Dan to help her prove her sister-in-law's innocence. As time went on, though, and other possibilities fell away, even she was forced to face the facts. But she refused to condemn Isabel. She kept trying to help Dan see the person beneath the despicable deed. She was a very loyal and loving friend.'

Jess remembered the way her grandmother always took her mother's side if Jess were driven to complain. Even when Nora finally told Jess about the incident when she was a baby, she'd insisted on mounting a defence of her daughter. 'She didn't mean it . . . She didn't know what she was doing . . . Something desperate came over her . . .' It was true what Nancy said: Nora was the very definition of loyal.

And now Jess wanted to do the right thing by her. 'It would be really helpful for me to see the notebooks,' she said. 'Do you think it'd be possible?'

'I'm afraid I can't send them to you,' Nancy said apologetically. 'But I can certainly scan some pages and email them. I have a client meeting in a minute, but I could do it later this afternoon. What are you interested in especially?'

Jess considered. The most pertinent facts had presumably ended up in the book. There was no point doubling up just to assuage her constitutional curiosity. To be honest, Isabel and the story of Halcyon, while fascinating, was a side interest. Her focus had to be on her grandmother, finding out whether there was anything among Daniel Miller's notes that might explain what was troubling her, why she had attempted to climb the stairs to the attic, or why she'd suddenly started worrying about Polly's father appearing out of the blue to claim her. 'Do you think you could send me Nora's interviews?'

'Certainly.'

'And perhaps—' Through the phone, a doorbell rang distantly.

'Oh, shoot,' said Nancy. 'That's my meeting. Listen, I'm going to have to go. I'll send across the scanned pages as soon as I can. But if you think of anything else, just let me know.'

Jess spent a frustrating couple of hours working on her article for the travel magazine. It was not going well, and the more she looked at it, the less she liked what she'd written. She couldn't concentrate. Her thoughts weren't with her in twenty-first century Sydney; they were at Halcyon with Nora, waiting at the house on a hot Christmas Eve afternoon, the town of Tambilla yet to learn of the terrible tragedy that had played out on the banks of the creek on the Turner property.

Also: Nancy kept popping into her head, with her mentions of the Ghan and Uluru, and Jess couldn't shake the sense of herself as a fraud. What business did she have anyway to be writing about this place as home? She'd been away for twenty years. She'd never seen a flock of wild budgies take flight. What did it mean to be *of* rather than merely *from* somewhere?

Jess willed her phone to ping with an incoming email and put her out of her misery. Her conversation with Nancy had told her something of Daniel Miller's process, but it hadn't explained why Nora had pulled his book down off the shelf now.

She was curious, too, about Nancy's claim that her uncle had been instrumental in helping police to solve the crime.

Was it, as Jess suspected, because he'd reported to them whatever it was the reverend had told him?

When she caught herself glancing again at her email (still nothing new), Jess had to accept that she was no longer making progress – good or bad – on her article. With a short sigh of surrender, she put it aside and picked up her copy of *As If They Were Asleep*. Nancy had promised that she was about to meet the reverend . . .

As If They Were Asleep

DANIEL MILLER

PART TWO

12

It had just gone five o'clock when Reverend Ned Lawson finally capped his pen. He had been working on his Christmas Eve message for the past week, hours spent sequestered in the vestry of St George's Anglican church. Now, at last, he was done, and not a moment too soon. Above the door, his clock ticked forward another minute. In half an hour, the church would be overrun with excited children dressed in their festive best.

He had decided to speak this year about John 1:14, picking up on the virtues of grace and truth, and the sometime struggle to embody both at once; theirs was a peaceful town, but there had been an element of disharmony rumbling along beneath the surface lately. He wasn't certain whether it was simply a sign of the times, the modern age speeding things up and setting men's tempers on edge, or whether there were more specific elements at work, but if the conversations he'd had with members of his congregation were any indication, many among them would welcome a soothing remark. Reverend Lawson felt certain that if the right words could be found, he would be able to set things on an even keel.

An ability to find the right words was something Reverend Lawson might have prided himself on, if pride had not been a sin he took great pains to avoid. He enjoyed the performative aspect of his work, but it was here, at his desk, that he felt closest to his purpose. The Lord had given him the gift of wordsmithery, and thus it was his duty to put it to good use. His commitment to writing was one that predated his call to the ministry. No one knew it, but behind the cupboard door, in a neat set of file boxes, was every short story he'd ever written, along with the letters he'd received in return from magazine editors; also, the draft of his current work in progress, a novel in the pulp fiction style of Raymond Chandler. Reverend Lawson pulled the manuscript out in the evenings sometimes, tinkering around the edges while Mrs Lawson was tending to the little Lawsons and he was free to slip across the parking lot to the silent vestry.

At 5:00 p.m. on December 24, though, he was focused only on perfecting the evening's sermon. He had just started reading when a knock came at the vestry door.

'Come in,' he called.

May Landry entered, her high-boned cheeks pinker than usual, shoulders rising and falling as if she'd run all the way from her house on Thiele Street.

'Hello there, May.'

'Oh, Reverend,' she said, still trying to catch her breath. 'Something has happened.'

He looked up over his half glasses.

'At the Wentworth place. Something bad. I was due to collect young Evie Turner – she'd arranged with Kitty to come together to choir rehearsal – but when I got there, why, I could hardly move my car for all the vehicles.'

'Vehicles?'

'Police, ambulances – more than one. Something *very* bad's happened, I'm sure of it.'

Reverend Lawson was already on his feet. He removed his robe, shrugged into his civilian coat, and within minutes was reversing out of the church car park, having given May Landry instructions to welcome the early congregants.

Along the main street, he noticed, the shops had closed; the town was ghostly quiet. He turned into Willner Road and was soon edging his Morris Minor onto the verge near the entrance to the Wentworth place.

Mrs Landry had not been exaggerating. Reverend Lawson counted four ambulances, two police vehicles, and several unmarked cars. His stomach knotted. May was right: something very bad had happened indeed.

He noticed a young police officer walking purposefully along the creek and gathered that whatever it was would be found in that direction. When he opened the car door, he could feel the air moistening, thickening. The weather was coming in. Steeling himself, the reverend crossed the road, unlatched the gate, and started over the fields toward the darkening north.

It was at this point, Reverend Lawson was to tell the police officers who came to visit him in his vestry the following Monday morning, that he had experienced a premonition of what he was going to find.

'Not the specifics,' he hastened to add. 'I couldn't have begun to imagine what I'd see beyond the ridge. But as I drew nearer, a recent conversation came back to me.'

'A conversation with Mrs Turner?'

'I run an open-door at the church – a ready ear, an impartial mind, a loving heart – and my parishioners often arrive seeking counsel. Mrs Turner came to see me some weeks ago, and as I walked across that hill last Thursday, our conversation flooded back with a dreadful sick feeling.'

'What was it that Mrs Turner spoke to you about, Reverend Lawson?'

At this, he balked. 'People talk to me in confidence. I wouldn't normally breathe a word . . .'

'I think we can agree that the circumstances here are not normal.'

Reverend Lawson, remembering what he'd seen beneath the willow, gave a nod. 'She was drawn and tired; it was some weeks after the baby had been born and she said she hadn't been sleeping well. She talked generally for a time, but I could see that something was weighing on her. Finally, she came to the point. She wanted to know what it meant if a woman was driven to do something that meant her children would be left without her. If she was acting in a way that she believed was best for all, was it possible she could still be considered a good mother, even if it meant leaving them behind? I asked her whether she was talking about a brief separation, at which point, she made the strangest sound. Not a laugh exactly, but a dry noise at the back of her throat that startled me somewhat and gave me a cold feeling.'

'Did she answer you?'

'She said, "Not a brief separation, no." She was thinking of something more permanent than that.'

'Did she tell you what she was planning?'

Reverend Lawson shook his head and told them he was

sorry, he could offer no further information, whereupon the policeman who had been asking the questions let out a long sigh.

'Are you sure, Reverend? There isn't anything else you can think of that might help with our inquiries?'

He was sure.

It was only as he lay awake in bed at night, his wife sleeping soundly beside him, or when he found himself alone in the vestry, sharing a quiet moment with his God, that he caught himself scrutinizing the advice he'd given to Mrs Turner that morning.

Knowing that she hailed from England, aware that her husband was away more and more these days, he had assumed that she was lonely, that she was thinking about taking a trip back home, perhaps even a stay of extended duration. 'A woman should be with her children, Mrs Turner,' he had said, in his most reassuring voice. 'She shouldn't leave them behind. Wherever it is she plans to go, and no matter how difficult the logistics might seem, she would be well advised to find a way to take them with her.'

As Reverend Lawson arrived at the awful scene that Christmas Eve, back at the church, Mrs Landry was taking her deputation seriously. Her cheeks were still flushed, but she'd managed by now to catch her breath and had positioned herself at the open front doors of the church, where she was waiting to let the congregants know that the minister had been called away on urgent business and the service would therefore be starting later than planned.

She was half watching Kitty and a couple of the other choir girls who'd been sent along early for rehearsals, agonizing over whether to stop them from climbing on the stone wall, when a hearty voice called out from a distance, 'Hello there, May! The cavalry has arrived!'

May looked up to see Maud McKendry striding along the paved path, arms full of bouquets for the pew ends.

'Oh, Maud,' said May, twisting her lace-gloved hands together with relief. 'Just the person I hoped to see.'

'Why, you're so flushed! Where is Reverend Lawson? What on earth has happened?'

'That's half the worry. I don't know exactly.'

'Tell me what you do know. Quickly now, before anyone else comes along.'

Something maternal in Maud McKendry's stern manner inclined a person to obedience, and accordingly Mrs Landry began to recount what she had seen on her way to church – the ambulances, the police, the absence of Evie Turner. Mrs McKendry maintained an impassive expression, listening through to the very end before nodding sharply. At this point, she turned on her heel, her arms still full of the most beautiful rose bouquets, and began walking at a calm but purposeful pace along the path to the back of the church.

Few people would have felt comfortable entering the sacred space of Reverend Lawson's vestry without invitation, but Mrs McKendry wasted no time in letting herself inside. She set down the flowers, picked up the telephone receiver, and dialed the telephone exchange.

'Marian?' she said, when the call was answered. 'Marian, it's Maud McKendry. Can you put me through to the police station, dear?'

The Tambilla police station is little more than a pair of rooms inside a modest stone building on the corner of West Road. A few stairs at the front lead up to a small landing with a door in the middle, the sign above it reads simply: POLICE. It is a humble repository for law and order, reflecting the community's tendency toward temperance and moderation.

Miss Lucy Finkleton had been due to finish an hour before, but had stayed put when the new sergeant, Liam Kelly, and Constables Doyle and Jerosch leapt into action. She'd been left with a flurry of tasks to accomplish – telephone calls to the police in Adelaide, instructions to the ambulance service – but since then had been at a loss: pacing, peering through the windows, working herself into a state of some agitation as she awaited further word as to what was going on. She wasn't supposed to use the telephone herself for fear of tying up the line, but in truth the need to tell someone what she knew was burning inside her like a fever.

When the telephone began to shrill at ten past six, she darted behind the desk and picked up on the second ring. 'Maud,' she said, when she heard who it was at the other end. The next words tumbled out like convicts relishing release. 'There's been an accident. They all left here in such a hurry. I had no idea what was happening, but I put a call through to Mrs Hughes.'

'Mrs Hughes?' said Maud. Esther Hughes was one of the few townspeople who bore the honor – or ignominy – of having been neither born nor bred in Tambilla. A Sydney-sider who'd 'gone west' to work as a governess on a sheep station out beyond the Darling River, she'd met there a serious young solicitor from Adelaide, entering an earnest and chaste courtship before marrying and moving south. Discretion being central to her nature, she was rarely implicated in any of the happenings of the town, and to hear her mentioned now was a great surprise. 'What on earth does Mrs Hughes have to do with it?'

'It was her husband that telephoned the police. He was one of the first to find them.'

'Them?'

'The Turner family. Mrs Turner and the children. That's what I'm trying to tell you. Oh, Maud, it's ghastly. They're all dead, the lot of them.'

Mrs Landry, who had abandoned her post at the front of the church, was standing at the doorway to the vestry, not yet brave enough to step across the threshold. She watched as Maud lowered the telephone receiver silently back into its cradle and finally, when she could stand the suspense no longer, ventured, 'Well?'

Maud McKendry was staring at the desk, trying to make sense of the shocking news. Being caught short of words was not a condition with which she often suffered, but on this occasion, she was silenced.

'Maud! Please.'

Mrs McKendry took ahold of herself. It was her responsibility, she knew, to pass on what she'd learned.

Mrs Landry's hand leapt to her mouth as she listened, and there it stayed, long after Mrs McKendry had finished.

Like that the pair remained, frozen as still as the wooden figures in the nativity scene at the front of the church. Joyous strains of 'O Come, All Ye Faithful' drifted through the glass doors from the church: the choir were rehearsing for the service, and the heartbreaking wonder of innocent voices raised in song mingled with the horror of the news.

It might have seemed that things could not get worse.

But when the clock had turned a full wretched minute, Mrs Landry remembered. 'Oh my,' she gasped. 'Oh, Maud. Mrs Turner's sister-in-law. I ran into her during the week. She's staying through until she has the baby.'

Maud McKendry sank into the reverend's chair, the full weight of the afternoon's events descending on her. 'That poor woman,' she said. 'What news to receive. And in her delicate condition.'

It was 6:30 p.m., and the first drops of rain had just begun to fall when Sergeant Kelly and Probationary Constable Jerosch knocked on the door of the Turner family home.

Inside, Nora woke from a strange, nonsensical dream to the stifling atmosphere of a summer's day that had lost its light but retained its heat. In the dusky gloaming, it took a moment for her to remember where she was, let alone to realize what had woken her, but then came another knock, and she eased herself from the bed.

As she made her way along the dim landing and carefully down the stairs, she wondered why Isabel and the children were still not back. The house was held in a state of unmistakable quiescence. Bedroom doors stood sullenly ajar, objects maintained the place and posture of that morning's abandonment, lamps and lightbulbs were cold and dull. Through the large window on the landing where the staircase peeled off at right angles to reach the bedroom level, she could see that the weather had come in as forecast. The pewter sky was heavy with intent, and the landscape, the rolling hills, and the silver-trunked gums, already darkened by the dusk, were further smudged by rain's approach.

Beyond the glass panes in the front door, Nora made out two shadowy forms on the porch. She knew at once that it wasn't Isabel or any of the children – there was none of the attendant noise she would have expected from her nieces and nephew – but assumed that the guests were some of the neighbors bringing over a basket of vegetables from their garden, or a home-cooked pie, or a little Christmas cheer. Or perhaps it was a delivery from town, something Isabel had ordered for the dinner and forgotten to mention.

Whatever the case, as she reached the Bessarabian rug at the bottom of the stairs, Nora was experiencing no unsettlement beyond that of being newly awoken and heavily pregnant in a hot climate. Indeed, it was the pregnancy alone that occupied her thoughts as she crossed toward the front door. The baby had shifted into an awkward position over breakfast, one foot stuck beneath her rib, and try as she might, Nora could not get her to budge.

'You might have found a more comfortable position, little one,' she whispered, prodding gently at her rib cage. 'Not even born and you're bending me to your will.'

A big kick came then from the baby, as if in response, and Nora smiled to herself as she opened the door to admit the visitors. She would later recollect that this little back-and-forth with her baby was her last happy moment.

CHAPTER EIGHTEEN

Sydney, 12 December 2018

Jess sat with the book open on her lap, captivated by the image of young Nora sharing communion with baby Polly in her last seconds of innocence.

Miller's final scene drove home the great trauma her grandmother had suffered; the horrific tragedy that had suffused the arrival of her long-awaited child. No wonder it was on her mind now – it had probably never left. The scene also showed the intimate way in which Daniel Miller had come to know his 'characters'. Jess recognised Nora: even the dialogue at the bottom of the staircase felt familiar to her, as something *her* Nora would have said.

Of note, too, was Miller's handling of Reverend Lawson's role in the investigation. The reverend had told police that Mrs Turner came to see him in a poor state – drawn, not sleeping, weighed down with worry, and talking about 'doing something' that would deprive her children of their mother. But he'd held information back in his initial interviews; Miller's book said as much.

For starters, as the book revealed, Reverend Lawson had advised Isabel that, whatever she was planning, she should find a way to take her children with her. Jess was sceptical as to whether that would have been enough for the police to consider the intelligence a breakthrough; it was possible that in 1959, when evidence gathering was comparatively limited, police were more convinced by the oral testimony of close contacts, particularly from a minister of God in a small-town setting. But this was a murder case. One would expect that to find a woman guilty of murder required a significant quantity of proof.

There must have been more to it, something Miller had left out of his book, but which he'd taken to police – to Sergeant Duke, whom Nancy said he'd come to know well. Maybe Miller had even convinced the reverend to give evidence at the inquest. According to the internet, the coroner had suppressed the vital testimony; it wasn't hard to imagine that such an arrangement might have been struck on account of a clergyman being reluctant to be seen to divulge his parishioners' confessions.

Jess thought of the notebooks. Nancy's doorbell had rung before she could ask her to include copies of Miller's interviews with Reverend Lawson. She considered ringing back now, but a glance at the world clock on her phone told her it was after business hours in Vermont. She fired off a quick text instead.

Hi Nancy, just wondering whether you'd mind having a look for interviews with the reverend, too? Thanks so much – I really appreciate your help.

As she was pressing send, the reminder to call Polly appeared on her phone screen. Jess sighed. The conversation was going to require a gear shift, but she would simply keep to the basics: apologise for not ringing sooner, give an update on the patient, and suggest that Polly come down for a visit and a 'proper catch-up' when Nora was out of hospital.

The phone had locked while Jess was thinking, and a new notification now appeared on the home screen. An email

from Nancy. Jess opened it, noting the attachment at the
bottom. The message read:

> *Dear Jess,*
>
> *Please find attached, as promised, pages scanned from
> various points within the 'Tambilla Notebooks'. As I
> mentioned on the phone, my uncle spent a great deal of
> time speaking with Nora. Quite aside from the project he
> was working on, they became friendly. They were a support
> to one another, I think, both having lost someone close.*
>
> *My assumption, based on how the research presents, is
> that he met with her on many occasions, most of them
> without a notebook. From what I can gather, his practice
> was then to write up his memories of the conversation, his
> observations and impressions, when he returned home, in
> the form of scenes.*
>
> *I'm not sure whether he planned or contemplated
> including them in the book, or whether it just became a
> useful way to synthesise information and build his narrative
> (even if only in his own mind), but regardless, I hope the
> pages help and look forward to speaking soon.*
>
> *Wishing your grandmother a speedy recovery,*
> *Nancy*
>
> *PS Just saw your message about the reverend. Will
> have a look, but I seem to remember Dan saying their
> conversations were 'off the record' due to clergy privilege.*

Jess opened the attachment and found thirty-three scanned
pages of fine-lined paper covered with tiny handwritten
scrawl. Too hard to read on her screen, she decided, and sent
the document to the printer instead.

The day outside was beautiful and Jess felt the restless excitement of someone on the brink of a possible discovery. She determined to sit in the garden, and with the pages tucked beneath her arm and a pen in her pocket stepped out into the sunshine, crunching across the gravel of the turning circle.

The phone in the house started to ring as Jess reached the edge of the tropical garden. She considered running back to get it, but in the end decided to let it go. It would be one of Nora's friends and they would leave a message or call back.

When it began to ring again a few minutes later, Jess didn't hear it; she had already reached the garden seat overlooking the harbour. The air was filled with the fragrance of star jasmine and the bell-like music of magpie morning song. A shiver passed through her body. It was the strangest sensation: when she was a child, they'd have said someone was walking over her grave. Now, though, she recognised it as an instinctive sense that something momentous had just happened.

Or was about to. Without another moment's hesitation, Jess opened Miller's notes, oblivious to the fact that deep inside Nora's beloved house, the phone was ringing yet again.

PART SIX

CHAPTER NINETEEN

Brisbane, Queensland, 12 December 2018

Polly was in the kitchen when the phone started ringing on Wednesday morning. She had been standing with her favourite straw hat in hand, wondering whether to brave the sultry summer heat and walk up to the shops for a piece of fish to fry for dinner, or whether it was just too hot, and she'd do better to abandon the morning's plan and wait instead until the afternoon shade came over and she could raid the garden for salad ingredients.

The phone, when it shrilled on the wall, had surprised her. Her palm leapt to her chest in apprehension and her breath caught in her throat. Or had it? Perhaps it was only afterwards, when she looked back on the day's events, that she imbued her remembered self with the gift of presentiment. Because the news that came with the phone call had been momentous. Nora was dead. It had happened thirty minutes earlier; there'd been nothing they could do to save her.

Standing by the big windows that overlooked the steep, leafy Paddington valley, Polly had been vaguely aware that she was saying things, listening and responding, thanking the person at the other end for everything they'd done. She returned the telephone receiver to its cradle and let the air within the room settle around her.

She was motherless. Nora was gone.

'It's all right,' Polly said softly. 'Everything's going to be all right.'

The structure of the day disintegrated after that. The question of dinner forgotten, Polly passed an hour or so in drifting. She found herself in one room after another, sitting first here and then there, straightening cushions and adjusting potted plants, making a cup of tea and then leaving it on the kitchen bench.

It had all happened so quickly; she'd only learned yesterday that Nora was in the hospital. Janey had let her know. No-nonsense, reliable Janey Robinson, Nora's housekeeper, her tone so calm and matter-of-fact that before Polly could register how unusual it was to hear the other woman's voice at the end of the phone line, she'd delivered two pieces of news, each of which alone would have been enough to cause dislocation: Nora was in the hospital and Jess was back from London. And then she'd said something that had thrown Polly even further: 'Jess has been asking about the business at Halcyon.'

It was this piece of information that Polly thought of now. She was standing in the doorway to the second bedroom of her modest worker's cottage, looking at the single bed she'd made up the day before when she learned that Jess was in Australia. A silly, sentimental thing to have done: Jess never came north to Brisbane on her trips back home; she stayed in Sydney. Truthfully, Polly had felt embarrassed the last time Jess came to stay. Not because she was ashamed of her house, which suited her very well, but *because* it suited her so well. Through her daughter's eyes, she could see how ordinary her life was. How little she had aspired to and how little she had achieved. More perplexing, how little it had taken to satisfy her in the end.

But: the business at Halcyon. How strange that Jess should be asking about it all again. She had first mentioned the house after the funeral and wake for Thomas Turner, when they were walking home together along the water's edge. Polly had stopped on the shoreline, her thoughts focused on the move she was planning, away from Sydney, away from Nora, away from the ties of the past, and Jess had come and slipped a hand into hers (the way it had fit so perfectly! Polly had always been amazed and gratified by that fit) and asked, as a boat out on the horizon appeared to levitate, 'What is Halcyon?'

Polly had been struck just as surely as if someone had fired a bullet nearby. She'd managed to say something – it was a house in the middle of nowhere, far, far away – but Jess was bright, and she'd pieced together a picture pretty quickly: Nora's sorrow, her fierce desire to sell the property. 'Was it her brother's house?' she'd asked, and Polly had agreed that it was, but she hadn't expanded. There'd been no need to say any more. Jess had been satisfied with the suggestion that Nora's grief rendered her brother's house something to be erased from memory, to be got rid of 'at once'. The truth, of course, had been more complicated.

Polly's mother had told her about the terrible event ten years before that day on the shoreline with Jess. Nora had relayed the story under duress and with a clear directive at the end that it was something they would not speak of again. It had been an inclement Sunday afternoon in January 1978, and they'd met in the library at Darling House to have tea. It was a relatively new mother–daughter ritual Nora had instigated when Polly started university the year before. Mrs Robinson was even roped into serving, purely for fun, as if they were fancy ladies at a posh London hotel. This particular afternoon, Polly had been anxious but determined to hide it. She'd changed her outfit several times and paid extra attention to her hair; she'd wanted to look older, more sure of herself.

For as long as she could remember she'd been nervy, even as a child. 'You're sensitive,' her mother used to say whenever Polly called out in the night or cried for fear of the dark or froze on the first day of a new school year. 'It's not your fault, just something in the way you were built.' Polly always felt strange when her mother said things like that; as if she hadn't been born in the usual way but had been put together in a workshop by a less-than-kindly stranger. That was her imagination running away from her. Another of her foibles. 'Such fancies,' Nora would say, clicking her tongue fondly and stroking Polly's head.

But today Polly was determined not to give her mother a chance to click her tongue. She had something important to say and she didn't want anything to knock her off course. She'd debated whether to wait until after they'd had their tea, but knew that if she left it too long she'd lose what little courage she'd gathered. And so, when Mrs Robinson was still in the kitchen, she said, 'I have news,' and the fingers of her right hand found the piece of jewellery on her left, a fine band of white gold with six delicate diamonds inlaid, turning it backwards and forwards.

Nora had been stunned. 'Engaged? But you hardly know him.'

'I know that I love him.'

'Love! Oh, Polly—'

'And he loves me.'

They had met at the University of Sydney a couple of months earlier. November, and she'd been reaching the end of her first year; the jacarandas were in full, purple bloom. She'd had car trouble on the way to the campus and been late for her Intro to English Literature class. She was so embarrassed at having to let herself into the full-to-brimming lecture theatre, spot her friend Diane waving at her from the middle of a distant row, and make her way up the centre stairs, that she didn't realise they had a guest lecturer until she was in her seat. Polly was still hunting through her book bag for a pen when the unexpected accent caught her attention.

He was a doctoral student, he said, visiting from Harvard, and his name was Jonathan James. His lecture had been a passionate argument that a thousand years of English literature could be read as an ongoing attempt to understand the eternally vexed relationship between civilisation and the wilderness. He took them on a journey from the primal fears of *Beowulf*, through the chivalric values of *Sir Gawain and the Green Knight*, the mock-heroic *Rape of the Lock* and the travels of Gulliver, the turbulence of *Frankenstein* and *Wuthering Heights*, to arrive finally at the fin de siècle Gothic wilderness-within of Jekyll and Hyde and Dracula. Polly felt that a light had been lit beneath everything she thought she knew about the world – humanity, literature, nature – and by its brilliance she glimpsed, in previously dark places, new connections and possibilities within herself.

Afterwards, she fussed with her books and fumbled her pens into her pencil box with such painful slowness that Diane grew tired of waiting and said she'd catch up with her in the cafeteria. When at last Polly started making her way down the stairs, she was one of the few remaining students in the theatre. She stopped at the lectern, her heart hammering against her ribs, certain that surely he must hear it, too. 'I liked what you said,' she managed. It was not a particularly clever offering, but this was new territory. She was not the sort of person who spoke to good-looking young American lecturers. His eyes were hazel, green-flecked, she noted.

Polly had read in books about people feeling themselves to be in a dream. Never in her life had she experienced the sensation herself, until now. Somehow, without effort or awareness, they fell into conversation, walking together out of the lecture theatre, beneath the cloister that ran the full length of the quadrangle, into the clear, warm day. They found a shaded spot on the main lawn, beneath a jacaranda, and didn't stop talking. She was no longer the shy girl her schoolmates had teased or ignored; conversation came naturally, he laughed easily, they ranked their five favourite Keats poems, agreeing to tie 'Bright Star' and 'To Autumn' for the top spot. Flowers rained down as the light breeze set them free, surrounding them in a purple haze. 'La Belle Dame,' he said softly, reaching to take a bloom from her hair. His expression was serious, his keen eyes studying hers. '*Full beautiful – a faery's child.* Have mercy on me.' Polly felt something turn deep inside her, like a key in a lock, and knew that there was no way back from here.

'I love him,' she said again, firmer this time, resolute.

'You're eighteen years old,' Nora replied with a flicker of her eyelids. 'Of course you're in love. That doesn't mean you should make hasty decisions. How does his father feel about him staying on in Sydney?'

His father was a United States senator, famous for his strong Christian values and handsome family. 'The Conservative Kennedy Clan' was a common media refrain when referencing his devoted wife, four adult sons, and sixteen-year-old daughter.

Polly hesitated. She hadn't planned on going into detail at this point, but she had no knack for dissembling. 'He's not staying here.'

'Then you're going to have a very difficult time of it. Long-distance relationships are—' Nora stopped short and Polly realised how seldom she saw her mother genuinely flustered. 'You can't mean to tell me that you're thinking of going with him to America? To live?'

Polly couldn't bring herself to agree, but her mother's face showed that she understood. Nora looked shaken, almost panicked.

'No. It's unthinkable. You're only eighteen years old, still a child. What about your degree?'

'He's going to help me transfer.'

'But, Polly, a life like that. All of the attention. How will you cope?'

'I'll be fine.'

'What about your health? You've always been fragile. My goodness, the worry I have for you – if only you knew!'

Polly did know. Her mother had been a constant presence in her childhood, watching closely whenever she attempted anything new. 'Please be careful,' Nora would say, and: 'Are you sure you wouldn't like to do something inside instead?' No doubt she'd just been mirroring Polly's own anxiety. She had been a nervous little girl, always imagining the worst, anticipating danger before it had a chance to surprise her, agonising about the world and her place in it. But she was older now; she had learned to manage. 'I'm stronger than you think,' she said.

'You have a support system here, people who love you. With one phone call, I can have an appointment for you with the top specialist in the country. Over there, you'd be all alone.'

'I met his parents when they were here for Christmas, and his sister. He has a huge family.'

As soon as she said it, Polly wanted to call back the words. A huge family was her mother's greatest dream, the lack of it her biggest lament. 'Of course, you'll come and visit,' she said quickly. 'Jon knows how important you are to me. His family will become yours too – the big family you always wanted!'

Nora sighed, and Polly wondered whether she was starting to come around.

'It will work,' Polly said vehemently. 'I know it will.'

Still her mother didn't answer.

'Mum?'

Polly watched as Nora went to the large window that overlooked the garden. There, she stood for what felt like an eternity, her arms crossed, her head bowed. Polly waited, daring to hope that her mother was on the verge of accepting the inevitability of her news. But when Nora finally turned, her expression was troubled. 'Come,' she said, gesturing with her hand as she returned to the sofa. 'There's something I need to tell you.'

'What is it?'

Nora reached for the silver box on the drinks table, took out a cigarette and lit it. This was of grave concern. Her mother did not smoke – she hated the habit, calling it a weak, self-loathing impulse. The match fizzed as Nora shook out the surplus flame. Her hands, Polly noticed, were quivering.

'What I am going to tell you,' Nora began, 'is a shameful family secret. I would have preferred to spare you from it – God knows I've tried – but I see no choice now. I know you're very keen on this young man; I've seen you together and I was young once myself. But when you talk about marriage . . . Well, before you make a decision like that, you should know the truth.' She drew on her cigarette and exhaled a stream of smoke, and then she began to speak, about her brother, Thomas, and the sister-in-law, Isabel, whom she had adored, and a brood of happy children in a big country house in the hills of South Australia. All of it was news to Polly, and she listened with great surprise and interest, until at length the story took a sharp turn. Her mother was talking about a picnic and the police and the storm that followed, and Polly wanted to press her hands against her ears to stop from hearing any more.

When at last Nora finished, she seemed spent. It was as if reliving the events by putting them into words and speaking them into the familiar room had wrung every last bit of energy from her. Polly also sat in silence. The things she'd heard had stunned her. The story was impossible to comprehend.

Mrs Robinson appeared then, carrying the tray of tea. 'Sorry to take so long,' she said. 'We had a delivery at the front door and a possum in the kitchen, if you can believe it. Cheeky thing.'

'Never mind, Jane, we've been busy here,' Nora said. 'We'll pour for ourselves.'

It was impossible not to pick up on the atmosphere in the room, and Mrs Robinson gave a polite, serious nod, setting down the tray and telling Nora to call out if she needed anything further.

Nora turned to Polly. 'So you see,' she said, 'why you can't possibly marry a man like him, a family like his.'

Polly was shaking her head, still trying to understand

what she'd heard, to grasp all of the ways in which it affected things. 'He won't care,' she said eventually, but even she could hear the hint of doubt that had crept into her voice.

'Not at first, perhaps, but in time.'

'He loves me.'

'How will he feel when your secret ruins his father? Blood is thicker than water, you know.' When Polly didn't answer – couldn't answer – Nora continued. 'I don't doubt that he loves you, Polly. The question is whether you love him enough to spare him from having to make that choice. One thing is certain: if you marry into a family like that, you will become a target. The press will dig into your history, and they'll find out. What do you think it would do to his father politically to have a daughter-in-law – the mother of his grandchildren, potentially – whose aunt was a' – she lowered her voice, and the word came out as a hiss – 'a *murderer*? It would ruin him. It would ruin all of you.'

CHAPTER TWENTY

A *murderer*. Even now, forty years later, sitting on the edge of the bed she'd made up for Jess, Polly felt the same kick of physical shock she'd experienced when her mother spoke the word that day. *Murderer*. It rolled around the room, echoing against the skirting boards, pooling in the corners.

'Maybe they won't find out?' she'd said. 'It was almost twenty years ago. I can't imagine the American media pay much attention to events over here.'

'I wish that were true,' Nora had answered, 'and perhaps it is generally. But in this case, news travelled. There was a book, you see. A very successful book, written by a journalist who happened to be visiting Australia at the time. It was a *New York Times* bestseller, all about the police investigation, the inquest, the crime itself.'

Polly had been defiant at first. She told her mother – she told herself – that she could hardly be held responsible for the actions of a woman who'd died before she was born, to whom she was related only by marriage. But that word changed things.

Murderer.

She'd broken things off with Jon. She'd said all the things her mother had suggested – that she wasn't ready, that she was too young, that she'd made a mistake – and then she'd given him back the ring.

She had never forgotten the look on his face. 'Tell me you don't love me,' he'd said.

She hadn't answered.

'Tell me you don't love me,' he'd said again, his voice a little less certain.

Polly closed her eyes tightly. It had been awful.

It took a moment for the colours of the room to normalise when she opened them again. The wooden boards ran horizontally in here; it had been a verandah once, enclosed some decades before. She'd painted the walls with glossy turquoise paint that had faded over time to a powdery hue. Outside, the morning magpies were carolling to one another across the valley. Polly loved that sound. Through the bank of louvre windows she could see the garden estate of Government House with its army of tall gums, the view partially blocked by the foliage of a large jacaranda that she'd been advised on more than one occasion to cut down to allow more light but had stubbornly retained. Once a year, like clockwork, the scene appeared: a mass of purple crepe against the crystal-blue sky, the dark summer storm clouds, confetti on the gravel. *Full beautiful – a faery's child. Have mercy on me.*

Polly glanced away. On the wall directly in front of her was one of her own paintings. She was not a great painter, but she loved the process and had become friendly with the small class she'd joined ten years before. She liked to paint pictures of rooms. Rooms through open doors. Beneath the painting was a Victorian highchair she'd bought when Jess was small and never been able to bring herself to give away. Polly liked the way old things looked. She found their small signs of damage reassuring: the scratches, the imprints from long-ago pens, the flaking paint. They understood that everybody had their bruised edges and private pasts.

She had seen Jon in the news occasionally over the years that followed. In relation to his father at first, and then, as his writing career took off, whenever he was promoting a new book. There'd been a photo spread in one of the women's magazines at some point; she'd pored over it, drinking in every detail. His wife and his children, all of them so good-looking. Polly had been alone by then, up in Brisbane, Jess back in Sydney with Nora, and she'd allowed herself the indulgence of despair. Nora had always taken a dim view of wallowing, but Polly had surrendered to it.

Her fingers went unthinkingly to the pendant on her chain, even as she reminded herself not to be melodramatic, that she had been the one to break it off with him. She could have told him the truth; maybe she should have. There was every chance he'd have taken her hands and said it didn't matter to him one whit, that he loved her anyway and they'd find a way through. Nora had anticipated as much. 'He'll tell you that Isabel's actions don't have any bearing on you,' she'd said the night before Polly was due to speak with him, as they sat together at the table in the kitchen of Darling House. Polly had found herself looking up at the portrait of her mother when she was young and wondering what it must have felt like to be so self-possessed. 'And for a time that might be true. But he'll carry the knowledge with him. You'll think everything's fine, and then one day you'll have a baby – trust me, having a baby changes things – and he'll look at you and it will be there in his eyes.'

Murderer.

Polly stood. The morning sun was high in the sky now and the roofing iron was expanding. A breath of warm muggy air came through the open window, laced with the ripe fragrance of star jasmine. Every summer, the humidity of

Brisbane was a shock. 'Welcome to the subtropics,' her neighbour Angie had said back when she first remarked upon it, chatting across the paling fence that ran between their houses, and then, gesturing towards her own swollen belly, 'Be grateful you're not pregnant with it.'

Angie had been digging. The speculative way she'd looked at Polly when she commented had made that clear. Perhaps she'd noticed the highchair when Polly moved in. Polly had only smiled without offering any further details.

She'd found out she was pregnant two weeks after Jon left for America. She'd been frightened to tell her mother. She'd felt so stupid and blighted. But in the end, Nora had surprised her. After she recovered from the shock, she'd been elated. 'But how could you have thought I'd be anything other than delighted?' she'd said, wrapping Polly in an embrace, stroking her hair. 'Babies are a blessing, no matter the circumstances.'

And while Polly was at a complete loss, Nora had known exactly what to do. She'd swept into action, buying vitamins and booking an appointment for Polly with a doctor friend of hers. 'Dr Bruce is the best. He's the one who helped me when I was pregnant with you.'

It was in Dr Bruce's chilly rooms, as Polly lay rigid beneath the stiff sheet within the curtain-lined cubicle, and Dr Bruce asked quietly after 'the father', that she first heard Nora match his low voice and say, 'Unknown, I'm afraid.'

The coldness of the lie had struck Polly hard. She reasoned that her mother was simply being discreet; there was no reason to share all of the private details with her doctor. Later, though, when Polly was wondering what she should write to Jon about the baby, Nora had looked aghast. 'Why on earth would you even consider it? Don't tell him anything – and later, tell your child you don't know who the father is. It's far safer that way. You'll never have to share her.' (Nora had been convinced from the start that the baby would be a daughter.)

Polly hadn't wanted to lie about the father. She didn't want her baby to think she didn't know who he was. It seemed a gross betrayal of the truth. She was angry with Nora for suggesting it, and hurt by the implication of promiscuity and carelessness. She was frustrated, too, because the more she cogitated on it in the dark of night, the more she saw that the reasoning behind the idea held some merit – if you looked at it in just the right way.

There was a lot of time to ruminate that summer. As the heat dragged on outside, Polly stayed in bed. 'It's not your fault,' Nora had soothed as Polly struggled to keep down her food. 'Some people are built for pregnancy, others aren't. I had a miserable time, too. You'll feel better soon.'

Not soon enough. In February, Polly realised she had no choice but to defer her return to uni. The nausea was constant. She struggled to stay upright. There was no way she could haul herself to lectures, let alone concentrate on her studies. Everything made her sad; she worried that the baby would be born sad.

Nora began to worry, too. She cut back on her work and social commitments, dedicating herself to Polly's care. During the day, she hovered; in the evenings, she positioned herself in the armchair in the corner of the room and made bright one-sided conversation about people she knew from her work, girls Polly had gone to school with – all moving ahead with their lives – and gossip from the neighbourhood. But the one topic in which Polly was interested, Nora refused to broach. Polly had found her thoughts returning again and again during those interminable weeks of confinement to Halcyon. To Isabel in particular: a woman so bereft, so out of place and distressed, that she could take her own life and that of her children. The story had become the locus for her own tragic narrative, and she wanted to know every detail.

Finally, sometime in April, Polly started to feel less bilious, and her thinking became more focused. But far from stepping back, Nora's attention tightened: she watched what Polly ate, she made sure Polly undertook no risky activities (like walking down the stairs too quickly), and she entreated her constantly to stay calm, relaxed, happy. Polly began to chafe. And then one day an idea came to her, a small act of defiance. She convinced Nora to drive her to the university library to return a couple of borrowings, and while she was there asked one of the librarians how she could go about finding a particular book – title unknown – about a real-life crime investigation. The librarian, who said she liked a challenge, had taken a list of the scant information Polly had – the name 'Thomas Turner', the approximate publication date, the fact that the journalist was American and the publication a commercial success – and promised to do what she could. A fortnight later, Polly received a message that the book had been found and requested from an interstate library and was now awaiting collection at the front desk.

A sudden thought sent Polly to her feet. She went quickly to the shelves that ran the length of her sitting room wall. She was sure she'd seen her copy of Daniel Miller's book recently. It was easy enough to spot among the rest; the spine still bore its library classification sticker. She hadn't been able to bring herself to return it; in the end, she'd pretended it was lost and paid the fine.

Tucked away at Darling House, Polly had devoured *As If They Were Asleep*. She'd had to be careful; Nora was everywhere. But the illicit nature of her reading made the experience more intense. The weave of Halcyon was shot through with threads of pregnancy and babies and summer and heat, of long days and twisted dreams, of her life and theirs, of now and then. She thought of that period in her life as 'the Halcyon summer', even though the months had leached into autumn.

One of the strangest aspects of reading the book had been experiencing her mother as a character – herself, too, as the baby born to 'Mrs Turner-Bridges' on Christmas Eve. In various scenes Daniel Miller described Nora with her baby – at the community meeting held by police or in the main street of Tambilla, taking her first tentative steps back into 'normal life' after the tragedy that had befallen her family. This Nora was younger and less experienced than the woman Polly knew, but still quite recognisable. Daniel Miller had captured her as the perfect, attentive, 'good' mother, in contrast, presumably, to Isabel. Polly could remember lingering on those passages when she first read the book, her own baby starting to move in her belly, hoping against hope that she, too, would be a good mother. But she'd had her doubts even then.

When she started to dream about Halcyon, Polly was dismayed to find that it wasn't her mother whose part her unconscious mind took, but Isabel's. She would wake in the mornings, having visited the house in her dreams, briefly certain that were she to look from the window she would see paddocks and roses and cockatoos in a walnut tree, instead of Sydney Harbour. She told Dr Bruce that she was having vivid dreams, but he didn't ask what they were about, saying only that it was normal to experience 'excitement' during pregnancy and murmuring something about hormones.

She wondered what was wrong with her, to feel any sort of empathy for someone like Isabel. To feel lonely and isolated, almost homesick, even though she was in her own home. Was that the fault of hormones, too? Nora had been right to warn her against telling Jon. Perhaps she was like this mysterious aunt in some way; maybe Nora had perceived it? Polly had so many questions, but Nora was resolute. She didn't want to talk about it.

Polly recognised the familiar yellow spine with its library classification and slid the book from the shelf. It was a stylistic cover: of its era, with a sixties font declaring just the title and the author's name. But in its simplicity, Polly felt that she could glimpse Daniel Miller's decency, the authenticity of his approach. He hadn't sensationalised events; his affection for his characters had been evident as he sought to show the ways in which a shocking event leaves its mark on everyone, individually and as a community. She still thought sometimes about Percy Summers, the man who'd found the bodies and whose comment to police – that the family had looked 'as if they were asleep' – had given Daniel Miller's book its title.

Polly had met the author once. He'd come to visit her mother at Darling House around the time of Jess's first birthday. Nora had been quiet all morning, and when the doorbell rang, Mrs Robinson went quickly to answer it. 'Daniel Miller is here,' she'd said, hurrying into the room off the kitchen where Nora was playing with baby Jess. Polly had been sitting on the carpet with them; the shock of the name, the illicit nature of its familiarity had made her skin heat.

'An old friend,' was all Nora said by way of explanation. 'Passing through Sydney.' And then she disappeared into the hall and up the stairs to the library, taking Daniel Miller with her and closing the door behind them.

They were in the library for over an hour, and by the time they emerged Polly had taken Jess out into the garden. She was sitting on the stone edge of the pond when the front door opened and Daniel Miller appeared: a well-preserved fifty-year-old with dark hair and a leather jacket, carrying a large satchel over his shoulder. He was wearing jeans and boots and was taller than Nora, who followed him out; there was an unmistakably American manner in the way he held himself. They spoke for a short time, and then Nora seemed to remember something, hurrying back inside the house, leaving the door ajar.

Daniel Miller, alone on the gravel turning circle, surveyed the garden and then walked across the lawn towards the harbour view. He was almost at the pond before he noticed Polly. 'Oh, hello there. I didn't mean to sneak up on you. I'm Daniel.' He extended his hand.

'Polly,' she said, dusting her own on her jeans. 'Nora's daughter.'

His expression seemed to change then, and she felt as if he were studying her face. Recognition lit his eyes.

'You're American,' she said, not knowing what else to say. She couldn't admit she'd read the book; that would be a betrayal of Nora's trust.

'I am. But I spend a lot of time in Australia. I have family here.'

'In Sydney?'

'In South Australia.'

Polly waited, hoping he would say more. When he didn't, she ventured, 'My mother used to have family down there, too.'

Daniel Miller smiled but didn't take the bait. 'This is a beautiful home,' he said, shifting his gaze to take in the water view. 'It must have been a nice place to grow up.'

Disappointed, but not surprised, Polly said neutrally, 'It was. It is.'

Jess had crawled back around from the other side of the pond. It was getting close to her lunchtime, and she knew it.

'Hello, who's this?' said Daniel Miller, laughing as she grabbed at his trouser leg, pulling herself up to stand.

Polly gathered her daughter in her arms. 'This is Jessica.'

'Hello, Jessica,' said Daniel Miller. 'What a sweet little baby.' His eyes met Polly's again. They were dark brown – kind and insightful. She liked him, she realised. She could see why he was good at his job. She could imagine him being the sort of person in whom people would happily confide. 'You both live here with Nora?' he asked.

Not that it was any of his business. Polly nodded.

'That's nice. Three generations together. Must be good to have your mom on hand to help.' His brow furrowed slightly, as if he were deciding whether to continue, and then: 'I knew her when you were small. She doted on you.'

'Yeah, she's great,' Polly agreed, but the comment was lost as Nora re-emerged from the house and Daniel Miller turned to answer her call with a wave.

He smiled at Polly. 'Well,' he said, 'it was good to meet you'; and to Jess, 'You too, little one.' And then he bid them both farewell and started back up the hill to where Nora was waiting. He cast a final glance over his shoulder as he neared the crest, and Polly, who'd been watching him retreat, lifted a hand to wave. Jess mimicked her before remembering she was hungry and starting to grizzle, and Polly experienced the same surge of panic she always did when Jess began to cry.

This was the point at which Nora usually swept in and Polly realised that whatever it was she'd thought to do in response had been wrong. But Nora wasn't there to fix things, so Polly started to sing 'The Grand Old Duke of York' – Jess's favourite – and they headed back to the house.

She took the path through Nora's special garden because Jess always calmed down when she had the chance to grab at the star jasmine tendrils in the arbour, and that's how she arrived near the spot where Daniel Miller's car was parked. He hadn't left yet, but was standing by the driver's-side door, talking with Nora. Polly paused as Jess reached in wonder for a leafy vine.

Something was wrong. Nora had her face in her hands, her shoulders hunched. She was speaking, shaking her head, and then, suddenly, she clutched at Daniel Miller's arm, looking up to meet his eyes. They stayed like that for what seemed an eternity but was probably no more than five seconds, until finally he shifted forward to enclose her in an embrace . . .

Polly slid the book back into place on the shelf. Even now, the memory of that moment made her uncomfortable. In part, it was the dissonance of what she'd seen. The gesture had been close, almost tender, but from where she'd stood, it had seemed to Polly that Daniel Miller's expression had been stony.

She had hoped that her mother would tell her about his visit that evening, but Nora had been more withdrawn than usual: pale and preoccupied. Thinking about Isabel and the children, Polly supposed, and her brother, Thomas, all of the loss.

Late that night, Polly had found Nora watching over Jess's cot. Even in the half-light, Polly had been able to see that the look on her face as she gazed down at the sleeping baby was of fervent love and concern. She heard Polly and looked up.

'Who was that man who came to see you today?' Polly asked.

'I told you – someone I used to know a long time ago.'

'Visiting from America?'

'Yes.'

'Nice that he could come to say hello.'

Nora nodded but said no more, and Polly joined her beside the cot. Together they stood, looking down at Jess's sleep-pinked cheeks, her baby lips pursed ripely, until at last Nora spoke. 'She can never know.' Her voice was very quiet. 'Promise me you'll never tell her what happened in South Australia, to my brother's family. A thing like that – it taints a person, a family. Promise me you'll never tell our girl.'

Polly went back to the kitchen and found her cup of tea sitting where she'd left it an hour ago. She took a sip, but it was cold. She started making another, but when she went to get the milk, her eyes alit upon the bottle of Corona standing on the top shelf. It was a new habit, and one she'd been enjoying very much over the summer. On hot afternoons, she took a cold beer from the fridge, put a wedge of lime in the top, and drank it outside in the garden, straight from the bottle.

She glanced at the clock. Nowhere near midday, but on the day one's mother died, she supposed it was close enough.

Beer in hand, she wandered the narrow paths within the dense garden. She had planted it herself. There'd been nothing but long grass and a rusted car body when she moved into the house thirty-odd years ago. It surprised Polly sometimes how willing things were to grow. The roses in the old claw-footed bathtub were doing very well this year. They shouldn't be doing well, not in this climate, but Polly had always had luck with roses. It seemed she was better at raising plants than people.

Nora had promised her she'd improve as a mother, but Polly had been nervous, worried that she'd do things the wrong way, and perhaps Jess picked up on it, because she was a fractious baby, until Nora came along and put her in a special hold and rocked her back to sleep. It was only when they moved into the flat that Polly had started to find her feet. Things had got better then, as Jess grew out of being a baby and into being a little person. She had been a delightful child: bright and challenging, full of questions and opinions and eminently sensible ideas. Sometimes Polly thought those had been her happiest years: just the two of them in the Art Deco apartment at the top of the promontory near the playground.

Jess. Standing in her sunny garden, a cold bottle of Corona in hand, Polly experienced an all-over shiver. Nora had died and the nurse who'd telephoned had said they were calling Polly because they hadn't been able to get on to Mrs Turner-Bridges' next of kin. They'd tried Darling House to no avail, and there'd been something then about an international number, but Polly had been in too much shock to make sense of it at the time.

Realisation made the fabric of the world seem suddenly tenuous: they had telephoned Polly because they couldn't reach Jess.

Nora had died and Jess didn't know.

Polly took another swig of her beer and then set it down. She wiped her hands on her overalls, drying them, and picked up her mobile.

CHAPTER TWENTY-ONE

Sydney, 12 December 2018

Jess had finally finished reading all thirty-three pages of the notebooks and her head was filled with Nora. Nancy was right when she said that Daniel Miller had a gift for understanding other people. Jess recognised Nora from the notes, at the same time as the Nora in these pages was new to her. This Nora was at least a decade younger than Jess was now, and Miller's notes showed a side of her that Jess had never known: vulnerable, less certain of herself, grief-stricken, but also a new mother, passionately in love with the baby who'd arrived in the midst of a family tragedy.

As Nancy had foreshadowed, some of the scenes were written in close third person, as if Daniel Miller had listened to Nora speak about herself and then, rather than write down the interviews precisely as they'd occurred, with his questions followed by her answers, taken the next step of interpreting the memories, history and personal feelings she'd shared, *showing* the things she'd described. The resulting scenes spoke of many conversations, not just one or two; there were too many diverse details – some of which Jess recognised from Nora's stories, others that were new to her – to have been gleaned in the formal setting of an initial interview.

Jess's phone began to ring. She glanced down, saw that it

was Polly, and even as her heart sank – frustrated, disappointed with herself – she switched the phone to silent, promising herself that she would call from the taxi on her way to the hospital. She didn't have long before visiting hours and still needed to go back over Miller's pages: she'd read them in one gulp, but there were a couple of scenes she wanted to look at with a closer eye to see whether they shed light on why Halcyon was back in Nora's mind.

DM Notes: Nora Turner-Bridges, December 1959

The journey from Sydney had been dreadful, but it was a joy to be at Halcyon. When Thomas first announced that he'd bought the house and was moving himself and his new young bride and baby daughter halfway across the country, Nora had been devastated. She'd told herself it wouldn't last. That it was just the latest in a long line of her brother's madcap plans and adventures. That just as he had shifted and changed between so many other ideas, so too he would abandon this fancy.

But then she'd come to visit and, even as her spirits soared at the beauty of the place, she'd felt her hopes deflate. From the first, she'd understood the spell that Halcyon and its garden cast. She had been helpless to withstand it herself. The grand English-style country house in the middle of a verdant garden was an Eden. But that wasn't what convinced Nora that her brother would never leave. She had seen beautiful houses and gardens before – she and Thomas had grown up in one on the eastern seaboard of Australia. What made Halcyon intoxicating, she knew, at least as far as Thomas was concerned, lay beyond the plush cushions and curtains of the grand house, the stone and marble and shiny brass fittings, the green lawn and the irrigated garden; it was the situation of the property, set as it was in the middle of the stark southern landscape.

The contrast between the formal garden and the native bushland was electric. It took Nora's breath away to stand on the corner of the verandah as the setting sun darkened the clipped hedges to a lush deep green while simultaneously bleaching the trunks of the candlebarks on the ridge beyond. The friction between the two was what Thomas craved. To possess an estate of unequaled civilization and comfort but know that it stood on the precipice of danger: therein lay the charge. Her brother had never found reassurance in the ordinary, the organized, the well-trodden path. That's how Nora knew, from that first visit, as she watched the sun set like fire on the nearby hills and the moon rise to illuminate the gums, a line of ghosts carrying old stories of the ancient landscape, that Thomas would never give up this place.

Nora's ambitions were comparatively modest. She'd grown up in a quiet house with cool, distant parents and a stream of stern nannies. Thomas had been her only light, and when he left – first for boarding school, and then for the war – Nora had suffered his absence like a death. Upon reaching adulthood, her greatest aspiration was not to be lonely. She planned to surround herself with love and laughter and lots of children, who would not be hidden away in a nursery and raised by strangers, but rather would bring their noise and clatter, their games and stories, into the heart of the home.

Soon after Thomas and Isabel left, Nora's parents had died suddenly, leaving Darling House (and a mountain of debts) to Thomas. Immediately, he'd signed over ownership of their childhood home to Nora.

'I've been luckier than most,' he'd said with a shrug. 'It's your turn.'

Nora married the first man who asked her, the friend of a friend of her brother named Richard Bridges, and started work at once on creating her family. But things had not turned out the way she'd planned. Falling pregnant had not been the problem; it was keeping the baby safe until old enough to be born that proved impossible. On and on the trial went, a never-ending cycle of hope, excitement, anxiety, and then grief, over the course of years. One doctor had spent an eternity leafing through her medical notes, before reclaiming his cigarette from the ashtray on his desk, leaning back in his leather swivel chair, and announcing – as she teetered nervously on the edge of her own far-less-comfortable seat – that some people just weren't meant to procreate.

She had been determined to prove him wrong. Wrong about her, at any rate. And at last, she had. With the help of Dr. Bruce, her great miracle worker, she had not only fallen pregnant, but kept the little one safe and well into the third trimester. Success, though, had not come without cost: Nora had been cursed with 'morning' sickness that lasted all day, for months. *Hyperemesis gravidarum* was the official name, though knowing what to call it didn't make a jot of difference. Still, she determined never to complain: to do so would have felt far too much like tempting fate.

Besides: 'It's a good sign,' the nurses had told her repeatedly, each offering a different variation on the theme.

'That's a lovely strong baby you've got there, showing Mother who's boss.'

'Get used to it – the baby's just preparing you for the long slog ahead!'

Nora had heard this sentiment several times: that being a mother was a difficult and thankless task. She noted that it was generally the privileged position of people fortunate enough to call themselves parents. She smiled along when she heard it – those who said such things were generally well-meaning – but privately it strengthened her resolve. When she was lucky enough to be blessed with a child, she would never let it be a thankless task.

But seven months of daily nausea and deep weariness was not pleasant, and the prospect of spending the remaining six weeks of pregnancy at Halcyon with Isabel and the children was too great an opportunity to pass up. When the invitation came, Nora had steeled herself for the journey and banked on the restorative powers of the property, her family, and the company of her dearest confidante.

It had been worth it. From the first moment she arrived, Nora had felt a weight lift. She hadn't realized until then how unsupported she'd felt at Darling House, how constrained. The ongoing cycle of pregnancy and loss had been grueling – and she'd grown increasingly desolate. Over time, her husband had started to waver in his allegiance to her vision of a household filled with children. Oh, he still wanted a child – an heir – very much, but he was happy to stop at one. Nora was confused at first, and then disappointed. She realized that she hadn't seen him tested before. They hadn't known one another well before they married, but what couple did? She started to perceive him as weak, lacking in commitment. She began to feel contempt when she looked at his satisfied face, his rounded shoulders, the crumb in his moustache at the other end of the breakfast table.

She had been thinking along such lines as she sat by the bedroom window on her first morning at Halcyon, watching the sun rise over the gums. Her baby had woken her early, as was becoming habit, with sharp kicks to the rib cage, and she'd been waiting for an acceptable time to go downstairs and take a walk among the roses. When she'd seen Isabel appear outside on the lawn, cup in hand, her muddy thoughts had lifted and she'd felt more energized than she had in months. She decided to join her sister-in-law.

'Good morning,' she said, crossing the lawn beneath the walnut tree.

Isabel turned and, seeing that the fellow early riser was Nora, smiled. 'Hello, dearest. What a pretty smock. Did you sew it yourself?'

Nora said that she had. In fact, she'd sewn herself several pregnancy smocks many years before. It had been a great pleasure to dig them out from where they'd been stored.

'I was about to make myself a second cup,' Isabel continued. 'Why don't I make one for both of us and meet you at the chairs on the northern side?'

Nora walked a circuit of the rose garden while she waited, taking it slowly for the sake of her aching hips, stopping to smell the delicate fragrances as early sun warmed their petals. She arrived at the set of chairs at the same time as Isabel.

'How's the little one today?' asked her sister-in-law, handing her a steaming cup.

'She's a good girl,' Nora replied, rubbing the fabric that stretched across her taut belly. 'I'm going to name her Polly.'

'A daughter,' Isabel said with a wry laugh. 'Be careful what you wish for.' Perhaps Nora frowned, for she went on quickly, 'Oh, don't listen to me. I'm sure your daughter will be far more obedient than mine. Each is more pigheaded than the other lately. Never happier than when they're managing to subvert my will.'

'A spirited girl is a joy to behold,' said Nora. 'I'm sure someone wise once told me that.'

'Oh dear.' Isabel grimaced. 'How one's words come back to bite. It's true, of course, but it certainly doesn't make things easier when one is responsible for them.' Her mouth tightened ever so slightly as she added, '*Solely* responsible.'

Nora took a sip of tea. She was aware that Thomas had been away more than usual this year. Isabel hadn't complained exactly,

not in so many words, but she made occasional jibes that
suggested she would have preferred him to do less of his business
overseas. Nora never knew what to say in response. She had a
fierce instinct to defend her brother, and yet she understood
more than anyone how lonely was the experience of missing him.

Nora's cheeks still burned when she thought back to the
extravagant way she'd behaved when he went away to the war:
twelve years old, but she'd wailed and raged like a distraught little
child. Four years later, when the letter finally arrived to say that
the war was over and he was coming home, she felt as if she'd
been reborn. He had written again from London on the morning
he set sail, promising a big surprise. Nora had hoped for a
portion of Liberty fabric, suspected he would bring a book, but
in truth wanted nothing more than to have him back.

She doubted anything could have prepared her for what he
brought with him. 'Are you ready?' he'd said, on the morning she
met him off the boat at Circular Quay. Nora had followed his
gaze when he glanced over his shoulder, expecting to see a porter
bringing a trolley with his bags. Instead, a woman stepped
forward, and Nora was immediately conscious of the slipped
stitches in her own hand-patched dress. The other woman was
elegance personified. Her skin was like alabaster, and Nora was
reminded suddenly of the admonishments of various governesses
over the years to wear a hat in the scorching midday sun.

'Nora Turner,' Thomas had said, with the broadest of smiles,
'meet Isabel Turner.'

Funny to think about it now, but Nora's first thought was how
extraordinary it was that this woman, this friend of Thomas's from
England, could possibly share their surname. (Her second, third,
and fourth thoughts were all to do with the tiny bundle in the
other woman's arms.)

Also amusing in retrospect: Nora had refused initially to give away her allegiance. For her brother to marry was bad enough, she'd felt, but to do so without her – that was impiety, plain and simple. To have a baby? Unthinkable. But Isabel was like no one Nora had met before. She was beautiful, of course – the otherworldly clarity of her English skin! – and possessed of the sort of poise Nora could only dream about. Beyond that, she was magnetic. Try as Nora might, she couldn't resist her brother's new wife. First, there was her voice when she spoke, that crisp accent and authoritative diction that made Miss Perry (strictest in a long line of governesses) seem like a drover's wife by comparison; next, there was her laugh, which rose like bubbles in a glass of champagne.

And then there were her stories. True tales of adventure and daring, rivaling anything Nora had read in her *Girls' Crystal Annuals*: during the Blitz, Isabel had handled secret papers in Whitehall and later worked in some sort of capacity that she wasn't able to speak of at length (at least not then and there). Even more excitingly, she was an orphan – a real one, just like a girl in a book, whose parents had died in tragic circumstances when she was only young, casting her out of the nest and into a childhood of boarding schools and midnight feasts and hockey sticks and daring japes. Nora couldn't think of anything more romantic.

Finally, there was baby Matilda, Nora's very own niece, born en route to Australia and the most precious child imaginable. Little wonder Nora had come to love Isabel like a sister. An older sister, just that bit further ahead on life's path: a sympathetic ear, a giver of advice, a funny, clever co-conspirator who always had the courage of her convictions yet could send Nora into peals of laughter with an unexpectedly ribald joke. It wasn't her fault that things came easily to her – her marriage to Nora's brother; her charm; her beautiful, healthy children, one after the other. If it were anyone else, Nora's admiration might have curdled into envy, but never with Isabel.

'Have you been feeling any better?' Isabel asked now, as Nora took a sip of tea.

'Better now than I've felt in months.'

'Well, there's no remedy as certain as country air, so on that front, you've come to the right place.'

From inside the house drifted the faint sound of a crying infant, as soft as a newborn lamb. Isabel glanced at her wristwatch. 'Right on schedule. I shouldn't tempt fate, but it seems that I've finally given birth to a child who read the manual.'

She disappeared through the front door, and when she returned, she was carrying a small, cotton-wrapped parcel in her arms.

'Baby Thea,' said Isabel, 'meet your Aunt Nora.'

'Oh, Isabel . . .' said Nora, taking the precious bundle and resting her atop her own considerable bump. 'She's perfect.'

The baby stared at Nora's face, her small, neat lips forming an O of concentration. Nora blew gently on the little one's eyelids and smiled as the tiny child flinched and then blinked with wonder.

'She's different from the others,' said Nora, pulling back the edge of the blanket to observe the baby's fine wrist and smooth velvet skin. 'Daintier.'

'They're all individuals,' said Isabel with a shrug. 'It's quite astonishing how children born of the same mother can be so distinct from one another. You wait and see. Just as you think you've got this mothering thing worked out, the next baby comes along and upends everything you thought you knew.'

Nora smiled. Isabel was trying to be kind, but Nora knew by now that it was likely she was only going to have one child. Even without the stern admonishments from doctors, Richard would never consent to try again. He'd made that clear, in one of the last arguments they'd had before she left for Halcyon. Thank God this child – this precious little girl, kicking against her ribs – had defied the odds to flourish where doctors said none would.

'I'm so happy that our babies are going to have one another as they grow up,' she said. 'They're going to be as close as cousins can be.'

Isabel smiled, but for a split second Nora thought she sensed something forced about the gesture. Isabel's eyes had always been more green than hazel, but when she was troubled, they seemed to lose their light, turning a sober shade of gold. Nora could have sworn it happened just now.

Then again, perhaps she had only imagined it, for when she looked again, her sister-in-law seemed her usual self.

CHAPTER TWENTY-TWO

Jess set down the pages. The scene had interested her in the first place because it offered a glimpse into Nora and Isabel's relationship (how much more shocking the loss must have been for Nora, having known, loved, and even idolised Isabel since she was just a girl), but also because it hinted at how and why Isabel could have done such a thing. When she talked about motherhood, she sounded tired, jaded even, and although the sentiments were nothing Jess hadn't heard her friends express over post-school-drop-off coffee, context is everything, and this was a woman who would be found only weeks later lying dead beside her poisoned children on the sunburnt edge of a quiet creek.

Of additional significance to Jess was the confirmation that things had not been rosy between Nora and her husband, Richard Bridges. According to Mrs Robinson, Nora was at Halcyon because she'd suffered severe morning sickness and longed for the comfort and company of her beloved sister-in-law, recently delivered of her own baby. Fair enough. Daniel Miller's pages seemed to back that up. But contrary to what the housekeeper had said, Miller's scene intimated that the marriage was already in trouble before Nora reached the end of her pregnancy.

It was possible that Miller was simply making an informed guess. Nora had stayed on alone at Halcyon in the weeks following the Turner family deaths and Polly's birth, while her husband remained in Sydney. Without knowing any of the details of their marriage, it seemed safe to assume that this wasn't the behaviour of a happy couple celebrating the arrival of their first child. But the particulars of the scene were so specific – Nora's contempt for the man at the other end of the breakfast table, her disappointment at what she perceived as a lack of shared values, reference to the specifics of their arguments; these suggested that Nora had confided in Daniel Miller.

And although Miller didn't say as much, Jess wondered whether there had been even more driving her grandmother's actions than general unhappiness with her marriage. *Issy, help me*, Nora had said at the hospital on Monday when she woke upset. *Issy, help me . . . he's going to take her from me.* She had sounded scared. Had Nora fled to Halcyon and remained there for as long as she did because she was frightened? Worried that if she ended her marriage, the husband she no longer loved, who had been waiting a long time for an heir, would fight to take her baby from her?

Considering the possibility almost sixty years later, it seemed feasible, except for one sticking point: Richard Bridges didn't appear to have sought any custody or visitation rights for Polly after Nora finally returned and the pair separated. In fact, Mrs Robinson said he had seemed to want very little to do with the baby at all.

Jess glanced out across the harbour, frowning thoughtfully against the glare. In a way, whether or not Richard Bridges intended to take Polly away from Nora was beside the point. It was enough that Nora had feared and believed it possible. She was nearing the end of a difficult pregnancy, a stressful period of life – the human mind was capable of all manner of misconceptions . . .

But something to do with Halcyon had worried Nora recently and sent her up to the attic. Patrick was adamant that her agitation had been sparked by the arrival of a letter from a solicitor in South Australia. Was it possible that Nora had consulted someone for legal advice while she was at Halcyon? Perhaps even found a way to prevent her husband from seeking and gaining custody rights over Polly? Did that explain his sudden about-face when she returned to Sydney?

Daniel Miller's book had mentioned a solicitor, she remembered. A neighbour of the Turner family, a man with horses to whom Becky Baker had sometimes fed apples on her way up Willner Road. Howard, Hunter, Hughes? It was a long bow to draw (there was, for a start, the blinding question of 'why now?'), but could the letter have come from him?

Jess glanced at her watch. Whatever the situation with Polly's custody, there was no doubt her birth had taken place in remarkable circumstances, and little wonder Nora had felt connected to her baby in a unique and powerful way. To that end, there was one more scene Jess wanted to read closely before she left for the hospital. She found the page she was looking for and slipped back into the confusion and horror of that stormy Christmas Eve night.

DM Notes: Nora Turner-Bridges, January 1960

Nora woke up to the end of the world. She was surrounded by pitch-darkness, flashes of silvery-mauve light, constant low rumbles of thunder. The smell was everywhere: a salty, animal scent of soil and decay. The destruction was inside her, too, a burning, muscular agony, blindingly painful, trying to break her apart.

Nora was lost; she had no idea where she was. In the intermittent light she saw a room of unfamiliar walls and angles. Paintings she could not place, mysterious curtains, a crystal ceiling light, the shards of which jingled and jangled, setting her nerves on edge.

All around her was the noise of a train, a tunnel, a torrent. A witch's brew of wind and rain and spite. One thing Nora knew for certain: she was alone.

And then, like leaves being thrown in the hurly-burly, it came back to her: she was at Halcyon. She'd fallen asleep in the late afternoon, after tossing and turning in the heat, and she'd had a dream, a wild and wicked dream, in which she'd been woken by a knock at the front door.

Down the stairs she'd gone and into the empty front hall, where dusk had been winning its battle against lingering afternoon, shadows lengthening across the sunlit floor.

Another knock, jarring, urgent, and Nora had opened the door to find two policemen standing there. Out of place, shadowy, yet just as in a child's fairy tale she'd been helpless but to invite them in.

The policemen stepped across the threshold, bringing with them a deep sense of menace, and Nora was newly nervous. She begged the officers to tell her why they'd come, but as soon as they began, she wanted them to stop. The words they spoke were impossible to comprehend.

'Dead?' her dream self had said.

'I'm very sorry, Mrs Turner-Bridges.'

'But I just saw them. They just left. A picnic. A picnic down by the creek.'

'That's where they were found.'

'Found? By whom?'

As is so often the case in dreams, she hadn't been able to

make her mind and mouth line up. Her words were imprecise, her thoughts scattered.

'Is there someone we should call to sit with you, Mrs Turner-Bridges? Somewhere else you'd rather stay tonight?'

Thomas would sort it out, he'd be able to deal with these two men. 'My brother,' she said. 'My brother, Thomas . . .'

'One of our officers is contacting him, you mustn't fret now; we'll come back tomorrow to see how you're going.'

'Tomorrow is Christmas Day,' she remembered.

'All the more reason. Don't you worry – we'll be back.'

There was something ominous in his comment, and when he went on to ask if one of them should perhaps stay with her at the house that night, she shivered and found herself rushing them toward the door, telling them no; no, thank you; she was fine, just fine. She'd had the strongest sense that they must leave. That all of this would end, if she could just get these harbingers of doom out of the house . . .

Time skipped, and in this new dream fragment, darkness had fallen. The policemen's voices had long since faded, replaced by nighttime noises: crickets teeming in the cooling black spaces of the garden, cows lowing in the fields beyond, the eerie still that precedes a storm. Inside, the absence of human voices seemed to heighten the rest, as if permission had been granted to the other things, the secret hidden things that lurk in dark places, to emerge from the corners and shadows.

Nora was still alone in the house, standing motionless in the center of the sitting room. Her gaze moved stiltedly from one item to the next. All of Thomas and Isabel's possessions, beautiful objects, selected with pride and care, arranged just so. Her brother had always enjoyed beauty, nothing but the best. The record player and speakers, the Herend vase on the side table by the sofa, the sterling silver photo frames. Her attention came to rest on one picture in particular; she had a copy of it in her own home in Sydney. Her brother's family on a trip to visit her, the children in their finest clothing, the Harbor Bridge behind them.

A terrible noise rose to fill the room, an awful, alarming keening sound. Nora only understood it had come from her when she realized that her mouth was stretched wide open in a painful cry.

She wanted to wake up, she wanted this dream to end, but she couldn't seem to break through to the surface. The secret hidden things had fled and were cowering now in the looming, lengthening shadows . . .

The dream skittered again, and she was running, trying to run, scrambling through the dark house, her limbs – in the way of dreams – refusing to do as they were told. She was looking for her family. They were here somewhere, she knew. They were hiding and she had to find them. When she did, she would wake up and know the nightmare was over. Upstairs she went, from one bedroom to the next, throwing open doors, searching, hunting, turning over the artifacts of her loved one's lives . . .

And then she was awake again. Here and now, alone in the dark, a storm underway. But she wasn't in her bedroom at Halcyon at all. There was no window on the wall to her left, the ceiling was farther away, the chest of drawers was gone.

Another flash of light and things clarified. She was in the middle of Isabel and Thomas's bed, the covers in disarray around her, the pillows strewn. The drawers were open, clothing was on the floor. The windows were open, and the wind outside was shaking them in their sashes, making the curtains flail, whipping rain into the room.

In the next flash of light she noticed a book on the bed beside her. She recognized it at once – it was one of Isabel's journals. Nora had seen her sister-in-law writing in it most mornings. Nora was reaching for the book when the world was plunged once more into darkness and her own body seized again with pain. She was frightened, suddenly, and alone. She needed to get back to her room, where everything was familiar.

Nora staggered across Isabel's room toward the landing. She paused in the doorway, leaning against the jamb, as another surge of blinding pain convulsed her body. That's when she finally realized what was happening. Because she wasn't alone at all. Her baby, her little Polly, was coming.

Jess leaned back against the garden seat, short of breath. She'd read the pages fast. Daniel Miller must have spoken to Nora at length to synthesise so much into a single scene: the police visit, Nora's reaction to it, her actions afterwards and the surreal, terrifying start to her labour with Polly. It seemed that Nora had dissolved into a state of panic and terror after the policemen left, even if she'd evidently maintained a brave public face as they delivered their news. Jess could just picture her grandmother telling the officers she didn't need anyone to stay, that she'd be just fine, thank you very much. That was Nora to a tee. Proud and as strong as nails.

And then there was Isabel's journal. She couldn't assume that Nora had given the journal to Miller, just because she was the one to find it. Her grandmother placed great value on privacy; it would have taken a lot for her to break those bonds of loyalty, especially where Isabel was concerned. But for Miller to depict it in his scene, she must have told him about her discovery that night in the storm . . .

Jess glanced at her watch and saw that it was well past time to leave for the hospital. She'd brought everything she needed with her when she left the house and now packed Miller's notes into her bag.

She hurried towards the Darling House driveway, pulling out her phone to call a taxi as she went. As soon as she'd made the booking, her phone began to ring again and Jess felt a stab of guilt when her mother's name appeared on the screen. Readying herself to apologise for being so late to get in touch, she pressed the button to answer.

Later, she would look back on the day and struggle to remember the order of everything that came after. It was as if a mirror had been shattered, and the sharp, clear shards could not be put back together to form a whole.

There was:

The lonely taxi ride to the hospital. The surreal staleness of the warm back seat, the hot wind buffeting her face through the driver's open window, the smell of carpet deodoriser and petrol fumes.

The shock of the tiny body in the bed, so frail, so quickly reduced, so empty.

The cold fingers, decidedly lifeless. The ribbon of memories of other versions of the same hand, warm.

The kindness of the nursing staff, whose work as caretakers of the dead Jess had never truly appreciated before.

There was a lot of business to be seen to after a death. The hospital had reassured Jess that they would keep Nora's body safe until Jess had made arrangements with a funeral home; they had given her brochures to help. She had called Nora's solicitor, who'd confirmed that Jess was her grandmother's executor and suggested they meet in a week or so to run through Nora's last wishes in more detail. Somehow, Jess had found herself able to converse quite articulately, hearing terms like 'the body' without flinching.

Now, though, back in her grandmother's house, a cold

shudder passed through her. Darling House felt different. Jess had been staying there by herself since Monday, but that had been in the knowledge that Nora was only away temporarily, soon to return. Everything seemed to have lost its lustre; the curtains, the cushions, the paintings on the wall had all slumped their shoulders in despond. Jess moved self-consciously among them, aware of herself as an interloper on their grief. She didn't think she'd ever felt so alone in her life.

She wanted to ring someone, to hear a familiar voice. She considered calling Rachel, but it was still only four in the morning in London. She'd be sure to wake the kids and for what? To tell her best friend, a busy working mother, that her grandmother had died? Even saying the words in her mind, she knew that they failed to convey the gravity of the situation. It wasn't just that her grandmother had died. Nora had died.

The afternoon stretched ahead interminably. Jess knew there were people she *should* tell – Mrs Robinson, Patrick, Nora's friends – but she preferred to live in denial for just a little bit longer. When Polly had first told her, all those hours and deserts ago, Jess had made her repeat the news, thinking, as her shock-shattered mind sought a way to put things right, that perhaps it was a dark joke of some sort. Polly did not make such jokes, as a rule, but the only other possibility was that her mother was speaking in earnest and that was impossible to accept.

Jess was aware of every minute increment of the clock hands, making their way around the dial above the doorway. Eventually, desperate to turn her attention somewhere – anywhere – else, she took out Miller's book and opened it to where her bookmark lay. Here was the start of the investigation, just as Nancy had foreshadowed. It was something concrete and structured for her to lose herself in. Wasn't this the theory about crime and mystery books? That their appeal lay in the promise of order restored in a disordered world?

Jess couldn't remember. All she knew was that Daniel Miller's book was what her grandmother had been reading when she died, and within its pages she would find Nora, still alive and with her whole life ahead of her; still able to surprise Jess with the things she said and did.

As If They Were Asleep

DANIEL MILLER

13

The South Australia Police Force Headquarters stands at 1 Angas Street in the middle of Adelaide's central business district. Even at its busiest, Adelaide, with its wide streets and elegant two-story buildings, is more like an amiable country town than a bustling metropolis. On the afternoon of Thursday, December 24 1959, it was a ghost town. Inside the police offices, a small but cheerful Christmas tree in the corner of the reception had been stripped of its edible decorations and the office staff sent home. Only Sergeant Peter Duke, who'd stayed behind to tackle a mountain of paperwork, was on deck to take the call when it came through. 'Jesus,' he said when his Adelaide Hills colleague, Mounted Constable Hugo Doyle, finished his brief report. 'How many kids did you say?'

His first call after that was to the government analyst, where he was met with a distant ringing that fell away eventually to dial tone. He glanced at the clock above the portrait of Her Majesty and, seeing that it was only quarter past five, tried the number again. Drumming his fingers on his desk, he sat through the ringing all the way to the end before pressing the receiver buttons to clear the line.

His second telephone call was to the West Terrace

morgue, where Dr. Larry Smythson picked up on the first ring, just as Peter had expected he would. The two men had started in their prospective fields at the same time, two decades ago, and enjoyed a mutual respect, each having recognized in the other a similarly dogmatic attitude toward duty. 'Larry,' said Sergeant Duke. 'Glad I caught you.'

'G'day, Peter. I take it you're not ringing to wish me a happy Christmas?'

Peter Duke's third call was to his wife, Annie, who was at that moment putting the finishing touches to the crystal compote of glazed cherries she was readying for the dining-room buffet table. She'd bathed Samantha and Pete Jr., and the pair were playing with the new puppy on the front lawn, waiting for their father to get home and the guests to start arriving for the annual Duke family Christmas Eve dinner. The tradition was one that Peter's Lutheran family had brought with them on the boat from Germany, and Mrs Greta Duke, Peter's mother, took its proper continuation very seriously indeed.

Annie wiped her sugar-dusted fingertips on her apron and took up the telephone receiver from the kitchen wall, tucking it beneath her chin. 'Duke residence.'

'Annie, it's me.'

'Oh, Pete, no—'

'I'm sorry, love.'

'Peter!'

Such calls were not unfamiliar to Annie Duke. Her husband was as dedicated to his job as a man could be, and the fact that thirty of his closest relatives were due to descend upon their bungalow within the next twenty minutes and she still had a kitchen covered with flour, sugar, and duck fat was irrelevant. There was no point in arguing; she'd learned that long ago. He would simply hear her out with unstinting patience and then tell her that he was sorry, that he understood, but there was no one else to take his place.

And so, as movement in the front garden drew her gaze through the glass to where the puppy was pawing the white skirt of her ever-punctual mother-in-law, she said only, 'What time should we expect you?'

The light was golden as Peter Duke drove himself up into the Hills. The road was busier than usual, as cars loaded to the ceiling with children and suitcases headed toward their Christmas holidays. Sergeant Duke followed the hairpin turns of Greenhill Road and outside Tambilla took a left onto Willner Road. His colleagues had arrived already, as had several ambulances. He parked among them and made his way toward a driveway with a sturdy farm gate across it and a fancy sign reading HALCYON.

'You'll find them if you hug the creek.'

Sergeant Duke turned around to see a young mounted constable tending his horse. The fellow indicated north. 'There's a water hole that opens up about a quarter mile along.'

Peter hadn't expected to be walking an overgrown creek bed that afternoon, and his footwear was not ideal, especially for a man in a hurry. He went as quickly as he could, clutching at the long sheafs of grass that lined the steep, slippery banks of the narrow waterway whenever he lost his footing. At last he turned a corner and arrived at the scene.

MC Doyle, who'd put in the call to headquarters, had been short on details, but Peter had gleaned enough to know that they were more than likely going to find themselves in front of the coroner on this one and they couldn't afford to miss a thing. He'd told the young constable to get a police photographer on the scene as quickly as possible and then given him the telephone number for the best. 'If he says it's not his shift, tell him I gave you his name.'

Chris Larkin had been working with the South Australia Police Force for near on fifteen years. Not only was he a first-rate photographer, but he also possessed the ability to survey a crime scene with the eye of an investigator. He could anticipate what they'd need to focus on later and without needing to be told. The older Peter Duke got, the more he appreciated working with people who didn't need to be told.

Larkin was already on-site, Peter noticed while he received a briefing from the local sergeant, Liam Kelly. As he listened to the other man's account, Duke took in the scene. He'd been told over the phone that the man who found them said the Turner family looked as peaceful as if they were asleep, but it was eerie to see it for himself.

Kelly beckoned over another officer with a wave of his hand. 'This is MC Doyle,' he said, as the other man joined them, 'one of the first to respond.'

Duke decided the fellow had a plain but honest face. 'No signs of a struggle?' he asked.

'No, sir.'

'Wounds suggesting a weapon?'

'No.'

'Dirt stirred up around them? Skid marks in the dust?'

'Nothing like that.'

'Marks on the bodies? Bruising, punctures?'

'Not that we can see. The medical examiner might find something.'

'Discarded needles, pill bottle?'

The constable shook his head. 'Nothing so far, sir.'

Duke nodded. 'Thank you, Doyle,' he said, placing a firm hand on the other officer's shoulder as he moved off to take a closer look.

Whoever it was that said they'd seemed to be asleep hadn't been wrong. At first glance, from a distance, that's exactly how they looked. Not once he got nearer, though, Duke realized. Only a careless eye would have failed to spot the difference. Careless or kind. It was Duke's habit to look in on his children at night – the last thing he did when he was heading down the hall to bed. Sleeping children flinched and sighed, smiles flickered like lightning on their lips, their chests rose and fell. These children did not look to be asleep. They were cold and empty. They looked dead.

Duke shifted his attention to the woman, the mother, who was lying on her back on a plaid rug, one arm bent at the elbow to encircle her head, the other folded across her middle. She had fine, slender fingers, he noticed, a wedding band slipping toward her knuckle.

'The husband?' Duke asked.

'Out of town on business,' said the other young constable, Jerosch, who had rejoined the group. 'Overseas, I think.'

Overseas at Christmastime. Peter noted the fact with interest. 'Get me his name?' It was one of the oldest rules in the policing handbook: in the case of a sudden death, look first to the next of kin. For all that 'home' was considered a word of warmth and comfort, policemen knew better. Home is where the heart is, and the heart could be a dark and damaged place. 'Let me know when and where you find him.'

A gust of wind lifted the hem of the woman's dress. Her

feet were bare, her sandals by the picnic basket on the edge of the rug. None of the children were wearing shoes either; both the boy and younger girl had bathing towels wrapped around their middles. The girl's hair was drying now, but the pigtails had clumped the way his daughter's did after a day at the beach.

'They've been swimming.'

'We think so. It was hot enough today.'

Duke exhaled contemplatively. He started making a summary of what was known; people didn't just close their eyes and spontaneously die together. Something – and possibly someone – had killed them. But there was nothing to indicate violent force. No blood, no obvious bruising, no suggestion of a weapon. There was always suffocation, but unless a group of assailants had descended as one and pulled it off without a struggle, it was hard to see how. Which left poison. There was an outside chance it was something environmental, an accident, but otherwise, they'd been killed. The question was why, and by whom.

The ambulances were waiting, and the team was working fast. The weather was drawing in, and although no one was unprofessional enough to say so, it was Christmas Eve; everyone was meant to be somewhere else. Once Duke was satisfied that the scene had been thoroughly searched and photographed, he would have the bodies of the Turner family transported to the West Terrace morgue, where Larry Smythson was standing by. Everything would be clearer when they knew what had killed them; until that time there was little Duke could do but wait.

Or so he thought. Suddenly, the young probationary constable came running.

'There's one missing, sir.'

Sergeant Duke turned to face him. 'One what?'

'One child, sir.' Jerosch pointed to a hanging basket in the lowest bough of a nearby willow. 'There was a baby, but she's not here now.'

Annie was in the kitchen when he got home, washing up a pile of dishes. It was late and, although she was facing the sink, he could tell from the set of her neck that she wasn't happy. Peter stopped in the doorway; he took off his wet hat but didn't hang it.

'Your dinner's in the fridge,' said Annie as she dragged dirty plates through suds to the clean pile on the other side. 'Along with the rest of your mother's stollen.'

Mention of his mother so soon was not a good sign.

'Sam and Petey are in bed. Asleep at last, though they've given me the devil of a time.'

'Too much excitement? Too much sugar?'

'Too much everything.'

'I'm sorry about the dinner. Things took longer than expected in the Hills.'

'Mmm.'

'It's a bad business what's happened up there, Annie. You'll see it in the news tomorrow. A woman, three children as well, all of them dead. A baby still missing.'

She turned around at that.

'Looks like dogs. We've been searching, but the weather's no help.'

Something changed in her expression. 'You're drenched.' She came to him, pressing her hands against his wet sleeves, his shoulders. 'You need to have a warm shower. Go on. I'll heat your plate and you can tell me about it.'

Her voice had softened. She was still angry – he could

only imagine his mother's mood at the dinner table when he failed to materialize – but she understood that he'd had to stay.

Policemen grew tough skins. The job required them to confront the worst of humankind while somehow keeping enough of themselves tender to remain good husbands and fathers, decent members of society. Peter Duke was a first-rate policeman; he could run his eye over a murder scene and look beyond the loss of life to a cool list of evidence and possibilities. But since Sam and Pete Jr. came along, something inside him had changed. He could be professional about it, but dead kids were his Achilles' heel.

They sat together, he and Annie, late into the night, wrapping the final Christmas presents as Peter described the scene that had met him when he arrived at the Turner place. Annie shook her head and frowned and asked him whether he had a theory. It was a bit early for that, he told her; they hadn't even started their investigation – but at his core, in the place from which one's instincts and assumptions rise, he was nursing something dark and troubling. As he'd stood there looking down at them, a mother and her children, her husband – their father – away, a word had come into his head: *Kilburn*. And with it the beginnings of a grim idea.

Kilburn is a suburb in Adelaide, once known as 'Little Chicago', situated about seven miles north of the central business district. For Duke, it had a different resonance, as the place where five years back a woman had tried to kill herself along with her two youngest children. She'd kept them home from school, given them each a capsule of sleeping powder, and turned up the gas in the kitchen.

Luckily, the lad, though drowsy, had been able to wait for his mother and sister to fall asleep before getting up to turn off the gas and sound the alarm.

Peter had been sitting in the Adelaide Police Court on the day the psychiatrist gave evidence. Dr. Harper stated that in his view the woman had been rational in her day-to-day life but had suffered a bout of 'sudden acute depression' leading to the attempted poisoning. Peter had listened as the assistant police prosecutor, Sergeant Randall, recounted for the judge the woman's police interview: 'Under questioning, she said that she'd just reached the end of the road.'

The case had got beneath Peter's skin in a way few others did. He couldn't comprehend how a mother could even consider doing such a thing, killing children she'd brought into the world. When he told Annie about the day's hearing over dinner that night, he'd expected her to be outraged, but she'd surprised him. She'd seemed to understand, even to sympathize. 'The poor woman didn't want to leave her children behind,' Annie said, her choice of words a disturbingly close echo of the Kilburn woman's police interview. 'She couldn't face going on, but she didn't want to leave them without a mother.'

The rain that had set in on Christmas Eve continued as drizzle through all of the next day and the one after that, making for a wet, gray Christmas. Peter Duke's Boxing Day was spent pacing the hallway and helping Pete Jr. build his new Space Station Morse Code Signaling Set while Sam put her 'Barbie' doll, sent all the way from America courtesy of Annie's sister, through a series of elaborate social paces. All the while, Duke kept an ear out for the telephone, waiting to hear from Dr. Larry Smythson. The call came through finally on Sunday afternoon: Larry had nothing conclusive to report.

Also regularly on the telephone were the police officers from Tambilla, who gave an update on the search – no sign yet of the baby, but a dead dog had been found in the field behind the Turners' shed – and informed him that the man who'd discovered the Turner bodies had come back to the station to tell them he'd thought some more about it and now remembered walking past the crib as he arrived on the scene; he couldn't say for certain, but he hadn't noticed a baby in it at that time. They also reported a high degree of general concern in the local area. The telephone had been ringing off the hook, they said, with folks wanting to offer 'suggestions' and 'clues', and others worried that there might be 'a murderer on the loose'. After some consult-ation, it was agreed that a community meeting would be called for Monday morning so the citizens of Tambilla could be briefed.

Sergeant Duke drove up to the Hills early. He had timed his journey to take in traffic contingencies that hadn't eventuated, and so he crossed the railway line and arrived in Tambilla with half an hour to spare. He found himself turning onto Willner Road and detouring past the entrance to the Turner property. Except for a bunch of cut Christmas bush that had been leaned against the gate, one would have been hard-pressed to guess that anything untoward had happened there.

The location for the town meeting was the stone Insti-tute building in the middle of the main street. It is difficult to find a town, large or small, in South Australia that doesn't have a building bearing the name INSTITUTE above

its large double doors, along with a date of construction
during the latter half of the nineteenth century. These had
been intended as places for community gatherings and further learning, arts and culture and civility. Sergeant Duke
couldn't decide whether it was the perfect site in which to
conduct the meeting, or a desecration. In the end, he
decided it didn't matter; it wasn't his decision anyway. He
had a job to do, and the room that he did it in was
immaterial.

In a small antechamber at the back of the Institute
building, Duke and the local police officers were instructed
by a busy woman named Maud McKendry, who was helping
to organize the event, to wait until everyone had arrived.
'There's quite a crowd expected,' she said in a purposefully
hushed tone, handing around cups of tea. 'We're all eager
to do our bit. There's no town without its tragedies, but
here in Tambilla this sort of thing just does not happen.
Not without someone knowing something.' She hesitated,
before mentioning the journalists from Adelaide and
beyond who had gathered at the back of the room. 'I hope
they understand that we're not that sort of community.
You'll tell them, I trust, what a shock this has been for all
of us.'

It had been agreed that Sergeant Duke would lead the
discussion, seeing as the investigation was being run out of
Adelaide, and so a few minutes after eleven, when Mrs
McKendry returned to give them the signal, he led the
other officers out into the hall. He hadn't given many of
these briefings before, not to the public, and his palms were
damp.

'Good morning,' he said. His voice, louder than usual,
hit the walls of the room with a wash of importance.

'Thank you all for coming. Our purpose here today is to give you an update on our investigation. We have not yet drawn any conclusions as to what happened, so I am going to limit myself to what we know: around lunchtime last Thursday, the twenty-fourth of December, Mrs Isabel Turner set out for a picnic with her four children: Matilda, fifteen years of age; John, thirteen; Evie, ten; and a baby, Thea, six weeks old. They walked together across the paddocks of their property until they reached the water hole on the northern side. There, they laid out their lunch in the shade of a willow tree. The bodies of Mrs Turner and her three eldest children were discovered around five in the afternoon. The cause of death has not yet been determined.'

'Was it murder?'

Sergeant Duke straightened his glasses and gazed out across the rows of those assembled until he attached the question to an unfamiliar man with a notebook and an expensive suit, leaning against the wall at the back of the room.

'Robin Clements,' said the man, 'reporting for the *Sydney Morning Herald*. Was it murder, sir?'

Duke returned his attention to the notes he'd brought with him to the podium and hesitated a little longer than he might have otherwise, signaling that he would be going at his own pace, thank you very much, and not to meet the expectations of an out-of-state reporter. 'We're not excluding the possibility of accidental poisoning, but for the purposes of the investigation the deaths are being treated as suspicious and murder has not been ruled out.'

A rumble of conversation went around the room, just as Sergeant Duke had known it would. Maud McKendry, sitting on the end of the front row, sealed her lips in a firm line of concern, her arms folded tightly across her middle.

'You think there could be a murderer at large?'

Duke spotted the reporter who'd asked the question in the back corner of the room: Cedric Barker, a local news-paperman, dogged but fair, with whom he'd spoken on numerous occasions in the past. 'That's not what I said.'

'You think the person who did it is among the deceased?' This was Clements again.

'I'm here to tell you what I know, Mr Clements, not what I think.'

As a matter of fact, although he had no intention of sharing it here and now, that was exactly what Sergeant Duke was thinking. He'd mused over the Kilburn case all weekend, along with what he knew of the Turners, and his initial suspicion had only strengthened. It seemed clear that the Turners had been poisoned, even if pathology had not yet been able to provide knowledge of the poison used; as to the poisoner, while it always paid to keep an open mind, he was keen to learn whether Mrs Turner had motive, opportunity, and capability.

'Can you at least tell us what comes next?' Barker this time.

'We will begin our investigation as soon as we're finished here,' Duke replied. 'No effort will be spared. We will learn what happened to the Turner family. No matter what it takes, we'll learn the truth.'

CHAPTER TWENTY-THREE

Sydney, 13 December 2018

Jess had slept poorly, woken frequently, and lost all track of time. When she did manage to sleep, her thoughts were filled with scenes from the past, half-remembered, dream-embellished, in which she inhabited various versions of her younger self. She was a toddler on the beach, a ten-year-old left with Nora, a bright-eyed graduate arriving in London to begin her big adventure.

When she finally awoke for good on Thursday morning, she lay in the dark letting the dreams disintegrate until only the awful events of the day before remained. The long dawn lay ahead, and Jess was imprisoned by lethargy that made her limbs as heavy as lead.

She was still lying in the same position when first light started to colour the room mauve, when the bright morning sun made it hard not to squint, and at ten past nine when her mobile began to ring. Jess fumbled her phone from the dressing table and saw Nancy Davis's name on the screen.

She answered and, after thanking Nancy for sending through her uncle's notes, paused momentarily before saying, 'Nancy, I have some very sad news. I feel I have to tell you. It's Nora. I'm afraid . . . I'm afraid she . . . yesterday . . .'

'Oh my God,' came Nancy's voice down the telephone line. 'Oh, Jess, I'm so sorry. I can't quite believe it.'

'Neither can I.' Jess could see on her bedside table the small box the hospital had given her containing Nora's jewellery. She hadn't been able to open it yet; she knew already what she'd find inside and how grotesquely out of place the familiar items would look.

'You know,' said Nancy gently, 'one of the things that always made me smile when I read my uncle's book was his depiction of Nora trying to cover her unborn baby's ears when her niece and nephew were bickering on the landing.'

Jess gave a strangled laugh; almost a sob.

'Even then, her instinct was to protect those she loved. Just as she tried to protect Isabel's reputation after the terrible events at Halcyon.'

'She was very loyal and caring,' Jess agreed. 'Too caring at times. I had to plead with her not to come to some of my school functions. She was often the only adult there other than the teachers!'

'Sounds like she was a very proud grandma.'

Jess closed her eyes. She'd been more than that. 'Nora all but raised me.'

'Did she?' The fondness was still there in Nancy's voice, but it now took on a note of concern: 'I hope . . . Jess, I hope nothing happened to Polly?'

Jess hurried to reassure her that Polly was fine, it was only that mother and daughter had grown estranged over time.

'But that's so sad,' Nancy said, genuinely upset. 'Nora was completely committed to her baby. It was one of the things that left a deep impression on my uncle. What happened between the two of them?'

Jess didn't really know how to explain. Not in brief, not to a virtual stranger. To be honest, the details were a little vague. She knew that she and Polly had lived with Nora at

Darling House when Jess was born, that they'd moved down the road a few years later, and that Polly had taken off for Queensland without a backward glance. Nora said that Polly had ever been nervy and unreliable (though she always defended her daughter if Jess dared to criticise), and then there was the incident when Jess was small. Nora tried to pass it off as one of those things – upsetting, certainly, but not decisive – yet Jess knew it had affected her deeply, changing the way she looked at Polly, and focusing her protective attentions on her granddaughter. 'I guess they just grew apart,' she said, aware of how insufficient the explanation sounded.

'It happens,' said Nancy sadly. 'Listen, I don't want to take up your time, especially in the circumstances. You must have a lot on your plate. I only rang because I just found another series of scenes within Dan's notebooks that might be of interest. Nothing on the reverend yet, I'm afraid; these are to do with Nora. I was in a bit of a rush last time and overlooked them. They're not written from Nora's point of view, you see, so they were hidden in plain sight.'

Jess was intrigued. 'Whose viewpoint is it?'

'Well, now, that's the interesting thing. The scenes are written from Uncle Dan's point of view.'

'They're in first person?'

'No, third person, as if he's writing about someone else.'

'Someone called Daniel Miller?'

'That's right. The scenes take the form of observations of, and conversations with, Nora. I can't tell you much more than that – I've been so busy today I haven't had a chance to read them again, but I know you said time was of the essence . . . Though of course with Nora, with everything that's happened, I totally understand if—'

'I'd love to see them,' said Jess.

'Then I'll scan and send them over and get out of your hair. Would you mind giving me your street address, too?'

She wanted to send flowers for Nora, Jess realised. 'That's very kind, but you don't have to do that.'

'No, I do,' said Nancy, her voice taking on a slightly urgent strain that Jess hadn't heard before. 'I really do.'

When Nancy's email arrived an hour later, Jess was sitting on the rocks overlooking the Darling House cove. This was the beach, she remembered, where she'd had her run-in with the soldier crabs all those years before, and Nora had rescued her.

The sun was shimmering in the sky; it was going to be another warm day, and Jess had been turning over the conversation with Nancy in her mind, wondering why Daniel Miller would have written himself into a research scene. He had been present at every interview; why treat these differently? It made her wonder whether perhaps these scenes weren't notes at all, but rather, as Nancy had suggested, drafts that he'd written for his book. The notion was intriguing: it suggested that he'd had an active role to play, beyond the standard function of the writer. It implied that something had happened in the unfolding story of Tambilla and the Turner tragedy to warrant 'Daniel Miller' walking onto the page. Perhaps even something worth telling the police . . .

As her phone sounded its cheerful ping, Jess shifted her screen out of the sunlight and swiped open the new email. The writing was small, and it wasn't the easiest way to read the attachment, but Jess knew she wasn't going to wait to get back to the house.

DM Notes: Nora, DM, January 1960

The first time Dan saw her was from a distance, on Monday, December 28, 1959, at the community meeting held by police officers running the Turner investigation. After days of rain, it had dawned hot and dry and the air inside the Institute building crackled as much with heat static as it did with the residents' anxiety.

Dan had gone with his uncle, who provided useful cover as the two of them took seats on the edge of a row near the back of the room. Being the lone stranger at a community meeting called to discuss the deaths of a local family was not an ideal way to carry out inconspicuous research. Thankfully, several members of the press had made the trip from Adelaide and beyond and were taking heat as people craned their necks to stare curiously, even suspiciously, at the outsiders in their midst. The journalists, for their part, were undeterred, standing shoulder to shoulder against the back wall of the building, notepads and pens at the ready.

Dan had decided to forgo such tools himself. Over the years he'd learned that there were two types of witnesses: those who lit up at the promise offered by that pristine sheet of blank paper, and those who zipped their mouths shut in its glare. A chatty witness could be a blessing, no doubt, but only for as long as they resisted the temptation to embellish. On balance, he'd found it preferable to engage his witnesses in a more natural style of conversation; he'd trained himself to rely on his memory, transcribing the interviews later when he was alone again. In so doing, he'd discovered an additional benefit he hadn't expected. It turned out that when he wasn't staring at the lines on his notepaper, pen racing to scribble down everything he heard, he was better able to absorb the atmosphere in the room, to notice the tiny gestures and mannerisms that oftentimes told far more than the words being spoken.

On December 28, as the blank-faced clock near the kitchenette ticked past the hour, Sergeant Peter Duke from the police headquarters in Adelaide emerged from a room in the wings and approached the lectern on the small wooden stage. It was the sort of hall where children would perform ballet concerts and the local youth orchestra would squeak through carols in the lead-up to Christmas, which made its function this morning even more sobering. Dan would have bet there were people in that room who'd seen the Turner children take their turn on that stage in happier days.

Duke cleared his throat and made a waving gesture with his hands that called the room to order. He thanked everyone for coming before outlining the situation in careful detail and then assuring the community that they were doing everything possible to find answers. Dan's first impressions of Duke were of a stand-up fellow, experienced but not yet jaded. Understandable that he was cautious about the information he imparted – for a crime like this one, where everyone remained a suspect until they weren't, police had to be careful how much they gave away.

As Sergeant Duke reached the end of his account, he reiterated that the search for the baby would continue alongside the investigation into the deaths, and that if there had been foul play, they'd find whoever was responsible; but he answered in the affirmative when asked by a reporter whether dogs were suspected.

'We found prints at the scene, and you all know how bad they've been this year.'

He turned when he said it to look down at a figure in the first row as if in apology. Dan had noticed the young woman dressed

all in black and understood now that she must be related in some
way to the Turner family.

'That's Mrs Turner's sister-in-law,' his uncle said, leaning to
speak quietly into Dan's ear. 'I hear she's been down from Sydney
for the past month. Came to stay for Christmas.'

Afterward, Dan had watched from afar as the woman was
ushered out of the room by one of the local ladies. She was
holding a bundle in her arms, he realized, a tiny new baby,
born – as he was later to learn – days before, on Christmas Eve.
He was able to get a better view of the haunted look on her face
as she left and felt something inside his own chest tighten. Her
expression, her hollow cheeks, the evident strain, were exactly as
one would expect of someone who had suffered the worst sort of
trauma. Dan knew that pain firsthand, and as she passed he felt
its echo deep within his own heart.

In the end, it was she who contacted him. A couple of days after
the community meeting, he received a message at his uncle's
house to say that Mrs Turner-Bridges wished to speak with him.
Curious, and unable to believe his luck, he'd shown up at the
specified time and date.

Mrs Turner-Bridges had been waiting for him on the verandah
at the top of the driveway. He hadn't seen her at first. He'd stood
for a moment, taking in the sight that greeted him as he broke
through into the formal garden. He had heard about the Turner
place, Halcyon, in his conversations with the townspeople –
stories that seemed hyperbolic in their extravagance, as if the
grisly nature of the family's deaths must necessarily find its
opposite in the paradisal description of their former home. But he
saw now that the reports had not been exaggerated. To emerge
from the dense driveway was to find oneself in Shangri-La.

An instinct alerted him to a human presence, so he wasn't

surprised when he saw her sitting on a wicker chair, observing him. She was dressed in black, and looked the model of Victorian grief, except – he realized as he drew near – for the addition of a swathe of fabric across her chest, forming a pouch within which slept her tiny babe. Dan was briefly taken aback: he had seen native women carrying their babies that way, but not ladies like Mrs Turner-Bridges.

'I hear that you've been speaking to people in town about my family,' she said, as he made his approach. Her voice was dry and airy, and he guessed that she'd been crying.

'I have,' he agreed, and then offered nothing more, waiting instead to see if she'd continue. This was his preferred mode of interview: to let the subject lead.

She held his gaze longer than was usual, which gave him time to perceive what an extraordinary-looking person she was. A rare sort of beauty – pale skin, paler than it normally was, he guessed, with freckles sprinkled across her high, round cheekbones, as if an artist had drawn them using a fine, point-tipped brush. 'Would you like a glass of iced tea?' she said.

'I'd like that very much, if it's not a bother.'

He sat opposite her on the matching chair, looking out toward a tree house and a laundry line and the crest of a hill that sloped away, he knew, in the direction of the water hole.

Nora already had a tray set out with a jug and two glasses, and she reached around the sleeping baby to pour them each a long, cool drink. 'You're from New York City,' she said. 'What's it like? I've never been.'

Dan was surprised at first by the question, but then he recalled the learned politeness of his Southern relatives and their friends. He reminded himself that the meeting was hers to guide and started telling her about his home, painting a picture of a shimmering city of towering buildings and underground jazz bars, neon signs glistening in grease-streaked puddles and lovers strolling arm in arm through a park that stretched for miles. It was a version of New York City that people who hadn't been there longed to imagine. The antithesis, he realized, of this place they were in now.

Nora listened, letting her eyes close, but she did not otherwise react, neither did she sip from her iced tea.

Finally, he ran out of things to say. As if on cue, a dog appeared on the sun-drenched concrete at the corner of the verandah, a big old golden retriever with a lion's paws and a permanent smile. He loped over to Nora, gazing up at her imploringly, and she reached unthinkingly to stroke beneath his chin.

'Poor thing,' she said. 'He keeps looking for them.' She tilted her head to consider Daniel. 'I hear you're planning to write about what happened.'

'Yes, ma'am.'

'Are you a good writer?'

He wasn't sure how to answer that. If this were a job interview, he'd have said he liked to think he was, but in this instance, as she regarded him with her somber eyes, her delicate drawn face, promoting himself didn't seem appropriate.

She didn't wait for him to answer. 'Has anything terrible ever happened to you, Mr Miller?' she asked.

The question caught him off guard. 'Yes, ma'am,' he answered. And then he found himself telling her about his kid brother. It was the first time he'd spoken of Marty since he'd arrived in Australia. Even his uncle had known better than to probe him on the matter. But something in the dignified grief of the woman across from him, the direct way in which she'd asked him, her exquisite aloneness, sitting there dressed all in black like a widow in a Henry James novel, made him open up. He described their childhood, their matching haircuts, the times he had been unkind and regretted it. Things he had never told anyone else. Things he hadn't known he felt or feared until he heard them coming from his own mouth that morning on the verandah of the Turner house.

She hadn't offered platitudes or assured him that he'd be all right, or that his brother was smiling down on him, or – God forbid – that all things happened for a reason. She listened intently and gave the slightest nod before turning to gaze out over the chattering trees.

'That's a sad story, Mr Miller. I don't know what would make a young man feel so hopeless. You have my sympathy for your loss.' Her words tapered off and she sat for a time, watching the leaves in the breeze, her hands moving gently across the mound of her baby. Dan was beginning to think she'd forgotten he was there, when she said, in a soft, almost musical voice, 'I have heard what they're saying in town, the rumors about Isabel . . . It isn't true. Isabel would never have done that – never. She loved the children. She loved her life. She had frustrations, like everyone, but she would never – could never – have done a thing like that.' She turned back to face him. 'If you're going to write about them, Mr Miller, you must make sure to tell that truth.'

It was to become a common refrain, and Dan had to walk a cautious line. He couldn't help but care for Nora. They were both outsiders, tied together by their recent personal losses and the Turner case itself. He looked forward to his visits with her, and he could sense the feeling was mutual. She was glad for news of the town, glad too for his company. But his duty was to his work. He believed in listening to all points of view, and telling a story that found its truth beyond the black-and-white details; he held wholeheartedly to the view that writers of nonfiction should have recourse to the same scene-setting tools as novelists. But he had to maintain his objectivity when it came to the facts of the case.

Nora was a smart woman. She heard the hesitation in his noises of support, and she didn't like it. 'I'm telling you: she wouldn't do a thing like that. She wouldn't have been capable of imagining it, let alone enacting it. If you'd only known Isabel, you would be as confident as I am.'

Dan promised that he'd keep an open mind, which was the best he could do, but her acceptance was grudging. He could see she wanted to prove it to him. And then one afternoon, when they had reached something of a stalemate, she excused herself and went inside. When she returned, she had a book in her hands. 'I found it quite by chance.' She flushed. 'I never would have read it, but for the circumstances. I didn't read all of it, just enough to know it was important.'

He looked more closely and registered the soft scuffed leather of the book, the gilt wearing off on the sides from frequent use, the unraveling ribbon placeholder peeking out from the bottom. 'Isabel's journal,' he said.

A thread of vindication plucked at Nora's lips as she noted his interest. 'She used to write in it every day, sitting right here in these chairs.'

'Have you shown it to Duke?'

'I want *you* to read it,' she said. 'I want you to hear from Issy. To see how funny, how kind, how alive she was. You'll know then that she could never have done what they're accusing her of.'

Dan's mind was racing. By rights, he knew, the police should have the book, but what she was offering was irresistible.

'There's nothing in there that would help Sergeant Duke. Quite the opposite, and that's my point.'

Dan reached down and let his fingers graze the cover. 'If there's anything that Duke should know . . .'

'If you find something that would help the police, I'll consider letting you show it to them.'

It was good enough. Dan took up the journal, letting it fall open naturally in his hands. The lines were covered with elegant handwriting. He ran his fingertip over a couple of torn stubs in the binding and glanced up at Nora.

'I'm sure we've all written things that embarrassed us later,' she said, with a sad smile. And then, with the baby growing fractious, she excused herself to go inside.

Dan spent the day with the journal, his head bowed as he read it line by line. Nora appeared every so often, bringing him a cup of tea or a slice of cake, and each time he was dazed and surprised to see her.

At the end of the day, when he was preparing to leave, he sensed her hovering by the door to the verandah.

'Do you see?' she said hopefully. 'Do you see how wrong they are? Do you see what kind of person she was? Wry and ironic at times, but a happy person, in the main.'

Dan nodded agreement, as he knew she needed him to, but all he could think about were those missing entries. It plagued him the whole way home and all through the night, wondering what had been written on them, and why they'd been ripped out.

He didn't say as much. He let Nora think the journal was watertight evidence of Isabel's good character. The problem was, Dan had been speaking with Sergeant Duke, and knew that as the police conducted their interviews and investigated further, they were becoming increasingly convinced that they were dealing with a murder-suicide. He couldn't help but wonder if the missing entries had contained guilty sentiments, or a confession of some sort, or even a description of her plans.

He didn't tell Nora any of this. It wasn't his remit to convince

Nora of her sister-in-law's possible guilt. And he'd noticed a real improvement in her condition since she'd shown him the journal. On the first morning he'd met her, she'd been utterly bereft, but she'd begun to rally. If the test of resilience was a person's ability to find a chink of light even in their darkest days, then Nora Turner-Bridges was a master of it.

Dan knew better than to give himself any credit for her renewal. The answer did not lie in the friendship they'd forged. Nora's glimmer of light, the place she'd found to channel every bit of love and hope she could find for the future, was her new baby. Her face was radiant as she shone attention on Polly, whispering softly in the child's tiny ears. It was divine. The infant was always in her arms. Understandable, Dan reasoned, given what had happened to her baby niece. The fate of the child preyed on everyone's mind. No one wanted to think of the little one denied the dignity of a proper resting place. But Dan's aunt Nell was family to the tracker working with police, and she said the heavy rain on Christmas Eve had washed away any hope of following the path of the wild dogs.

In the end, it was an unpleasant event in the village that caused the blinders to fall from Nora's eyes. Her precious baby was threatened in the episode, and the shock of what might have been refocused her. Dan had learned through his work never to be surprised at the way cause and effect played out; in Nora's case, her abiding determination to defend Isabel shifted, and she began to think more of her nieces and nephew.

When Dan arrived the morning after, she seemed different: nervous, but also decided. Even as he emerged from the driveway, he could see that something was afoot in the rigidity of her neck, the set of her shoulders, the clip of her gait as she paced the verandah.

As he approached, a hand leapt to her throat. 'Oh, Mr Miller, there you are. I was awake half the night with a thought that won't leave me.'

Dan sat down. Close up, she looked wretched. Her face was drawn and her eyes bloodshot. He could well believe she'd hardly slept.

'You must promise me that you will not put this in your book. You must keep it to yourself.'

'What is it?'

'Do you promise?'

'Sure.' She was so worked up, he found himself speaking slowly to calm her down. 'Of course.'

'It's only that I have no one else to talk to here, and I feel – I don't think wrongly – that you and I share a friendship of sorts.'

'We do.'

'I still don't believe that Isabel could ever have done what they're saying.'

'I know.' Dan waited and then, when she didn't continue, prompted gently: 'But?'

Nora glanced down at Polly, her hands caressing the tiny back. 'I haven't told you what I went through to have this little baby. I've only known her for a matter of weeks, but she is my world. Even now, I know that on my deathbed I'll be able to look back and say that I did everything I could to protect her.'

'I can see that,' said Dan softly.

'I loved Isabel, but I loved those children, too, and I have to honor them. Sergeant Duke asked me something the other day. Whether I'd ever seen Isabel behave violently toward any of them. I said, No, of course not. I was offended by his question. To harm a child, in my view, is the greatest evil. Only, later . . .'

'Yes?'

'I remembered something. It came to me, not in a flash – people say that, but it's not a flash, it's more gradual than that; I think I'd convinced myself that I'd imagined it. But when I first arrived here, back in early December, I knew almost at once that Issy wasn't herself. I've heard of women suffering with low spirits after a birth. One afternoon, I heard the baby crying. That girl, Becky, who comes in to help, had already left, and Isabel didn't seem to be responding. I thought perhaps I could help. I reached the nursery, and when I got there, I saw Isabel by the crib.' Nora swallowed the last word as she uttered a sob. 'Oh, Mr Miller, something must have possessed her, it's the only explanation.'

'What was it? What did you see?'

'It makes me ill to say it, ill to remember it, but she was holding a pillow – a cushion – and she was . . .' Nora's eyes met his beseechingly. Then, her voice little more than a whisper: 'She was lowering it toward the little one's face.'

PART SEVEN

CHAPTER TWENTY-FOUR

Brisbane, 14 December 2018

As a flight attendant reminded the man beside her to tuck his bag beneath the seat for take-off, Polly tightened her seatbelt and made sure her phone was switched to aeroplane mode. It was only a short trip – a little over an hour – and the weather was fine today down the east coast of Australia. Nothing to be nervous about, yet her stomach was in knots. She couldn't remember the last time she'd flown. Usually, Polly drove the coast road south to Sydney, but her car was at the garage this week having its transmission replaced and, with the funeral on Monday, she'd had no other choice.

Polly had never liked flying; she'd even done a course once, in which an ex-pilot instructed white knucklers on the basics of aerodynamics, an attempt to counter fear with reason. Turbulence? Nothing to worry about; just a change in air temperature. But learning such facts had done little to quell her anxiety when the plane she was trapped inside started shaking at thirty-six thousand feet.

Fear of flying wasn't the problem today, though. Ever since the hospital rang to tell her that Nora had died, Polly had felt herself cast adrift. She couldn't concentrate, her thoughts were clouded, she was suffering from a pervasive sense of disconnection from her own life. She'd been lying awake the night before, listening to the wind slapping the fronds of the palm tree outside her bedroom window, when she realised that the creeping, gnawing feeling that had wrapped itself around her like a pair of dark, damp wings was loneliness. A deep and profound loneliness.

Polly wondered why she should feel such a thing. She and Nora seldom spoke; they rarely saw one another anymore. Her mother's death made no demonstrable difference to her daily life, yet something inside her had plunged since receiving the news. She had come to the conclusion that being lonely wasn't the same thing as being alone. Polly had been alone for decades. She didn't mind it. Even as a young girl, she hadn't been the sort to crave company. But loneliness was different. One could be lonely in a crowded room.

Polly glanced through the plane window to where the men who'd been loading luggage were finishing up on the tarmac. It was normal, she assumed, to feel an absence after the death of one's mother, but with Nora it was something more. The world felt less stable without her in it.

She was an orphan now, Polly realised as the flight attendant started the safety briefing. That was part of it. For she had lost more than Nora. With her mother's death, she had also lost her father.

Polly was five years old when she realised that she was different from the other children. As with so many things, it was starting school that enlightened her. Until that point, she had passed a blissful period at Darling House with her mother. She had been spoiled, completely indulged. She had heard the stories many times of how wanted she was, and that was precisely how she'd been treated. She had never doubted how much she was loved.

But when she began year one and was brought into regular

communion with a large group of peers, like all children, Polly began to define herself by comparison. The other girls had fathers, and if they did not have them living at home, they were out in the world somewhere, with names and faces and relationships with their daughters, good or bad.

Early on, before Polly came to realise that the topic was off limits, she had asked her mother outright. 'Do I have a father?'

'No, my darling,' Nora had said, without skipping a beat. 'You're all mine and I'm all yours.'

This had been in accord with Polly's life to date and she had accepted the answer. She had also, when called upon to do so, repeated it at school. The derision of the other children had brought her straight back to Nora.

'Where is my father?'

'I told you, my love, it's just you and me.'

'But Ruth and Susan said that everyone has a father.'

'Did they?'

'They said that you can't be born without one.'

'Well,' Nora said airily, 'that might be true for Ruth and Susan, and I'm sure they meant well when they said it, but little girls don't know everything.'

'But if I don't have a father, how was I born?'

It was not like Polly to push, and briefly she saw exasperation in the flash of her mother's eyes. But the moment passed quickly, and Nora smiled conspiratorially, her eyes twinkling now as they always did when she was about to suggest something fun. 'Well, I don't often tell the story, because one must be careful with magic. But the truth is, I longed for a little girl so deeply, and for so long, casting every wish I could into every wishing well I passed, until one day, when I least expected it, there you were, at the bottom of the dahlia patch.'

'Here at Darling House?' Polly had played in the dahlia patch many times, and the idea of magic being transacted there was of great appeal.

Nora, sitting in the chair beside Polly, warmed to the telling. 'I had headed out to do a session of weeding, gloves on my hands and a basket on my hip, when I knelt near the thickest patch of flowers and what should I hear but the softest of cries. I thought at first it was a kitten, but what I found was even more of a surprise: the sweetest little baby I'd ever seen. The very daughter I had wished and hoped and prayed would one day be mine. A gift from the garden fairies.'

Later, Polly had run the story over in her mind, picturing herself in the midst of the dahlia patch. It was one of her favourite parts of the garden, which is no doubt why her mother had chosen it, and the story made her happy, but she hadn't repeated it at school. When Ruth and Susan asked about her father, which they had taken to doing on an almost-daily basis, she told them that he was an explorer whose ship had been lost in a great storm at sea as he approached the Arctic Circle and he had not been seen again since.

But no matter how much she enjoyed the idea of being left by fairies, or how well her mother loved her, a little hole had opened inside Polly where the answer to her question should have been. And, like so many of life's blights, it grew in the shadows without her realising it.

As she got older and stopped believing in fairy tales about babies in dahlia patches, the situation became more vexed. 'What difference does it make?' Nora would say, or, 'I told you, you're all mine,' or, if Polly happened to catch her in a hurry, 'I really can't remember.' Once, she had even lost her temper, her manner anguished: 'Why are you carrying on like this? Am I not enough for you? I've given up everything to be your mother. You are my life, Polly. *My whole life.*'

That much was true. Polly had often heard the stories of how devoted her mother was. She began to wonder whether perhaps the reason her mother wouldn't discuss the matter was because the truth was too terrible to confess. Was her father a criminal? A thief? A pervert? Was her mother trying to protect Polly with her silence?

And then, just after she started high school, Polly overheard a conversation that changed everything. Like all those starved of information, she'd become practised at pilfering scraps of illicit intelligence, and her ears pricked up when the voice of one of her mother's friends drifted through an open door, insisting on what a wonderful mother Nora was, even to the point of having sacrificed her marriage.

With those words, several seemingly unrelated gleanings came together, and for the first time ever Polly realised that her mother had once been married. She was aware, of course, that strangers referred to her as 'Mrs' Turner-Bridges, but Nora had so effectively removed 'Mr Bridges' from her life that it had not entered Polly's mind that the title might reflect an historical marriage. Now, at last, she had her answer: her father was Mr Bridges, the man whose name she, too, had been carrying all of this time.

But who *was* Mr Bridges? She scoured the house for evidence of him, yet although they had apparently been married for a decade, Nora had managed to excise every hint of the man from Darling House. Even the single image she'd kept from her wedding day was a framed portrait of a young, wide-eyed Nora, captured in profile as she gazed from the library window, out across the harbour.

Growing desperate, Polly asked Mrs Robinson for help,

but the housekeeper wouldn't be drawn. 'Don't ask me questions I can't answer,' she said. 'There wouldn't be a luckier girl in the world than to have a mother like yours.'

That she was lucky, Polly already knew. How could she not? She had been told over and over throughout her childhood. Her schoolfriends had been emphatic on the matter. They all admired Nora, wishing their own mothers could be just like her. She was the only one who would host actual high tea parties in the dining rooms of expensive hotels, or with Mrs Robinson in a maid's uniform at Darling House. Girls clamoured for invitations, despite having no time for Polly when she was on her own at school.

Polly knew that she was not as charming or as fun or as good at friend-making as her mother; now she noticed all of the other ways in which they were different. Nora was a confident person who relished attention, and Polly was not. Nora's complexion was pale with a tendency to freckle, whereas Polly's was light olive. Nora was unmoved by music, where certain songs made Polly weep. Polly started to keep a list of their differences in a notebook, wondering whether they were traits she held in common with her father, and under this consideration the negative space began to grow and take on a shape.

Eventually, Polly worked up the courage to ask her mother directly about Mr Bridges.

'Who told you about him?' Nora demanded, and then, 'Never mind. He's nothing.'

'He's my father,' Polly dared to venture.

'He's not your father! He could never have fathered a wonderful child like you.'

But Polly didn't believe her. She had been lied to for too long. Besides, there was no other explanation. She continued to raise the subject. Every birthday she wondered whether she was finally old enough for her mother to trust her with the truth. Her proximity to answers made the lack of knowledge agonising. She would walk into a room where her mother was entertaining friends and a hush would fall over the group, followed by a greeting, artificial in its cheerfulness, and she would torture herself with the possibility that they all knew. She began to feel less of a full person, as if she were see-through. She became withdrawn and silent; she felt herself disappearing.

And then, one day, when she was eighteen and pregnant with Jess, she found him. She had learned by then how to use the library resources, and she tracked him down. On a breezy afternoon in May, she waited for him outside his office at Crows Nest, and when he emerged, briefcase in hand, she approached from the other side of the street.

He smiled cheerfully when he saw her – courtesy, no more – and, for want of a better introduction, she blurted out, 'I think you're my father.'

A moment's hesitation and then, 'Polly?'

Her legs felt as if they might collapse. She nodded.

Richard Bridges walked closer, his gaze taking in the features of her face as hers did the same to his. At length, he smiled again, more warmly this time. Polly realised that his eyes had glazed. 'I wondered if I'd ever see you,' he said. 'Would you like to have a coffee?'

Polly didn't drink coffee – didn't drink much of anything during that stage of her pregnancy – but of course she agreed.

'She told me you weren't mine,' he explained, as they sat on opposite sides of a table at a nearby cafe. 'She was very firm about it. She had a solicitor write to me, telling me not to contact you.'

'Well, I'm an adult now, and I'm the one contacting you.'

They talked pleasantly, but politely, about their lives, and about Nora and the past – a strange social experience. She told him a little bit about her school years, and he told her that he'd married again and had a son and two daughters. Polly's heart clenched at the prospect of half-siblings. For a moment she'd glimpsed what it might feel like not to be so alone.

When it was time to go, Richard Bridges said, 'I suppose we should have one of those tests, shouldn't we?'

He meant a DNA test. It made sense, Polly considered, given what Nora had told them both, and he offered to pay, so they did.

The test came back negative. So, whatever else could be said against Nora, she had been telling the truth when she said that her daughter had been conceived with someone else.

Polly was bereft. But as the truth of the result sank in, she realised that she wasn't completely surprised. If she were honest, no matter how deeply she had wanted to belong somewhere and to someone, she had felt no sense of recognition when she met Richard Bridges. Nothing in his face, or in his gestures, genial as they were, had reached out and connected with her, given her a sense of kinship, of coming home.

Richard Bridges was as flummoxed as Polly. 'She said you weren't mine, but I never truly believed it. I couldn't work it out at the time and I'm afraid I still can't. How could you be anyone else's?'

The answer seemed self-evident, and Polly felt a wave of embarrassment for him, followed quickly by sympathy. He was trying to save face; he was humiliated by the proof that his wife had once upon a time been unfaithful to him. Polly didn't know what to say and settled on, 'I'm sorry.'

He appeared not to have heard; he was deep in his own thoughts and memories. 'She was desperate to conceive,' he continued with a frown. 'We'd lost a few pregnancies already. It happens, I'm told. I was never sure exactly what the problem was. We had all the tests, she made sure of that.

'But there was no one else but me. I suppose that sounds terribly self-confident, but that's not how I mean it. At the risk of being indelicate, she had seen a doctor, the most recent in a long string, who gave her a window of days and said she needed to make sure she gave herself every chance.

'She didn't leave the house that week and she didn't let me leave either. She saw no one except the housekeeper, Jane Robinson, and Dr Bruce, who made house calls. Afterwards, she stayed in bed for a fortnight because she said it gave the baby a better chance of "sticking". And, say what you will, it worked, she was pregnant. But I was there that month – it couldn't have been anyone else.'

It was an awkward farewell, and Polly had the sense, as she turned to watch him walk away, of sliding doors. There went the man who might have been her father, with whom she had shared the rather intimate experience of having their DNA compared, reduced now to the status of a stranger, someone she would probably never see or speak to again.

The flight attendant was still demonstrating the life vest and whistle, and Polly tried to pay attention. She had seen it all before, of course, more than once, but watching the woman's presentation seemed to be the least one could do. She couldn't help her mind wandering, though.

Polly hadn't told Nora about her meeting with Richard Bridges, the test they'd done. What would have been the point? But he had left her with a problem to puzzle over. In the evenings, when she sat on the garden seat overlooking the harbour, she would recollect their conversations; in particular, she remembered Richard Bridges' insistence that Nora couldn't possibly have betrayed him.

His argument had been one of reason rather than emotion. Nora hadn't left the house, he'd said; as far as he was aware, the only people she'd seen during the month that Polly was conceived were him, her doctor, and Mrs Robinson. But where Mr Bridges drew one conclusion from that set of facts, Polly came to another.

Nora had laughed uproariously when Polly asked whether Dr Bruce was her father and told her not to be so ridiculous. 'Honestly, Polly, I don't know where you get these ideas. Dr Bruce is a very handsome man, and you could certainly do worse, but he is not your father.' She'd sobered before continuing: 'Darling, it really isn't wise to make wild accusations like that.'

'It's not an accusation.'

'Wild guesses, then.'

'I wouldn't have to guess if you would just tell me.'

'I have told you: I found you in the dahlia patch.'

Polly, who never became angry, was incensed. 'I deserve to know the truth. I deserve to know who I am.'

'You're you! You're mine! Isn't that enough?'

'No!'

Nora sighed then, irritated. 'Well, I don't know why not. Look how fortunate you are.'

'Please, Mummy!' The childish moniker had come from nowhere; Polly hadn't uttered it in more than a decade and was as surprised as Nora by its appearance. It sat between them, a declaration of desperation.

A maddening placatory look came across her mother's

face then, and she softened her voice to say, 'I'll tell you one day, I promise, when the time is right. But you must stop asking me now. It's my story to tell and you're upsetting me. You're upsetting yourself, too – it isn't good for the baby, you know.'

Inside her hand luggage, Polly dug about for her earplugs. The leather bag was ever so slightly too deep, and everything became lost inside it. Her fingers brushed against the dream-catcher, which she'd brought with her wrapped in a tea towel. She took it out and inspected her long-ago knots, the drift-wood she and Jess had found on the beach. Silly and sentimental, but she'd seen the thing propped on the shelf as she hurried down the hallway to leave and run back to get it. She was nervous about seeing Jess. Particularly seeing Jess without Nora, being alone together at Darling House. She found herself besieged with memories of the other period of her life in which it had felt like the two of them against the world, back when they moved into the apartment on the promontory.

A lot had happened since then. Polly had been so positive when she finally took that step. The decision to move had been inspired, in part, by her mother's refusal to answer her questions. After Jess was born, knowing the truth had felt even more urgent. Polly couldn't shake the feeling that parts of her daughter were a mystery. She would stare at Jess's sleeping face and see elements of herself, and Jonathan, but there were other traits there, too: fleeting expressions that her baby had inherited from unnamed people further up the chain.

The unknowing created a distance between Polly and Jess, a gap that Nora didn't suffer. The more Polly faded, the brighter Nora shone. The love between them started to curdle; what had once seemed protective now began to suffocate. Polly felt trapped by her mother's attention, particularly her confidence and expertise with Jess. She started dreaming about going away. The idea came to her that she might somehow, with a little extra space, find it all a bit easier.

Polly sighed and returned the dreamcatcher to her bag. She continued grasping about, hoping her fingers would find her earplugs. She needed to take her mind off the flight and what would confront her at the other end. She had meant to buy a magazine at the airport but had been unable to bring herself to select anything on offer. All she had with her was the copy of *As If They Were Asleep*, which she'd brought because Mrs Robinson said that Jess was asking questions about the events back then. Polly had hoped it might serve as a bridge; a way to assuage some of the grief she knew Jess would be feeling after Nora's death. And, if she were honest, a way of pleasing the daughter with whom she could never quite seem to connect.

The familiar cover, the yellowing paper, the library barcode – all of it brought back memories of the first time she'd read it. The spell that the book had cast – its tragic atmosphere of summer and heat, the big old house and magpie songs, the ill-starred children on their final day – returned to her now, like an old coat she'd forgotten in the back of the closet. As the plane started to accelerate, Polly put in her earplugs and let the old library copy of Daniel Miller's book fall open.

As If They Were Asleep

DANIEL MILLER

14

Peter Duke knew in his heart that Mrs Turner had poisoned her family on the edge of the creek that baking Christmas Eve. Any policeman worth his salt developed an instinct for crimes and those who commit them. But convinced as Duke was, a hunch meant nothing if he couldn't prove it.

The report hadn't yet come from the government analyst, but there was a good chance, Duke knew, that his team would uncover what poison she'd used before Larry Smythson finished his tests. Initial searches at the house had left him hopeful. In the days following the discovery, Duke sent two of the local officers up the hill to look around. Mrs Turner's sister-in-law answered the door. The poor woman, who had been expecting a time of restful family engagement as she waited out the last weeks of a difficult pregnancy, had instead found herself coping alone with a family tragedy. Little wonder the shock brought forward her baby's birth.

'How's the little one going?' Mounted Constable Doyle asked as she admitted them to the house.

'A bit dazed. Like all of us, I'm sure.'

Noticing suddenly how tired the young woman looked

and remembering back into the distant past of his own children's births and his wife's refusal to get out of bed for the first seven days after each, Doyle said: 'You should have your feet up. Is there someone we can call?'

'Thank you, but Mrs Summers has been helping, and Mrs Pike will be here later in the week.'

They found the barbital bottle first, in the bedside table drawer in Mrs Turner's room. The unexpected name on the label caused Doyle and Jerosch to exchange a glance. They both knew Eliza Drumming – Doyle had been at school with her – but as far as either was aware she'd been down at Parkside for as long as the Turners had been around. Even Jerosch, the more imaginative of the pair, had a hard time coming up with a plausible explanation as to how Mrs Drumming's pills might have wound up in Mrs Turner's bedside table.

Henrik Drumming was ashen-faced when asked to explain. He confessed to having supplied Mrs Turner with a bottle of his wife's barbital tablets because 'she was having a terrible time sleeping', and Doyle, who knew Henrik as well as one could know such a private fellow, took the explanation at face value. Henrik was a good man, devoted to his wife, and just the sort to render assistance where and when he could. But Duke's expression when he heard the admission was one of curiosity and inference.

In Matilda Turner's room, they found a jar containing a dried plant sample that piqued their interest. A hand-written label featuring the initials M.S. marked it the property of Merlin Stamp, and Probationary Constable Jerosch, drawing the short straw, was sent back.

The interview didn't last long. 'He's not one for talking,' Jerosch explained late that afternoon when the officers met again in the small back room of the Tambilla police station to make their report to Duke. 'But he said it's pennyroyal.'

'Deadly?'

Jerosch was a fresh young officer whose ears protruded just enough to suggest boyish alertness and an eagerness to please. At this, he gained a slight pall of queasiness. The tips of his ears were pink. 'Yes and no.'

'What's that supposed to mean?' said Sergeant Kelly from where he was standing with his elbow resting on the file cabinet. 'Either it kills, or it doesn't.'

'I think I understand,' said Duke, lifting the jar to inspect the sample inside. 'A luckless girl's best friend. But not our poison.'

Then, in a bin at the back of the Turner house, police found five identical empty bottles. 'Bingo,' said Jerosch, calling Doyle over to have a look.

Sometimes referred to by police as 'the poisoner's poison', thallium is a colorless, tasteless, and odorless substance, the ingestion of which causes symptoms in common with many other ailments. Being easily obtained – used often in rat baits – in the middle years of the twentieth century, it was the poison of choice for those inclined to domestic murder, and, in the 1950s, a rash of crimes in which wives killed their husbands had lit up investigative bureaus across Australia.

Meg Summers was able to confirm that Mrs Turner had bought the Thall-Rat back in the winter. The shopkeeper, who had been called from the house to speak with officers, had the disorientated air of a busy person nonetheless inclined to helpfulness. 'If you give me a minute, I'll be able to look it up in the register. A half dozen or so, from memory.'

'Is that an unusually large quantity?'

'I didn't think anything of it at the time. Most people around here have trouble with rats in the winter, especially in a house that size.'

Duke was closing his notebook when another idea occurred. 'Did Mrs Turner usually make purchases of that sort?' he asked. 'It seems more the purview of a farm manager.'

'I suppose it's a little odd. Henrik has been working up there for as long as I can remember, and he usually keeps things shipshape.'

Duke thought of the bottle of sleeping pills. There was something intimate in it: the act of a man giving another woman his wife's pills. He thought, too, of the missing entries from Mrs Turner's journal. Duke had been handed the journal by a secret source a couple of weeks after the deaths and had read it from cover to cover. The entries themselves didn't offer much in the way of motive, but those stubs made him wonder – a guilty confession hastily made and then removed? – and he pondered whether there might be a reason for the shift in dynamics between Mrs Turner and her farm manager.

Having ascertained by now that Meg Summers was a repository for community confidences, Duke pushed his luck; alas, he had misjudged her commitment to discretion. She looked like she'd been slapped.

'Sergeant Duke, I'm sure I have no special insight into the intimacies of Mrs Turner's life and no intention whatsoever of raking over the coals of the dead.'

It had been a misstep, and Duke retreated hastily. Whether or not Mrs Turner and Henrik Drumming had been romantically involved was probably immaterial to the investigation, and it wasn't wise to put his witnesses offside. The copious quantity of empty Thall-Rat bottles was their biggest lead; if a betting man, Duke would've put money on the fact they'd found the poison they were looking for.

Marcus Summers, who'd been making a delivery to Halcyon as picnic preparations were underway, recalled seeing Mrs Turner stir 'lots of sugar' into the iced tea she was preparing for her family. 'There was a cake, too,' he added, 'with thick frosting.' Nora Turner-Bridges, who had also witnessed her sister-in-law assembling the lunch, didn't dispute the claim but scoffed at the idea there was anything untoward in it: 'Issy had a sweet tooth, as did young Evie. My niece couldn't be made to drink anything unless it had a pound of sugar stirred through.'

The theory had appeal for Duke: the thermoses had been empty when the family was found, and only crumbs of cake remained. A sticking point was the time thallium took to kill. More usual was three weeks of slow application, a little in the victim's cup each evening; it wasn't traditionally the sort of poison that could be used to induce deaths in an entire family in an afternoon. Duke made a note to speak with Larry Smythson about the likelihood that Mrs Turner had found a different way to administer the drug. It was certainly possible that thirsty children on a hot summer's day could be convinced to drink more than a tiresome husband taking a teaspoon in his daily tea.

While he waited impatiently for Larry to complete his tests, Peter Duke wondered about motive: What could incite a woman to kill her own children? There was the mercy defense that Annie had intuited in the Kilburn case, in which the woman had lost the will to live but couldn't bear to leave her kids without a mother, but there were other colors in the palette of human motivations that warranted consideration.

It was his office receptionist, Helen, who put him in mind of revenge. She was stirring milk into the tea she'd just poured in the kitchen of the police headquarters, tapping the spoon on the rim of her cup, when she said, apropos of nothing, 'That situation up there in the Hills reminds me of Medea.'

'What's that?' Duke, who had been scanning the newspaper for coverage of the Turners and only half listening, wondered whether she might be referring to an old case that had slipped his mind. 'Medea?'

'The daughter of King Aeëtes of Colchis.'

Peter frowned.

'The niece of Circe. Granddaughter of the sun god Helios.'

And then he realized. 'It's a myth.'

'In a play, by Euripides, one of my dad's favorites, Medea kills her children to punish Jason.'

'Her husband.' Duke was catching on.

'He'd abandoned her for another woman. She kills his new wife, too, which obviously didn't happen here.' She gave her teacup a final chiming strike.

Sergeant Duke supposed that for a woman who'd spent the first half of her life on the other side of the world, being abandoned to a farm on the outskirts of Tambilla while her husband headed abroad might feel a bit like banishment. And certainly, the consensus in the public bar at the Tambilla Hotel was that Thomas Turner hadn't any business leaving his pregnant wife alone for so many months on end.

Talk was rife that the man had taken up with another woman overseas.

Reverend Lawson tried to persuade his flock that they must avoid being 'tattlers and busybodies'. 'Let us all remember Proverbs 11,' he beseeched from his pulpit. 'A man who lacks judgement derides his neighbor, but a man of understanding holds his tongue.' But although the good people of Tambilla took in the message on Sunday morning, by Monday they were back to speculating. And thanks to a telephone call from officers at Charing Cross station, Duke's men determined that they weren't far wrong: Mr Turner did indeed have a girlfriend in London, one Miss Rose Spencer, with whom he'd been consorting on and off for the past twelve months.

Whether Mrs Turner knew about her husband's dalliance, Duke wasn't sure. There was no evidence to that effect, and while young Matthew McKenzie was able to confirm that John Turner had discovered the infidelity, he did not know whether the boy had shared the information with his mother. Nora Turner-Bridges was adamant that Isabel hadn't mentioned a word. 'Not only that; I can't believe it of my brother. There were always women chasing after him, but it meant nothing – Issy wouldn't have let that bother her.'

Evidently, if Mrs Turner was concerned, she hadn't felt comfortable disclosing the fact to her husband's sister.

Duke asked around town, in the hope that Mrs Turner might have revealed the secrets of her heart to someone else. But while it wasn't easy to find anyone to say a bad word against her, neither did he turn up someone who might be labeled a confidante. In fact, it was noteworthy, as far as Duke was concerned, how few close friends Isabel

Turner seemed to have. Meg Summers frowned when he asked about it and looked almost guilty by the time she arrived at her answer. Duke had seen this before, the regret of good people who have failed to spot another in need. 'Now you mention it,' she said, 'I wouldn't say she was especially close to anyone around here.'

That Isabel Turner had been admired was not in doubt. Duke and his team had conducted extensive interviews in the days following the deaths and were told variously that Mrs Turner was 'energetic', 'clever', 'beautiful', and 'kind'. Mrs Summers, trying perhaps to repair the impression that she'd failed to notice the other woman's plight, added that Mrs Turner had come to see her in the shop some years ago 'for tea and sympathy', and that she'd confessed to feeling lonely and isolated with her husband away so often for work.

There was a flare of excitement within Duke's team when the new lead came from Reverend Lawson that Mrs Turner had spoken of doing something that would deprive her children of their mother – it wasn't proof, but it helped to reinforce the theory they were working with. For Duke, it also echoed what Annie had said about the Kilburn case: 'The poor woman didn't want to leave her children behind.'

While Mrs Turner's journal was not the smoking gun Duke might have wished it to be, there was some debate among the officers as to whether more could be read into the daily weather notes than met the eye. And then there was the possibility presented by the missing entries. They had been removed for a reason; perhaps if Duke's men could find them, they might contain a confession. A search was instigated, but police knew they were clutching at straws.

And then, finally, it came. The evidence Duke had been hoping for. It didn't always happen that way, but every so often the right piece of information fell into place like the key to a jigsaw puzzle. This testimony was an account from a source 'close to the parties', whom police refused to name publicly due to the sensitivity of the subject matter. The witness described having recently had to stop Mrs Turner from harming her own baby.

Duke called upon the psychiatrist who'd given evidence in the Kilburn case, and the gentleman provided a compelling description of a condition called postpartum psychosis.

'Far more than the so-called baby blues,' he explained, 'the symptoms can include delusions, agitation, paranoia, confusion, disconnection from the baby, and insomnia. In some cases, sadly, it can lead to depression and hopelessness.'

Could a woman suffering in such a way behave violently toward her baby? Duke asked, to which the doctor assented.

'It's just a pity she didn't consult a professional,' he couldn't refrain from adding. 'We might have been able to save the lives of those poor kiddies.'

Duke was often surprised at how quickly townspeople caught wind of what was happening in an investigation. Like any small town in which tragedy has occurred, the social fabric of Tambilla tore a bit that Christmas and needed mending. The people were rattled, tired of having their town written about in newspapers, of looking askance at one another, of trying quietly to convince themselves – and loudly to convince one another – that they couldn't have done anything more. Once the citizens of Tambilla realized police were looking seriously at Mrs Turner, it was as if a tacit agreement was reached whereby they could alleviate their own remorse and assuage their community's guilt in one fell swoop.

When Duke and his officers conducted a further round of interviews, it seemed that people had begun to see things through a different lens.

'And really,' Mrs McKendry added to an account she'd just given of Mrs Turner's 'unusual' contributions to the Country Women's Association cake stalls, 'it's a bit odd, isn't it, to marry a man who approaches you on a bridge, to agree to move to the other side of the world. It isn't . . . well, it isn't *stable*.'

'I'll tell you what I've been thinking about,' said Mrs Fisher, who was interviewed in her kitchen, a flyer from the recent Billy Graham tour on the fridge behind her. 'I told her there was bad luck attached to that house and she didn't so much as blink. Completely unaffected! She thought she knew better. If only she'd listened.'

Mrs Pigott voiced sad agreement: 'She should never have renamed that house. They were tempting fate.'

Even Mrs Pike, who had heretofore remained stubbornly loyal to her former employer, appeared to reconsider. 'The way she took against the portrait of Mr Wentworth. That struck me as odd – paranoid – to mind so much about a painting. It makes you wonder whether she had some reason. I'm not saying what it might be, just some sort of guilty conscience.'

Mrs Pigott noted that Mrs Turner had sent and received more packages through the post office than the other residents of Tambilla. 'International, most of them.' At that, she raised her thin eyebrows as if a conclusion could easily be drawn. 'There were more lately than ever.'

Mrs Pike agreed that Mrs Turner had seemed unusually occupied over the past weeks and months. 'I didn't think much of it at the time, but it's different when you look back after something like this, isn't it?' When asked to expand, the housekeeper frowned and said, 'It seemed to me that she was busy putting her affairs in order. Sorting papers, throwing things away.'

'Pages from a journal?'

'I couldn't say for sure – I never looked; I'm no snoop – but it's certainly possible.'

Perhaps no event demonstrated the restive state of the community quite like what occurred when Nora Turner-Bridges came down from the house one day in early January, bringing her new baby, Polly, into the main street.

'I'd only meant to take a walk,' she was to say later, still clearly shaken by the experience. 'I'd been up at the house since before Christmas, and I needed to get out, to have a change of scene. I wouldn't have gone if I'd known what was going to happen. I didn't mean for anyone to get upset. I didn't need any more upset myself.'

Since the baby's birth on Christmas Eve, Nora had been carrying her in a fabric wrap; having waited a long time to call herself a mother, she wasn't about to let her tiny girl out of her arms. But there's nothing as sure as that babies grow bigger, and within a few weeks, when she wanted to take a longer walk into town, she realized that it had become impractical to bear the child all the way, especially when there was a perfectly good perambulator sitting up at the house.

Nora had no way of knowing the immensity of affection that Becky Baker had for the contraption, nor how wretchedly the poor girl had suffered since news of the deaths reached her at the brewery. No way, either, of anticipating that Becky would be visiting her aunt Betty at the teahouse that very morning and was indeed watching from the window when Nora began her walk along the main street.

Mr Ted Holmes, who was taking a tea break from the sign-writing work he was doing for Patterson & Sons Mechanics down the road, said that he wondered what on earth had come over the lass when she stood bolt upright, 'as if she'd seen a ghost!' She ran, 'hell for leather', he said, out of the teashop, before her aunt could stop her, setting upon poor Mrs Turner-Bridges.

'She was as flustered as I've seen a person look,' said Mrs Pigott, who'd heard the screeching and come outside the post office to see what was going on. 'Mrs Turner-Bridges is a dignified woman, and her face was a picture of agony. Becky's a good girl, but she looked like a banshee. She ripped the child from the pram – my heart was in my mouth; I thought she was going to drop her.'

The altercation was sorted out by police who, as good luck would have it, were on hand, having just finished another round of interviews. Mrs Summers, too, was there to separate the girl from the baby, and afterward put in a kind word. 'She cared for baby Thea very much. She never would have meant to frighten Mrs Turner-Bridges, and certainly could never harm little Polly.'

But there was a note of concern in Meg's voice; she'd been shaken. And even Becky Baker's parents, her greatest defenders, were mortified by the trouble she'd caused. Charges weren't laid – 'Good Lord, no,' said Nora, 'that's the last thing I'd want' – but it was agreed quietly that something had to be done, and the local GP, Dr. Ralph McKendry, was called upon to prescribe a gentle sedative for the poor girl.

Duke, when he learned of the event, recognized that community anxiety had reached a fever pitch; with a glance at the calendar, the weeks that had passed them by, he reached again for the phone.

Since Christmas Eve, Dr. Larry Smythson had been working solidly on the Turner case. By the first week of February, he was fielding calls from Peter Duke at least once a day. Every time he was summoned to the telephone, he said the same thing he'd said the day before and the day before that: he had nothing yet to report; he'd be sure to get in touch as soon as he did. Dr. Smythson understood the pressure the police were under, and he wanted answers, too. But science couldn't be rushed, and results would not be obtained any faster than the tests allowed.

Larry Smythson had worked at the West Terrace morgue for just over two decades but had stopped telling people what he did years ago. Not because he was embarrassed, but because he quickly became tired of the look of thrilled horror that would animate his questioner's face when they learned of his occupation. He had trained as a doctor but never regretted his choice to work with the dead. He knew others in his field who had become inured to the sights and smells, who could chat as they worked about the film they planned to see on the weekend and the funny thing their kid had said before school that morning. But not Larry. Although he would never say it to anyone else, he considered his job sacred. The dead had lost their ability to communicate in any of the usual ways, yet many times they still had a story to tell. For some, it would be the most important story of their life. His was the great responsibility to coax from them their secrets, and he was good at it.

But although Larry made sure to use his calmest, most methodical tone when he spoke to Duke, the truth was, this case had him more puzzled than most. His job wasn't to determine who; that was for police to decide during their investigation. His role was to supply credible, supportable answers as to how. And therein lay the problem. The bodies had come in all but untouched. He'd given each one a careful physical examination and found no evidence of trauma or violence. They hadn't been shot or stabbed or strangled or suffocated, and yet they were all clearly dead. As Peter Duke had reasoned, the only sensible option was poison.

But neither Larry nor his deputy found any evidence of injection sites and, so far, all pathology results were negative. (Even Matilda Turner's fears of impending maternity were confirmed as groundless; if conception had occurred, pregnancy had not.) Their kidneys and livers had been swollen, suggesting the digestion of a toxin, but no trace remained as to what that toxin was. This was unusual. In fact, he had only seen it once before, when the Somerton Man's body was brought in. That case had been his greatest career failing, and the reason the Turner family deaths carried an additional burden.

On occasion over the course of their long working lives, Peter Duke and Larry Smythson had met for a drink on Friday afternoon at one of the hotels in town. The occurrence was not regular enough to be called a habit, but – perhaps because each man was, in his own way, a stickler for routine – the meetings were immediately comfortable and always fell along familiar lines. On the afternoon of February 5, 1960, an astute observer would have noted the pair at a back table of the Wellington Hotel on the square, looking for all the world like a couple of old friends shooting the breeze. A listener, though, would have drawn a different conclusion. Larry had just finished running through an exhaustive list of the tests he'd completed and the negative results they'd returned. Wearily, he said, 'What about Mrs Turner? Have you found anything in her past that would point to knowledge of a toxin of this kind?'

Peter Duke, who had been sitting back in a leather lounge chair listening, recognized in the question the depth of Larry's defeat. Here was a man whose life's work had been built around letting science speak for itself. That he was looking now toward the biography of the suspect, considering speculative factors like motive and capability, was a tacit admission that he had lost faith in science to find the answer. Duke brightened; he faced no such constraint – indeed, he put great stock in the role of deduction to arrive at a solution. 'As a matter of fact,' he said, 'it turns out her father was a well-known naturalist, and she herself a budding scientist.' He leaned closer. 'Furthermore, a colleague in London rang me in the middle of the night and said he wasn't supposed to know anything about it – official secrets, war business – but he had it on good authority that she'd been involved in a special unit operating in France.'

'That might explain it,' said Larry thoughtfully. 'All manner of experimental chemicals were used during the war. To source and apply a poison like that – rare, untraceable – implies knowledge above and beyond what's normal.'

'A spy in our midst.'

Thinking again of the mysterious Somerton Man on the beach, Larry gave a hopeless wave of his hand. 'She wouldn't be the first.'

Summer became autumn. The risk of fire in the Hills receded and the porous hours that wrapped around the end of the days grew shorter and cooler. On a fine, crisp day in April, Henrik Drumming traveled on foot, as he always had, up the long, winding driveway to the house. He'd brought Barnaby with him, for old times' sake. After Mrs Turner-Bridges and her baby finally returned to Sydney and the house stood quiet and empty once more, Henrik had stepped in, offering to adopt the old retriever. 'We're a right pair,' he told an acquaintance. 'We sit together in the evenings and reflect on happier times.' (He'd have taken Smarty, too, but the ginger tabby had already been rehomed with the Baker family over at the brewery, where he'd put on a sour show of pique before yielding to the irresistible temptation of the grain store rats.)

The wind had picked up since dawn – the sort of wind that would be a worry in February, when the temperatures were soaring and the fields were covered with tinder-dry grasses, but in April gave him a job to do. Brown leaves were falling from the plane trees near the house and for the next few weeks it would be a daily task to gather and then cart them to the dumping ground at the top of the east field, near the line of gums. Henrik hadn't been paid for a couple of months – he wasn't sure if he was still employed – but he couldn't bear to think of the leaves piling up. He had worked at the Wentworth place from before the Turners arrived; he'd been one of the men engaged to get it ready for them. Henrik knew the property as well as he knew his own. Better in some respects.

Autumn became winter, and in July the coroner began an inquest into the Turner deaths. Duke and his team, including the police prosecutor, presented their arguments.

Larry Smythson's medical evidence was frank but disappointed. He described the postmortem examination of the bodies and opined that death was by heart failure, which, given the otherwise normal condition of their hearts, could not be from natural causes. The most likely cause of death was by a poison that could not be found on analysis.

Mrs Turner's state of mind proved a central part of the police case, and evidence was given by eighteen witnesses, including one unnamed person whose testimony the coroner kept sealed due to its sensitive nature. That Mrs Turner could execute such an intricate plan was supported by her history of service during the war, along with character references from former friends in England describing her as 'resolute' and 'determined' and 'capable'. That her mother had died by suicide when Isabel was at an impressionable age was not without relevance; so, too, her father's familiarity with rare and exotic fungi.

Toward the end of the hearing, the Misses Edwards, who had sat through every day, were determined to say their part, each of them offering testimony on a similar theme.

'She was a proper English lady. Those children were always well dressed, and she had them put their shoes on for lessons. You don't like to think of a person suffering in such a way, but if anyone could pull off something like this, so neatly, it was her.'

The coroner was unable to make findings, so the cases

remained officially open. But it was merely a formality. Everyone knew by then what had happened: the sorry story of a woman – an outsider – driven by a combination of loneliness and temporary psychological illness to commit the most unspeakable crime.

Epilogue

On a Saturday in late August 1960, Peter Duke found himself driving the bends of Greenhill Road to meet a man about a trailer he'd seen advertised and hoped to buy. He was early, and without consciously making the decision to do so, turned toward Tambilla, headed along Willner Road, and parked out the front of the farm gate with its fancy sign: HALCYON. He walked up the driveway, taking in the birdsong and the sound of water rushing. It had been a wet season. The creek was full and the sky was heavy.

The house, when he reached it, was not the place he remembered. It had taken on the air of abandonment that all empty houses do after a time. The rooms no longer rang with the busy noise of a family going about their lives: the clatter of the piano, the squeal of children playing, a new baby's cry. The doors were sealed, and a haze of wind-blown dirt rendered the windows dull.

The garden, too, was bare-boned and still. If autumn was the busiest time, winter was the quietest. The roses had been pruned, leaving only their gnarly stumps, and the plane trees had lost their leaves, their naked branches cold and gray.

Movement in his peripheral vision drew Duke's gaze up and toward the east, where a small, distant figure stood at the top of the field beneath the gums. Somehow, before he even noticed the retriever standing behind the man, he knew that it was Henrik Drumming.

Henrik was unaware that he was being observed. He was leaning on the wooden handle of his shovel, taking in the pile of leaves he'd built over the autumn; he'd been waiting weeks for a dry enough patch to set it alight, same as he did at this time every year. Mrs Turner was on his mind, and the poem she used to recite each August, about the bleak midwinter and the frosty wind moaning and the earth as hard as iron. She would get a wistful look when she delivered it, and he knew it was because she spoke of home.

As Henrik Drumming struck the match and threw it onto the heap, Duke began his walk back down the driveway. When he reached the bottom he saw a couple – a man and woman – leaning over the fence, gazing up toward the house as if observing a weird and wonderful display at Barnum's American Museum.

'Did you know the family?' called the man, who was old and well-dressed enough to have known better.

The woman was holding a bunch of golden wattle that Duke figured she'd picked from the trees lining the street beyond. 'We read about it in the papers,' she said, 'and wanted to see where it happened.'

'I never met them,' said Duke truthfully.

He didn't add that he nonetheless knew them very well. That he would never forget the Turner family of Halcyon, their lives and terrible deaths beside the creek that Christmas Eve.

Instead, he turned and walked back to his car, and left the couple gawping at the house, and he wondered idly if he would ever learn what poison Mrs Turner had used, or turn up the remains of little baby Thea, so that she could be laid to rest with her family and so be brought back home.

CHAPTER TWENTY-FIVE

Sydney, 17 December 2018

Polly had set two places at Nora's dining table and was preparing a meal. It seemed like a constructive thing to do. She was keen to be constructive. When she'd left Brisbane for Sydney on Friday, she'd envisaged herself supporting Jess in her grief, the two of them working over the weekend to prepare for the funeral on Monday. She'd consulted the internet and drawn up a list of what needed to be done. She had forgotten, though, how capable Jess was, and how independent. The first words from her mouth as a baby had been, 'I do'; in retrospect, she'd been giving voice to what would become her mantra.

Evidently, Nora had also been confident in Jess because she'd named her as executor, and by the time Polly arrived in Sydney, most of the funeral arrangements had already been made. As Polly listened to Jess and the minister converse knowledgeably on the order of service, she pictured her own handwritten note at the bottom of her bag and wondered how on earth she could have been so foolish.

Jess had done a brilliant job. The funeral had been dignified and elegant, the minister genuine in his eulogy, the reading beautifully rendered. Polly had watched her daughter, a woman of forty now, the picture of grace in a fitted black dress with a square neck and cap sleeves, speak the

words of Christina Rossetti's 'Let Me Go'. The poem's spirit
had lingered in the church like a violin's closing note. The
wake, too, had been exactly what Nora would have wanted.
A garden party at Darling House, all the people she cared for
invited to enjoy the terrace and the view, a final experience of Nora's famous hospitality. Polly had been filled with
pride as she observed Jess moving among the guests, before
chastising herself for the misplaced emotion. Admiration,
perhaps, but she'd forfeited the right to pride a long time
ago.

Polly sliced cheese finely and fanned the pieces around
one side of Nora's porcelain platter. Dinner wasn't going to
be elaborate – neither of them was in the mood for that –
but she'd noticed that Jess had hardly eaten all day. She'd
been busy performing the role of host, but Polly suspected
there was more to it than that. Over the weekend, she'd
noticed a sporadic distraction in Jess, at odds with the focus
she was applying to Nora's arrangements. Polly was an
astute observer, a skill honed over a lifetime of invisibility.
Jess was grief-stricken over Nora, but something else was
bothering her. Polly wondered whether it related to Mrs
Robinson's report that Jess had been asking about the Turner
family and Halcyon. 'She's been very insistent,' Mrs Robinson had said over the phone. 'Wanting me to tell her
everything I know.'

'Is she upset?' Polly had asked, remembering how dis-
tressed she'd been herself to learn of the family connection to
a famous murderer.

'Not upset, no, I wouldn't say that. More curious – the
way she used to get: fixated on discovering everything she
possibly can about a subject.'

Polly finished putting the cold plate together and debated

briefly whether to set it on the table or leave it at the bench so they could serve themselves, buffet-style. The latter, though casual, seemed a bit ridiculous when there was only one platter and two diners. She carried the dish to the middle of the table and then sat at one of the places to wait for Jess. After a few seconds, she got up again and retrieved the copy of Daniel Miller's book that she'd brought with her from Brisbane. She was going to give it to Jess tonight and had carried it downstairs wrapped in a fabric bookstore bag. Polly had been surprised at first, to think that Nora had confided in Jess about Halcyon after being so adamant that she must never know the truth, but Mrs Robinson had confirmed that wasn't the case. 'As far as I can tell, your mum said something about it in the hospital, when she was in and out of consciousness. Jess was there and put two and two together. Not sure how, exactly – you know what she's like.'

Polly hooked the bag over her seat and sat the book on the table beside her place setting. She *did* know what Jess was like: curious and committed. As a child, nothing had escaped her notice. It had been a challenge and a delight. When Polly was planning the move to Queensland, she'd had to include Jess in the preparations well before she'd wanted to, because her daughter had gleaned something was afoot and started making scarily accurate guesses.

A foolish decision, as it turned out: she should have tried harder to keep things under wraps until she'd finalised the details. Jess had been a little girl of ten – it was natural that she should get caught up in the excitement of the adventure – but Polly ought to have known better. She'd failed to consider the realities of moving a child away from the only place she'd ever called home. Nora had been the one to make her see that there was more at stake than she'd imagined. On the morning Polly finally worked up the courage to tell her mother she'd taken a new job and they were heading north, Nora had appeared to receive the news dispassionately, saying only, 'But you can't mean to disrupt Jessica in her final year of primary school? Not when she's just won the lead role in the musical.'

It had been the first crack in the beautiful glass bauble of Polly's dream.

'Why don't you leave her with me,' Nora had urged, 'just until the end of the school year? Let Jess finish with her friends. You'll have a lot to organise up there. It's bound to be a bit stressful. She's better off here, where I can help.'

Eventually, Polly had agreed. It wasn't going to be for long, she told herself. It would give her a chance to find her feet and work out a plan for school. So she moved north, started her job, set up the house, and then waited at night for the clock to reach eight-thirty – Nora's nominated time – so she could ring and find out how the school day had been. Jess was always full of stories and Polly would listen with equal parts joy and sadness; sometimes, though, Jess was still at rehearsal, or else she'd gone to bed early because she was exhausted from her many extracurricular activities. 'I can wake her, if you like,' Nora would say. 'I'm sure she'll want to say hello. She was expecting to hear from you, but she was just so tired I didn't have the heart to make her wait up.'

'Of course, of course,' Polly would always reply. 'It's far more important that she gets enough sleep.'

It was her own fault, Polly knew: her job was new so she didn't like to say no to later shifts, and she couldn't call long distance from work; but she still should have found a way to speak with Jess, as she'd promised.

One night she worked up the nerve to ask Nora how Jess was *really* doing – was she missing her mother too much, did she feel abandoned, was she fretting? But Nora brushed away her concern. 'You mustn't worry, darling,' she said. 'Jess is fine – better than fine; she's thriving.'

Polly couldn't think what to say to that. It was a good thing, she decided. She didn't want Jess to be unhappy and pining for her. She was glad.

'You did the right thing letting her stay through to the end of the term.'

Polly had made a small noise of acknowledgement.

'I know how difficult it must be, my dear. You're a wonderful mother to put your little girl's needs before your own.'

Polly swatted a fly away from the platter. All of that was old news now. She shouldn't be dwelling on it. There was no going back, and it had all worked out. Nora had been right: Sydney was the best place for Jess, Darling House the better home. Polly couldn't have offered her daughter half the opportunities Nora had, and the proof of the pudding was in the eating: Jess was a magnificent person.

Polly straightened the book in line with her fork and listened closely for movement on the stairs. The house creaked in reply, but otherwise sat silent. Ever since the night of Daniel Miller's visit, when Nora had stood over Jess's crib, impossibly pale and wretched, and implored Polly to keep the secret of what had happened in South Australia to herself, Polly had done as she'd been asked. It hadn't been difficult at first: she would never have wished upon her young daughter the anguish she'd suffered when she learned the truth, and by the time Jess was old enough to be told, their relationship was no longer of the sort to encourage confidences.

But now Jess was asking about their family history and Nora was gone. The decision was no longer Polly's to make, the secret not hers to keep. As in all the best fairy tales, she felt herself released from her promise by Nora's death.

Polly eyed the book again. After a moment's deliberation she slipped it back inside the bag. Better to give a small pre-amble before presenting it to Jess, she decided. She glanced at the clock and wondered whether she ought to call out that dinner was ready. She'd said earlier that she was going to prepare something; Jess had said that sounded good. But perhaps she'd forgotten? Polly shook her head and chided herself for overcomplicating a very simple arrangement. She had put together a meal, her daughter would be downstairs in a minute or two, and then they would eat. She just needed to relax.

Jess was still wearing the dress she'd chosen for the funeral. It was one of Nora's. She hadn't brought anything remotely suitable with her from London, and the idea of shopping for clothing over the weekend had been abhorrent. Besides, the vintage Carla Zampatti at the back of Nora's wardrobe was perfect. There was a photograph of Nora wearing it at the opening of a theatre production in the eighties; the image had been printed in the newspaper and the photographer had sent Nora a print as a gift. People, as a rule, liked to please Nora. Jess could remember admiring the framed picture when she was a little girl, standing at her grandmother's chest of drawers, inspecting the exotic items that graced its surface, and thinking that the woman in the black dress was the height of adult chic.

'Aim to be decorative, dearest, but always on your own terms.'

Jess closed her eyes tightly. The memory of her grandmother's voice was so close it seared. How was she ever going to accept that Nora was gone? There had been moments since the horror of last Wednesday when she'd felt the solid earth disappear from beneath her feet. She had found herself casting about for something familiar to hold on to, and yet at the same time doing so numbly, without panic; she had struggled to find the right word to describe the emotion she was feeling, before realising it was grief. Not only for the loss of Nora, but for herself, her life, for all of the things that she had once counted on that now seemed lost.

Her career, a source of pride and solidity, was in tatters: for the first time that she could remember, she'd missed a deadline. And while to an outside view her grandmother's death might seem to offer a valid reason, Jess knew it was more than that. She'd been struggling with the article beforehand. Never had she felt her work to be so pointless.

She had no family to speak of; her home was a house she couldn't afford, standing empty in a faraway street on the other side of the planet. She felt as if the strings that tethered her to the world and everyone and everything in it had been severed.

To top it all off, she was suffering a chest-hollowing guilt at the thought that she'd let her grandmother down. She had not honoured Nora's wish to die at Darling House. She'd told herself that it had all happened so fast; now, though, she wondered whether she had simply been too slow to understand what the doctor and nurses had been trying to tell her at the hospital. She should have brought Nora home sooner;

she should have been more observant, more insistent. The one time that Nora had relied on Jess to advocate for her, she had failed.

Jess had never before considered herself a failure, no matter the setbacks she'd endured. 'One step at a time,' Nora used to say if Jess suffered a disappointment at school. 'Anything can be overcome, any distance travelled, just put one foot in front of the other and keep on going until you get there.' But what if one didn't know where 'there' was? What was a person to do when she was stuck in a place she didn't recognise, with no signposts, and no idea where to put the next step?

'What am I going to do, Nora?'

The room met her question with a resounding silence.

Downstairs, a piece of cutlery fell to the tiled floor. The noise was a sacrilege. Jess sat very quietly, as still as she could, tamping down the resentment she felt that Polly was clattering away in the kitchen, being careless with Nora's things, when Nora herself was not.

Her mother had said she'd make dinner, and although Jess felt neither like eating nor engaging in polite conversation, she hadn't had the heart to say no. As a rule, Polly's efforts were to be supported: it was a fact, sometimes tiresome, of her 'vulnerability'. Allowances were to be made, and not merely because Nora said so. The part of Jess that remembered when it was just the two of them in the flat further up the peninsula, the part that recollected laughing together with joy, feeling safety and comfort, the sunlight and warmth before hurt had hardened her heart – that part could never allow her to express frustration towards her mother, no matter how strongly she felt it.

At length, Jess found the impetus to move. She went to

the ensuite to wash her hands and ready herself for the next hurdle. Her hair was coming loose; she brushed it. Her face was pale; she pinched each cheek. The dress smelled like Nora; she left it on. And then, putting one foot in front of the other, she started making her way downstairs.

CHAPTER TWENTY-SIX

It was unsettling being back at Darling House. Polly was beset with memories; the past appeared at every turn. Just over there, for instance, on the sofa below the wall of family photographs, she saw herself at twenty, her face in her hands. It was her birthday, and Nora had served lunch outside on the terrace. She'd invited a number of Polly's friends from school, girls Polly hadn't seen in months, all of them dressed beautifully, fresh with stories of university and travel and plans for the future.

Polly hadn't wanted a party; she'd been feeling a bit overwhelmed. Just when she'd started to get the hang of having a baby, had gained some release from the constant fear that she was going to damage this perfect child they'd sent home with her from the hospital, Jess had morphed and grown and gained with her new mobility an instinct for danger.

Polly cried some evenings from sheer exhaustion and loneliness, and Nora listened as she outlined all that had gone wrong in the day. Her mother's face would be as a mirror to Polly's own sorrow, and then Polly would feel worse. 'A mother is only ever as happy as her unhappiest child,' Nora was fond of saying. 'And I only have one child, so you have to be jolly.' Nora was joking when she said it, but jests are often used to mask the truth and Polly knew that this was such a time: her mother had sacrificed an enormous amount to have her, and had dedicated herself to Polly's upbringing.

That's why, when Nora suggested a birthday dinner – 'to cheer you up!' – Polly had agreed; it had seemed the least she could do. But the occasion had been as awful as she'd feared. She wasn't good at being with people anymore – not that she'd ever been a charming hostess. She'd messed up Jess's feeding time, forgotten to rebutton her own dress when she returned to the table, and then everyone had wanted to hold the baby and Jess had become overtired and refused to settle and Polly had stood and jiggled her and cooed and felt all eyes on her as she failed this most basic of tests.

Thank God Nora had been there with her magic hold. 'Guaranteed to tame even the crankiest baby,' she'd said with a smile for the party guests.

Sure enough, Jess had calmed almost at once. Her red baby face, stuck in an attitude of deep surprise and indignation, wide eyes, juddering mouth and tearful hiccoughs, had felt like an indictment. Relief and embarrassment had swirled together with self-loathing to form a sick knot in Polly's stomach, and there'd been something else with it – a feeling she was tempted to call rage, only it couldn't be that, because Jess was an innocent little baby who just wanted to be comforted and cared for, and only a monster, an absolute monster, could be angry with a helpless child.

It was later the same night that Nora found her crying into her hands on the sofa.

'Oh, Polly,' she'd said. 'My dear Polly. Everything's going to be all right.'

'I don't know what I'm doing. It's so hard.'

'It feels that way because it's new. Being a mother doesn't

always come naturally. It's like anything – one must learn the ropes.'

'Was it like that for you, too?'

'To a degree. Though some women are born mothers.' The implication being that some women were not.

'She hates me.'

Nora laughed. 'She doesn't hate you! She's a baby; she doesn't know what hate is.'

'Then why won't she settle when I hold her?'

'You're nervous. Babies can sense these things.' Nora had paused then, before saying delicately: 'Listen, have you thought about seeing Dr Westerby again?'

Memories of the weekly after-school sessions in the cloying office of Dr Westerby flooded back. The stale air conditioning, never quite cool enough; the sense she always had that the air was thick with other people's problems. The frailty of her wrists, the softness of her voice, the insubstantiality of her whole being. The truth was, whenever she considered opening up and telling Dr Westerby how scared and uncertain she felt, she would remember him laughing and raising a glass at one of Nora's parties and know that there was no way she could trust him.

'I don't need to see Dr Westerby,' she said.

'Well,' Nora replied, 'you can always change your mind. And in the meantime, I'm here, aren't I? You're not to worry – our little Jess is in the safest of hands.'

Polly shook the memory away. It had been an awful time, but it was in the past. Things had got better, just as Nora said they would. Polly had grown in confidence and proficiency, so much so that by the time Jess was three and starting kindergarten, she had a job she loved at a local bookstore, some savings in the bank, and was starting to think about moving out.

It was in this room, she remembered now, that she'd told Nora her plans. Though no, that wasn't quite right; she hadn't told Nora – Nora had asked her to explain. Polly hadn't meant to be sneaky or underhanded, it was rather that she'd known, even as the idea first started to take shape, that Nora wouldn't like it.

The decision was hard enough to explain to herself. Nora was the perfect mother, everybody said so, and Darling House was the most beautiful home a person could hope to live in. And yet, for all its rooms, Polly felt herself running short of space. Everywhere she turned, she was confronted with Nora's possessions, and they were so definite, so permanent, so established. Polly wanted to stretch out, sometimes in different directions, to form shapes other than the ones that Nora left for her; she wanted to have time with Jess that belonged to the two of them alone.

Perhaps it was because such desires felt selfish and ungrateful, or else because she didn't have much experience going against Nora's wishes and it was difficult to break a lifetime's habit – maybe even because there was a part of her that knew even then that Nora was used to things going her way and her bonhomie was not entirely without expectation – but when she began to consult the rental section of the newspaper, Polly did so secretly. She was only looking, she told herself. There would be plenty of time to talk to Nora if, and when, her search for a new place became a reality.

When she'd found a few options that she thought she could afford, Polly had made appointments to inspect them. The first agent was a woman by the name of Sue Haley who kindly offered to drive Polly around and show her some of the other properties on her books.

It had been foolish, in retrospect, not to realise that word would get back to Nora.

'I ran into a colleague at the shops today,' Nora said one evening. Polly had been at the kitchen bench shelling peas, and Nora was sitting on the sofa, bouncing Jess on her knee. 'She mentioned that she'd shown an apartment to a Polly Turner-Bridges and wasn't that a coincidence.'

Polly's heart sank, but her mother didn't seem angry. 'I just wish you'd told me,' she said. 'I felt so embarrassed. To stand there while that awful woman looked at me, glee-ful to realise that my daughter hadn't included me in her plans.'

Polly felt a wave of shame. 'I'm sorry. I didn't want to upset you.'

'I'm more upset that you thought you couldn't trust me. I don't expect you to live with me forever. I know how lucky I've been to hold on to you both for as long as I have. You're always welcome here, of course, but I understand – you're twenty-two years old, an adult in your own right, and a mother, for goodness' sake!'

Polly had felt awash with relief and gratitude. All of her worry had been for nothing. Her workmate, Sharon, with whom she shared most shifts at the shop, had frowned when she said she was nervous about what her mother would say, and Polly had felt foolish when she tried to explain that her mother was different, that they were very close. It had sounded stupid, even to her own ears, more so when Sharon said, 'Wouldn't she be happy to see you enjoying your inde-pendence?' Polly hadn't known what to say to that, and in the end she'd said nothing; obviously Sharon had missed the point.

'Have you found anything you like?' Nora asked.

'Not yet. They were all a bit . . .' Polly lifted a shoulder.

'I can imagine. If you'd spoken to me, I'd have warned you about Sue Haley. She's well-meaning, and there's a market for every kind of property, but an agent's list is only as good as the agent herself.'

'I don't need luxury,' Polly protested.

'I might be able to help,' continued Nora, as if Polly hadn't spoken, lifting Jess onto her hip and going to her desk in the small office off the kitchen. 'Something of a coincidence, but one of my favourite little apartments is becoming available next month. It would be perfect for the two of you. You probably wanted to do this all by yourself – I can remember being your age – but it's right around the corner from Jessica's kindergarten. I know you wouldn't want to move her. This way, you'd still be able to walk there.' She held out a brochure.

Polly looked at the photograph. She knew the apartment block. It was one of the nicer ones up near the playground. Not brand-new, but a significant improvement on the flats she'd been looking at with Sue Haley.

Nora was right; Polly had wanted to do it by herself. She thought back to the thrill she'd felt, almost of danger, when Sue Haley had slowed her car out the front of a six-pack brick block of flats in a part of Sydney she'd never been to before.

But in choosing such an apartment just to avoid having to ask her mother for help, was she hurting Jess in some way?

'What's the rent?'

'One fifty a week.'

'For an apartment with an ensuite?'

'It's very small. The second bedroom is little more than a glorified cupboard.'

Polly wasn't sure whether her mother was telling her the truth or not.

'Why don't you look, at least?' said Nora. 'If you don't like it, or it's not suitable, you can give Sue Haley another call.'

Polly thought about it and agreed that she would go to see the apartment the following day. And of course, as her mother said, if she didn't want to take it, she didn't have to.

'Wonderful,' said Nora. 'You can be independent without having to make Jess live in squalor. And, if you need me, I'll be just around the corner.'

Jess arrived at the kitchen to find Polly lost in thought and clutching a handful of cutlery. She appeared to be in the process of un-setting the table. Jess felt a wave of frustration and quickly quelled it. She was tired and desperately sad; the surge of resentment she felt as she registered the disarray, the hint of uncertainty and dithering, had nothing really to do with her mother. At least, that's what she told herself.

'Oh, Jess, hello,' said Polly, noticing her, gesturing uncertainly towards Nora's table. 'I've put a cold platter together. I thought that might be best for dinner. Something light?'

Jess ignored the hesitant rising inflection at the end of what was a perfectly reasonable statement. 'Sounds good.'

'I know you probably don't feel like anything heavier.'

'No.'

'But it's important to eat.'

Jess smiled grimly. Fifteen minutes of patience, she told herself, and then she could go back upstairs and be alone.

They engaged in an awkward exchange about the day's events – how much Nora would have liked it, how well the minister had done, Mrs Robinson's catering prowess. It was a relief when they'd finally wrung the last possibilities from the conversation and silence was allowed to fall. Jess nibbled on the edge of a water cracker and glanced at the clock. She was aware of her mother's sterling silver cat tinkling every time she moved, knocking against the small wooden bird pendant. The sound grated. Jess was preparing to make her excuses when Polly took a deep breath and said, 'I have something for you.'

Jess felt a wave of confusion. She didn't want a gift. She was no longer a child of ten. Nora had died and a trinket would not make it better. But Polly reached into a bag that was sitting on the table beside her and took out a book, sliding it across the surface.

Jess recognised the cover at once, and the dissonance of the moment was dizzying. Disparate elements of her life came together in a most unexpected and inexplicable way. Nora in the hospital – *Halcyon . . . Issy, help me . . . He's going to take her from me . . .* – the strange immersion in Daniel Miller's book of the past week, and Polly, the mother she rarely saw, staring at her now with great expectation. 'I . . . I don't . . .' stammered Jess. 'Where did you . . . how . . . ?'

'Janey – Mrs Robinson – told me you'd been asking about it all. I had this book sitting on my shelf at home.'

But that hadn't been what Jess was going to ask at all. What she'd wanted to know was, how did Polly know about Halcyon and the Turner family? Nora had considered the secret too deep and dark to share. How had Polly found out?

'It was written at the time by a journalist who was living

nearby,' Polly continued. 'I thought it might answer some of your questions.'

'How do you know about what happened at Halcyon?'

'Nora told me. When I was pregnant with you. In fact, I . . .'

Jess was reeling. She didn't know whose betrayal was worse: Polly's, for having known all this time and said nothing, or Nora's, for trusting Polly with the truth and not Jess. But it was impossible to feel angry with Nora – to do so would have made her seem even more absent and Jess couldn't cope with that; and so, the needle settled on Polly, who was still chattering away as if nothing were wrong.

Jess stood abruptly and pushed her stool back towards the bench.

'Jess? Are you all right? You haven't finished.'

'I'm not hungry.'

'But you haven't eaten all day.'

'I'll be fine.' Jess paused, hesitated, failed. Her voice was unrecognisable, even to her own ears. 'And to be frank, I think it's a little late in the day for you to start playing the concerned mother. Or the caring daughter, for that matter. You abandoned both of us a long time ago.'

By the time Jess reached the top of the stairs, the brief glow of self-righteousness was already giving way to a sense of guilt. Her mother's expression had been one of surprise followed by uncertainty, and then her cheeks had reddened and she'd looked crestfallen.

But really, it had been more than Jess could take. The realisation that Polly had known about Halcyon and the Turners all along, that Nora had told her, and Jess had been kept in the dark by both, was blinding. The hot ball of

emotion and upset she'd experienced as a little girl when she
realised that her mother didn't want her, that she'd been
tricked into thinking she was moving to Brisbane, too, that
she wasn't being told the whole truth, was back.

And the incident when she was a baby – one of the most
reliable sources of hurt and anger towards her mother – had
returned as well, but muddied now by a sense of confusion,
because ever since she'd read Daniel Miller's notes and realised the nature of his tip-off to the police, Nora's account of
what she'd seen Isabel do, Jess had known deep inside her
gut that something wasn't right.

She followed the corridor past the library, but instead of
going upstairs to her bed, she turned into Nora's room. She
lay down and pressed her face into the soft edge of her
grandmother's pillow.

After a time, she grew restless. She still had Polly's copy of
Daniel Miller's book in hand. She lifted it up and inspected
the familiar jacket. It was a little different from Nora's. For
one thing, it had a clear plastic cover and a Dewey decimal
library classification on the spine.

A piece of paper had been stuck adjacent to the title page
with columns of dates stamped in rows. Jess remembered the
analogue borrowing system from trips to the library when
she was a girl. The last date was 4 April 1978: six months
before Jess was born. Another stamp inside the jacket read
LIBRARY OF SOUTH AUSTRALIA. Interesting. Nora might
have been the one to tell Polly about Halcyon, but it
appeared that Polly had gone looking for more information
herself.

There was something else distinctive about this copy, Jess
noticed. Now that she looked closely, she saw a protrusion,
an item tucked inside the back cover. Within the sleeve of

protective plastic were some sheets of folded paper. She took them out, opened them, and saw that it was photocopied text. Someone had written neatly at the top in blue biro: *Addendum, 1980 edition.*

Jess sat up straighter against Nora's pillows. This, then, was the final chapter that Nancy Davis had mentioned. Written after Daniel Miller returned to Australia, when Thea Turner's remains were found in the garden at Halcyon, ending a twenty-year mystery.

As If They Were Asleep

DANIEL MILLER

Addendum: Halcyon Revisited

It was said that poor Percy Summers, who'd made the grim discovery, was never the same again. Edith Pigott was told by Maud McKendry, who'd heard it from Meg Summers herself. He'd thought they were asleep. He almost went right by, but his horse, that loyal old girl, Blaze, was hot and tired and in need of a swim – she'd done the walk from the Station down near Meadows, after all – and that's how he wound up at the water hole and saw the distressing sight. He'd never been able to forget it, especially the youngest girl, the line of ants marching busily over her wrist.

On the first anniversary of the shocking events, Reverend Lawson prepared a special sermon, with prayers at its end for baby Thea. It was his tradition to give a roundup of the year, the community's struggles and successes, the lives lost and gained; it would have been unthinkable not to mention the Turner family. Besides, everyone in town, each member of his flock, had lived through a trauma that year. The situation itself had been difficult enough to bear, but until the coroner handed down his findings, there'd also been fears that a murderer walked among them. Ned Lawson knew it was his calling to bring peace of mind back to his flock. And how often did the opportunity to tell a local story about sinners and innocents combined present itself?

The following year, Christmas Eve 1961, Reverend Lawson eulogized the Turner family again, but less lyrically this time, and with a restraint to his delivery that conveyed reserve. It was one thing to tell stories that inspired gratitude for community and life while warning against evil, and quite another to dwell on tragedy.

By the third year, mention of the family had been reduced to inclusion in the prayer list for church donors past and present; by year four, an administrative error caused their names to drop completely from the group.

Over the next five years, the Turner family slipped out of everyday conversation. It wasn't that people forgot so much as that they didn't always remember. Locals found that they could walk past the end of Willner Road without immediately thinking of the way the four ambulances had formed a convoy that day, driving their sorry load slowly away from the farm; months could go by without anyone mentioning the tragedy, until a news report about wild dogs or a warning about poisonous flowers in the woods or plans for a summer picnic caused someone to sigh with sad recollection and say, 'Remember the poor family that used to live up at the Wentworth place?'

And then, in early 1966, two things happened. First, on a blistering summer's day, January 26, as the people of Adelaide, in step with their countrymen, marked Australia Day, three children from a single family caught the tram from their home in the sleepy suburb of Somerton Park to the carnival fun of Glenelg Beach. After a day spent exploring the sand and the sea, having been spotted with a man who bought them ice-cream cones, the children disappeared into thin air.

The nation's attention was captured by the investigation. Day after day, newspaper reports dissected every detail, printing each rumor and false lead. When new developments were thin on the ground, the papers ran reports about other unsolved crimes instead. The Somerton Body was resurrected, as was the Turner Tragedy. Editors hoped that the latter, with its lost child element, might satisfy readers hungry for more newsprint tragedy, but fresh reports about the Turner baby did not gain traction. The coroner had ruled, no further evidence had come to light, the times had moved on; and so, the mystery of the Beaumont Children replaced the Turner Tragedy in the collective imagination.

The other thing that happened was closer to home for the people of Tambilla. Mr Thomas Turner, choosing to stay in London, decided at last to sell the house and surrounding farms. Local farmers took on the outer fields quickly enough, but Mr Turner did not succeed in selling Halcyon. It seemed there was a limit to the number of people simultaneously wealthy and romantic enough to buy a Georgian manor house on the edge of a small, dusty town in rural South Australia. Not to mention, there were few folks willing to overlook what had happened there.

The house sat empty for a time, until finally, after more than a decade of being unable to sell for a price that came close to its value, Mr Turner succeeded in renting Halcyon. The arrangement was less than ideal – he would have preferred a single well-to-do family – but by then he had waited so long, and he knew that beggars could not be choosers. The lease was taken up by a young couple, new to the area, who had decided to leave the city and – in the spirit of the seventies – set up a commune for like-minded people.

The other residents of Tambilla watched on from afar with characteristic interest, but over time stopped talking incessantly about the new people at the Wentworth place. It became quite usual to see one or two of them making the walk into the village for groceries and other essential supplies, dressed in tie-dyed shirts, their hair long and knotty, their faces clear and bright. Mrs Pigott at the post office, who could never resist voicing every question that sprang to her mind, asked them how things worked up there at the house, which is how folks gleaned that there was some sort of roster at play whereby everybody in the Nirvana Commune took turns making sure the cooking and the cleaning were done, odd jobs completed and work undertaken in the garden.

They were trying to grow as much of their own food as they could, said Mrs Pigott knowingly. They'd been told that once upon a time there was a kitchen garden at the house, but if that was the case, it had turned to weeds and thistles. Never mind, they were determined to build their own. One of the commune members had been a legal clerk before changing her name to Moon-Petal and retained enough respect for the law that she wrote to the landlord to ask his permission. He had written back a short, typed consent notice, very dry in tone, in which he noted that the garden had been a whim of his wife and, as she was now deceased, he didn't care what they did with it.

The group of five that had been assigned to outdoor work in the spring of 1979 had been striking tomato plants in the old greenhouse for weeks by then, the seeds gathered from fruit on the leggy vines that were spreading wild and unstaked in the gardens when they'd arrived. Sonia M, who had been 'reborn' and chose not to speak about her past, seemed to know a lot about gardening and growing, and she said that they were heirloom tomatoes and would respond well to drying and potting; sure enough, green shoots had sprouted, and now the time had come at last to plant them outside.

After much observation and discussion, and a meeting at which everybody had their say, the group decided to build their vegetable garden in a plot that seemed to have been a formal garden bed once, with a few arthritic rosebushes still in evidence. The patch, surrounded by overgrown hedges, was protected from the worst of the winds that tore up the driveway, while being close enough to the kitchen to be practical. Janice S, one of the leaseholders, who had some experience with communal living, spoke with calm authority on the need for practicality, even – especially – in an enterprise of free living such as theirs. The only drawback was an old walnut tree nearby that brought the cockatoos at dusk, but a scarecrow would take care of that, she assured them, with a confidence that could not be ignored.

And so, as the last frosts disappeared, and spring began to brighten and lift the sky, the group of intrepid outdoor workers started to dig their trenches. It was Ash P who made the chilling discovery. 'Hey,' he called out, setting down his spade. 'There's something here.'

'Treasure? Are we rich?' Angel K joked, before remembering that she'd taken a vow to forsake all worldly possessions. 'What is it?' she added quickly, adopting a more serious, quizzical tone.

Ash was on his knees by then, staring down into the hole he'd dug.

The group had gathered around and were avid in their attention, all but for a skinny boy named Henry R, who had a habit of finding himself and his interests out of step with those of other people and had chosen that very moment to gaze skyward at a pair of wheeling kites, wings outstretched as they soared in perfect synch. It was a choice for which he later said he'd be grateful for the rest of his life.

He watched, transfixed, as a breeze bearing the first hint of summer's warmth kissed his cheek and he was transported back to a childhood memory of another pair of circling birds above another garden, and he heard his mother's voice in his memory suddenly and clearly, singing a long-forgotten lullaby about a mockingbird, and his removal from the here and now was so complete that by the time his housemates' horrified cries pulled him back, the hole had been covered with a spade, its heart-wrenching contents hidden once more from view.

Daniel Miller, 1980

PART EIGHT

CHAPTER TWENTY-SEVEN

Sydney, 18 December 2018

The light was bright and warm on her face, and it took a minute for Jess to remember where she was. She had been dreaming about babies and rose gardens. The first thing she saw as she opened her eyes was the deep green foliage of an overgrown forest. Wallpaper, she realised. This was Nora's room. She was still wearing Nora's dress.

She felt sluggish. Every day now started with the fresh weight of Nora's death, but today something else was mixed in. A door closed downstairs and, after a momentary flicker of surprise, Jess remembered that Polly was also at Darling House – that she'd be staying another couple of days through until Thursday for the meeting with Nora's solicitor. With the recollection, details from the evening before returned and Jess understood her malaise. She had snapped at her mother after Polly gave her a copy of Daniel Miller's book.

Jess felt about for the book. She'd been reading the 1980 addendum the night before and had fallen asleep with the lamp still burning on the bedside table. She sat up and checked the quilt either side of her. Just as she was beginning to wonder whether she'd dreamed the whole thing, she looked over the edge of the bed and saw that the book had fallen into the wastepaper basket.

As Jess retrieved it, a striking letterhead in the rubbish pile caught her eye. The address that ran beneath the company name was in Adelaide.

With an inkling already as to what she was going to discover, Jess took the piece of paper from the bin and opened it out flat.

Sure enough, it was the letter she'd been looking for, addressed to Nora from a firm of solicitors in South Australia, signed by one of the partners. Jess recognised the name immediately. Marcus Summers, the younger son of Percy and Meg; one-time resident of Tambilla, on-again-off-again friend to John Turner, part-time helper in his mother's grocery shop.

With growing excitement, she read:

Dear Mrs Turner-Bridges,

Re: Mrs Isabel Turner and family, formerly of Tambilla, South Australia

I am writing to you on behalf of a client who has asked me to ascertain whether you would be willing to speak with him about the Turner family, formerly of Tambilla, South Australia.

Specifically, my client wishes to speak with you about the death of Thea Turner.

If you are amenable, I would be pleased to arrange a meeting at your convenience.

Kind regards,

Marcus Summers

Jess read the letter again. Included among the list of tasks to complete in her grandmother's diary had been the initials

M.S. A reminder to Nora to telephone Marcus Summers. The box beside the initials had not been ticked.

It was still only seven in the morning: too early to ring him herself. But Jess knew exactly what she could do to fill the time. She should have done it sooner. Nora had died because she went upstairs to the attic; Jess was more determined than ever to find out why.

The last time Jess had climbed these stairs had been the night before she'd left for London. Apprehension had kept her awake, her thoughts electric, her legs restless, until finally she'd had no choice but to get out of bed. Wandering the hallways of the dark house, willing the hours to pass, something had drawn her upstairs; when she reached the rickety flight leading to the attic, she'd understood why. Despite – or perhaps because of – Nora's repeated admonitions that it wasn't safe, that she should find elsewhere in the house to play, in the decade that Jess had lived at Darling House, the attic had been her favourite, special spot.

After Polly left her behind, she had craved a nest in which to lick her wounds, and where better than the quaint, peak-roofed room at the top of the house? The dormer window provided a vantage point from which she could survey the garden and, beyond it, the harbour; the walls were close, the space always warm. Even the smell of old dust had been a comfort. The attic had remained her first port of call when things went wrong at school, if she argued with a friend or missed out on a place in the debating team, if she just needed to be alone for a time.

That night, Jess had curled up on the small round carpet in the centre of the raw pine floorboards and closed her eyes; a decade of her previous incarnations had gathered around, bringing with them a return to certainty. Apprehension had tilted towards excitement, and when Jess woke up to first light spilling through the window and across the ceiling, she had been ready.

Twenty years later, it wasn't versions of her former self that climbed the stairs with her towards the attic, but echoes of Nora. Halfway up, Jess was hit with a fresh wave of grief, and needed to pause to absorb its force. When it had passed, she continued.

The door opened easily.

In Jess's experience, very few things matched one's memory of them, particularly meaningful places from childhood. They were invariably smaller, plainer, and shabbier than remembered. The attic of Darling House was a rare exception. As she was hit by the familiar scent of dust and time, Jess was reassured to see that everything was exactly as she'd recollected. The rug was still on the floor, the antique glass of the dormer window was still mottled with age, the old ship's clock was still stopped at twenty past two.

She surveyed the room, wondering where to start. The set of shelves on the eastern wall was loaded with once-treasured toys and books, the south wall was lined with plastic storage tubs of curtains and blankets and other remnants of material 'too good to toss', and a hinged full-length mirror stood in one corner. Beneath the dormer window was the old steamer trunk that had once belonged to Thomas Turner.

It was difficult to imagine that a toy or book might hold the clue. Far more likely, Jess decided, as much for its function as its provenance, was the steamer trunk. She opened the lid and blinked as mothball fumes made her eyes sting. The trunk, she saw, was still filled with piles of old dresses.

She took them out, one by one, checking the pockets, the seams, the sleeves. Her progress was slowed somewhat by nostalgia as she held up first one and then another, recalling the times she'd clambered into them as a teenager.

But Jess had turned up nothing of note. She ran her fingers around the inside panels and joins of the trunk, searching for a trick base or a hidden release. Alas, there was none.

Sitting on her knees on the floor, Jess surveyed the rest of the room, this time with a more scrutinising eye. The books caught her attention. Thinking of the photocopied addendum she'd found at the back of Polly's edition of *As If They Were Asleep*, Jess took each one from the shelf, checking inside the covers, agitating them by the spine. Aside from a faded shopping list and a dry-cleaning receipt, there was nothing. The careful investigation of each toy also yielded naught. Jess even checked the battery compartment of the train engine and pressed the old teddy bear's fur belly, neck and ears in search of something tucked within the stitching.

She opened the storage tubs, studying every piece of fabric individually, shaking the blankets loose and then discarding them in a heap. She looked beneath the rug, she paced out the floor, she combed the wide pine boards in case she found one that lifted to reveal a secret hiding place. Finally, she performed a close inspection of the windowsill.

Nothing. An hour spent searching, destruction wrought, and she was no closer to knowing the truth.

Back downstairs, showered, and ready to face the day, Jess reasoned that a random search of the attic had always been a long shot. This was real life, not a *Famous Five* story. Of far more promise was the link to Marcus Summers in

South Australia. Patrick had said how much the letter had upset Nora, and having read the contents, Jess was not surprised.

When it was at last office hours in Adelaide, Jess sat at Nora's desk in the library and dialled the number for Marcus Summers' firm. She waited impatiently for someone to pick up, and when the phone was eventually answered gave her name to the receptionist. At length, there came the clunking of a handheld receiver and a cordial voice at the other end of the line: 'Hello?'

'Marcus Summers?'

'Speaking.'

'It's Jess Turner-Bridges here, calling from Sydney. My grandmother was Nora Turner-Bridges.'

He didn't reply at first and, in the absence of a response, Jess heard the melancholy notes of a windchime in the background. She was beginning to wonder if he'd forgotten writing the letter at all, when belatedly he said, 'Good morning, Jess. Pardon me, did you say your grandmother *was* Nora Turner-Bridges?'

'Yes, I should explain – Nora passed away last week.'

'I'm so sorry to hear that.'

He really did sound disheartened by the news, and Jess wondered whether Marcus Summers, like Daniel Miller, had come to know Nora personally when she was living at Halcyon over the summer of 1959. She considered asking outright but decided to do so would reveal too much of her own interest too soon. 'I'm my grandmother's executor,' she said instead, 'and I've been trying to get her affairs in order. You wrote a letter recently, in which you said you had a client wishing to speak with her about the death of her niece, Thea Turner.'

A pause, and then, 'Yes.'

'I was wondering . . .' What was she wondering exactly? Whether the client would speak to her instead? If there was anything Marcus Summers could tell her that would shed light on her grandmother's final weeks, why Nora had been freshly upset about a long-ago tragedy, whether her ex-husband had sought custody of their daughter . . . She wondered all of those things, but how was she to explain to Marcus Summers without sounding breathless?

While Jess was trying to find the words, Marcus took the lead. 'I'm sorry – you said you're Mrs Turner-Bridges' granddaughter?'

'Yes.'

'And you're her executor?'

'That's right.'

'Are you Mrs Turner-Bridges' only surviving descendant?'

He was being a careful lawyer, seeking to ascertain that she had authority to speak to him on matters relating to Nora. As if somehow intuiting that she'd become the subject of conversation, even if only tangentially, Polly chose that moment to walk past the closed library door. Jess stayed silent, waiting until she heard her mother on her way downstairs before saying, 'My mother and grandmother weren't particularly close; Nora all but raised me. She trusted me with her affairs.' She added the whitest of lies: 'In fact, my grandmother spoke to me about your letter before she died. She had been meaning to contact you.'

There was a beat of silence but, whatever his considerations, when Marcus Summers spoke, his tone was decisive. 'Are you familiar with what happened to your grandmother's family in Tambilla all those years ago?'

'Understandably, my grandmother didn't speak of it often,

but I've read Daniel Miller's book. If there's something your client wanted to discuss with Nora, then I'm able to speak in her stead.'

Marcus Summers let out a long, considering sigh. 'I wrote to your grandmother because I have it on good authority that her niece, Thea Turner, wasn't taken from the picnic that day by wild dogs.'

'What?' It was on the tip of Jess's tongue to ask how his client could possibly know such a thing, but she paced herself. 'You're saying that Daniel Miller – and the police, and the coroner – got it wrong?'

'That's what I'm saying.'

'Do you know what *did* happen?'

'I'd prefer not to speak about it further over the phone. I have business in Sydney next week. Perhaps we can meet then?'

She could hear Polly downstairs in the kitchen, fishing out cutlery again. Thursday, the day of her mother's return to Brisbane, suddenly seemed a long way off. Jess didn't need to think longer than a second. 'I've got a better idea,' she said. 'I'll come and see you. Are you free tomorrow?'

CHAPTER TWENTY-EIGHT

Adelaide Hills, 18 December 2018

The country road was narrow, and dusk was falling faster now that she had left the freeway. Jess proceeded quickly but carefully, one eye on the unfamiliar road, the other glancing sideways to the passenger seat, where she'd put her phone with Google Maps and the sheet of paper listing directions she'd jotted down on the plane to help pinpoint the house. She'd rented the car at Adelaide Airport and, after a shaky start, was getting used to it, even if she still hadn't stopped engaging the windscreen wipers whenever she wanted to indicate a turn.

The drive up into the Hills had been easy enough, the freeway surprisingly uncongested. The stark gums and long scrappy grasses that had punctuated the parched earth either side of the road on the flats had given way to lush maples and giant cedars when she approached the villages of Crafers and Stirling, before opening out again to farmland as she headed east. Now, having taken the Hahndorf exit, Jess was winding along the Onkaparinga Valley Road, passing tiny country schools, and fields planted with grapevines, and stone houses with long driveways.

At last she saw signs pointing the way to Tambilla, where she'd managed with some difficulty to find herself an Airbnb at short notice. Check-in was scheduled for eight, but Jess had no intention of spending the night in South Australia without first catching a glimpse of Halcyon. She'd been hampered by her flight's late landing and was now in a race against the setting sun. According to the directions she'd put together, she needed to make a left turn approximately four kilometres beyond the town of Verdun.

Ahead of her, the road appeared to diverge. Slowing slightly, Jess leaned forward, her chest pressed against the steering wheel. She spotted a street sign, obscured in part by a low branch, and squinted to see what was written on it. Willner Road. Jess recognised the name with satisfaction, flicked on the wipers by mistake, then switched quickly to the blinker and took the turn.

She drove for what felt like a long time, her impatience growing in step with her anticipation. The road, which had been narrow to start with, thinned further, bitumen margins unravelling on either side so that any pretence of two lanes was soon abandoned. The gum trees were giants, and although the faraway sky continued blue, and late sunlight was turning the trunks silver, evening had already arrived in the cool, shaded underbrush at their base.

Jess flinched as an animal – a kangaroo, she guessed – lurched in the verge to her right, a dark flash of motion, before darting back into the bush behind. The shock made her slow the car almost to a standstill. She had been away too long. Driving the gentle country lanes of England, where a stray sheep taking a gentlemanly stroll was the gravest risk one might face, had made her forget the danger of kangaroos at dusk.

Daniel Miller's description was all she had to go by: 'The house on the hill, in the middle of the steep-rising fields at the end of Willner Road.' She'd lost track of how far she'd gone but was running out of road and beginning to suspect she'd missed the property. She was looking for a wide enough shoulder to turn the car around when she noticed, among the dense grove of tree trunks to her right, something running parallel to the road: masses of ivy had tangled with other voracious climbers, covering what must once have been a fence. Thick clumps of agapanthus grew sporadically at its base, long glossy leaves and a celebration of bright purple flowers shooting skywards.

Jess let the car crawl forward, looking for markers, until finally she reached a pair of old farm gates shut tight across what had once been a gravel driveway. Each gate was anchored to a stone pillar with a concrete sphere on top, barely visible anymore as creepers had grown unimpeded, tendrils adhering to every surface. Jess brought the car to a stop, scanning for some signal that she was in the right place. At last, on the left-hand pillar, she saw the edge of what appeared to be a property name.

She parked the car and climbed out. The foliage was pulled aside easily enough, revealing beneath it a rectangular sign of black metal on which spotted silver lettering spelled out the single word HALCYON. A large padlock bound the two gates together and a quick shake confirmed that it was locked. Though not brand-new, the lock appeared to be in working order. Jess wondered who might hold the key.

She shot a look back down the road. Parrots chattered excitedly in the treetops, and far above her the branches basked in the last lingering rays of sun. A group of cockatoos arced across the sky towards where the house presumably stood – descendants, she supposed, of the birds Nora had watched in the walnut tree from the window of her bedroom at Halcyon. No one else was around. Before she could think better of it, Jess hoisted herself up and climbed over the top of the gate.

She walked along the shaded driveway, expectation making the tips of her fingers tingle as she drew further away from the road. The driveway went steeply up the hill, enormous trees all around. Birds moved loud but invisible in the canopy and somewhere, a distance away, Jess could hear the faint rush of water. She remembered Daniel Miller's chapters about the crime scene, the picnic laid out beneath the willow where the creek widened to a waterhole. All at once, she was struck anew by the gravity of past events.

Jess had travelled far enough that the gate, her car, the path back, could no longer be seen; the bush through which she'd walked was thick and the effect from where she now stood was as if the trees had closed to encircle her. There was something quintessential about the landscape here. This place was new to her, and yet the clarity of the light, the air, the smell of the earth beneath her feet, was deeply familiar.

The driveway wound on through a profusion of changing foliage, lusher and denser than the bush through which she'd already come. Enormous hydrangeas with vibrant pink sponge-like blooms, rhododendrons and impatiens, tall spears of flowering oyster plants jostled together with Jurassic-looking philodendron leaves and tree ferns, a mixed bag all tied by a wild creeper with bell-shaped blue flowers. The damp smell of the garden reminded Jess of places she'd visited in Cornwall, like St Just in Roseland, where fertile ground spoke of layers of different generations, civilisations past.

At last, beyond the tangled greenery, Jess could glimpse the jutting white chimneys of a large roof. She realised she was holding her breath. She turned a final corner, just like

Daniel Miller had done on his way to meet Nora, and there it was. Grand and magnificent, yet even from a distance she could see that the house was in a state of disrepair. It was perched upon a stone plinth that rose about a metre off the ground. A clinging ficus with tiny leaves had grown to cover most of the stones and moss stained the rest, so that the house appeared to sit upon an ocean of greenery. Jess was reminded of the houses in fairy tales, hidden and then forgotten, ignored by the human world only to be reclaimed by nature.

Protruding from one corner of the plinth was a lion's head, its mouth open to reveal a void from which a stream of spring water must once have flowed. On the ground beneath sat a stone bowl, half-filled with stale rainwater. As Jess watched, a blue-breasted fairy wren flew down to perch upon the edge of the bowl; after observing Jess for a moment, the little bird made a graceful dive across the surface of the water, skimming himself clean before disappearing once more into the folds of the garden.

Jess skirted the house. It was an uncanny experience. She was for the first time visiting a place that, courtesy of Daniel Miller, she already knew quite well. The line of plane trees leading up towards the shed, the Hen Hilton, the plant pot man – lying in pieces now – where the vegetable garden had once been laid out in rows. As she rounded the southern corner and arrived in the overgrown back area, she recognised at once that she was standing in the spot where Isabel Turner had created her rose garden. It was here that Thea Turner's remains had been found in 1979, by the outdoor work group of the Nirvana Commune.

Jess wished she'd remembered to grab her phone from the car seat; she could have done with a torch. She longed to stay, to see whether she could open any of the doors to the house, but it was already getting difficult to see. The browns and golds and olive-greens of before had darkened, and if she didn't start making her way back now, she would be caught in the bush when night fell.

Jess went quickly, aware of the changing mood of the landscape. Trees that had been full of birds were quiet now. She sensed animal eyes watching her from the shadows. When she was very small, one of Jess's favourite books at the library was *The Bunyip of Berkeley's Creek*. She'd found it frightening, and yet been hopelessly drawn to its eerie illustrations and story. Jess hadn't thought of it in decades, but now the cover came back to her, with its scaled and feathered creature, born from the mud, emerging from the place where the dark things lived, lonely and unlovely.

By the time she neared the gate, Jess was almost running, and it was a relief to slip into the car, turn on the headlights, and drive away.

Home for the night was a small but cheerful bedsit above the garage of a modest brick bungalow off the main street of Tambilla. Jess was half an hour later than she'd arranged when she made the booking, but the woman meeting her was not put out. 'I don't live far,' she said, nodding towards the place next door. 'It's no problem at all.'

As they were parting, Jess asked about local dinner options and the woman frowned at her watch. 'You'll be pushing it at this time of night, especially mid-week. The hotel might be your best bet, unless you fancy driving into Mount Barker.'

Jess thanked her and set off on foot along the main street, which was lined with huge oak trees, strings of yellow light bulbs scalloped between them. Jess thought, as she walked, of the descriptions of the town in Daniel Miller's book. She passed the intersection where the churches of St Peter's Lutheran and St George's Anglican faced off against one another, the stone Institute building inside which Peter Duke had conducted his community meeting in the days following the Turner deaths, and she picked out the buildings where Betty Diamond's tearoom and Summers & Sons Grocers had once been.

So vivid in her mind was the book that Jess half-expected to see the businesses from back then thriving still, and she felt her heart sink when she saw there was now an artisan cheesemaker on the corner across from the hotel, and that the only grocery in town was a modern-looking IGA. A Portuguese friend had once given her the word *saudade* when she was trying to describe the feeling of being overcome by a weighty sense of absence for something that couldn't be had or experienced again; Jess had never forgotten it. That's how she felt now. She *missed* the Tambilla of Miller's book with an intensity that was visceral.

The Tambilla Hotel, at least, looked almost identical to the historical pictures she'd seen online, as did the Centenary Garden across the street. Jess, who was warned that the kitchen was closing in five minutes, placed an order quickly. The pub was decorated with a mix of German and Australian paraphernalia and offered a lot to look at, but there was still enough warmth in the day that she preferred to find a seat outside at one of the tables on the pavement.

Tambilla was pretty; Australian country towns were often a motley collection of different architectural styles, but the uniformity and preservation of the stone cottages along this main street reminded Jess of villages in the Cotswolds. Be that as it may, the spirit of the place had certainly changed since the time when Thomas Turner brought his family here. Daniel Miller had described an insularity – a town for local people – but it was clear from the type of shops that now occupied the settlers' cottages along the main street that Tambilla did a busy line in tourism. Sheepskins, handwoven baskets, alpaca clothing, cheese, wine, jams – Jess was willing to bet it was all but impossible to get a parking spot along this street on weekends.

A young waiter brought her the drink she'd ordered, and she pushed aside the straw to take a sip. Visiting Halcyon had left her melancholy; the decrepit state of the place had been objectively dispiriting, but Jess found herself overlaying the property she'd seen with images evoked by Daniel Miller's book, of sunshine and light, children and picnics and Christmases. That was the world Nora had known; a world she had never been able – or wanted – to share with her granddaughter.

Jess suffered a sudden wave of dislocation. A week and a half ago, she'd been sitting with Rachel in a Hampstead tapas bar, oblivious to Tambilla or Halcyon or the Turner family. What must it have been like for Isabel, she wondered, who had also travelled around the globe from the place she'd called home; who had lived through the chaos and noise of the Second World War only to find herself in a quiet town like this? The sense of country was so strong out here. Isabel must have felt herself a stranger in a strange land. The newspaper reports from the time had certainly made a lot of her 'otherness'. Daniel Miller had mentioned it, too, as had the coroner. It had become a central narrative: that homesickness had made her 'do what she'd done'.

As Jess ate her dinner of Coorong mullet, she read articles

on her phone and wondered how she was going to gain a look inside Halcyon. When the young waitress came to clear her plate, Jess asked her what she knew about the house on the hill outside of town.

The girl, eighteen or so, tilted her head, uncertain.

'It's called Halcyon,' Jess prompted. 'Or maybe you know it as the Wentworth place?'

The girl shook her head and smiled ruefully. 'Never heard of it, sorry. I'll ask someone inside if you like.'

Jess was packing up to leave when an older waitress came out to the table. 'Nikki said you were asking about Halcyon?'

'Do you know it?'

''Course I do. Big house out on Willner Road.'

'I was wondering who owns the place these days.'

'There hasn't been anyone living there for as long as I can remember. It was a hippie commune back when I was born.' She looked at Jess enquiringly. 'Do you know the history?'

'I know about the Turner deaths.'

She nodded. 'After they discovered the baby's remains, the hippies moved out. Decided it had bad energy. It was the end of the seventies anyway. They all had haircuts to get and Reeboks to buy. The place sat empty for a decade or so after that and then it went on the market. Bought by someone who lived overseas, from memory, but no one moved in. It's changed hands a few times, but nothing ever seems to happen. Up for sale again, I think.'

Jess glimpsed an opportunity. 'Do you know the agent who's listed it?'

'That'd be Deb Green. Hang on a minute, I've got one of her cards inside.'

*

Next morning, as Jess sat in Marcus Summers' office near the University of Adelaide, she thumbed the edge of Deb Green's business card. Her flight left at two that afternoon, but she was hoping to be able to get back up into the Hills to explore the house before she left. It was going to be tight. Her meeting with Marcus had been scheduled for nine and it was already half past. It was a forty-five-minute drive back to Tambilla and another forty-five from there to the airport. She had no baggage to check, but the car would need to be returned, and that always took longer than it should.

She glanced again at the clock and then at the young man behind the desk. He was an interesting choice of assistant, around twenty years old, with shaggy hair, earnest blue eyes, and a goofy manner of whistling while he worked. She supposed he was a law student helping out. 'Won't be long,' he said with a smile, catching her looking at him. 'Cup of tea?'

Jess told him again that she was fine.

Marcus Summers' office was comprehensively and eclectically full. Two walls were lined with bookshelves and the others hosted an array of artwork, some from nations of the Pacific, most by Indigenous Australian artists. She'd googled Summers the day before and knew that he had impressive qualifications and experience. He'd started out as a young lawyer helping on Mabo and been instrumental in various Native Title cases throughout the Northern Territory and South Australia. The only recent photograph she'd found online was from his website, a beautiful shot of Kakadu, a plunging waterfall with a tiny human figure standing at its base. The bio itself described a man who found professional and personal meaning in nature. In one of the interviews she'd found on the web, he'd said, 'Morality is a funny thing.

It often has little to do with lawfulness.' She supposed a lawyer was in a good position to know.

Finally, the door burst open and a man with a bulging stack of manila folders bumbled busily into the office. 'Jess?' he said, peering at her over his blue-framed glasses.

Jess nodded.

'Wonderful. Have you met my grandson, Jasper?' He was beaming at the young man, who rolled his eyes fondly before taking the files from his grandfather. 'I hope he offered you tea.'

'He did. Twice.'

'Marvellous. Won't be a moment – I just have to make a note of something.'

As Jess looked on, Marcus Summers produced a pen from his shirt pocket and stooped over the desk. He was tall and slim with white hair and wild, thick sideburns, and the air of a septuagenarian undergraduate: interested, avid, energetic, but at the same time wise and intelligent. He was wearing pale denim jeans, sneakers and, although it was summer, a knitted vest over his T-shirt.

When he'd finished scribbling, he handed the small square of paper to Jasper, then turned to Jess. 'It's a beautiful day,' he said. 'I thought we'd go for a walk.'

They set off together towards the university campus, and Jess broke the ice by thanking him for making time to meet with her.

'Nonsense,' he replied. 'I'm the one who should be thanking you for coming all this way. I've overseen more than my fair share of estates – your commitment to your grandmother's affairs is admirable.'

'Actually,' Jess began, deciding that she didn't have the time or the inclination to dissemble, 'I have more than a passing interest in my grandmother's family history. I think something was troubling her before she died, and receiving your letter was part of it. Finding out why – it's personal for me.'

'It's personal for me, too,' he said. 'I'm glad you got in touch. I've waited a long time.'

Jess was momentarily confused. His letter to Nora had been recent; in it, Marcus Summers said that he was writing on behalf of a client; on the phone he'd mentioned being in possession of new information. 'Your client . . . I thought you said . . .' She broke off, unable to make the pieces fit together.

'Jess,' said Marcus, coming to a stop. He scratched his head thoughtfully. 'I think we're both aware that I don't have a client. Not in the usual sense. I contacted your grand-mother because I know certain things about that night, Christmas Eve 1959, and the days that followed; things that I've carried with me for a long time. I sometimes think I've spent my whole life trying to balance the scales. My dad felt similarly, but he's not here to tell his story anymore. I know he'd reached out to Nora in the past – he wanted her to know the truth – and I thought it was worth another go.'

Jess was aware of being at a juncture. Nora hadn't wanted her to know about Halcyon; she'd chosen not to hear what Marcus and his father had to say. But it was no longer Nora's decision to make. 'You said that Thea Turner wasn't taken by dogs?' Jess prompted.

'I said she wasn't taken by dogs *that day*.' He gave a slight smile, almost of apology. 'Let me explain.'

And as he launched into his father's story, Jess knew she wasn't going to be making it back up to the Hills that morning.

CHAPTER TWENTY-NINE

Adelaide Hills, 24 December 1959

From the dark wet street, the house looked warm and welcoming, a beacon of tranquillity in a sea of trouble, but as soon as Percy stepped inside, he could feel that something was amiss. It was too quiet. He knew the sounds of his own house; it was a place of noise and movement, atoms in constant motion, swirling currents of energy. Tonight, everything was in a state of suspension. It was as if this *place*, the only home he'd ever known, sensed that he was steeling himself to deliver Meg the terrible news of what he'd found.

A single light was on in the kitchen and Percy walked towards it.

The first thing he saw when he entered the room was the glass of sherry on the table, and then his wife sitting very still behind it. He realised immediately that she already knew what had happened. But of course she did: it was inconceivable that such a thing could occur in Tambilla, that a family could die on Christmas Eve, that a baby could go missing, that a search party could be organised and dispatched, without word reaching Meg. He wondered whether she knew the role he'd played.

'Perce,' she said, when she saw him. 'Oh, Perce.' She stood and came to him, studying his face as he let his kit bag fall to the ground. 'Was it awful?'

He felt a dark wave of the day's horror rising to over-whelm him. He didn't want to have to talk about what he'd seen, he realised, not now, not yet. Not with Meg. A picture came to him of the lost wren. 'I've been at the police station,' he said instead.

She nodded quickly. 'I spoke with Lucy. The boys are out. They're with the search.'

He should have known they'd be helping; Percy felt a surge of pride. 'Kurt?'

'Devastated.'

'I'll talk to him when he gets back.'

'The police?' she asked. 'What did they say? What do they think?'

He gave her a summary of the interview, leaving out any mention of the questions about their son. She looked dis-tressed already; Percy saw no reason to concern her further. He was worried enough for both of them.

When he finished, Meg was silent for a moment. At last she said, 'Can I fetch you something? Cup of tea? A bite to eat?'

A faint baking smell hung in the air, but it curdled his stomach even to contemplate eating. 'Think I'll have a wash first.'

She hesitated then. 'Perce, before you do,' she said. 'There's something . . . Come with me.'

He followed her along the hallway and outside down the path that led to the coach house. A hair-width strip of dull light was coming through the closed curtains. That was sur-prising; since his mother's death, they hadn't had much use for the small building. Percy couldn't think when he'd last set foot inside.

Meg opened the door. The room was empty. Just the bed

the two of them had shared long ago, and the elegant cedar settler's chest of drawers they'd restored when they were young. The bottom drawer, he noticed, was missing. Meg walked to the other side of the bed and beckoned him, motioning that he should proceed quietly.

Later, he was to see that the sherry should have been the tip-off. Meg didn't touch alcohol – hadn't for as long as he'd known her.

He joined her at the far side of the bed. On the floor near the wall, beneath the curtain-cloaked window, illuminated by a warm circle of soft lamplight, was the missing drawer, and in it, swaddled in white cotton, a sleeping baby.

A thousand words presented themselves, but each slipped away before it could be uttered. 'Who?' he managed at last, even though of course he knew full well.

Meg didn't answer the question. 'She's sleeping so soundly. You wouldn't know any of it had happened.'

'How?' he said. 'How did she get here?'

'I found her.'

Percy couldn't understand how it was possible. 'When? Where?'

'The waterhole. I was out walking.'

Fragmented images flashed like cards in a dealer's deck: the family on the picnic rug, the wicker basket in the tree, ants crawling across the little girl's wrist. It wasn't possible that Meg had been there, had seen it all, that she'd taken the baby from the crib.

'I couldn't just leave her. Anything might have happened.'

'The boys?'

She shook her head.

That was something at least. 'Meg,' he began, his thoughts starting to come into line. 'Meg, we have to—'

'She's safe here. Look how soundly she's sleeping.'

His wife had gone mad, he realised. The shock of what she'd seen had driven her mad. 'We have to give her back,' he said. 'We have to take her home right now.'

Meg looked at him as if he'd spoken a different language.

Even as he said it, he knew they couldn't just give the baby back. The knowledge made him tired. Bone-weary. He sank onto the end of the bed.

What he wanted was to pick up the telephone, to call the police officer in charge and tell him to come at once, that the baby had been found. But to do so would turn the spotlight of investigation onto them, onto Meg. She would be implicated. How could she explain how she came to be in possession of Thea in the first place? Anything that took her near the picnic site was going to be trouble. Four people were dead. Percy had already been interviewed, there'd been interest in Kurt. God only knew what someone else in town might volunteer about the connections between the Summers and Turner families. And now, for police to learn that Meg had been there, had found the child and brought her home, all without reporting the scene?

Why on earth had she done it?

Percy stood up suddenly. He ran his hands through his hair. *Jesus.*

'Will they find her, Perce?' said Meg. 'Will they figure out what happened?'

Percy noticed an element of panic in her voice, and it struck him that it was the first such note he'd heard. Before that, when she was showing him the baby, she'd sounded almost excited. Adrenaline, he supposed; wasn't that what happened when a person was in shock? He considered her question: what were the chances that the search would lead them here? It depended on how careful she'd been. 'There's no finer tracker out there than Jimmy,' he said cautiously. 'Young Eric Jerosch is no slouch either. But this weather will make things difficult. That's serious rain and it looks like setting in.'

'Perhaps someone saw something?'

'Perhaps,' he allowed. God knew, she was best placed to answer that one. Why had she been out walking anyway, with so much to do? But anxiety had started to knot her features and, because it had been his life's role to smooth them, he said only, 'Though you have to think they'd have come forward by now.'

'I'm so worried, Perce. I'm so very frightened.'

In the half-light, he saw the little girl from the disused mine all those years ago, when he'd told her he was leaving and she'd tried to look brave.

'What's going to happen to that dear child?'

They both looked down at the sleeping baby, and as if on cue she squirmed in the makeshift crib, screwing up her face the way babies do when they're suffering with wind. Meg crouched to lay a flat palm upon the baby's tum, rubbing gently until the pain eased. 'She reminds me of our boys,' she said softly.

'All babies look alike.'

Meg didn't answer and Percy experienced a surge of unexpected anger. 'Meg,' he began, 'you know she has to go back.'

'Where? To whom?' she said, in the same gentle tone she'd have used to soothe the baby. 'Her family is gone.'

Percy's blood chilled at that. There was something challenging in the way she said it. If not her tone, then in the words themselves. Because for all intents and purposes, it was true. Thomas Turner was in England and a man whose interests lay outside the paternal. It was hard to see what would become of the child now, what was the best thing for her.

The little one lifted her knees, squirming this way and that until the wrap was loose around her middle; her hands were balled into fists. Even in the lamplight Percy could see that her face was bright puce.

'There now.' Meg reached in to scoop her from the drawer. She stood, patting the baby's bottom, swaying in that innate way of mothers everywhere. When she pressed her lips against the downy head, whispering sweet nothings, the soft consoling sounds he remembered from when the boys were young, Percy glimpsed how much trouble they were in.

'I'm going to go back inside the house,' he said, surprised by how normal he sounded. 'Take a shower, wait for the boys.'

'Yes, all right,' she said, without looking up. 'I'll stay here with this little treasure. She needs someone to love her.' And then, to the baby, 'Isn't that right, dearest one?'

Some hours later, Percy stood out on the narrow back verandah that ran the length of the coach house, smoking the last of Esther Hughes's cigarettes. The boys were both asleep in their rooms. His plan to speak with them had not gone as he'd hoped; he'd managed to gather his thoughts together, but neither lad had been in the mood for talking when they got back from the search. Never mind, there'd be time for that in the morning. He'd sat down and cleaned their boots instead.

The biggest challenge over the coming days was going to be keeping the presence of the baby from them. The less they knew, the better. Percy had been trying to remember everything he'd told the police about Meg. He'd said she knew Mrs Turner, and that they'd made deliveries to the house for as long as the family had lived there; he'd also mentioned that Meg counted everyone in town a friend, that's just the sort of person she was. Nothing in that, surely, would bring suspicion upon his wife?

Percy's gaze alit upon the line of trees that grew along the main street of Tambilla. His life, he suddenly saw, had been like one of Meg's precious Christmas ornaments, hand-blown glass globes, hanging inside on the tree: imperfect but integral. The perceived stability had been deceptive, though; it had all been far more fragile than he'd thought. He wanted to put that precious orb back together, contain everything important safely inside, make it all as it had been before.

But that was magical thinking and Percy didn't have time for it. He wasn't the Mayor of Casterbridge or Jude the Obscure; this wasn't a Victorian novel about a good man's fatal flaw, his tragic fall from grace. He had a family to think about, and a baby too.

The baby was asleep now, curled up on the bed next to Meg. His wife had been exhausted, crashing fast. Percy had sat on the side of the bed, listening as her breath slowed, as the baby shifted beneath the cotton sheet, sucking her fist, sighing and gasping as babies do. As he sat there, his back turned on the pair, a plan had started to form. They would wait a few days, until the police search cooled, and then he would find a way to take the baby somewhere she'd be found, a place he could leave her safely, without being observed.

The rain had got lighter as he paced the verandah. Percy could see it falling in the glow of the streetlamp on the far side of the street. He finished his cigarette. He still struggled to understand how any of this had happened. 'I was out walking . . . I couldn't just leave her,' was all Meg would say when he'd asked her. But the thought didn't sit easily.

He feared that the police knew more than they'd let on. His mind was racing, trying to picture the scene, because something about it, he worried now, had made the sergeant from Adelaide suspicious. 'You didn't see any evidence that the picnic had been disturbed? Any sign that someone else had been there?'

Percy had replied that he had not. It was hard to know if Sergeant Duke was simply canvassing every possibility, or whether he'd already formed a theory.

'Did you notice any prints?' the sergeant had asked.

Percy had assumed he meant from dogs, but what if the police had found Meg's footprints at the scene?

Percy needed to move. He'd finished his cigarette and now he needed to get free of this place. He went quietly through the house to collect his boots and then onwards along the tight path that ran beside the shop towards the street. Once, he wouldn't have been able to make his escape so easily; Buddy-dog would have been at his heel, eager to run alongside him. Percy dug his hands deep into his pockets. On a night marked by such extraordinary loss of life, too much to comprehend, thoughts of old Buddy were a tipping point. That had been his fault, too. He hadn't been watching closely enough. He should have known that when the long hot days stretched on and on, and the blue-green algal blooms grew thick, there'd be pufferfish washed up on the beach. So much loss. Percy slipped along the lonely path and out into the dark night.

*

The first thing he noticed when he reached the waterhole was how sodden the earth had become. It was a mess, where the Turners had been, even right up close to the tree's trunk. Rain had washed away any prints, he realised, and for a split second he felt a flood of relief. Surveying the muddy ground, he pictured them all lying there, remembered the lack of breath on his fingers, the ants on Evie's wrist, Matilda and her necklace; he recalled the way Sergeant Duke had made a note of his son's name.

It started to rain again, and out there in dark, hidden places dingoes sent their howls into the stormy night. Hearing them, Percy was overcome with a sudden deep and profound grief. Events of the day, but even more than that, at an elemental level. It could do that to you, this country. The sounds, the colours, the stories of make and break – there was something brutally stark about it all. It could cause you to feel hollow and lonely, just by virtue of its vastness, its scale, the stretch of earth that went on forever. Only – Percy had the realisation suddenly – he wasn't alone. He sensed it beneath his skin; he was being watched. The sky lit up silver and Percy felt himself exposed. When darkness returned and thunder shuddered around him, he started for home.

He didn't travel fast, and by the time he reached the house, dawn was less than an hour away. Percy took his boots off on the landing and let himself in by the back door. He crept along the hallway towards the front room. His boots were muddy, and he couldn't leave them until morning to clean. He didn't want to risk anyone knowing he'd been out.

As quietly as he could, Percy took out the cloth rags from the wooden box in the cupboard. Just enough of a tidy-up to remove the mud. He reached to pick one up and froze. His sons' boots were set out in a line near the wall as they always were, where he'd left them earlier after cleaning; but one pair was as muddy as his. Fresh mud, wet and cold.

Percy pictured the stirred-up ground beneath the willow tree on the bank of the Turners' waterhole. He had a memory of the same spot earlier that afternoon, everyone moving about the site, the police officers, the photographer. Rain might have erased most signs of earlier activity, but the photographer had caught and preserved the scene on film.

Did you notice any prints? the sergeant from Adelaide had asked, and then he'd enquired as to whether Percy had gone over to the baby's basket. *A woven thing, hanging in the tree.* Percy had told them no, but they'd taken a measurement of his boot, and that's when the officer from Adelaide had mentioned Kurt. Not Meg, but Kurt.

And then, suddenly, Percy understood. They hadn't found women's footprints near the crib; they'd found prints the size and shape of a man's boot. That's why they'd taken his measurements. He grasped, too, Meg's reluctance to give details of her afternoon. She hadn't been obfuscating. She'd been vague because she was inventing.

Percy didn't know for sure which one of his boys she was covering for, but he could guess, and he realised, grimly, as he looked at the matching sets of boots on the ground, that he was going to have to amend his police statement.

Next morning, Percy called ahead and went into the station first thing. It was still raining, and Hugo Doyle's uniform shirt was wet in patches.

'G'day, Perce.'

'Hugo.'

'Lucy said you wanted to add something to your statement?'

'That's right.'

Doyle was looking at him, waiting for him to go on, and Percy was aware of his own cadence, foreign to him suddenly, as he spoke. 'I was thinking about it later. Sergeant Duke asked whether I'd gone over to the crib, and I said no.'

'I remember.'

'Only, that wasn't right. I did go near the crib. I didn't recall it when I was answering last night. It was the shock. I wasn't thinking straight.'

Hugo was nodding in a not unfriendly way, and yet to Percy, straitened by guilt, the gesture was concerning.

'Sure,' said the policeman, 'I get that. Terrible shock. Easy to forget the details.' He wrote something on the notepad and looked up. 'Just to make sure I've got it clear, you're still happy with the rest of your statement – your horse needed a swim, you came to the creek, you saw the Turner family and thought they were asleep, and then you went closer?'

'Yes, but on the way, I walked past the crib.'

'Walked past it.'

'Around it. I didn't know that's what it was at the time. Just seemed like a basket to me.'

'Didn't look inside?'

'No. I could see the Turners on the picnic rug. I knew something wasn't right. I went directly to them.'

Doyle wrote another couple of sentences on the notepad. 'Didn't see or hear anything?'

'I only wish I had. There was nothing to suggest – I'd have gone to check if I'd thought for a second . . .'

Doyle was nodding, and when it became clear that Percy was going to leave his regret unspoken, the policeman set down his pen. 'Well, thanks, Perce,' he said. 'I'll get Lucy to type this up and we'll add it to your statement.'

'Thanks.'

'Good of you to come in, especially on Christmas Day.'

'Of course.'

'And you're not to worry, we'll get to the bottom of it. Whatever happened, if someone out there had a part to play in it, we'll find him. Make no mistake about that. Owe it to them all, don't we?'

Percy nodded his agreement.

'And we'll find that baby, too. I've got men out there now and they're getting close.'

'You've got a lead?'

Doyle tapped the side of his nose. 'Let's just say, if she's still out there to be found, we'll find her.'

CHAPTER THIRTY

For the next few days, Percy struggled to keep his head above water. Meg was unreachable, neither of his sons was speaking to him, the Turner family lay dead in the morgue. The police were interviewing everyone in town – Percy had taken Kurt along to the station himself, getting in early before the eye of suspicion had a chance to land; the search for the Turner baby continued.

Some of the regulars had started to comment on Meg's absence from the shop counter, and Percy told them she was resting, having taken the news hard. They all made noises of understanding; she was known to be an especially empathetic woman. In reality, though, Meg was very busy. When at home, she barely left the baby's side; there was a new infant formula they'd ordered for the shop some months back that had sat on the shelf unsold. Meg put it to good use now, sitting for lengthy feeding sessions with the baby, crooning and singing, comforting the child, who responded well to the constant attention. The only other place she went was Halcyon, where she'd taken it upon herself to keep an eye on Mrs Turner-Bridges, whose own baby had arrived under such difficult circumstances.

Percy grew increasingly uneasy. The baby – Thea – needed to be found soon, and not in his wife's arms. He had been turning over his options in the days since Christmas, and finally, during the community meeting at the Institute, he'd perceived an opportunity. He'd gone alone, leaving Meg at home with the baby and the boys helping in the shop, and that's where he'd glimpsed the woman people were referring to in pitying whispers as 'Mrs Turner's poor sister-in-law'.

He'd already met her once before, a couple of weeks earlier, when he'd made an early morning delivery up to Halcyon. She had still been heavily pregnant then, her skin glowing with a fine sheen of perspiration as the day was already warm, despite the early hour. 'You must be Mr Summers,' she'd said with a smile when he appeared at the kitchen door. 'Issy said you'd be along with the groceries today. Would you mind bringing them inside for me?'

Percy had done as she requested and then stepped back, trying to think of something to say. He hadn't been expecting to see her. This woman, the sister-in-law, reminded him so much of her brother, Thomas Turner; they shared the same manner, effortlessly charming, a confidence born of privilege. Percy felt awkward by comparison. The sister-in-law's expression had turned quizzical as Percy continued to stand there, before she smiled suddenly and said, 'Oh, forgive me!', and she'd gone as quickly as a heavily pregnant woman could to retrieve her purse. She reached inside and plucked out a couple of coins, holding them out to him. 'For your trouble,' she said. 'Coming all this way on a day as hot as this one.'

Even now, Percy felt his face heat embarrassedly at the memory. He'd waved away the coins. 'It's no trouble at all,' he'd said quickly. 'No trouble. I'll leave you to it, then, if you'll be all right with these?'

'We'll be fine. Thank you again.'

She accompanied him to the door, and he had just stepped out into the golden dazzle of morning light when he spotted a figure walking down the sloping drive from the upper shed.

'Oh, there's Issy now!' Mrs Turner-Bridges lifted a hand to wave.

She'd been in the vegetable garden, Percy realised as she joined them; there was a smudge of dirt on her cheek and a dainty teacup dangled lazily from her fingers. 'You're early, Mr Summers,' she said with a smile. 'Have you two met?

'We have,' replied Mrs Turner-Bridges. 'Mr Summers was good enough to carry the groceries inside.'

'I'm sorry I wasn't here – I became distracted.' She motioned knowingly towards Mrs Turner-Bridges' pregnancy. 'I'm going to have to stop doing that. It won't be much longer now.'

'I certainly hope not,' Mrs Turner-Bridges responded. 'I know I sound impatient, but the sooner she's in my arms, the better. I'm doing my best to move things along.' She glanced at Percy a little coyly, as if in acknowledgement of having broached the female mysteries of birth. 'A brisk walk every morning with the dawn. It's an old habit.'

'Nora is the only person I know who can reliably be counted on to wake before I do, and the greatest creature of habit. Rain, hail or shine, she always takes a turn about the rose garden before the day begins.'

'It's restorative,' said Mrs Turner-Bridges. 'Better than any vitamin you care to name. God willing it will soon bring forth this child!'

She had got her wish on Christmas Eve, and when Percy saw her at the community meeting on 28 December, she was carrying her babe in arms. As Sergeant Duke ran through the evidence for the assembled group of townspeople, Percy kept one eye on Mrs Turner-Bridges. She was grief-stricken, that much was clear, and exhausted, and preoccupied with her baby. He watched the way she cradled her child, tucked within a fabric wrap against her front, leaning her cheek to rest it lightly against the little one's head.

That gesture, the instinctive devotion it conveyed, convinced him. His plan might not be perfect, but he was out of time. He had to separate Meg from the baby, and sooner rather than later.

Percy braced himself for a difficult conversation, but Meg surprised him.

'Yes,' she agreed. 'The baby needs to go; she should be with family.'

Meg said she'd come to know Mrs Turner-Bridges – or Nora, as she called her now – in the days since Christmas, when she'd been going up to the house to help. 'I've observed her to be a kind and capable woman. The dear little child will be in good hands.'

Relieved and glad, Percy told her his idea. After considering it carefully, she gave a serious nod. 'Yes,' she said. 'I think that should work well.'

The weather was forecast to be fine on Thursday, 31 December. Percy decided to go just before dawn. It would be dark enough that he could remain concealed, but close enough to daylight that the child wouldn't be alone outside for long. It sickened him, the riskiness of what he was doing, but no matter how many times he thought it over, no matter how many ways he tried to get the pieces of the puzzle to fit together, it was the best he could come up with.

He carried her against his chest in the delivery sling, riding carefully and slowly up the back way towards the house. Despite the burst of sunny weather since Boxing Day afternoon, there was still a lot of water around and the ground was marshy. The last thing he needed was to get stuck up here.

He made his way up the last paddock, through the gate and into the grove that led to the southern side of the rose garden. When he was close enough, he dismounted and slipped the reins over the post, looping them tight. The lulling motion of the ride had sent the child to sleep. Percy found himself staring at her in the light of the full moon. She was a beautiful baby – Meg was right in that. The moonlight on her face reminded him of when his boys were new. People said it all the time; it was a cliché because it was true: you forgot how small they were.

Percy crept across the garden. It was divided into a quadrangle – four floral plots with grass paths making the cross, and a large stone urn in the centre. He was going to leave the baby in the furthest quadrant, near the walnut tree: that way, when the back door opened, the corner of the garden would be visible. All he had to do was wait until the light lifted just a little more, and then stay until the child was found.

He placed the baby down carefully, smoothing the ground first. Percy had made sure to wrap her well for the ride but loosened the blanket now, so she didn't look too neat; he pulled the edge to cover the dirt beneath her head. The night, thank goodness, was not cold. He hesitated for a moment, gazing at the little face, the eyes wide open again, blinking at him; her mouth twisted at the corners, almost a smile. Percy grazed the top of his knuckle gently against the plum of her cheek. 'Be well, little one. Won't be long and you'll be back home.'

He returned to the spot where he'd left Blaze and crouched behind the hedge. The first hint of light was breaking pink beyond the gum trees on the ridge, but the rest of the sky remained dark.

There was a noise behind him. Percy froze, listening. He quietened his horse.

He must have imagined it. No one else would be out now.

But there it was again.

He had to check. If anyone saw what he had done, if anyone could place him with the missing child, it would lead police to his family, to Meg or Kurt.

With a last glance over his shoulder at the white blanket on the ground, Percy skirted around the bush, careful not to slip. He shone his torch into the dark glen; he was sure he saw something moving.

'Hey,' he called out guardedly, a chill passing through his body as he did.

No one responded. Percy stood motionless and listened.

The rustling sound of something in the foliage, the thud of footfall.

Percy went deeper. He shone his torch once more. Here, then there. Nothing. The only thing making noise, movement, now was him. Whatever – whoever – it had been was gone.

He tucked his torch back into his pocket and returned to his vantage spot. Blaze, waiting patiently, nosed Percy's shoulder as he took up position. Percy trained his eye once more on the furthest garden bed.

His heart caught mid-beat as he scanned the rosebushes in the breaking dawn, and he felt a spike of adrenaline. The baby was gone.

All day, back at the shop, Percy waited. It made him nervous that he hadn't seen Mrs Turner-Bridges find the child, but he knew she walked a lap of the rose garden each morning with the dawn; the whole plan had been predicated on that fact. His back had been turned for a few minutes, five at most; surely in that time she had emerged from the house, seen the baby, and taken her inside. Any hour now, word would come that the child had been found and the search could end.

Information spread like plague in Tambilla and Percy spent that first day on tenterhooks, certain that each person who came through the door would bring with them the good news. As the afternoon waned, and still no announcement came, he told himself that the police must have lots of official things to do in the event of a missing child turning up; there was nothing strange in the delay.

But it was the same again the next day. Percy waited, he listened to the news on the wireless, he even saw the police officers conducting interviews in the main street, eating lunch at Betty's. No word. Not even a hint of it.

He checked the newspaper daily, he and Meg each in silent competition to bring the bundles in from where the delivery had been left on the doorstep before dawn. Under the pretence of getting the grocery shelves stocked, whichever of them got there first would release the papers from their ties and scan the pages.

'Anything of interest?' Meg would say.

'Doesn't seem to be.'

With every day that passed, as he remained stuck in a quagmire of uncertainty, Percy waited for Meg to reproach him, to say: 'I trusted you,' and, 'What went wrong?' But to her credit, she never did.

Even so, Percy berated himself. It made no sense. He had returned the child. He had looked away, yes, he had pursued whatever it was that had followed him into the glen, but he had only been gone for a matter of minutes.

Percy held on to the last shreds of hope for as long as he could, until the day he saw Mrs Turner-Bridges and the perambulator in the street. She was still in mourning dress, and it was apparent that nothing about her situation had altered from when he'd glimpsed her at the community meeting. He knew then that things had not gone as he'd planned. She hadn't found the baby, and he had made a terrible, terrible mistake.

CHAPTER THIRTY-ONE

Sydney, 19 December 2018

It was eight on Wednesday night when Jess arrived back at Darling House; the last of the day's light was cooling to purple and the dusk birds were gathering in the cove. She'd spent the entire two-hour flight from Adelaide mulling over the conversation with Marcus Summers, transported back to Tambilla on that stormy Christmas Eve of 1959: the horrifying discovery; the long, rain-drenched hours at the Summers' house; the agonising days and decisions that followed.

Marcus had been relieved to have finally told the story. His father had carried a heavy burden of guilt, he said, and now, at last, it was discharged. For Marcus, too, there'd been a personal comfort in taking up his father's confession.

'I'd got back from making a delivery that afternoon,' he explained to Jess, 'and I was telling my mum about the gift that I'd passed along to Mrs Turner, but she was distracted, baking a cake for my dad's birthday. She looked overwhelmed, and I felt bad for her – she was always doing things for other people. I decided that I wanted to head out to meet my dad on his return and make sure that he came straight home.

'I must have just missed him. Going on what I learned later of the timing, I must have arrived at the scene beneath the willow soon after he'd been and gone. I was in complete shock at what I saw – but then I heard the baby crying. She was in her crib, hanging from a branch of the tree. I wasn't thinking straight. I was still wearing my delivery sling, so I slipped her inside and got out of there as fast as I could, through the paddocks, avoiding the roads, back to my mum, with all the confidence of a fourteen-year-old lad that she'd be able to fix things.'

And Meg had tried to do so. 'She telephoned the police station,' Marcus continued, 'but they were too busy to take the call – told her there was an emergency and hung up the phone. She already knew all about it, of course – I'd told her what I'd seen – so she sent me to bring my brother Kurt home. He'd been seeing Matilda Turner and I suppose Mum had an inkling that the police were bound to start looking his way. She wanted him close.'

His father had held on to hope, Marcus said, for as long as possible, imagining that the child had somehow survived – that someone else had come upon her and snatched her away, and she had led a happy life elsewhere, none the wiser. But in 1979, when her remains were found in the rose garden, not far from where he'd left her, Percy had been forced to accept the truth. Marcus said that his father had tried to contact Nora then, but she'd wanted nothing to do with him.

'And so you made one last attempt to tell her,' said Jess. 'That's why you wrote the letter. It was on behalf of your father.'

'It was the anniversary of his death and I figured it was worth another try. I owed it to him – I was responsible, after all, for everything that happened.'

'Because you brought Thea home from the picnic.'

'And because I was the one who followed him that night,

when he took her up to Halcyon. I was a busybody at that age. I was trying to understand the adult world, and I saw a damn sight more than I should've.'

Jess remembered from Daniel Miller's book the reverend's admission that young Marcus Summers had come to talk to him, confused and upset, having witnessed Kurt and Matilda together.

Knowing that he had distracted his father at the vital moment, so that neither of them saw what happened, that they weren't then able to protect the baby, had changed the course of Marcus's life.

'It's why I pursued the law,' he told Jess. 'I committed myself to putting things right. I couldn't change what happened to Thea Turner, but I could help fix other things. I had a bloody naive view of the legal system back then – took me a while to learn that what's lawful and what's right aren't always the same, but I've done my best.'

Jess had the sense, honed over decades of asking questions for a living and drawing together an airtight narrative, that there were loose threads to be teased out. But she'd wanted to consider this new information first – and she'd needed to run for her flight. She wondered what Nora had made of Marcus Summers' letter. What had she thought he wanted to tell her? She had thrown it away, but it had caused her to take up Daniel Miller's book and brave the stairs to the attic. And she'd written Marcus's initials in her diary, implying that she'd meant to call him. If only she had. Perhaps she'd be here still, walking beside Jess as the two of them returned together from a visit to Tambilla.

Instead, Jess was by herself and, as she approached Darling House, such thoughts dissipated and the problems of the here and now returned. The light was on in the kitchen and the shadows of her last conversation with Polly came back to her. A lot had happened since their previous interaction; Jess had all but forgotten what had made her so angry in the first place. The feeling was familiar. This was how it always went with Polly: on the rare occasions when Jess got justifiably annoyed, her frustration would diminish over time, and she'd invariably come to feel that she'd been too quick to react, that she hadn't been fair, that her mother deserved another chance. 'She's watched over by the angels,' Rachel had once said knowingly, when Jess described the phenomenon. Jess must have looked perplexed, because her friend went on to explain: 'We all know someone like that. They're less careful, less capable, and yet somehow the truly terrible things never happen to them. People want to help; they attract kindness – they're looked after by guardian angels wherever they go.'

The idea had resonated with Jess. It certainly fit what she'd observed of Polly.

She steeled herself for the awkwardness of her return. She didn't want to continue their animosity: she was too tired. She would go straight to the kitchen, say hello, and then she would withdraw. The best thing for each of them was to get through the remaining day and then return to their separate lives.

Polly was just finishing washing up when Jess surprised her in the kitchen. A single plate and set of cutlery occupied the drying rack, and Jess felt a pang of sympathy, even though – as she reminded herself – she frequently ate alone. And this was exactly what she meant – Polly attracted sympathy for things that other people took in their stride.

'Hello there,' Jess said with a brittle cheerfulness. 'Had a good day?'

After a split second of uncertainty, Polly smiled in greeting. 'I have, thanks. You, too? You've been busy?'

'Yes.' Jess chafed at the coy indirectness of the question, declined to share more, and the pair fell to silence. 'Well,' she said, after a couple of empty beats, 'I'm very tired. I'm going to turn in early.'

'Before you go,' Polly said quickly, as Jess made to leave, 'there's some mail for you.'

This was a surprise. 'For me? Here?'

Polly nodded, wiping her hands on the tea towel, and indicated the dining table. Two packages sat near the fruit bowl, both bearing US stamps. Jess could see that the first was the copy of Daniel Miller's book she'd ordered via Abe-Books. The second, she gathered from the return address scribbled on the international mail slip, had come from Nancy Davis. She remembered now that Nancy had wanted to send something after Nora's death. Not the bunch of flowers she'd assumed, apparently.

She was curious to know what was inside, but for a reason mysterious even to herself, she wouldn't allow herself to seem even remotely intrigued in front of Polly. She gathered up the parcels and said a polite, 'Thanks,' before heading upstairs to her room.

She opened the AbeBooks parcel first. An irony that within the space of two weeks she had managed to obtain three copies of Daniel Miller's book. This was the 1980 edition and contained the addendum that Polly had photocopied and attached at the back of her book. Jess opened it and flicked through the pages. There was rather more evidence of past use than she'd expected. Whoever had owned it previously appeared to have fancied themselves an amateur sleuth, using a pencil to annotate throughout, jotting down character observations, posing questions in the margins – and, most intriguingly, a list on the title page of poisons and possible murder methods. *Sola dosis facit venenum*, they'd written at the bottom: *The dose makes the poison!* Jess nodded as she saw the rat killer that Meg Summers had sold to Isabel Turner and the specimen that Evie had obtained for Matilda, but at the bottom of the list, with a question mark, was written a word she didn't immediately recognise: *Cyanotoxin?*

Jess frowned. What was cyanotoxin? She typed the word into her phone. Streams of links appeared, from Wikipedia to the EPA and various scientific publications. A quick scan revealed that cyanotoxin was another name for blue-green algae. Jess read enough to glean that the toxin, produced by cyanobacteria, was found in all manner of places but especially waterways with a high concentration of phosphorus conditions. Cyanotoxins were among the most powerful natural poisons known to science, and in concentration could kill animals and humans. Some experimentation had even been done to investigate their potential military use as a biological weapon.

A bell started sounding faintly in Jess's mind. She searched 'blue-green algae' and 'South Australia' and landed on the SA Health government website, which stated that water resources in South Australia were routinely monitored for blue-green algae. It went on to note that public health advice would be issued if blooms occurred. The Adelaide Hills was an agricultural region, Jess knew, and had been in the fifties – there was every chance run-off from phosphorous fertiliser and septic systems might have caused algae to bloom locally in December 1959. Further, if, as Jess suspected, Isabel had aided the Resistance during the war, it was possible she'd been aware of the poison's experimental use as a weapon . . .

Then again, the Turner family had been swimming when Percy Summers found them. What if they'd filled their water bottles from the creek and the whole thing had been a ghastly accident, not a case of murder at all? Had the police and the medical examiner considered cyanotoxins? Would they have known to look for them back then?

Jess hadn't heard back from the professor at the university, but she pulled up her previous email and sent another, apologising for making contact again so soon, but asking whether blue-green algae might have been the culprit and, if so, whether it would have been detectable at the time.

She was eager to pore over all of the book's previous owner's notes – who knew what other helpful ideas might be scribbled in the margins? – but Nancy's parcel was playing on her mind. Jess had avoided opening it, knowing that it would relate to Nora's death and not sure whether she wanted to have her spirits dragged back to the place of fresh condolences, but it had been sent by courier – Nancy had been determined that Jess should receive it, and fast.

The parcel was soft, with an inordinate amount of tape sealing the padded envelope. Jess had to use her nail scissors to break into it. Inside she discovered a bubble-wrapped package and a letter.

Dear Jess,

I hope this letter finds you well, even as I know you will be dealing with immense grief at the loss of your grandmother. I wish I had the words to make it better, but you and I both know that there are no shortcuts where

*grief is concerned. Instead, I will simply say how sorry I am
and send you solidarity along with my sincere and selfish
gratitude that we were able to speak.*

*In writing to you now, I am also completing a promise
made to my uncle. Enclosed with my letter is a package that
turned up when I was cataloguing Dan's shed after his
death. He had a safe deposit box, inside of which was this
package and a note containing a set of instructions. In the
event of Nora Turner-Bridges' death, if contact was ever
made by either her daughter Polly or granddaughter Jessica,
the package was to be sent to them. Dan's preference was
that Polly receive the package.*

*I know that your mother and grandmother had become
estranged, while you and Nora remained as close as can be,
and I am afraid that carrying out Dan's instructions will be
hurtful. But Dan was quite specific that the package was to
be opened by Polly, if possible. I am forwarding it to you in
the hopes that you will be able to pass it on to her, and
with my apologies that I have no choice but to do as my
uncle instructed.*

*I hope you will understand and look forward to speaking
with you again soon.*

Sending all my best wishes,
Nancy

Jess realised that she'd been holding her breath and she
now let it out in a long, slow sigh. She scanned the letter
again and then, after a moment's contemplation, set it down
and turned her attention to the accompanying package. No
one would ever know if she were to open it herself. Nancy
wasn't here to see, and Polly had no idea who Nancy Davis
was.

But – she smiled ruefully to herself – even as she had the thought, she knew she wasn't going to go against Daniel Miller's wishes. She pressed on the bubble wrap. There was something hard inside. Jess gave it a light shake and detected a rattle. The sound was vaguely familiar, but she couldn't place it.

Jess set the parcel down at arm's length. It struck her, suddenly, that Nancy's letter had quoted Daniel Miller as having mentioned Polly and herself by name. That he knew her mother's name she could understand – he had met Polly as a baby – but how had he known hers?

Jess needed to know what the parcel contained. More than ever, she was convinced that some of the answers she'd been seeking were inside.

There was only one thing to do.

She swept up the parcel and went back downstairs.

'Tell me again who sent it?' Polly was still trying to understand. Jess had come barrelling into the kitchen with a determination Polly recognised from when her daughter was a child. She'd been waving a small package and delivering a hurried explanation from which Polly gleaned only that someone somewhere had sent something and that she was somehow involved.

'Her name is Nancy Davis.'

'I don't know anyone called Nancy Davis,' Polly said, puzzled. 'Why would she send me a parcel, and how did she know to send it to me here? And why was it addressed to you?'

Jess exhaled impatiently. 'Nancy Davis is Daniel Miller's niece.'

'Daniel Miller who wrote the book I gave you?'

'Yes, exactly. Daniel Miller died some years ago and Nancy was his executor. He left a package with instructions that if Nora died, and contact was ever made by one of her descendants, this package should be passed along.'

'But I didn't make contact.'

'No, but *I* did. I rang Nancy Davis.'

'Then why has she sent the package to me?'

'That I don't know. But Nancy said the instructions were explicit. The package was for you.'

Polly sighed. Her inclination was towards trepidation. She had brought Daniel Miller's book for Jess because she wanted to help her daughter at a difficult time, but she wasn't keen to reopen the whole affair. It had caused such a rupture in her life: the shock of learning what Isabel Turner had done; Nora's demand for secrecy; her insistence that Jess should never be told . . .

And yet here they were. No matter Nora's wishes, a package had arrived for Polly, the train set in motion by Jess herself. The three of them were like the figures in an old fairy tale: the spell cast atop the baby's crib, the promise extracted to prevent the child from learning a secret, the inevitability of truth's return.

'The instructions were explicit,' Jess said again. 'It's yours to do with what you will.'

Polly took up the parcel. No matter how uncertain she remained, one thing was very clear: Jess was desperate to know what it contained. She steeled herself and said, 'Shall I open it, then?'

'If you like.'

Polly concealed her amusement at Jess's attempt at nonchalance. Indifference had never been her natural state. 'All right,' she said. 'Let's see what's inside.'

The sticky tape holding the bubble wrap together was old and had started to yellow. It came away easily. 'It's a cassette,' Polly said. 'I haven't seen one of these in years.'

'What's on it? What does it say?'

Polly turned over the case to look at the label. *Nora Turner-Bridges, 14 December 1979.* The date rang a bell, and it took less than a second for the pieces to come together. That was the day Daniel Miller had visited Nora at Darling House. She said as much to Jess and then frowned: 'But I don't know what that's got to do with this cassette.'

Jess drew breath. 'It's the interview he did with Nora.'

Polly listened as Jess explained about Daniel Miller's return to Australia after the discovery of Thea Turner's remains. 'He was here to write the addendum that appears in later editions of his book, but Nancy told me he also made recordings. He couldn't in '59 – the technology wasn't good enough – so he spoke to the residents of Tambilla again.'

'I had no idea. So that's what they were doing in the library. And then afterwards, he came out into the garden.' Polly remembered the large satchel he'd been carrying; it had contained an early tape recorder, she supposed.

'And that's when you met him?'

'You met him, too. He was much taken with you.'

Jess was nodding; her eyes widened in realisation. 'That's how he knew my name.'

'I suppose it is.'

'May I?' Jess indicated the cassette.

Polly watched as Jess turned the plastic case over in her hands, cracking it open and running her finger ardently along the top of the cassette.

Taking in her daughter's excited face, Polly's mind returned to the day she'd met Daniel Miller. She saw herself standing by the fountain, chatting with the sophisticated, leather-clad American writer as baby Jess crawled over and pulled herself to standing. Polly had liked Miller. Something in his eyes had communicated genuine interest, even when he was asking the most mundane questions about her life at Darling House and making small talk about how much she must have enjoyed growing up there, how nice it was for the three generations to live together, how Nora had doted on Polly as a baby.

Sitting here with Jess, Polly felt, as she so often did, the melancholy of time passed and opportunities missed. Her daughter's childhood features were still visible in the adult face, but only to those who knew where to find them. The wide brows that had made her seem clever, even as an infant; the thoughtful mouth and dimpled chin; the slight tilt of the head when she was concentrating. Polly had spent countless hours memorising the heart-shaped lines of her daughter's jaw. A cruel fact of life, that parents and children shared so many fundamental experiences but only one of the pair retained the memories. It was a lonely position to occupy, the sole rememberer.

'What?' Jess had glanced up and caught her staring.

Polly had certainly made some wrong turns – strange how easy the signposts were to see in the rear-view mirror – but she had learned long ago that it was pointless to give in to the black temptation of regret. She smiled instead and said only, 'Come on then. Shall we see what's on the tape?'

CHAPTER THIRTY-TWO

It was lucky, they were to agree later, that Nora was one of the few people in Sydney to have retained not only her VCR player, but the then state-of-the-art stereo system she'd purchased in the eighties and had installed, with much fanfare, in the Darling House library. The brushed silver casing contained a cassette deck and two VU meters measuring the output of each massive speaker.

Jess had only been allowed limited access to the special device when she came to live with Nora, and it had therefore retained an air of prestige. Watching the VU needles quiver, backlit in orange, had been a religious experience. Now, she checked which side the tape reel was on and dropped the cassette into the deck. Her finger was trembling slightly as she pressed down the play button.

'Is that thing on?'

Nora's voice came blaring from the speakers and Jess startled, retracting her finger so quickly that the play button released, and the tape stopped rolling.

Although she'd expected it, hearing Nora speak had been a shock. She sounded so present and yet, at the same time, as if she were a blithe spirit, inhabiting the air of the library after death. It was surreal to realise that the tape had been recorded in this very room.

Where had Nora sat that day? Jess wondered. In her chair by the window? At her desk? And what about Daniel Miller?

He'd have had his tape recorder to consider. Had he, perhaps, taken the desk? Or had his aim been to relax his interview subject by removing any impediment, speaking to her in the manner of a confidant?

Polly was waiting patiently for the tape to restart.

With a deep, unsettled breath, Jess pushed play, and as the tape began once more to roll, and a man's voice said, 'It certainly is,' she went to sit in Nora's chair and waited to hear what her grandmother would say next.

'Do I need to speak into it?'

'Not at all.' The clarity of Daniel Miller's warm, American-accented voice suggested that he was closer to the device than Nora. 'In fact, it tends to work out best if you forget that I'm recording. Just talk to me and ignore the machine entirely.'

What followed was a pleasant interview, sad at times, between two people whose bond had been forged through having known one another during the progress of a harrowing event. The barrier that might have been expected to exist between journalist and subject was bridged, and although they had not seen one another in twenty-odd years, their conversation flowed, with evidence in the pauses and shorthand, from a place of shared knowledge and experience.

Nora wept when talk turned to the recent discovery of Thea Turner's remains, and Daniel Miller could be heard consoling her before their discussion continued.

'It's just been such a long time,' she said at last. 'I had come to believe they'd never find her.'

'It must be a relief, of sorts, that she can now be laid to rest?'

'Of sorts,' Nora allowed. 'But it does rather bring it all back.'

'Have you been sleeping?' His voice was gentle, concerned.

'Barely.'

'Will she be buried in Tambilla?'

'I don't – My brother will make those decisions.'

'Have you spoken with him?'

'Briefly.'

'Does Polly know?'

'No. No, I don't speak to her about such things. What good would it do her to have such horrors in her mind?'

'She knows about Halcyon, though?'

'She knows enough.'

'She must be twenty now.'

'Yes. Nearly. On Christmas Eve.'

'It's hard to imagine.'

'What is it they say? The days are long, but the years are short.'

'What's she like?'

'Polly? Oh, she's a good girl. Sensitive and kind, clever at school, quite a beauty. But she's naive; romantic, delicate – the sort of girl to read a lot of books and poetry and imagine that life might really be like that. I have to save her from herself sometimes; watch carefully to make sure people don't take advantage. I don't mind. It's what I signed up for: having a child is a job for life.'

'I remember the two of you back then. I didn't realise it, but you made me think of my sister-in-law and her baby. Your Polly was a lovely child, so calm.'

Jess glanced at Polly, but her head was bowed, her emotions difficult to read.

Daniel Miller asked Nora then whether she had been back to Tambilla since 1960.

'Good God, no. Certainly not. I couldn't bear to go near

the place again. It haunts me, all of it.' There was a pause then, and Daniel Miller wisely left it to expand. When Nora spoke again, her voice faltered: 'Have you . . . Did you visit the house while you were there?'

'I did.'

'Was it in poor condition? I don't know who's looking after it, whether Thomas organised someone. There were those hippies, the ones who found her – God only knows what they've done to the place with all their digging and interfering.'

'It looked okay. The worst they've done is to hang tie-dyed sheets across the doorways. The garden has suffered, though. Henrik Drumming looked after it for as long as he could – despite Thomas's instructions to let it alone – but he had a stroke a few years back and it all got too much.'

A lull fell, and Jess was aware of the shuffling of feet, the squeak of leather as someone shifted position, and then Nora's voice, tight, unnatural: 'Her roses?'

'They fought valiantly to hold on, but at some point, a bird must've dropped a cherry tomato seed into the garden and the vines have grown wild since then. The roses are pretty much suffocated.'

'She'd have hated that. The rose garden was her pride and joy. To think of those philistines digging it up! Once, it was a sacred place – no one would have dared.'

'Do you think your brother will sell the house now?'

'He has no reason to keep it.'

'Maybe this will be the closure he's been waiting for? It must have been horrific not knowing for certain what happened to his child.'

The suggestion sounded sensible to Jess, but Nora said only, 'Is that everything you need? I'm getting tired of talking.'

'It is.'

Jess heard packing-up noises – briefcase clips being popped, the rattle of a pen skittling across a surface, a glass being lifted and returned to a tabletop; and then, suddenly, Nora's voice again, as if an afterthought: 'How were they all? The others down there?'

'Well enough.'

'Who did you meet with?'

'Peter Duke, Percy Summers – he'd lost his wife, sadly.'

'Meg died?'

'A year or so ago.'

'I didn't know.' Nora spoke so softly that Jess leaned forward as if it would help to hear her better. 'She came to help me, do you remember? Turned up on Christmas Day to bring me food and insisted on staying to clean up the kitchen.'

'She was a kind person.'

'And now she's gone. She's really gone.' Nora's tone was tender, but there was something else there, too. Disbelief, Jess decided: she could imagine how disconcerting it would be to learn of the death of someone who had shown such kindness in a time of tremendous anguish.

'Her son Kurt was still around,' said Daniel Miller, 'and I spoke with Betty Diamond and Becky Baker.'

Nora made a hissing noise at the mention of Becky's name, and Jess remembered the altercation between the two women described in Daniel Miller's book.

'That girl was a menace,' Nora said. 'Far too attached. I sensed it as soon as I arrived. Always lurking about, behaving as if Isabel's baby were her own.'

'She was very upset during our interview,' Miller replied. 'She didn't want to believe that the remains had been found.

I don't think she ever gave up expecting Thea to turn up alive.'

'Well, she was simple. No doubt she had all manner of stupid ideas in that head of hers.'

Jess was taken aback by the severity in Nora's voice and the unkind sentiment expressed. Evidently, she'd been very wounded when Becky Baker set upon her in the street. Fair enough, Jess supposed, she was only human, she'd suffered a massive trauma; but the rationalisation sat uneasily. Jess couldn't help feeling it was a cruel comment on which to end the interview.

But alas, that was where it ended. Daniel Miller had stopped the tape recording at that point, so there was no way of knowing what he had said to Nora in reply.

Now, in the lamplit library, Jess said, 'Well,' into the silence. The recording had left her disappointed. She had hoped – more than hoped; she had believed – that the tape would contain the answers to her questions. Why send the tape to Polly at all, particularly with such secrecy and explicit instructions? The conversation offered nothing new, covering old ground on a topic Miller had written and published about. Neither did it paint Nora in a particularly glowing light, in a way that could comfort her loved ones.

Jess glanced at her mother to see whether she was feeling the same way, but Polly had her head bent over a sheet of paper.

'What's that?' Jess asked.

'A letter.'

Jess was confused. 'Another one? From Nancy?'

'From Daniel Miller. It was inside the cassette container, folded beneath the track list. I found it just now. I don't have my reading glasses. Here.' She handed it to Jess. 'You read it out loud.'

Jess took the letter from her. The paper was ultra-fine – old-fashioned airmail paper, by the looks of it, from the time before email, when people had to consider the weight of their stationery when they wanted to communicate with someone far away. Jess angled it towards the spill of lamp-light and started reading.

Dear Polly,

I am sitting on a plane, about two hours out of JFK, having agonised the whole way home from Sydney about what to do. By the time you receive this letter, if you receive this letter, it is likely you will have forgotten me. But as I write, your face is vivid in my memory.

I met you only a few days ago, by the fountain at Darling House, where I had just interviewed your mother about the recent discovery of human remains at the house called Halcyon, once occupied by her brother and sister-in-law, and the closing of a missing person's police investigation that had stood open since the disappearance of her baby niece, Thea Turner, twenty years before.

I'd been glad to see Nora. We got on well in 1959 and I liked her very much, so the visit had a social element as well as being professionally important. When we finished our interview, she walked me to the front door, and as we reached the driveway, she remembered that she'd been going to show me a photograph of her garden when it was new. She went back inside to fetch it, and I took the opportunity to walk down across the lawn.

I came upon you at the fountain. I hadn't expected to run into anyone, so it was a surprise to find myself suddenly in your company. I experienced the strangest feeling of vertigo; I had last met you as a tiny baby in your mother's arms. I asked you about your life, whether you were happy, and you told me that you were. I met your daughter, Jessica, and learned that the two of you lived with Nora at Darling House.

I couldn't shake the odd sensation, though, and my mind was still ticking over when Nora returned and called me back. With every step I took, the cogs tightened, until finally it came to me as clear as day, the cause of my discomfort. Nora was shocked when I asked her outright, and for a split second I could see that she was tempted to deny my charge. But it has been my experience that guilt shadows a person like a most reliable friend, urging them to reveal the truth when opportunity at last presents itself.

She broke down, begging me to understand, to forgive her. Her distress was heartrending. I suggested that we go inside again where we could talk. She made me promise not to breathe a word and I agreed. Neither will I, though I will wonder forever what else I missed or got wrong, in which other ways I was misled. Nonetheless, I did something that day of which I am not proud.

I cannot say what made me do it, other than a deep-seated professional need to keep the record. The tape from our previous interview had already been turned over and rewound, ready for the next time I needed it. Without telling Nora, I recorded our second, private conversation. Afterward, I considered destroying the tape. I had already decided that I wouldn't publish what she told me. I'd promised her – and more than that, I couldn't think that it would help anyone, whereas I knew it had a great potential to cause harm.

I could see only one person whose life would be changed by what she'd said. Nora asked me to forgive her, but her actions were not for me to forgive. And so I decided to put this tape aside for you, Polly. I don't know whether you will ever read this letter. It depends, I suppose, on you – on your determination to know the truth. If you never seek it, I will assume that you preferred not to know, and I did the right thing in keeping Nora's secret. If you do find your way to me, then the truth is waiting. It belongs to you. I have simply been its keeper.

Daniel Miller

The truth! Jess's mind was racing. Here, at last, she glimpsed, were the answers she'd been hoping for. She felt incredibly eager, and yet – Miller's reference to guilt made her anxious. For the first time, Jess began to worry that Nora had done something seriously wrong. She folded the fine piece of paper in half and waited for Polly to react. The letter, the tape, the decision, were hers. It was a lot to take in, particularly for someone who hadn't spent the past week immersed in the world of Halcyon and the Turners.

Still . . . 'What do you think?' she prompted. 'Should I flip the tape?'

Her mother met her eyes, and when she gave a solemn nod of agreement, for a split second Jess felt a sense of déjà vu, an old memory of togetherness, of feeling bonded and safe, no matter what terrifying spectre might be waiting around the corner.

CHAPTER THIRTY-THREE

'Do you want to tell me what happened?' This was Daniel Miller. Only half an hour had passed since they'd finished the last interview, but his voice was changed. It was strained now: serious and careful. Jess recognised the note of caution; she had adopted it herself during interviews where she knew she had to tread carefully lest the subject withdraw their agreement to talk. His words were muffled – he must have left the tape recorder in his bag – and the effect was to make them both seem further away. 'Why don't you start with the night she was born,' Miller suggested.

Jess held her breath as the library speakers crackled and hissed with the static of distance. She did not meet her mother's eyes. Finally came Nora's faded voice: 'I gave birth to her in the middle of a violent storm. It was Christmas Eve, the day of the disaster down at the waterhole. I went into labour after the policemen left. It was the shock, I think. It took me a while to understand what was happening. I was out of my right mind.

'It wasn't meant to be like that – Isabel was supposed to be with me. I was relying on her. I remember very little of the birth, I just remember the storm, the hellish storm. I thought the walnut tree outside my window was going to snap in half; wind howling through the gaps in the window, rain like spite against the glass. In my mind, it was as if I had become the storm, or else it had become me.

'I felt possessed, like I might be stuck inside that moment forever, but somehow, she was born, and although you might have thought I'd never be able to sleep again, after that day, the nightmare of it all, I was exhausted, and passed out with my baby in my arms.

'When I woke, I thought I'd dreamed it all, until I glanced at her tiny face in the crook of my elbow and everything came back in a rush. I couldn't hold it in my head all at once, the utter joy and the sickening horror that had preceded it, and so I focused on her, on that delicate sleeping face, the minuscule movements of her lips, the softness of her velvet skin, her impossibly small, perfect fingers. She was remarkable. She was mine. She was everything I'd ever wanted and dreamed of. So pretty and peaceful. One of the policemen commented on how quiet she was when they came to check on me that day. "You've had your baby," he said, when I opened the door.

'"Last night," I heard myself reply. My voice was strange to my ears, as if it belonged to someone else.

'"You'll have to call her Noël."

'"Or Joy." This was the other officer, the younger one.

'"Her name is Polly," I told them.

'"Well, whatever the name, that's a good one you've got there. Couldn't get any of my three to sleep like that. Sleeping like a baby, that's what people say, isn't it? Not any of the babies in my house."

'They were right. She was so sleepy, so quiet and still. I wasn't worried, not at first. I'd never had a baby before. I didn't know any differently. And when Mrs Summers came to check on me and help around the house, she said that they were all unique, and she'd arrived at a difficult time. Babies could be sensitive like that.

'But as the days went on, my concern grew. I couldn't get her to feed. She would cry when I tried, meek and soft, as if she were already weary with the world. I couldn't understand. I knew she needed milk, but I couldn't bring her comfort. My body ached; I felt as if a clamp were squeezing shut inside my belly, my chest, my head. I wished more than anything for Isabel to be there. She was supposed to be there, helping me.

'My baby would cry in my arms and then finally fall asleep, and I would cradle her like that for as long as I could, only placing her in the crib when I needed both hands for something else. It was after one such period that I went to check on her. I'd fallen asleep myself – I was so tired; more tired than I'd been before or since. But when I woke, I saw that the light had changed and knew she'd been sleeping for hours and hours.

'She was lying in her crib, a blanket covering the small mound of her body, her face turned to the side, little eyes sealed shut; she was so very still. As perfect as a porcelain doll. I've never been able to get that picture from my mind. I stood at the doorway, admiring her for a time, and then something twigged and I pounced forward, planting my hand on her back, desperate to feel the rise and fall of breath, to startle her awake.

'But there was nothing. Nothing. I picked her up; I thought maybe if I rocked her, or walked her, or fed her, everything would be all right. But it wasn't. She wasn't. It wasn't all right at all.'

The tape continued to play, but the voices had disappeared. There was only the ambience of the long-ago room, a claustrophobic airy sound. Jess chanced a brief look at Polly, but her mother was staring at her hands, her thoughts impossible to read. Jess turned up the volume, focused on the hissing and popping. Just as she was beginning to think the recording might have ended, Nora's voice returned. It was different again, recognisably Nora, and yet Jess couldn't think that she'd ever heard her grandmother sound so . . . vulnerable.

'It's hard to remember how much time passed. I held her to me as if maybe, just maybe, I might that way give life back to her. I wouldn't put her down. I couldn't let her go – while I held her, there was hope. I was still cradling her the next day when Meg arrived, and later, when the policemen came to take me to the town meeting.'

Jess remembered Daniel Miller's account of Nora at the community meeting, a model of dignity, grieving for her family while caring for her newborn child. To know the truth behind that picture was disturbing, the unfathomable depth of her new loss, devastating. Jess willed Miller to prompt for more, even as she knew he was right to let the story come out at Nora's pace.

Finally, her grandmother continued: 'It was just before dawn the next morning, or perhaps the one after that, when I went outside for a walk. I used to do that quite often, to move my legs, to clear my head. I hadn't since my Polly was born, but that morning, I did. I stepped outside, and almost at once I heard it. Like a small animal crying. I went over to where the roses are, the bed nearest the house, and the noise got louder. That's when I saw her. I thought I'd gone mad. Babies don't just appear. But there she was, in the middle of the roses.'

'Thea,' said Daniel Miller.

'I snatched her up and took her inside with me – what else could I have done? The blanket was muddy and torn, but inside it she was perfect. There wasn't a mark on her. Initially, she wouldn't settle. She was hungry, of course – God knows how long it had been since she'd eaten, poor little lamb. I fed her from my own breast, and it was the most natural thing in the world. She was so eager.

'I didn't mean to keep her, not then. But there was no one for me to tell, no way to tell them. The telephone lines were still down after the storm on Christmas Eve, and I was all alone. I wasn't up to walking into the town. We were alone, the two of us, for days. Amid so much loss, we were the sole survivors. It was a miracle.

'It was some days later that one of the policemen gave me the idea. They came to the house, and she was sleeping peacefully in her pram beside me. She cried and I nursed her, and the policeman said, "She's doing well. Getting bigger quickly, isn't she?"

'I wondered for a moment what he meant and then I realised his mistake. "She's a very hungry baby," I said. Which was true. And it was all so normal, so right.'

Nora's tone had shifted into defensive mode, sounding more and more like the grandmother Jess knew well. Confident and beyond reproach, justified. But what she was saying was shocking. Jess glanced at Polly, wondering how on earth she was taking this news, but her mother's face was impassive, revealing nothing.

'There were times,' Nora continued, 'when I forgot what I'd done. She was my baby, my Polly. Other times, I reasoned, what better option was there for this little person who had done nothing wrong? Would I have been doing her a favour to tell the police? To have word spread as to who she really was? To make her live with the ignominy of what Isabel had done?

'No. I was her mother, and I would be the best mother to her, to that perfect little girl. A baby should always be with her family. Who else would have loved her as I did? What harm could it cause to anyone?'

Jess thought of Percy Summers, who had lived the decades wondering what had happened, and then believing himself responsible for the baby girl's death. Nora wasn't to have known, of course, though she must have wondered how the baby arrived in the rose garden. Had she really believed that wild dogs had taken the child from the picnic and then delivered her, unscathed, to Isabel's rose garden near the house? Perhaps it was possible to believe anything if one wanted to badly enough.

Daniel Miller had evidently been considering Nora's rhetorical question as to who might have been harmed. 'What about your brother? It was his child, too.'

'What would he have done with a tiny baby?' she scoffed. 'He didn't have time for the family he had! No, she and I belonged together. We had survived together.'

'Did he ever recognise her?'

'He never saw her. He abandoned us both – started fresh in London and never returned to Australia, and of course I never took her to see him. I went home to Sydney a month after their deaths, taking my baby girl, my Polly, with me. I was spared from answering questions. People don't know how to behave around tragedy. They don't know what to say, and they don't want to say the wrong thing, so they make sure they're not in a position to say anything. I didn't see a soul, except Mrs Robinson. I didn't mind. I couldn't have been happier than to spend time with my little baby, just the two of us.

'When enough time had passed, and people finally came to visit, they didn't talk about Isabel and what she'd done. Oh, I'm sure they gossiped avidly among themselves, but they knew better than to engage me. They focused on the baby instead, my baby. Everyone knew how much I'd wanted her, and certainly no one suspected that she wasn't mine.

Why would they? I had gone to South Australia, heavy with
pregnancy, sick, intending to stay with my sister-in-law until
I had my baby. That Isabel had committed that awful crime
was dreadful timing, but there was no reason for anyone to
see anything in my return with a baby other than what they
had expected to see.'

A pause, a silence, and then Daniel Miller said: 'There's
one thing I don't understand. When Becky Baker set upon
you in the main street and swore that it was Isabel's baby in
that pram you were carrying, she was right, wasn't she?'

'It was no business of hers.'

'But Meg Summers vouched for you. She must have
known. She'd been up at the house with you, she knew
Isabel, she'd seen baby Thea in the past. She was a mother
herself – she'd have known the difference.'

'Your point, Mr Miller?'

'I'm wondering why she'd have done that. Why did she
keep your secret?'

'You'd have to ask her. She was beloved in town – a mother
to everyone, that's what people said. Perhaps it was as simple
as she knew I was the best person to care for the baby.'

Daniel Miller made a noise of consideration and was
silent for a time, pondering this. His voice, when he spoke
again, was low. 'And what about Polly, your baby; what happened to her?'

'I kept her safe in the wicker crib for a time. She looked
so peaceful, so perfect. And then I buried her.'

'In the rose garden?'

'It was the most beautiful place. You remember. They
should never have been digging there, it was sacrosanct. She
should have been safe there, safe to sleep peacefully forever.'

PART NINE

CHAPTER THIRTY-FOUR

Sydney, 20 December 2018

Dawn was breaking when Jess heard the front door close downstairs. From her bedroom window, she watched as Polly disappeared over the crest of the hill in the direction of the Darling House cove. It was no surprise that her mother couldn't sleep. Hearing Nora on the tape had been shattering enough for Jess; she could only imagine what it must have been like for her mother.

They hadn't spoken of it yet. When the recording finished the night before, Polly rose from her seat, muttering the usual perfunctory goodnight wishes before heading off directly to her room.

What Nora had said, what she'd done, was unfathomable – the confession, delivered so frankly, had landed like a stone in a pond, sending ripples rolling on and on towards the bank. Jess's thoughts had cycled all night, ranging across her own life, settling briefly on various interactions she'd had with Nora, small things she'd seen, heard and felt, but coming to settle eventually on what she'd learned over the past week.

She kept revisiting the conversation she'd had with her grandmother in the hospital: *You . . .* Nora had said when she opened her eyes to see Jess. *I've missed you . . . You came from England . . .* It was clear now that her grandmother, in her confusion, had thought she was speaking to Isabel; when she'd said, *I've looked after her* . . . she'd been promising she'd taken good care of baby Thea; and when she woke in a panic, grabbing Jess's wrist and hissing: *Issy, help me* . . . *He's going to take her from me*, it wasn't Mr Bridges she'd feared; it was Marcus Summers. The sudden arrival of his letter, expressing a desire to speak with her about Thea Turner, had filled her with terror, sufficient that she had braved the narrow stairs to the attic.

But to do what? What had Nora feared from Marcus? He hadn't mentioned anything about Polly being Thea; in fact, one of the reasons he claimed to be telling his story was to assuage his guilt, and that of his father, for the part he believed they'd played in Thea Turner's death. It was only Marcus's mother, Meg, who had known the truth, having been up at Halcyon in the days following Nora's delivery. Which begged the question as to why she hadn't told the rest of her family. Nora's tone when Daniel Miller asked why Meg had kept her secret had been noncommittal: '*You'd have to ask her.*'

Perhaps Nora was right, and Meg had simply decided Nora was the best person to take care of the baby, though Miller's silence at that point on the tape suggested he was dissatisfied with the answer. Maybe he'd just been upset by the whole turn of events. That would explain why he'd disappeared from view after the publication of his revised edition with its addendum. It was bad enough to make errors in journalism; to publish a true crime book to great acclaim and fanfare, only to discover later that a central tenet – the fate of a missing baby – had been completely wrong, would have been hard to bear.

As for Nora, no matter how calm she'd managed to sound

on the tape, Jess knew she must have lived with great anxiety that someone, someday, would hold her to account. She had managed to convince herself she'd acted in the baby's best interests, but there was surely a part of her that grappled with the horror of what she'd experienced, guilt over what she'd done. Jess knew there was: how else to explain the roses? Nora had hated them: one of the first things she'd done when she inherited Darling House was to tear every specimen from the garden. It had once seemed an endearing idiosyncrasy, because who on earth took so violently against a rose? But now, knowing that Nora had buried her tiny newborn baby in Isabel's rose garden, the antipathy took on a far more sinister stain.

An alert sounded on Jess's phone, a reminder that the meeting with Nora's solicitor was scheduled to begin in two hours' time. They'd arranged to get together at eight, before he went into the office, early enough to accommodate Polly's flight back to Brisbane that afternoon.

Jess stared at the reminder for a moment. It was almost impossible to believe that life could go on as normal – appointments, paperwork, meetings – when the night before had brought such revelation.

As if to underline the fact, a fresh email notification appeared on her screen. It took a moment for Jess to recognise the sender, Rowena Carrick, as the university professor she'd written to about poisons. The response was informal and direct:

Hi Jess,
    Happy to assist. To your second question first, algae bloom toxins are more than capable of causing death to

humans – indeed, they're among the deadliest we know.
I'm not overly familiar with historical post-mortem, but
cyanotoxins had certainly been discovered by 1959 and
both gas chromatography and liquid chromatograph
detection methods were in early practice then. I'd have
thought the medical examiner would've run this test.

Re your original question: there are various poisons that
wouldn't have been discernible in 1959, not because they
weren't recognised as toxic, but because the science to
isolate them wasn't yet established. Take tetrodotoxin, a
specialty of mine. Recognised as toxic for hundreds of
years – even shows up in Captain Cook's logs for 1774 –
but the structure wasn't elucidated until 1964. Extremely
toxic to humans, a thousand times more than cyanide.
Found in the livers, ovaries and skins of porcupine fish,
triggerfish, puffers, toadfish etc., aka the parts fed to Cook's
pigs in Haiti.

I've attached a (not-exhaustive) list of possible
contenders, but it pays to remember that dose is key.
Sodium chloride is toxic, but you'd have to eat a lot of table
salt for it to kill you . . .

Cheers,
Rowena

Jess read the message a second time but was left deflated.
She hadn't realised until now how invested she'd become in
the idea that the Turner family's deaths had, in fact, been a
case of accidental poisoning by blue-green algae. She didn't
want to think that Isabel had intended to kill herself and her
older children, that she'd abandoned her newborn child to
fend for herself in the world. Knowing that the baby left

behind in the white wicker basket had been her own mother made the whole thing even more abhorrent.

What must Polly be making of all this? If Jess was finding it impossible to fathom, Polly, who was already fragile, must be suffering terribly. Jess wished they were closer. Her instinct was to provide comfort; she'd have liked to receive some in return. But in all of the important ways, they were strangers to one another. Nonetheless, Jess decided to walk down to the cove. They could at least be alone together with the news.

Polly was standing by the rocks with her eyes closed, listening to the waves slap against the shore. She knew this place: the smell, the sound, the salt in the air. She knew it in the pores of her skin. This fact was some comfort, as her thoughts scattered around her like a thousand grains of sand.

Thea Turner.

The words came softly, quietly from her lips; she tried to find something solid in them, something real. She felt strangely reassured. The contents of the tape had explained certain things she'd struggled with all her life. How different she was from Nora, for one; but more than that, Nora's constant fear of losing her, the way she'd held on so tightly that Polly felt sometimes that she struggled to breathe. It hadn't been intrinsic to Polly, after all; she wasn't fundamentally fragile. The anxiety in their relationship had been driven by Nora.

And how ironic that amid so many untruths told to her by her mother, the single anecdote she had known to be an invention had turned out to be true. She *had* been found in a flower garden. Not the dahlia patch of Darling House, perhaps, but the rose garden of a house in a town called Tambilla.

Polly removed her necklace and then her dress and stood in her underwear. The air brushed warm against her skin, its fragrance of bruised gardenia and brine. She walked down to the shoreline and when she reached it kept going. The water was a welcome shock.

Refusing to allow herself the time to hesitate and change her mind, she raised her arms and dived forward, disappearing beneath the surface, rejoicing as the water found her fingers, her shoulders, the skin between her toes.

When she came to the surface she rolled onto her back, floating like a starfish. Her eyes were on the faraway sky, lightening now, warming.

Jess didn't know it, but Polly had been to Tambilla once before. She had planned to tell her daughter about it the other night, after the funeral, when she'd handed over Daniel Miller's book, but the conversation hadn't gone as she'd expected. Jess had been overwhelmed, grieving the loss of Nora, upset at receiving the book, put out that Polly had known the family story and failed to tell her; she had then charged Polly with abandoning both her and Nora.

But it hadn't been like that at all. It had happened incrementally. Polly had thought she was doing the right thing. Sometimes, in those early days in Brisbane, she'd been convinced that nothing was more important than that she and Jess stay together. But then she would think of all the things she couldn't afford to give her daughter, comforts and opportunities that Nora could offer, and she would see her desire to keep her daughter for herself as selfish. She'd thought about moving back to Sydney, living in Darling House with Nora and Jess, but she withered in proximity to Nora; she became all of the things she'd been told she was – weak, forgetful, delicate, nervy. Polly knew she could be more than that, a better person, a better parent, out from under Nora's thumb. But would Polly herself be enough for Jess?

And so it went, her thoughts going round and round and round, until two years had passed, Jess lived in Sydney and she in Brisbane, and the time for decisions was over.

Strangely, it was their separation that had led her to Tambilla. Polly had visited the place almost twenty-nine years ago to the day, December 1989. She hadn't meant to go anywhere that summer. Jess was booked to come to Brisbane for a fortnight and Polly had taken the whole glorious two weeks off work. Nora's phone call had been devastating.

'But I need her to come,' Polly had said, sounding, even to her own ears like a petulant teenager.

'Darling, I know you're looking forward to seeing her, but it's the NIDA summer school. Places are as rare as hen's teeth – I had to pull strings to get her in.'

Silence fell as Polly bit down hard on the words she wanted to say.

Finally, Nora broke the impasse: 'Of course, if it's important to you, I can cancel the course. I'm sure Jessica will understand . . . in time.'

Polly felt the prick of tears. It *was* important to her that Jess come to Brisbane, desperately important.

'How's the new job going?'

Somehow, Nora had intuited her strain.

'It's good,' said Polly, trying to sound confident. 'I've got a lot to learn, but I like it.'

'Not too stressful?'

'It's okay. I'm okay.'

'That's good, so long as you're taking care. Now, what would you like me to tell Jess? Would you like me to send her north?'

Polly had closed her eyes. 'No.' The word was bitter in her mouth.

'What's that?'

'No, she should do the summer school.'

'Are you sure?'

Polly had twisted the phone cord tightly around her finger. 'It's a great opportunity.'

She'd wept when she hung up. Hot, angry tears of disappointment and resentment, even as she told herself it was the right decision. There was nothing to be gained by putting herself and her own needs above her daughter's. Jess loved drama. To be the cause of cancelling the NIDA course would have cast a pall over the whole visit.

Polly was determined to be the very best mother she could, even if that meant spending less time with Jess. Work *was* fine. But Nora was right – it was stressful at times, being new; there was a lot to learn. Stress, she knew, was not to be taken lightly. Polly had not always been the best mother. On one occasion, she had even been a harmful mother. It was Nora who'd stopped her and rescued Jess. For a long time, Polly hadn't even remembered the incident. That was one of the scariest parts. She'd argued with Nora and insisted that it wasn't true.

'I'm glad you've forgotten,' Nora had said kindly. 'It's not uncommon, apparently. It's a type of psychosis, usually only postpartum, but something to be mindful of in times of stress. You mustn't worry, though. I won't let it happen again.'

No, she couldn't risk it. She would miss Jess like mad, but it was much better that she should enjoy the drama school without the distraction of a visit from Polly.

But Polly had already put in for the time off and hadn't

fancied sitting at home for two weeks feeling sorry for herself. For a day or two she moped, noticing how quiet the house was, tripping over the mother–daughter art canvases she'd bought, ticking off the activities she'd planned to do with Jess.

And then, on a whim, she decided to go for a drive. She threw a bag into the boot of her car with a couple of changes of clothes and set off west, with no plan beyond heading out through Warwick and down into New South Wales. She travelled through Goondiwindi, Moree and Dubbo, tuning her car radio to whichever station she could find; when there was only static, she pushed in the mix tape she'd made for Jess. With Belinda Carlisle, Roxette and the B-52s for company, she made her way through Parkes, Forbes and West Wyalong, towards the north-western corner of Victoria; there was a lot to be said for the healing properties of shout-singing 'Like a Prayer' as one drove through ever-changing countryside, all of it new to her eyes, the window down and the breeze blasting her hair back.

Somewhere near Mildura, she realised she was getting close to the South Australian border. She studied the map and plotted a course, and before she knew it she was in the Riverland and the landscape had changed from green to red. She arrived in the Adelaide Hills two days after she'd left Brisbane, approaching through the back of Murray Bridge.

Had she always been heading towards Tambilla? Looking back, she wondered whether it had been some sort of unconscious way of dealing a blow to her mother for keeping Jess in Sydney. For having the money and the thought to enrol her in the perfect activity to prevent her from travelling to Brisbane. For having once observed Polly doing an unforgivable thing.

Whatever the case, as she followed the street signs, glancing at the open map on the passenger seat beside her, she felt gripped with a strange sense of rightness about the journey. It was as if she were taking back something that had held her captive for as long as she'd known about it.

She had visited the waterhole. She had walked along the creek, inspecting beautiful stones and leaves that caught her eye, and gone right up to the willow tree, stroking the woody trunk. She found that she was easily able to imagine the scene as it must have been that day. The picnic rug, the family members, the white crib hanging from the strongest bough. She ate her sandwich on the grass, lying on her back afterwards and closing her eyes, listening to the birds calling and the cicadas ticking, and water tumbling in the distance. A terrible thing had happened there, and yet Polly had felt at peace.

Now, floating on her back in the December-warm water of Sydney Harbour, Polly thought about how that visit had been her second time at the waterhole. The first time, of course, she'd been asleep in her crib, in the shade of that very willow tree. She wondered what had happened next – how she'd ended up with Nora. And she wondered whether the reason she'd so often felt alone when she was young, as if something were missing or misplaced, was because at an intrinsic level she had known that once upon a time she had belonged to another, larger family. Or whether it was because the fear and the guilt Nora carried had caused her to focus on Polly to the exclusion and denial of all else, encircling her daughter so completely that Polly couldn't help but end up hopelessly isolated. Nora's secret had severed Polly's relationship with Jonathan; ultimately, it had divided her from her own daughter, too.

From the corner of her eye, Polly caught movement on the beach. It was Jess waving at her from the sand. She swam back slowly.

She felt self-conscious when she reached the shore, not for herself, but for Jess, who was, perhaps, unaccustomed to seeing a sixty-year-old woman emerge from the ocean in her underwear.

But Jess didn't seem concerned by Polly's attire. 'How's the water?'

'Lovely.' Polly joined her daughter on the sand and reached for her dress.

'I wasn't sure if you remembered that Leo Friedman is coming this morning?'

Polly smiled and pressed her dress against first one ear and then the other, drying herself. She was used to Jess and Nora thinking that she struggled with the basics. It was another of those old narratives that had existed for so long as to have calcified. Polly was actually very good at remembering times and dates. Her neighbour, Angie, was always asking for reminders about important neighbourhood events, shaking her head admiringly and saying Polly had the memory of an elephant.

'Nora's solicitor?' Jess prompted.

'Yes,' said Polly. 'I know. I'm going to make iced tea when I get back to the house.'

Jess frowned slightly and Polly realised that the talk of refreshments must have seemed insensitive. Jess would be taking Nora's deception very hard. Her daughter had idolised her grandmother and must be suffering terribly now. She was going to need help, but not too overtly. Funnily enough, Jess was an awful lot like Nora: proud, strong, and fiercely independent. Perhaps she'd got it from Thomas Turner?

Polly pulled her dress over the top of her damp underwear and slipped on her necklace. She held the pendants in the palm of her hand. The silver cat, the jacaranda tree that had been a birthday gift from Jonathan, the bird she'd brought back from Tambilla.

There had been so many lies and secrets. She wanted to be honest with Jess, for better and for worse. To say something that would start to bridge the gap, maybe even soften some of the pain she was feeling in the wake of Nora's confession, address the charge that Jess had levelled the other night. 'There's something I want to tell you,' she began.

Jess looked at her.

But what could Polly say? *I didn't want to leave you here. I intended to take you with me. I was terrified, because a long time ago, when you were brand-new and I was not in my right mind, my mother caught me standing over your cot with a cushion. I never wanted to risk your safety again; I had to learn to trust myself. I'd give anything to go back in time and do it all differently.* What was done, was done. All of the explanations she ran through her head sounded like excuses, flimsy.

Jess seemed to recognise that there was nothing more coming. She gave a small weary smile and started back towards the house.

'Do you remember the time I brought you down here and the tide came in?' Polly said quickly.

Jess turned to face her.

'You were only two or three, completely absorbed in your game, and when you looked up, an island had formed where you were sitting, and hundreds of crabs were crawling towards you.'

It was among the few memories Polly treasured. It had

happened not long after she'd moved with Jess to live in the apartment further up the peninsula. She'd been sitting on the beach reading *The Color Purple*, glancing over the top at regular intervals to see what Jess was up to, when suddenly Jess had let loose a shriek of unadulterated terror and Polly had leapt to her feet, her heart galloping.

She'd run to Jess and scooped her up, and as she held her and whispered against her ear that everything was all right, she'd felt her daughter's little body, rigid with fear, relax. It had been one of the first times she'd acted instinctively and been able to bring comfort to her child.

'You were right over there,' she said, pointing further along the beach. 'I rescued you from that very spot.'

Jess looked to where Polly was gesturing and then shrugged.

She didn't remember.

Polly's sudden plunge of despair was unexpected. It was an overreaction, of course: her daughter had been no more than three years old, practically a baby – no wonder she couldn't remember. But Polly's eyes stung, and she turned her face so that Jess wouldn't see. Far more affecting than any-thing Polly had heard from Nora on the tape, Jess's denial of their shared moment made Polly feel, in that moment, com-pletely alone in the world.

CHAPTER THIRTY-FIVE

Jess turned Polly's story over in her mind as they walked back to the house from the cove. She was deeply unsettled by it. She *remembered* Nora rescuing her from the crabs – she could see her still in her mind's eye. A tall figure, enormously tall, reaching down to pick her up; strong arms wrapped around her so that Jess felt eminently safe and protected. It had to have been Nora. Maybe Polly had heard the story and become mixed up over time? Nora had often said that Polly was impressionable. Or perhaps she'd become a bit confused in the aftermath of what they'd heard the night before.

She wasn't the only one.

They parted ways at the entrance hall and Jess went upstairs to have a shower. She was still struggling to process what her grandmother had done, the secret she'd kept. No, not her grandmother, she realised – her . . . great-aunt? The correction sat uneasily.

Finding herself at a loss when she was dressed, and unsure how to pass the time until Nora's solicitor arrived, Jess went back to the list of toxins that Rowena Carrick had sent with her email. The mechanical task was comforting; she was glad for the distraction.

By the time an hour had passed, she'd googled half the poisons on the list, cross-referencing against Daniel Miller's book and the folder of contemporaneous newspaper articles she'd printed. It wasn't the most scientific way of conducting a cold-case investigation, but it was all she had. She wondered whether the police records could still be accessed, perhaps even the coroner's report.

The court had found that poison was 'likely' but 'further facts' were needed to determine what might have caused such a quiet death. The inquest was adjourned *sine die*, in the hope that the required further facts would be discovered, but the city coroner had said he would be 'prepared to find that the family had died from a particular poison administered by Mrs Turner'.

So far, none of the toxins from Rowena Carrick's list fit the bill for a swift, 'quiet' death. Jess had just eliminated *Penicillium roqueforti* (lethal to rats in lab tests, but the quantity required to kill a human being was too large to have been practicable) when the doorbell rang. Crossing it off, she closed her laptop and went downstairs to open the door.

Leo Friedman had been Nora's solicitor for as long as Jess had been aware such a person existed. He'd come to the house plenty of times while she was living with her grandmother and, as was the norm where Nora was concerned, the two had developed a friendship outside their professional relationship. 'Whether you need a plumber, a mechanic or an optometrist,' Nora was fond of saying, 'the place to start is in your own teledex.' No amount of outside research could sway her conviction that the people *she* knew were the best, the most qualified, the only options she ever needed to consider.

In the case of Leo, it was quite possibly true. He had always struck Jess as a kind and decent man, with the sort of crumpled face and dustpan-brush moustache that inclined a person to trust him. ('One of his greatest attributes,' Nora had said with a wink when Jess mentioned it. 'People always underestimate a kind face.')

Today, when he arrived, his face was arranged in a suitably sombre expression. 'Jessica,' he said when he saw her. 'Let me say again how sorry I am for your loss.' He took a handkerchief from his pocket to pat perspiration from the rim of his balding head. Only eight in the morning, but it was already very warm.

'Thank you, Mr Friedman.'

'Leo, please.'

'Leo.'

'Is your mother here?'

'She is. Would you like to come inside?'

Jess directed Mr Friedman into the kitchen, where they could all sit together at the table. She and Polly had agreed already that they wouldn't mention anything they'd learned from the tape. There was no need for Leo to know; it would only serve to complicate matters.

Polly brought over the jug of iced tea she'd made and set it on the table atop a tray with three highball glasses. It struck Jess as a quaint thing to do, something her mother might have observed on television, or gleaned from a book and been convinced was de rigueur in the boardroom. But when Leo Friedman reached gratefully for the jug, pouring himself a long drink and then complimenting Polly on the flavour, Jess had to admit that on this occasion her mother had got it right.

Leo Friedman took from his briefcase a cardboard folder with Nora's name written in black marker along the vertical tab. He opened it, setting the top page to one side, before launching into a long-winded summary of the will's rather straightforward contents. Nora had split everything between

Polly and Jess, with a few provisions relating to her business, trusts, and charities, and a small stipend each for Mrs Robinson and Patrick. Then he said, 'Your grandmother was very specific in her wishes. She came to see me some time ago – when she went into the hospital to have her gall bladder operation. She wanted me to make an addition to her will. It concerns you, Jessica. I think it's best if I read it, if that's all right with the two of you?'

Jess exchanged a glance with Polly; Mr Friedman's words were a surprise, his tone difficult to interpret. She nodded and he began to read: '*Finally, I have a special request to make of my granddaughter, Jessica Turner-Bridges. In the attic of my home in Sydney, Darling House, there is a bookcase. The bookcase conceals a doorway, behind which is a small storeroom. Inside the storeroom is a travelling case. In the event of my death, I would like my granddaughter, Jessica Turner-Bridges, to retrieve the case and destroy it. It is not to be opened; its contents are not to be inspected or retained. I make this request trusting that it will be respected and followed. We are all allowed personal matters in our lives, and I trust that Jessica will agree that one's right to privacy continues after death.*'

Likely, Leo Friedman had never had a meeting end so abruptly as the gathering that day at Darling House. Jess was on her feet almost as soon as he'd finished reading, thanking him again for coming so early and ushering him to the door. It was all she could do not to rush upstairs to the attic and push the bookcase out of place. As it was, she wasted little time once the door was closed in turning to Polly and saying, 'Should we go and have a look?'

'You should,' said Polly. 'I still have to pack for the flight this afternoon.' Her expression was one of delicate consideration as she continued: 'Nora entrusted this task to you. She loved you enormously; nothing will ever change that fact.'

The words struck a nerve. Jess had been trying not to think about how cast adrift she'd felt in the wake of Nora's confession. For as long as she could remember, being the granddaughter of Nora Turner-Bridges had been the steel in her spine. She knew that family was more than biology – but that was abstract knowledge. It didn't do much for how a person felt deep down.

Jess didn't want to admit weakness in front of Polly, though, and she wasn't ready to address Nora's confession front on, not right now, and so she nodded polite agreement and headed upstairs alone.

The attic was warm, and Jess felt a ripple of purpose as she crossed the circular rug and passed through the filtering dust motes to reach the bookcase. She assessed the piece of furniture, gave it a little shove, and was pleasantly surprised to find that it moved without too much trouble.

Once the door behind it was on full show, Jess found it almost impossible to believe that she'd never found it before. It seemed so obvious. Darling House was just the sort of place, and this just the sort of attic, that should feature a secret room. She remembered her grandmother's entreaties not to play upstairs, her warnings that it was dangerous. Evidently, Nora had nursed other reasons for wanting to keep her curious granddaughter from the attic.

The travelling case was old and beautiful, and when Jess saw the name stencilled in gold paint along the top she felt a frisson of excitement: *Mlle Amélie F. Pinot*. This was the trunk that Isabel Turner had inherited after her French mother's death, that had arrived at her flat in London and from which she'd unpacked the 'sea of heirlooms and trinkets', among them the favourite teacup that had travelled with her to Australia, only to be dropped and shattered in the vegetable garden at Halcyon on Christmas Eve morning, 1959.

Jess heard Leo Friedman's words – Nora's request – in her head. They had been very clear. And yet. Here, finally, was the answer to the question Jess had been chasing since she'd arrived back in Sydney; surely Nora had gone to the attic after receiving Marcus Summers's letter to hide or remove something from this trunk.

If she had not heard the tape, if she had not learned that Nora had kept an enormous secret from both Polly and herself, if things were as they had been a fortnight ago, Jess liked to think that she'd have done as Nora instructed and destroyed the trunk with no questions asked. But she *had* heard the tape, and she knew now what Nora had done, and these actions were not without consequences. This trunk had belonged to Polly's birth mother, and her mother before that; what business was it of Nora's to determine that such a precious inheritance should be destroyed?

She didn't have to think about it for long. With a determined intake of breath, Jess opened the lid.

CHAPTER THIRTY-SIX

The first thing to hit her was the smell; not awful, just different, of another place, another time. The trunk was full to the brim, its contents packed tightly. Jess started pulling them out one by one. She was overcome by thoughts of Isabel as a young woman in London, all those years before, receiving her mother's precious keepsakes.

Jess had expected to find personal items that had once belonged to Isabel; she hadn't considered that the trunk would contain tributes to an entire family. Neither had she anticipated how easily she would recognise them. Here was Evie's handwritten book, self-importantly titled *Flora, Fauna and Fungi of the Adelaide Hills*; piano sheet music for beginners, including 'Long, Long Ago', embellished with instructions and advice as to notation and finger placement in the persnickety but patient handwriting of the Misses Edwards; the rolled-up posters of John Coltrane and Ella Fitzgerald that had once adorned the walls of Matilda Turner's bedroom; a saxophone; a cricket ball signed by Donald Bradman; a pink woollen matinee jacket for a baby, beautifully knitted with neat, even stitches.

Jess had to pause there, feeling unexpectedly moved. She had been too quick to cast judgement; this was a sentimental collection after all. She pictured her grandmother alone at Halcyon after the deaths with only baby Polly for company, walking from room to room selecting the objects that had meant the most to her nieces and nephew and sister-in-law. And she wondered how often Nora had made the sad, solo pilgrimage to the attic of Darling House to unpack and inspect this shrine to her lost family.

She fingered the edge of the sheet music. The paper at the right-hand bottom corner was softer and smoother for having been frequently handled, and Jess let out a long, complicated sigh before returning to the remaining objects in the trunk. Any lingering guilt at having opened it against Nora's wishes had disintegrated and drifted away. These keepsakes were important. Polly, especially, had a right to see them. These were the possessions of her siblings – the pink garment had been knitted especially for her.

Here, wrapped carefully in silk, was an assortment of boxwood and ivory miniature sculptures, the netsukes that Isabel had inherited from her mother. Beneath that, another soft fabric parcel revealed shattered pieces of porcelain: Isabel's teacup, Jess realised. Finally, at the very bottom of the trunk, was a book, leather-bound. Jess took it up, searching as she did for a title or name or some other distinguishing feature.

Later, when she related the story to Polly, Jess would say that she'd known instantly what it was, and perhaps she had. For here was Isabel Turner's journal from 1959, its lined paper covered with beautiful handwriting that told the story, in her own words, of the last year of her life. Time had faded the ink on the journal's pages, and Jess had to move to stand beneath the window to make out what was written. *And so, a new year dawns*, read the first line. *I wonder what it holds?* Pictures came to mind of Isabel sitting on the verandah at Halcyon that Christmas Eve morning, of Nora waking in the storm late at night to find the journal on the bed beside her, of Daniel Miller receiving the journal gratefully as he started to research his book. And now, here it was, almost sixty years later at Darling House, in Jess's own hands. She had a sense of history concertinaing, the present touching the past.

Slowly, carefully, Jess turned the pages, reaching in time the stubs that Miller had noted, where Isabel had torn out entries. Like Miller before her, she ran her finger along their length and, as she did so, the journal teetered. Jess reacted quickly to stop it from falling, and the action caused something to dislodge from the back. A sheet of paper, she realised; more than one.

On a couple of occasions in her professional life, Jess had experienced the sensation of several disparate pieces of knowledge coming together in an instant, as if by alchemy, to form a complete picture. So, now, at the very same second that she realised there were loose pages stashed at the back of the journal, an echo sounded in her mind, Nora in the hospital worrying about 'the pages', and Jess knew that these were the missing entries that Daniel Miller had wondered about in 1959 and that her grandmother had sought to retrieve after the letter arrived from Marcus Summers. Nora had wanted them destroyed, she realised: that was the reason behind her attempt to climb to the attic, and the purpose of the special request in her will.

Without a moment's hesitation, Jess angled the top sheet to the light, scanning quickly, gleaning what she could. Something of interest, tucked within the rest of the entry:

> I know I must learn to live without him. He has a
> wife, he cares for her, they have known one another
> since they were schoolchildren. And I, too, am
> married. Such as it is.

On the next page:

> I think back sometimes to the day we met. I write it that way, because although we had known one another for the many years that he had been coming to the house, that day was like a new meeting, the real meeting.

And the one after that:

> He will never leave his wife. And how would I live with myself if I urged him to? He is a carer by nature. His sense of worth is determined by the fulfilment of his duties. He has sacrificed so much already to her needs. He would resent me if I encouraged him to forsake his responsibilities – he would hate himself. And so, an impasse. There are times when no solution can be found that suits everyone. But is it too much to admit here, unashamedly, greedily, that I have needs, too?

And then:

> He saw the baby today, his baby. I could see it in his face, all the words he could not say. But I observed them. I knew. His love for me, for her. Oh, but I agonise sometimes, seeking a solution! It does me no good, but every so often I let myself daydream along the lines of what might have been, if we were the only people whose happiness mattered, if neither of us had responsibilities elsewhere.

Followed by:

> I met with a solicitor in Adelaide today, a gentleman who is not known to Thomas, who has promised me

discretion. He is going to put things in motion. Now
that I have made the decision, I am impatient to get it
done. I will require a new passport – it has been so long
since I arrived here, and I haven't travelled since. The
children, too, will need official documents. They will
hate to leave, but after much soul-searching I know
that it is the only reasonable path. I cannot bear to stay
here, so close to him, and yet unable to be together.
I need to go home – I feel so far away, so alone, so
separated from my past. And how could I ever leave
them behind? I am their mother; we belong together.
Do I flatter myself that their home is surely wherever
I am? They will learn to love England, my little
Australian children. In time, they will make a new
home, we will make it together, and all will be well.

And on the final page:

I am going to give the netsuke rabbit to Becky. She
is not the person whom I will miss the most, but
she is the person who will, I think, miss us the most,
especially the baby. I like the idea of leaving my small
precious rabbit with the person who so loved my
small precious child.

Jess stared unseeing through the attic window, lost in
thought. In the space of a few minutes the landscape of
everything she knew had changed yet again. Some of the
words in Isabel's second-last entry resonated especially; she
had heard them before. She had read them in Miller's book,
she remembered, when Reverend Lawson made his report to
police. The morbid assumption had been that Isabel meant
to 'take the children with her' into death. But the journal

suggested something very different. She had been planning to leave Australia to return to England; that's why she had sought the reverend's advice.

Why would someone planning to start afresh in her home country decide instead to kill herself and her family? Had there been a problem getting the passports? Had the solicitor changed his mind and refused to help her? Had Isabel become overwhelmed by the hurdles and lapsed into hopelessness?

Or had the policemen, the coroner, Daniel Miller – history – got it all wrong? What if Isabel hadn't meant to kill herself? What if their deaths had been a terrible accident after all? The blue-green algae came once more to mind. Rowena Carrick, the university professor, was confident that the coroner would have tested for it, but there were other possibilities on the list of toxins. She needed to finish going through it – maybe something else would jump out and announce itself the culprit.

Jess experienced a vague, distracting feeling, almost as if she were remembering something she wasn't aware she'd forgotten. It was like catching a glimpse of a fluttering moth on the very edge of her vision. Irritating, sly, impossible to ignore; but every time she tried to look at it directly, it disappeared . . . When she couldn't pin it down, her thoughts cycled on to something else that was bothering her: why had Isabel removed the pages? It was possible that she considered them too sensitive to leave to chance and the eyes of snooping children, but then why *keep* the pages? Why not destroy the evidence? And where had she put them? Somewhere that Nora had been able to find them, evidently.

Unless . . . Jess felt the electricity of knowing she was right – it wasn't Isabel who had torn the pages out. Who else but Nora would have removed the entry about Becky Baker and the netsuke?

Nora had given the journal to Daniel Miller to prove to him that Isabel was a loving wife and mother with a happy life who wouldn't have dreamed of killing herself and her children. The last thing she'd have wanted him to see was that Isabel was having an affair, and that Thomas Turner wasn't Thea's father. It was such a Nora thing to have done. To remove the pages that contradicted the rosy picture she wanted the journal to paint. Nora, with her gift for positive thinking, for certainty, for looking forward and never over her shoulder . . .

But what about the entry outlining Isabel's plan to leave? Why would Nora have removed that one? If anything, it would have helped her cause, suggesting that Isabel was far from suicidal: she'd been planning a new life. Was it simply because it was personally upsetting to Nora that Isabel had been planning to leave her Australian life – and family – behind?

And why, after tearing them out, had Nora kept the pages?

Jess frowned. Maybe, once Daniel Miller's book was written and public attention had moved on from the Turner story, she'd figured there was no reason to fear what was written on them? Isabel's affair, Thea's true parentage – these were facts that need not have worried Nora until she received the letter from Marcus Summers referencing a client and a desire to discuss Thea Turner's death.

All the same, keeping them was an action. It would have been so easy to destroy them: throw them in a fire, watch them burn . . .

Jess's head was spinning. She was missing something.

There were so many moving parts. One thing, though, was clear. She needed to share what she'd found with Polly. The journal pages, and the notes that Nancy Davis had sent her, too – Nora's account of what she claimed to have seen Isabel do with the pillow that had convinced the police that she was guilty. It had been niggling ever since Jess read it, so similar to the incident Nora claimed to have witnessed when Polly was a young mother and Jess a baby in her crib.

Leaving everything else where it lay on the floor, Jess took up the journal and hurried downstairs, hoping against hope that her mother hadn't left yet for the airport.

'I was beginning to wonder if I needed to send a search party,' said Polly, when Jess arrived at the kitchen door. Her suitcase was packed and standing against the wall.

'Do you have a second?' Jess knew she had to be careful here. The journal was very big news, speaking as it did to Polly's parentage; she had no choice other than to reveal it, but her mother was sensitive, delicate. Jess had no idea how she'd take the information. 'I have to tell you something.'

Polly's face fell. 'Is everything okay? Did you find the trunk?'

'I did, and before I say anything else, I should tell you that I opened it. Not just opened it – I took everything out. I searched it. I'm sorry. I hope you're not too disappointed.'

Polly smiled. 'Neither disappointed nor surprised.'

'Really?'

'I don't think a Christmas went by that you didn't hunt out your presents well ahead of time. I'd ask whether you found any skeletons in the attic closet, but after the last couple of days, I'm a little frightened you'll say yes.'

'I didn't find a skeleton.'

'That's a relief.'

'But . . .'

Polly winced. 'But?'

Jess indicated that they should sit down together at the table, and although Polly obliged, she did so guardedly, as if preparing for bad news. When they were seated, Jess slid the journal across the surface. 'It's Isabel's,' she said.

Polly looked at it. She didn't open it. She didn't even touch it. After a few seconds she glanced up, her chin held high, an attempt at bravery that made Jess feel painfully fond. 'What does it say?'

Jess understood that her mother was asking her for the kindness of a summary. Important parts only; any blow dealt swiftly.

She took a deep breath and outlined what she'd read: Isabel had been having an affair, she'd been careful not to name her lover in the pages of her journal, but Jess knew who it was. Whether he was conscious of it or not, Miller's book had made the answer clear: Henrik Drumming, the farm manager. He had a sick wife for whom he cared deeply, they had met when they were children together at school in Tambilla, he was a good and decent man. Someone Isabel had known for a long time, as he'd been coming to the house for work, but whom she had evidently come to know much better. No wonder he had continued to maintain the garden after her death, even when Thomas Turner told him not to: he hadn't been able to accept that she was gone.

'She writes about some of their meetings. She really loved him. From what she wrote, it wasn't a sudden one-off thing, or an accident. It was a true meeting of minds. They loved one another. And' – Jess hesitated – 'she seems certain that he was the father of her baby.'

Polly absorbed this information, nodding slowly. It was impossible to tell by her expression how the news was landing and Jess was anxious. She found it difficult to imagine how she would feel, confronting so many changes over the course of twenty-four hours, let alone what it must be like for someone like Polly.

And then her mother said, 'I always liked him in the book. He seemed to be a kind man. The way he cared for his wife.'

Now, she opened the front cover of the journal, touching it gingerly, as if it might be hot. She pulled it closer and ran her fingertips over the pen-crinkled pages. She wasn't reading, rather turning page after page – thinking, Jess supposed, about the woman who had written it, recording her most intimate thoughts and confessions.

When she reached the end, Polly considered the inside back cover closely.

Jess realised her mother was worrying a fine crease at the top. 'What is it?' she said.

'I'm not sure.' Polly slipped the tips of her fingers into what had now revealed itself as a fine cut in the endpaper. As Jess watched, she withdrew an envelope, pressed flat over time. When she turned it over, Jess could see that a message was written on the front in large capital letters and underlined:

PRIVATE AND CONFIDENTIAL:
FOR THE EYES OF MRS ISABEL TURNER ONLY

Polly raised her brows at Jess, who nodded avidly, and then she opened it, sliding a folded sheet of paper from inside.

'Well?' Jess said, unable to keep her curiosity in check any longer.

Polly held it on an angle so that they could both read it at once. The message had been written in an irregular script with a black ink pen and read:

Dear Mrs Turner,

I know what you have been doing with another womans husband. I saw you. He is a father and has responsabilities to his family, just like you have to your own children. It is not deecent or right to behave as you have done. If you do not stop, I will have no choise but to tell your husband what you have been up to.

The letter was unsigned.

Despite the formal tone, there were a number of spelling errors that made Jess think it had been sent by someone who lacked education, or else someone young.

'It's been a long time since I read the book,' said Polly, frowning lightly. 'But I don't remember Henrik Drumming having children? Just his wife in the hospital.'

'Poor Eliza, yes, down at Parkside,' said Jess. 'But I don't understand. It must be a mistake. It had to have been him.'

Polly didn't answer. An absent look had come across her face as if she were watching something play out inside her mind.

'What is it?' Jess asked.

No answer.

'Mum?'

Polly looked up. Perhaps the word was as strange for her to hear as it was for Jess to speak. 'I just . . .' She frowned at the tabletop and then glanced back at Jess. 'It's just that . . . I think I might know who he was.'

CHAPTER THIRTY-SEVEN

Adelaide Hills, 15 December 1989

The man with the ride-on mower was driving it in careful lines, this way and that. Polly watched him for a while from her spot in the shade, and perhaps he sensed her presence, because he came to a stop, lifting a hand in acknowledgement when he saw her. He shut off the ignition and wiped his palms on the sides of his trousers as he approached.

'Hi there,' he said.

'I'm sorry to intrude. I was taking a walk. I got lost.'

'Easy enough to do.'

He was a decade or two older than she was.

'Is this your property?'

He laughed. 'I'm the groundsman – in an unofficial sense, anyway. This land is part of a larger estate. Big house up there on the hill. The owner's overseas. He doesn't always know when it needs attention, and I don't live far. It's no effort for me to mow it when the grass gets too long.'

Polly wondered about this. Her new neighbour in Brisbane, Angie, was nice enough, but it seemed improbable that she'd make her way across the fence to maintain the backyard while Polly was away.

Perhaps he, too, felt that the disclosure needed further explanation, because he added: 'It's a fire risk when the grass is let go.'

Polly could glimpse the peak of Halcyon's roof line through the trees, and its pull was strong. 'The house is for sale,' she said, and then, because she was conscious of sounding strange, 'I saw a sign on the fence by the road.'

'You interested in buying it?'

She smiled.

'It's a beautiful house,' he said. 'A bit neglected now, but still impressive.'

'I thought I might walk up and take a look.'

'I don't think anyone around here's going to mind. Like I said, the owner's overseas.'

'Thanks,' said Polly, but she didn't leave. She heard herself say, 'Actually, the owner was my uncle. His name was Thomas Turner. Maybe you knew him? I've never met him. He died last year. My mother – his sister – is the one selling the house.'

The man looked at her from beneath his hat and she saw something change in his face, almost like recognition. He wasn't recognising her, per se, she knew, but establishing a context. At last he said, 'I mow the grass here because I used to love the girl who lived inside that house.' And then, almost immediately: 'I'm sorry. I don't know why I said that. I'm not usually one to talk about myself. Kurt.' He held out a hand to shake hers.

'Polly.' Behind him, a duck had glided onto the creek, and ribbons of sunlight were sent rolling up the trunk of an overhanging willow. 'You were talking about Matilda Turner,' she said, struck by his admission.

He shrugged. 'It was a long time ago. We were kids. And yet I sometimes feel that everything in my life might have been different but for what happened to her. Probably sounds stupid.'

'Not to me it doesn't.'

He smiled, and then shook his head. 'I'm sorry. It's just . . . you remind me of her. Your voice – something.'

'She was my cousin, I guess. Not that I knew her. My mother didn't talk about them. Too sad.'

He nodded. 'I suppose you've read the book?'

'Only recently.'

'What did you think of it?'

'On its literary merits, it was fine. I had mixed feelings about the subject matter.'

He laughed.

'It must be strange to have been written about?'

'It wasn't published here. Only in America. Most of us didn't get our hands on a copy until sometime later. By then, life – people – had moved on.' He shrugged again. 'The event itself was far worse than the book. My brother was really thrown by it. He'd had a falling-out with his mate.'

'John Turner?'

Kurt nodded. 'He was out of sorts at home, too. It's a tough age, fourteen. Fifteen and sixteen weren't much better, to be honest. He got itchy feet and left as soon as he was able. He'll come home one day, though. People always do. I wish he were around more – I'd like my kids to know their uncle a bit. He's a good guy, Marcus. Always helping people. And not just by offering them his ute when they're moving house. Proper help. Fighting for justice, protecting the disenfranchised. He's a lawyer. It's funny – when we were kids, I was the "bright one". I was good at school, bound to go on to bigger and better things; Marcus was the "outdoorsy one".' He gestured towards the mower and grinned. 'Funny how things turn out.'

'But you're not unhappy.'

'Not at all. This is my calling. Stewardship. After Matilda died, I lost interest in school. There were other ways to learn the things I wanted to know – I didn't need the formal parts. I found that I didn't hold much with religion, either. I would sit in church, listening to Reverend Lawson, trying to feel something, to feel God, I guess . . .' He lifted his hands, indicating the garden canopy, the silver-grassed mountain on the other side of the valley, the white-trunked gums. 'This is my church. My dad used to talk about places overseas, like St Paul's Cathedral in London, the Notre-Dame in Paris – places he'd read about in books and wanted to see. But I always felt most connected when I was outside; not just surrounded by nature, but intrinsic to it, a tiny part of a system much larger than I was. Reverence. Grace. Meaning. Purpose. I feel those things when I'm working. Nature is my cathedral.' He frowned and shook his head bemusedly. 'Sorry – I didn't mean to rattle on. You staying in town tonight?'

Polly didn't have any plans at all. She hadn't intended to come here in the first place. 'Is there somewhere local you'd recommend?'

'The hotel's nice. New owners; they've done a good-looking reno.'

Polly remembered the Tambilla Hotel from Daniel Miller's book. She liked the idea of staying in one of the town's oldest buildings. 'I'll give it a try.'

'Hey, listen – I don't want to be too forward, but my family and I have dinner there most Friday nights. You're welcome to join us if you don't have other plans. My kids are as mad as meat ants, but they tend to clear off after they've scoffed their fish and chips.'

Polly was accustomed to thinking of herself as a shy

person, so it was a surprise to hear herself agreeing that she'd be glad to join them; not only that, but meaning it. She liked Kurt Summers; she found him easy to be with, and she wanted to know more about this place, its past.

'Great,' he said. 'I'll see you later. Around seven. We try and nab an outside table when the weather's this good.' He tapped the brim of his hat and started back towards the mower. He was almost there when he turned to call over his shoulder. 'My dad's coming tonight, too. Mum died a few years back, so we try and keep him busy. You'll like him.'

Polly knew who Kurt's father was – Percy Summers, the man who'd found the Turner family that afternoon and, in his description of the bleak scene, given Daniel Miller the title for his book. She was curious to meet him; he had known her aunt and uncle and would be able to give an adult perspective on Halcyon as it was back then. As seven o'clock drew nearer, though, Polly experienced her customary evaporation of confidence, anticipation turning to anxiety.

She showered and dressed and went down the broad, carpeted stairs of the Tambilla Hotel at five minutes to seven, pulling on her sleeve cuffs nervously. She was glad she'd thought to throw in a halfway decent blouse. She told herself that if she didn't see the Summers family in the first lap she did of the restaurant and its outside tables, she would keep walking down the street and grab herself a bite to eat at the little Thai place she'd spotted further along.

As it turned out, the Summers family was not only expecting her, they'd set a place at the table and taken the liberty of ordering her a drink.

Within seconds, Polly knew that she'd been worrying

about nothing. She had spent a lot of time observing families. Coming from a group of two, she'd always found the dynamics mysterious. The way siblings could fight tooth and nail, only to turn around and defend the other furiously if anyone else were to criticise them. But it turned out being with the Summers clan was easy. Kurt's wife, Sally, ran a stone fruit nursery, and their children, two sets of twins a year apart, went to high school in Adelaide. They had come to dinner straight off the bus and were still wearing their uniforms. Kurt's dad, a gentle-faced man in his early seventies, sat at the end of the table watching it all take place, his smile, Polly thought, tending towards the philosophical. She felt she understood that smile. It was how she felt sometimes: on the edge of things, but not unhappily.

He'd stood when Polly came to the table and nodded a greeting, but they were seated at opposite ends and hadn't been able to talk beyond the general, frenetic family discussion. Afterwards, when Sally excused herself to drive the kids to an end-of-term party and Kurt went to pay the bill, refusing Polly's offer to chip in, Percy said something she couldn't hear. There was a noisy table behind them, a group of friends celebrating an upcoming wedding, so she moved closer.

'What did you think of the house?' Percy said. 'Halcyon.'

'Beautiful,' she replied. 'Sad, grand. It reminded me of something out of Jane Austen.'

'Pemberley, I always thought.'

'Yes, exactly. Mr Darcy would have been quite at home there.'

He smiled, considering her. 'You like Austen?'

'I like most books.'

'Reading anything good now?'

'I just started *The Remains of the Day*.'

'Oh, excellent. Wonderful writer. How about *The Joy Luck Club*?'

'Last book but one.'

'On my list of favourites for the year.'

'Mine too.'

'*A Time to Kill*?'

'Loved it.'

He was nodding, a smile of satisfaction on his face. Polly, too, felt the bonhomie that grows quickly and strongly between like-minded booklovers. And then he frowned, leaning a little closer. 'That necklace,' he said.

Polly looked down to where her silver cat was hanging on the long chain. It needed a polish, she realised. She told him the story about the Victorian rattle, but when she'd finished he said, 'I meant the little bird. Where did you find it?'

Polly smiled. 'Actually,' she said, 'I really *did* find it. Today, just before I met Kurt. I spotted it on the ground while I was walking. The sunlight caught on a piece of silver ribbon that must once have been tied to it and drew my eye.'

He was nodding. 'Near the waterhole?'

She wondered how he knew, and then realised that of course Kurt must have told him where they'd met. 'I like to collect things from nature. I'm always on the lookout. It's a hobby; my daughter and I used to beachcomb when she was small . . . I thought it was a stone at first, or a smooth seedpod. But it wasn't. It was this most perfect little bird. A wren, I think.'

'A fairy wren. We have a lot of them around here.'

'A fairy wren,' said Polly, liking the name very much. 'There was something almost magical about it. It was just lying there, as if it had been waiting for me to find it. I suppose that sounds silly.'

'Not at all.'

'I can be a bit of a romantic.'

'A fine trait. We'd have no books or music or paintings if not for the romantics among us.'

He didn't look to be laughing and it gave her the confidence to continue. 'It had this little loop attached – see, right here – so I slipped it onto my necklace.'

'It's perfect.' His voice seemed to catch and his eyes looked a bit glassy, she noticed. Perhaps the wind was bothering him. It had picked up, and they were sitting outside. She realised he was probably tired. She could see Kurt making his way back.

'I've had such a lovely time,' she said. 'I'm glad I met Kurt today.'

'Are you leaving?'

'I should. It's been a long day and I've imposed on your time enough; thank you for having me at your family dinner.'

She stood to leave, and he reached to take her hand in a gesture that was somewhere between the formality of shaking and the familiarity of holding. His grip was surprisingly firm. 'You're very like your mother,' he said. 'It really is like seeing a ghost.'

He was being polite; Polly knew that she looked nothing at all like Nora. She smiled. 'It's been so nice to meet you.'

'Come back again, won't you?' he said. 'Please come and see us again.'

'I will,' she replied.

But she never did. He was a charming old fellow, and she'd fallen in love that evening with the whole Summers family. But Polly had no excuse to visit again.

CHAPTER THIRTY-EIGHT

Kurt drove him home that night. He was a good lad and he'd been making an extra effort since Meg died. The run to Port Willunga from Tambilla was almost an hour long and there were kangaroos to dodge in the late summer dusk, but Kurt wouldn't hear of his dad driving himself. 'I enjoy it,' he said. 'Besides, you've seen the circus I live with – it's the only quiet time I get.'

Percy had moved down to Port Willunga not long after Meg's funeral. He'd have liked to do it sooner, but Meg wouldn't countenance leaving Tambilla and Percy didn't have the heart to upset her. There were times in a long marriage for pushing and times when the victory of getting one's own way was not worth the price. Knowing how to tell the difference was key.

Caring for Meg in those final months was difficult and sad, but he'd been determined to see it through himself. A married couple owed one another certain things; balance sheets drawn up over a shared lifetime. Towards the end, Kurt and Sally had organised a nurse to help part-time, and Percy had been grateful to take an afternoon away every now and then.

One day, he'd come down to the beach, for old times' sake, and it was while he was walking back across the dunes from the water's edge that he'd seen a For Sale sign in the front lawn of a wooden shack with a narrow balcony and big windows overlooking the sea. It had a rainwater tank and a vegetable garden and a big orange tree in the front. He'd known at once it was the place.

Percy had been born and bred in Tambilla, he'd raised his boys there, experienced love and loss, tragedy and joy; he knew the sights and sounds and smells better than anywhere else on earth. But he'd been glad to move away. He hadn't a lot of life left, and it was good to try something new. He might not have made it to Greece or Canada or Spain, but he'd left Tambilla in the end, just as he'd always said he would. He'd sold the shop, too, even though he'd made a promise to Meg. There was a place, Percy thought, for a white lie like that one.

'Make you a cup of tea before I go?' Kurt asked, switching on the kitchen light as Percy let them inside.

The day's warmth had collected in the corners of the room and Percy pushed open the window above the sink to let it out. A dragonfly was panicking against the glass pane and he used his cupped hand to edge it free. 'How about I make you a coffee for the drive home,' he replied.

Once he'd seen his son off safely, Percy took his cuppa out onto the balcony and sat in his old deckchair. The sea was calm tonight: tide rolling in and then pulling away again. It was his favourite sound.

He had always liked to come down here; some of his happiest memories were of bringing the boys to the beach to camp when they were small. Those long, sweet days when there was nowhere they'd rather be than by his side. Strange the way life went. It really did happen while you were busy looking the other way.

As the heady fragrance of native frangipani infused the warm night air, Percy ran back over the evening in his mind.

When Kurt first told him about the young woman he'd met that day, and mentioned, so casually, that he'd invited her to dinner, Percy had almost keeled over.

He hadn't known what to expect. The reality had been disarming. He'd wondered over the years, made some attempts to find out for certain, but when he saw her, he'd known instantly. She was Isabel's daughter. The mannerisms were there, even if Polly carried herself with less confidence. Any remaining questions about what had happened that night when he'd taken the baby back to the house to be found were answered; what he'd sometimes suspected was now confirmed.

Time had a way of fading emotion out of memories, but Percy could still touch the terror and confusion of those days after he left the baby in the rose garden. As he'd waited for an announcement that never came, he'd begun to reproach himself. In the absence of any other plausible explanation, he came to believe that wild dogs had pounced when his back was turned. That in trying to save the child, he had put her in harm's way.

But then, a week or so later, a strange thing happened in the main street. He was loading boxes at the shop when he glimpsed Isabel's sister-in-law in town for the first time since the community meeting. She was dressed again in mourning black, but this time, rather than carrying her baby, she was using the old-fashioned perambulator that belonged to the Turner family. It was a dislocating sight. The pram – purchased from London and shipped to South Australia, unlike anything made or used here – was synonymous with the Turners, and new life, and it was jarring to see it in action after what had happened.

Percy was still processing these thoughts when he sensed

fierce motion in his peripheral vision. Becky Baker came flying out of the side door of her aunt's teahouse, letting the screen door slam angrily behind her as she barrelled over to the perambulator and snatched up the baby.

Mrs Turner-Bridges screamed – 'My baby! She's stolen my baby!' – as Meg ran out from the shop. 'Becky, love,' Meg was saying, 'let the child go. Let her go, love. That's not young Thea; it's Mrs Turner-Bridges' baby. It's Mrs Turner-Bridges' baby Polly.'

By now there was quite a scene. Betty had come out of the teahouse, closely followed by Eric Jerosch and Hugo Doyle, who, as good luck would have it, had stopped in for their tea break. The police officers helped bundle poor Becky away. Everyone knew how much she'd adored Thea Turner. The gossips said she'd liked to pretend the baby was her own, that she'd become too close to the family, and everyone knew she was slower than most, more apt to get confused.

Afterwards, Percy couldn't get the episode out of his head. He started to wonder; he remembered Isabel telling him that her sister-in-law was coming to stay. She had a long-held dream of becoming a mother, but to date she'd had a lot of trouble in that regard. 'The world isn't fair,' Isabel had said. 'But does it have to be so often cruel? Poor Nora has suffered so much, and she would be the most loving mother. If there were any justice in the world, she would have four or five children of her own by now. She doesn't have any problem falling pregnant, it's just that her babies don't seem to cling to life.'

What if Becky were right? Percy wondered. What if Mrs Turner-Bridges' baby hadn't survived, if the sad occurrence Isabel feared had come to pass? The child that he'd left in the rose garden, Isabel's baby, had been alive and well. It was not inconceivable that one might have been switched for the other.

But when he asked Meg, she'd put him straight. 'I'm sorry, love,' she said. 'I know how much you want it to be true – I'd have liked that, too – but I had a good look, and it wasn't Thea. It was Mrs Turner-Bridges' baby.'

Meg ought to know. Percy had woken Christmas morning and found her up and about already, in the shop putting together a parcel of food. 'It's for Mrs Turner-Bridges,' she explained. 'I kept thinking of her, all alone in that big house. Pregnant and grieving – she must be in utter misery. I can't bear to imagine her by herself.'

Percy had urged her to wait, even just a day. In the circumstances, he wondered whether she oughtn't to let someone else take a turn at being helpful. But Meg was having none of it. She had always been among the first to lend a hand when it was needed, and she was determined that this occasion should be no different. The more he tried to reason with her, the more agitated she became. 'She's all by herself, Perce.'

And so Percy had agreed to keep an eye on the baby while Meg went to check on Mrs Turner-Bridges and deliver some supplies. That's when she learned that Nora had given birth.

'She was struggling,' Meg reported later that night. 'I had no choice but to stay and help her. She'd handled it as well as could be expected in the circumstances – a natural mother – but the house was a mess – the kitchen still covered in food from the day they left. And the baby had come too early. She was tiny. Perfectly formed, but oh, so small and feeble. I had to stay and help. What else could I have done?'

*

The moon was the finest of fingernails tonight. Nothing more than a ghostly sliver. High above him, Percy located the Southern Cross and the two pointers: entry-level star-spotting, but old habits die hard. Isabel had told him once it was the night sky that caused her to feel the furthest from home. 'To look up and not see the Great and Little Bears – it makes me lonely at a cosmic level. It's all wrong.'

Percy wondered now at the flaw in his logic back then. He had acted as if returning the baby to her home would some-how save her from the shadow of a tragic, violent, and traumatic event. He'd expected that she would be found by family and that it would represent a happy end to the story, at least as far as her disappearance was concerned. But his thinking had been simplistic. All events, like all objects, cast a shadow; there was no way to escape it. That was physics. That was life.

At dinner that evening, Percy had observed that Polly was shy. He knew nothing about the rest of her life, but he won-dered whether her tendency to blush, the diffident way she had of speaking, the nervous habit of playing with the pen-dants on her necklace, were consequences of having grown up, even unwittingly, in tragedy's shadow. What Nora Turner-Bridges had lived through, what she had done, must have left its mark. How, Percy wondered, had it changed her? What sort of mother had she been?

It was Polly's habit with the necklace that had drawn his attention to the wooden wren. He'd recognised it at once and had instantly been spun back thirty years: the ride from Meadows, the shop in Hahndorf, the last day of his life before it had all fallen apart.

There'd been rain recently in the Hills. It must've churned things up. But how remarkable that Polly should have found the wren. How sly the gods. Percy had looked for the little sculpture many times since his first trip back to the picnic site that Christmas Eve, scouring the land by the edge of the waterhole, beneath the willow tree, to no avail. The wren had become a symbol for all that he'd lost, that night and afterwards. He'd figured it had vanished irretrievably. It seemed that he'd been wrong in that.

Percy had bought the fairy wren for Isabel as a parting gift. He could still remember the jolt of bittersweet pleasure he'd felt when he saw it, the certainty that she would love it. She adored miniatures; the collection of her mother's Japanese netsukes was her most prized possession. She had shown it to him once, when he was borrowing books from the library at Halcyon, back in the year before she died, when they were still politely tiptoeing around the attraction that was growing between them.

The love affair itself had been brief. A matter of weeks before they agreed that it had to end. Isabel had been distraught when she showed him the letter, which had been dropped through the mail slot on the door and bore no stamp. Percy had known at once from whom it came. He'd recognised the handwriting and it had brought into focus the inexplicable bad mood of his second son in recent weeks.

Once Marcus knew, the situation was untenable, the affair was ended. But love itself is not so easily defused. Incredible to think that if Percy hadn't run into Mrs Pigott from the post office while he was riding Blaze on the first morning of 1959, if she hadn't asked him to do her the favour of delivering a parcel on his way home, everything might have turned out differently.

But Percy had agreed to help, and so it was he who handed the parcel to Isabel that day. 'Hello!' he'd heard her call as he guided Blaze up the driveway towards Halcyon. 'I'm over here.' She was standing at the top of a ladder, holding a string of bunting, surrounded by foliage. She looked like Titania, Queen of the Fairies. 'Is that for me?' she said.

Spellbound, he held the parcel out towards her and gave a nod.

'Do you think you could do me a terrific favour?' she asked with a laugh – that laugh! 'I can't let go of this string – it's been the devil to get it this far – but I'm dying to open that package. Would you come and hold this for me?'

He did as she asked, climbing up one side of the ladder to take the string from her, their hands brushing as she let go. He watched as she tore away the wrapping to reveal brand-new books, hot off the press: *Breakfast at Tiffany's, Our Man in Havana, The Darling Buds of May.*

They got to talking. Reading shapes a person. The landscape of books is more real, in some ways, than the one outside the window. It isn't experienced at a remove; it is internal, vital. A young boy laid up in bed for a year because his legs refuse to work and a young girl on the other side of the globe, sent to boarding school because her parents had both died, had led completely different lives – and yet, through a mutual love of reading, they had inhabited the same world.

It was a bridge he'd never been able to cross with Meg. It hadn't mattered before. It didn't matter now. He and Meg had built a life together, children and a business in common, countless small daily joys and terrors. But meeting Isabel and finding that she, too, knew the places and people of his imagination was powerful. Intoxicating. To feel known was a revelation. To have to give it up was like being expelled from home.

Isabel had told him, just before he left for Meadows, that she'd decided to go back to England. 'What future is there for me here if you're not part of it?'

They'd been sitting side by side on the stone bench near Mr Wentworth's pond. He'd come up on the pretence of a grocery delivery and she'd slipped around the rear of the house to meet him as he made his way back down the driveway. A few final, precious, snatched moments. He'd wanted to be able to offer her more. In another life, with a different set of circumstances and values, he might have been able to do so.

She'd been to see a solicitor, she said, who was arranging passports. They were going to leave in the new year. She hadn't told her husband. 'He would only find a way to stop us. He's a very determined man.'

She hadn't told her children, either. 'Matilda will be the difficult one, and John. And Evie.' She'd sighed. 'None of them will be happy. Except, of course, little Thea. She's always happy. She's a delightful little person. She takes after her father.'

Percy's phone was ringing somewhere nearby, and it took him a moment to find it in his coat pocket. Kurt's name appeared on the screen. Percy checked the time and saw that it was half past ten. 'Hey, mate,' he said when he answered.

'Hey, Dad. Not too late, I hope?'

'Just counting the stars.'

'All still there?'

'So far, so good.'

There was a pause then, and Percy realised that his son had called with no purpose other than to check on him. He'd had more of these telephone calls in recent years. It was as if Kurt and Sally believed that he had lost the ability to take care of himself now that Meg was gone. Next would come a simple, random inquiry. Something like:

'Didn't leave my hat down there, did I? Black cap with the shop logo on the front?'

'Haven't seen it, but I'll keep an eye out.'

'Right-o, thanks.' Another pause, and then, 'Nice dinner tonight.'

'Very nice.'

'I think Polly had a good time.'

'She seemed to enjoy herself.'

'Such a strange thing, meeting her there like that.'

Another pause. Percy appreciated being checked on, but he wasn't ready to speak about Polly or the serendipity of her turning up by the waterhole that day. As it was, his son's continued maintenance of the place was a subject they rarely broached. They were alike, he and Kurt, each very private, nursing his feelings close.

'Have you had a think about the Lobethal Lights next weekend? Sal thought you might like to stay up here with us overnight. Marcus will be back in town by then. He said he'd come – bring the kids.'

'Sounds like a plan.'

Percy ended the call as a night-bird flew overhead in the dark. His eldest son was happy; he and Sally were one of those married couples who were friends and equals before anything else, his kids were terrific, he seemed to have found an occupation that brought him peace and fulfilment. But Percy wondered sometimes whether Kurt still thought about Matilda Turner each year when the signs went up for the Lobethal Lights. It often came to Percy's mind: the plans his son had made to see the lights with her that Christmas.

Percy was suddenly tired, ready for bed. He took up his

teacup, tossed the cool dregs over the side of the balcony, and went inside. He closed the door behind him and rinsed the cup beneath running water at the sink.

It was Marcus who had gone on to the university. Funny how things worked out in the end. A determination had gripped him after the Turner deaths, and he'd dedicated himself to a pursuit of the law. For a long time, they'd only ever seen him at Christmas. He'd come back, because it was important to Meg, and then he'd disappear again. They'd find him mentioned in the newspaper every so often, protesting for this cause, representing that one in court, angering those in positions of authority, championing the powerless. He'd always had a sharply defined set of values. He and Meg were alike in that: no room in either outlook for shades of grey.

It wasn't until after Meg's funeral that they finally talked for the first time about what had happened. Everyone had come to Summers & Sons for drinks – the whole town had wanted to pay their respects, cramming into the shop and spilling out onto the pavement – and then, after they left, Marcus, Percy and Kurt had sat with a bottle of whisky, reminiscing. Finally, Kurt had stumbled home, leaving just the two of them.

Marcus was in his thirties by then. He'd gained enough life experience to bruise the black and white out of his moral outlook. He wanted to apologise, he said, for not understanding how hard it must have been for Percy to lose Isabel. 'In among all the rest of it,' he said, 'I didn't perceive back then that you'd have been experiencing a personal grief, too.'

'Thanks, mate,' Percy said. 'I appreciate it.' And he had.

'I was so angry,' Marcus said. 'After I saw the two of you, all I could think of was Mum. I used to lie awake at night, listening to my records, plotting ways to punish Mrs Turner for coming into our family and ruining things.'

'It was a long time ago.'

'I know, I know.'

'There's no need—'

'There is, though, Dad. There's something I have to tell you.'

Percy had had a lot to drink by then. They both had. He wasn't ordinarily a big drinker, and it didn't take much to make his head swim. He was unprepared as Marcus continued:

'I went down to Port Willunga, and I caught a puffer. After old Buddy died, you'd warned us off them, said just as they'd killed Buddy they could make a person poorly. I had some vague notion it was just what Mrs Turner deserved.'

Caught a puffer? What she deserved? Percy heard the words his son was speaking, but his mind was taking longer than it might have to assign them meaning. He shook his head as if to clear it.

'God only knows how I thought I was going to make her eat it.'

Percy suddenly saw where this was going. 'But you didn't, mate? You didn't do anything as stupid as that?'

'No, thank God.'

Percy felt relief like a flood of nerves from one end of his body to the other.

'I could've, though. You remember what I was like.'

Percy did.

'Thankfully Mum found me in time. She was livid, I can tell you. Made me tell her what on earth was on my mind. I was so panicked – I told her, Dad. I told her why I'd been so upset, about you and Mrs Turner. She gave me a big hug and said not to worry. That everything was all right. And she took the fish off me and made me promise I'd never do anything so stupid again.'

Percy shut off the lights on his way to bed. He cleaned his teeth, plugged in his phone to charge, and then opened his window so he could listen to the ocean if he woke in the night.

Percy had never believed that Isabel had done it. It was impossible; besides, he knew that she'd been making plans to leave the country. But he had been in no position to be giving statements of that nature to the police, and someone else – an unnamed source was how they put it – had told them something that convinced them otherwise. He'd had no choice but to watch from afar and trust that they would figure it all out correctly in the end. As time went by, and they failed to uncover the truth, he told himself that it made no difference to him. The way the Turner family died, the open finding, the questions about the poison – what did it matter? She was gone.

And then, for years, nothing. Until the night after they buried Meg, and Marcus told him what he'd almost done. Percy had had too much to drink for it to hit him hard in that moment, but he had lain awake in bed afterwards thinking about the boy his youngest son had been: headstrong and loud, but good and kind and loyal to a fault. He'd thought, too, about the aftermath of the Turner tragedy and the white-hot fear he'd felt for Kurt. The irony wasn't lost on him, as he finally fell asleep, that all along he'd been trying to protect the wrong kid.

Marcus's story came back to him like a bad dream when he woke the next morning, like something he'd seen on television years before and only half-remembered. Now, though, it wasn't his sons he was thinking of: his thoughts fell on Meg. Marcus had mentioned that his mother took the pufferfish from him, and the recollection made Percy think of something else. Something Meg had said, right near the end.

It was a merciless, messy time. She'd been dosed up on morphine and the medication had knocked her sideways. She'd thought she was a little girl sometimes; at others, she'd believed they were just married. On occasion, she was angry with him. 'I know what you've been doing,' she'd say, with a bitterness so acute that it made him wonder. 'I see that dreamy look in your eyes. I know where it is you go.'

And then, one day: 'I took it from him, Perce. I stopped him.'

He'd had no idea what she was talking about, but the nurse said that was to be expected. That she'd speak nonsense and it was kindest just to go along with whatever she was seeing in her head. So, 'That's good, love,' he said.

'I took it from him, but I didn't throw it away. I made it for her specially. Take Mrs Turner her Christmas gift, I told him. You must make sure she gets it. He came back to the house and told me she was so happy with the gift. I only found out later that she'd given it to all of them. She never shared my fish paste – she told me a hundred times. "My one pleasure, all for myself," she said. She wasn't meant to share it.'

Percy climbed into bed. When he moved to the house at Port Willunga, he hadn't brought any of the old furniture. Kurt and Sally had raised their eyebrows and ribbed him gently for his extravagance when he told them he wouldn't need a moving truck, he was going to buy what he needed new. They hadn't meant anything by it; it was just the way young people treated the old when they didn't intend to be condescending but were nonetheless.

He had bought himself a king single. He didn't need more, and he liked the idea of taking up only the amount of space that he required. With the extra room he'd installed bookshelves on three walls. In the spare room, he put two sets of bunk beds so his grandchildren could come and visit whenever they wanted. He loved it when they stayed, watching them scramble over the dunes towards the beach, boards under their arms, kicking sand at one another and laughing as they went.

Most of the time, though, Percy was alone. Being old, he had come to realise, was like being stuck inside an enormous museum with hundreds of rooms, each crammed full of artefacts from the past. He understood now why the elderly could sit, seemingly still and alone, for hours on end. There was always something else to take out, to look at from a fresh angle and become reacquainted with.

He tried not to let his thoughts pull him back to the night he left the baby in the rose garden. She'd disappeared so fast, too fast. It was almost as if Mrs Turner-Bridges had been told to watch out for her. But the only person who knew was Meg, and Percy couldn't believe it of her. That would've meant she knew where the baby had ended up all along, and had let him go on believing himself responsible for the little one's death. She could never be so unkind.

Percy had blamed himself for a lot of things over the years. But he hadn't caught the puffer and he hadn't put it in the fish paste. He hadn't taken the baby from her crib, and he hadn't kept her. He had fallen in love and betrayed his wife. He had tried to be a good father. He had tried to make things up with Meg and had pledged to her the single thing he had to give: his service. Life was a journey, and it wasn't always smooth, and sometimes terrible things happened. Percy was under no illusions: he was aware of what he'd done, and of what he hadn't.

Tonight, Percy was tired, and he knew that he would sleep. He lifted his sore old legs into bed and straightened the sheet over the top, and as he closed his eyes he let himself into a room that was one of his favourites. He was a younger man, slipping through the fence on the hidden side of the Turner property, crossing the paddock towards the willow that stood by the waterhole. Isabel, he could see, was already waiting for him. Beside her was a small pile of books; he carried the one he'd borrowed in his knapsack. She must have sensed him, because she looked up and saw him, and when she smiled, he felt that everything was right with the world and always would be.

CHAPTER THIRTY-NINE

Adelaide Hills, 24 December 2018

The Banksia Bookshop occupied a stone building on the main street of Tambilla that, according to the real estate agent, had once been home to the town's only grocery shop. The bookseller, Margie, was new to the area, and took the information as an interesting but insignificant piece of local trivia of the sort often shared by real estate agents hoping to make a sale. She had a romantic view of history, though, and enjoyed the fact that if you looked hard enough, in a certain light, you could still see the old font beneath the new paint showing a pair of S's where 'Summers & Sons' had been written.

On Christmas Eve morning, the bookshop was doing a roaring trade. Carols piped through the sound system, children wearing Santa hats and reindeer ears slipped among the shoppers, and a staff member dressed as an elf was handing candy canes to people when they left. As Jess stepped out of the shop and onto the pavement, she was filled with the lightness of spirit and free-floating sense of possibility that always claimed her when she had a brown paper bag containing new books under her arm.

Across the road, she spotted a narrow path running through the grass away from the street between two buildings. She recognised it from Daniel Miller's book as the path that Becky Baker must have taken on her walk from the brewery to the Turner house each morning, when she left the narrow river that ran parallel to the town and appeared in the main street to greet Meg Summers and claim her morning apple.

Becky had enjoyed the tunnel of oaks and elms that grew along the street, and almost sixty years later, Jess was similarly struck. The trees were enormous, their deep green leaves as big as dinner plates, casting the road – which would otherwise be baking – into complete shade.

'You ought to visit in autumn,' the woman behind the counter in the Organic Market had told her when she'd picked up a coffee earlier. 'The colour of those leaves, you'd think you were in Canada.'

Jess had agreed to meet Polly at midday, which gave her fifteen minutes to fill. Her mother had been very mysterious at dinner the night before. She'd taken a phone call and, from what Jess could hear, made plans to do something this afternoon. She'd then asked Jess if she were free.

Polly had been very careful since they'd arrived – they both had – not to make any assumptions as to the type of trip it was, and what it meant that they'd decided to travel to Tambilla together over Christmas. In the wake of Nancy Davis's tape and the unearthing of Isabel's journal, each had her own reason for wanting to return to South Australia. Still, they'd agreed, it was a nice idea to have dinner together on the first night, and so they had.

It had been an unexpected event all around. From the first, Polly had been very particular about where they sat, choosing a table outside, in a corner overlooking the street. Only then had she revealed, somewhat sheepishly, that she'd been to Tambilla once before. 'I wanted to tell you the other night,' she said, 'after the funeral, but everything got a bit . . . confused.' As it turned out, by some sort of coincidence Jess was yet to understand, Polly had wound up eating dinner with the man she now suspected of being her father.

'You had no idea at the time?' Jess asked.

'None, though I liked him. I liked all of them. I remember driving away the next day and being struck by how comfortable I'd felt in their presence. At the risk of sounding ridiculous, I was changed in some way by that dinner; I became lighter, more resolved. Less constrained by the somewhat limited idea of myself I'd been carrying around.'

Polly said she'd already decided by then that she didn't want to live a life defined by secrets. 'That's why I'd left Sydney,' she explained, 'six months before I came down here.' She told Jess then about the night Daniel Miller had come to Darling House: she'd discovered her mother standing over Jess's crib in the dark, and Nora had turned and made her promise never to tell Jess what had happened at Halcyon. Jess saw now that it had provided a pivot point: Nora, Polly, Jess and their acidic family secrets, joined together in that moment.

'I agreed,' Polly said, 'and I shouldn't have. By keeping my own secrets, I did the same thing to you that Nora did to me – withheld important parts of your identity. But I want to do things differently.' Her fingers went to the jacaranda pendant on her chain. 'I want to talk to you about something important – I should have done it a long time ago. I want to tell you about your father.'

Jess had experienced the slowdown of everything around her then. The noise from the other tables had sucked away as into a vacuum, replaced by the ocean of her own pulse in her ears; there were instant pins and needles in her fingers. She had imagined this conversation a thousand times but given up hope of ever having it. In the end, her mother's story of love and wasted opportunity, of secrecy and shame, was simpler than she'd guessed, and therefore somehow sadder.

Perhaps because the story was sad, Polly sought to balance it by rolling into happier anecdotes of Jess's early years. 'Once,' she said with a laugh, 'when you were only about three or four, I took you to a local funfair. We went on the rides together, and bought fairy floss and a toffee apple, and later, in the evening, found a spot on the oval to watch the fireworks. Your little face was all lit up, your eyes as wide as I'd seen them, and as we left, you looked up at me in wonder and said, "But how did they know it was my birthday?"

'Another time, you must have been about five, and you and the other children at school were spending recesses racing around the sandpit. You were upset, because there was another girl – Fast Mary, you called her – who always managed to beat you. You never liked being beaten. You'd outgrown your sneakers, and when I took you to buy new ones you asked me if they'd make you fast. It was such a sweet thing to say, and you were so eager and earnest, that I answered, "Yes, of course," without really thinking about it. Well! The look on your face the next afternoon when I collected you from school and you told me indignantly that they were not fast shoes at all – you'd come second once again to Mary – I've never forgotten it. I never again answered your questions glibly.'

The memories were sweet and funny, and Jess could see that for Polly, who had been keeping them to herself for so long, it was a relief finally to share them; but for Jess, it was like being told stories about someone else. She didn't remember any of it. She'd been a child, of course, but there was more to it than that.

There was a truth observed by all good preachers, leaders, and salesmen: tell a good story, tell it in simple language, tell it often. That's how beliefs and memories were formed. It was how people defined themselves, in a reliance upon the stories about themselves that they were told by others. Nora had been the chief storyteller in Jess's life, which was how she came to know herself as strong, smart, and determined, as Nora's much-loved granddaughter, a true Turner.

Except that she wasn't a Turner at all.

Listening to Polly's fond memories of a little girl from decades ago, reflecting on everything her mother had said earlier about meeting Jonathan James and Nora's reaction to their engagement, the months and years that had followed, Jess had a lot of questions: about her father, the past, her history. But when there came a lull in Polly's stream of consciousness, she surprised herself. She was more aware than ever of how few memories she and her mother had in common; it seemed suddenly vital to repeat and celebrate those they did: 'I remember the crabs,' she said. 'On the beach that day? I remember them. I was terrified, and then I felt safe.'

She wasn't sure what she'd expected, but it hadn't included Polly's face crumpling as tears formed in her eyes and her hands came up to hide them. She wondered at first if her mother had misheard, or if there were something else about the matter that she'd missed. 'Are you okay?'

Polly had taken a tissue from her handbag; her cat necklace was tinkling against the bird as she dabbed her eyes. 'I'm fine,' she said. 'It's really nothing. It's nothing and it's everything.'

*

As Jess waited for Polly on the bench in the middle of the Centenary Garden, a group of crimson rosellas swept overhead in a flash of blue and red, disappearing noisily into the branches of the giant gum at the back of the hotel on the other side of the road. She was still experiencing a curious, though not unpleasant, culture shock. The last thing she'd expected when she set out from London just over a fortnight ago was to find herself spending Christmas with Polly in a small country town in South Australia.

For her part, Jess had a raft of things to do while she was here. The first related to Isabel's journal pages. There was a detail that hadn't made its way into the official account that Jess had been pondering. Isabel had consulted a solicitor about procuring passports: why hadn't he come forward during the police investigation, particularly when the finger of suspicion was pointing at his client? Jess had been trying to figure out how to track down his identity, when she'd spotted an article on the front page of a newspaper report she'd printed from the day the Turner bodies were found. It mentioned the death of a prominent Adelaide solicitor, Mr Alan S. Becker, in a car accident on Jetty Road. It was a long shot, but Jess had managed to ascertain that Mr Becker's business effects had been donated by his wife to the State Library of South Australia, and she planned to go and look as soon as they re-opened after Christmas.

She'd also arranged to meet again with Marcus Summers. Their previous conversation had been cut short and there was something she wanted to ask him. It was going to take a delicate touch, though. Jess had wondered why her grandmother hadn't destroyed the journal pages sooner, then, drifting off to sleep some nights before, she'd realised the nature of the moth that had been flickering on the edge of her memory when she was in the attic. It was the pufferfish. Rowena Carrick had mentioned its toxin in her email as one that wasn't isolated until the 1960s, and couldn't therefore be tested for in 1959.

She'd considered Percy – she'd even considered Marcus – but then, in a parallel line of thinking, Jess had found herself reflecting on Nora's change of heart about Isabel. In the beginning, Nora had been her sister-in-law's fiercest defender, vehemently insisting that Isabel could never have committed the heinous crime of which she'd been accused. But after her baby died, after she discovered Thea in the rose garden, after the run-in with Becky Baker in the street, Nora had 'remembered' seeing Isabel behave harmfully towards baby Thea. She had told Daniel Miller and he had felt duty bound to inform the police. His evidence had swayed their thinking and ultimately the coroner's view.

Jess wondered when Nora put two and two together. Had she seen Meg in the kitchen and wondered why she was taking special care to discard every remnant of the fish paste? Or was it only after Meg had stepped in and rescued her in the street that she started wondering why and realised what had happened. Either way, each woman had a guilty secret that the other had agreed – tacitly or otherwise – to keep. It hadn't been disbelief that Jess had detected in Nora's voice on the tape when Daniel Miller told her Meg was dead – it was relief. The only person who knew her secret was gone.

All speculation, of course, but it did explain why Nora would have kept the journal pages: they were proof of the affair and Meg Summers' motive. A very handy thing to have, in the circumstances. Jess felt sorry for Daniel Miller. It must have eaten away at him that he'd published something he knew not to be true. She had gone back to read the addendum again and noted that he'd got around it by taking the point of view of people who had no reason not to believe the evidence as it presented. In that way, the outcome of the book was authentic; the voices telling the story were doing so truthfully. But Jess understood why he'd felt unable to publicise the new edition. It would have involved a level of duplicity with which, from what she knew of Miller, he wouldn't have been comfortable. Already, he must have struggled with the ill feeling that he'd helped to propagate a falsehood; that he had been complicit in Nora's deception.

Jess glanced at her watch and saw that it was ten past twelve. Polly was late. She'd mentioned as they parted the night before that she was going to visit a stone fruit nursery on the edge of town this morning. It had seemed like a very specific way to spend time, but Jess had other things on her mind and figured maybe Polly had a penchant for peach trees. There was a lot she still needed to learn about her mother. And her father, for that matter.

She reached into the brown paper bag and withdrew the two books she'd purchased from the Banksia Bookshop. The first was a new copy of an old favourite: *The Bunyip of Berkeley's Creek*. Jess had seen the familiar cream-coloured spine on the shelf and been flooded with memories of being taken to the library by Polly as a child. The memories were new – not the library part, with its smell of pages and dust, the excitement of the small stack of borrowed books, the click-clack of the date stamp – but somewhere along the line, Polly had faded from the picture.

Now, though, Jess could see the two of them in her mind's eye, curled up together on the cushions in the warm, sunlit

corner, reading the much-borrowed copy of this book. She
was pleased to find that the illustrations, with their cross-
hatched mastery of the macabre, still had the power to
transfix her; she'd remembered them in all their glorious
detail. The story, though, was a surprise. She'd been frightened of it back then, but as she read it again today, Jess
wasn't sure how she'd missed the fact that the bunyip was
simply a lost soul, wondering what and who it was, where
and to whom it belonged.

The other book was also about loneliness, in a way: it was
called *The Meeting of Strangers* by Jonathan James and told
the story of a man who'd had a happy marriage and a good
life but couldn't stop thinking about his long-ago first love
who had broken his heart. The author's bio on the back of
the book described an accomplished writer, with a wife and
three children and a home in North Carolina.

Jess had googled Jonathan James the night before, back in
her hotel room after her mother told her, and pored over old
interviews, learning about him but also, she realised, searching for evidence of herself. Did she write because she'd
inherited the trait from him? Did she also like Jeff Buckley
because musical taste was coded genetically and passed from
him to her?

By the same token, she'd found herself thinking of Polly.
There was no handy online biography to read about her
mother, no interviews from newspapers, no website to trawl
through. She'd heard a lot of stories over the course of the
past thirty years, but they had all been told by Nora. The
same stories Nora had told Polly about herself: that she was
sweet but nervous, well-meaning but delicate, that she
needed her mother to look after her.

Nora. Even as Jess was hurt that her grandmother hadn't

trusted her with the truth, and shocked by some of the decisions she'd made, it was impossible to be truly angry with her. Because while Nora's focus had made Polly feel smothered, she had, through her care and attention, built Jess up, made her believe she could do anything and given her the confidence to spread her wings. Jess carried a complete set of Nora's Rules for Life inside her mind, applicable to every situation in which she found herself. She also carried decades' worth of memories of being encouraged and loved. She might not be a Turner in the genetic sense, but Jess would always be Nora's granddaughter.

Being part of a family was complicated. Jess wasn't sure whether she would ever completely understand how her mother could have left her behind, but she did see why Polly had to leave Nora – more precisely, Nora's version of herself – behind. Jess saw, too, that it couldn't have been easy. It must have taken courage and strength for Polly to break away from Nora, to leave everything she knew, the things she'd been told, and remake herself by creating a new life all of her own.

'Hello!' Polly had pulled up on the other side of the road and was leaning to call through the open passenger-seat window. When Jess looked over, she beckoned eagerly. 'I hope you haven't been waiting long?'

'A matter of minutes,' said Jess, sliding into the passenger seat and tucking her bag of books into the footwell. 'How was the nursery?'

'Wonderful,' Polly said, as they drove together down the main street and out of town. 'It was wonderful. I'll tell you about it later, there's a lot to tell – once we're finished here.'

An enigmatic enough response, but also a reminder to Jess

that she still didn't know where 'here' was. 'Where is it we're going?' she asked, but even as the words left her lips she noticed that the car was slowing. She saw the street sign and knew where they were; she had driven here herself just the week before.

A sporty red Mazda was pulled over on the verge at the end of Willner Road. 'I think that's her,' said Polly, peering over the top of the steering wheel.

A woman with a shoulder-length auburn perm waved at them enthusiastically before climbing back into the driver's seat of her car and starting slowly up the winding driveway. Polly followed, parking behind the Mazda on the gravel at the top.

The other woman met them with a dazzling smile. 'Hi there,' she said, 'I'm Deb – Deb Green. And you must be Polly?'

'I am. Thanks for agreeing to show us through on Christmas Eve.'

'No worries at all. It's a beautiful property.' She gestured with a wide sweep of her arm at the grand house behind her. 'A bit neglected over the years, but a wonderful project for the right person. Some history to it, like most places this age.'

'Is it all right to take a look?' Polly asked.

'Certainly. I've already been in and opened things up – you're free to wander. Take your time. I have some emails to send off before Christmas, so I'll be out here, but I'm happy to answer questions when you're finished.'

Being inside the house was every bit as eerie as Jess had anticipated it would be. Through the entrance hall, she reached the sitting room where police had spoken to Nora;

the dining room where the Turner family had eaten their final breakfast; the library, with its wall of bookshelves; and the good parlour, where the netsukes used to live. Much of the furniture was still in place: having removed the personal items, Thomas Turner had decided that, mostly custom-made, it belonged with the building. He had always, Jess remembered, held the provenance of the place in high esteem.

With Daniel Miller's account in mind, it was hard not to hear the echoes of John Turner running too heavily down the stairs, the piano starting up in the library, the happy noise of a family leaving for a picnic lunch. It had been fifty-nine years to the day. Jess ran her fingertips lightly along the banister of the wide, handsome staircase as she followed it up to the balcony level.

It never failed to amaze Jess, the power of the written word to impart not only knowledge, but experience. This was her first time physically in this house, but Daniel Miller had taken her to Halcyon in 1959 and thus she already knew it. She saw the door which led to the room that had been Nora's and went directly to it. Glancing across the balcony, past the telephone alcove towards Matilda's bedroom, Jess experienced a flash of what felt almost like a personal memory: Nora's observation of her nieces that last day. *Did you get it?* A nod. *Show me . . . Not out here!*

With a shiver, Jess pushed open the door to Nora's room and went inside. This was where her grandmother had slept in the last weeks of her uncomfortable pregnancy, and where she'd had her baby; from that window over there she'd watched Isabel in the garden below.

Jess went to the window now.

The property was very overgrown, just as the agent had said, filled with creepers and weeds, but Jess saw it as it had been back then. The roses, the walnut tree and, further up the bend of the drive, the henhouse and vegetable patch. But it was Polly, and not Isabel, who was wandering among the trees today; Jess wondered whether her mother was thinking about the night she was left there to be found, the dawn in which Nora had slipped out of the house and discovered her among the roses, and her life was set on a different path. No longer Thea Turner, but Polly Turner-Bridges.

Jess had a sudden urge to leave this room, to be outside. She went down the stairs and across the entrance hall, aware that she was walking in Isabel's footsteps from that long-ago Christmas Eve. As she stepped through the front door onto the verandah, a warm breeze brushed her face and she felt a heavy wave of deep familiarity: the smell of eucalyptus and sun-baked dirt, the light so bright it put creases around her eyes just to look at it. The slender blue gums on the ridge, ancient and watchful. This was the landscape of her childhood and she would never be able to escape its influence.

But just as Daniel Miller had brought her to Halcyon, the books that she'd read as a child, lying beneath the ferns at Darling House, had taken her to lands where trees with names like oak and chestnut and elm grew in great, ancient forests, and the soil was moist and the sun was gentle, where there were magical words like 'hedgerow' and 'conker', and snow kissed the glass of windows in winter, and children went sledding at Christmas and ate 'pudding' and 'blanc-mange'. And so, she had come to know another landscape, not just intellectually, but viscerally: a landscape of the imagination as real to her as the geographical landscape in which she moved. When she first arrived in England as a twenty-year-old graduate, she had stepped off the plane and known it already.

Standing here now, looking across the valley towards the facing hill, Jess could imagine how homesick Isabel must have felt at times. She herself had been thinking about 'home' a lot. Home, she'd realised, wasn't a place or a time or a person, though it could be any and all of those things: home was a feeling, a sense of being complete. The opposite of 'home' wasn't 'away', it was 'lonely'. When someone said, 'I want to go home', what they really meant was that they didn't want to feel lonely anymore.

She had put away the travel article. Instead, she was going to write something different, more ambitious. The ideas were a bit random yet, but had to do with home and belonging, connection and family; and Polly had said something at dinner last night about Isabel and setting the record straight. 'She's been remembered in the most horrific light, and none of it is warranted or true.' Somehow – Jess wasn't sure exactly how yet – it all fit together.

Across the gravel, Jess noticed that Polly was accepting a glossy sales brochure from the agent. She had assumed that they'd been looking out of curiosity, for history's sake. And perhaps Polly was just being polite. Though it was possible, Jess realised, her mother's interest was more serious than that. She didn't know the secrets of Polly's heart, but she realised that she wanted to.

Polly smiled in greeting as Jess joined them. 'Deb was just saying it's okay for us to take a walk around the grounds and down towards the creek.'

'I can't stay much longer, unfortunately,' the agent explained. 'My daughter's singing in the Christmas Eve service tonight and I need to get her to rehearsal. I've locked up the house, but the two of you are welcome to wander around. The gardens have been let go, but I'm sure you'll be able to see the potential. I should mention' – her smile wavered, and Jess noticed a flicker of hesitation in her eyes as she lowered her voice – 'there was something of an incident on the property, a long time ago.'

'Yes,' said Polly with a smile. 'Thank you, we already know about that.'

Deb Green's bonhomie returned. 'That's good. And I have to say, I couldn't agree more. I've always felt what's past is past. No need to dwell; look forward, not back.'

It wasn't exactly what Polly had said, but neither she nor Jess made any attempt to clarify.

Deb Green shook their hands, wished them a happy Christmas, and then took off in her red Mazda.

In the wake of her departure, Jess and Polly stood without speaking, letting the sounds of the garden resettle. A flock of tiny fairy wrens darted busily in and around the base of a nearby plum tree, crickets ticked in the long grass, and a sense of timelessness, of nature, older and more pervasive than anything human beings and their histories could generate, grew thick and warm around them.

'Shall we walk down together?' said Polly.

Jess noticed a new note of self-possession in her mother's voice. Summery air threaded across the back of her neck, and she felt a pull, suddenly, deep inside her. She didn't know whether it was being here, in this place, or the beautiful weather that evoked long childhood days in which the hours stretched away to be filled only with pleasure, or the fact that it was Christmas Eve, or that her mother was standing here with her, solid and present in a way she hadn't been before, so that Jess was seeing her as if for the first time. But she felt a sensation in her chest that was quite the opposite of loneliness.

'Are you with me?' Polly was searching Jess's face, waiting for an answer.

Jess gave a nod and smiled. 'I am.'

ACKNOWLEDGEMENTS

Thank you to my agent, Lizzy Kremer, who brings both knowledge and wisdom to my publishing life; to Kay Begum and Maddalena Cavaciuti; and to the DHA international rights team, especially Margaux Vialleron.

Thank you to my editors, Maria Rejt, Kate Nintzel, and Annette Barlow, all of whom challenged and helped me to make this book much better than it might have been; to Gonzalo Albert, who sent his unmatched enthusiasm at just the right time; to Nita Pronovost; to Ali Lavau; to Marian Reid; to Christa Munns, Charlotte Tennant, and Laura Brady (indefatigable all!); to Chloe Bollentin and Janet Rosenberg; and to my various translators, who made me look even more closely than usual at my complicated, flexible, and fascinating mother tongue. I am lucky indeed to have so many word-loving allies, eager to consider plot and character, structure and ideas, synonyms, homonyms, and even, when pressed, the virtues – or otherwise – of the Oxford comma.

Beyond editorial, numerous people played a part in publishing this book and I offer my sincere thanks to everyone at A&U, Mantle, Mariner, and Simon & Schuster Canada, who brought their significant talents to bear, and to Robert Gorman, Joanna Prior, Liate Stehlik, and Kevin Hanson for their ongoing support. Thank you to Ami Smithson (UK), Elsie Lyons (North America), and Sandy Cull (ANZ) for their creative wizardry in making sure *Homecoming* was so well-dressed, with special mention of Bec Bartell for her beautiful original artwork.

Thank you to Diane Morton, Julia Kretschmer, and Lisa Patterson for reading early drafts of the manuscript. Julia, in particular, has my immeasurable gratitude for her willingness to discuss my characters over the course of years, as avidly and sincerely as if they were real people in our lives.

Thank you to Associate Professor Nick Osborne from the School of Public Health at the University of Queensland, and Kym Hardwick APM, Vice President of the South Australian Police Historical Society, for answering my research questions. Thank you to the State Library of South Australia. All errors of fact in this book, intentional or not, are my own.

The first ideas for *Homecoming* came to me in the Adelaide Hills, the magnificent traditional land of the Peramangk people, and a place of refuge for my family during the great unsettlement at the start of the Covid pandemic. Removed from the bustle of London to a remote farm in South Australia, from late winter to the last long days of summer, as global events churned and swirled, I thought a lot about home and belonging, and kept returning to the T. S. Eliot line about 'the still point of the turning world'. I am thankful for this place, in awe of its beauty, and grateful for my own connection to it.

I also consider it a privilege to introduce the Hills to readers not yet acquainted with them. For Tambilla and its inhabitants might be inventions, but Hahndorf, Stirling, Mount Lofty, the Onkaparinga Valley, and Greenhill Road are not. As a novelist, I have taken creative licence here and there, but I hope nonetheless that the place rings true for those readers who *are* familiar with it. Certainly, the residents of Tambilla have woven themselves into the fabric of my daily life, so that when I am travelling the winding roads of the Hills, I often catch glimpses of them from the corner of my eye.

This book is in part about stories and their tellers. The story that Percy recalls being told about the origins of Mount Lofty comes from the Kaurna people, the Traditional Custodians of the Adelaide Plains to the west of the Hills, and I reference it here with utmost respect.

Homecoming is also about books and booklovers, and a number of writers and works are mentioned within its pages. Charles Dickens, Thomas Hardy, and Jane Austen are names well-known around the world, but it was a pleasure to include among them Percy's introduction to fiction, *The Magic Pudding* by Norman Lindsay, and Jess's childhood favourite, *The Bunyip of Berkeley's Creek* by Jenny Wagner, illustrated by Ron Brooks. I still have my own well-thumbed copies of each sitting on my bookshelf.

Thank you, in anticipation, to every bookseller, librarian, and reader into whose hands *Homecoming* will fall – this book was a home of sorts for me over the past few years and it is a joy at last to welcome you inside.

Thank you, in memory, to Herbert and Rita. What I wouldn't give to arrive in their front garden on Tamborine Mountain, call 'Hello' from the porch, and hear that welcoming reply from inside the cottage: 'The door's on the latch!' I miss them with an abiding longing and sadness that grows deeper every year.

Finally, I am a person who feels a profound connection to places, and I have been known to fall in love with buildings; but my true home – my still point in the turning world – is my family. Thank you to Davin, Oliver, Louis, and Henry. This book is for them, with endless, timeless, limitless love and thanks.